PRAISE FOR
Revealed

"*Revealed* is not just a simple romance novel, it is a damn good one."
—*The Book Smugglers*

"Noble crafts an exciting, witty, and highly entertaining tale about an unlikely duo caught in a killer's web."   —*Romantic Times*

"Full of action and adventure . . . *Revealed* has it all . . . Ms. Noble has real talent."   —*Romance Junkies*

"*Revealed* is . . . fresh and lively and utterly delightful. *Revealed* will enchant lovers of the Regency novel, but I highly recommend it even for those who usually avoid this genre. Somehow, I think you'll be hooked by this story as securely as I was."   —*Fallen Angel Reviews*

"[A] terrific tale of 'love and war' that contrasts . . . Regency High Society with the dangerous world of espionage."
—*Midwest Book Review*

Compromised

"Noble's clever and graceful debut Regency romance is simply sublime."   —*Booklist*

"*Compromised* is a delectable and delightful debut! Every word sparkles like a diamond of the first water. I can't wait for Kate Noble's next treasure of a book!"
—Teresa Medeiros, *New York Times* bestselling author

"Kate Noble's writing is smart and sparkling. Wonderfully entertaining, delightfully effervescent romance."
—Amanda Quick, *New York Times* bestselling author

"An amusing historical romance . . . A lighthearted late-Regency romp."
—*Midwest Book Review*

"Ms. Noble is a talent to watch. I look forward to her next book."
—*Romance Reviews Today*

The Summer of You

KATE NOBLE

BERKLEY SENSATION, NEW YORK

THE BERKLEY PUBLISHING GROUP
Published by the Penguin Group
Penguin Group (USA) Inc.
375 Hudson Street, New York, New York 10014, USA
Penguin Group (Canada), 90 Eglinton Avenue East, Suite 700, Toronto, Ontario M4P 2Y3, Canada
(a division of Pearson Penguin Canada Inc.)
Penguin Books Ltd., 80 Strand, London WC2R 0RL, England
Penguin Group Ireland, 25 St. Stephen's Green, Dublin 2, Ireland (a division of Penguin Books Ltd.)
Penguin Group (Australia), 250 Camberwell Road, Camberwell, Victoria 3124, Australia
(a division of Pearson Australia Group Pty. Ltd.)
Penguin Books India Pvt. Ltd., 11 Community Centre, Panchsheel Park, New Delhi—110 017, India
Penguin Group (NZ), 67 Apollo Drive, Rosedale, North Shore 0632, New Zealand
(a division of Pearson New Zealand Ltd.)
Penguin Books (South Africa) (Pty.) Ltd., 24 Sturdee Avenue, Rosebank, Johannesburg 2196,
South Africa

Penguin Books Ltd., Registered Offices: 80 Strand, London WC2R 0RL, England

This book is an original publication of The Berkley Publishing Group.

PRINTING HISTORY
Berkley Sensation trade paperback edition / April 2010

Berkley Sensation trade paperback ISBN: 978-0-425-23239-2

Library of Congress Cataloging-in-Publication Data

Noble, Kate, 1978–
The summer of you / Kate Noble.—Berkley Sensation trade pbk. ed.
    p. cm.
  ISBN 978-0-425-23239-2
  1. Nobility—England—Fiction.   2. Brigands and robbers—Fiction.   3. Mistaken identity—
Fiction.   4. Lake District (England)—Fiction.   I. Title.
  PS3614.O246S86   2010   2009050827
  813'.6—dc22

PRINTED IN THE UNITED STATES OF AMERICA

10 9 8 7 6 5 4 3 2 1

*To the residents of Martin Lane—
past, present, and future—for a lifetime of summers.*

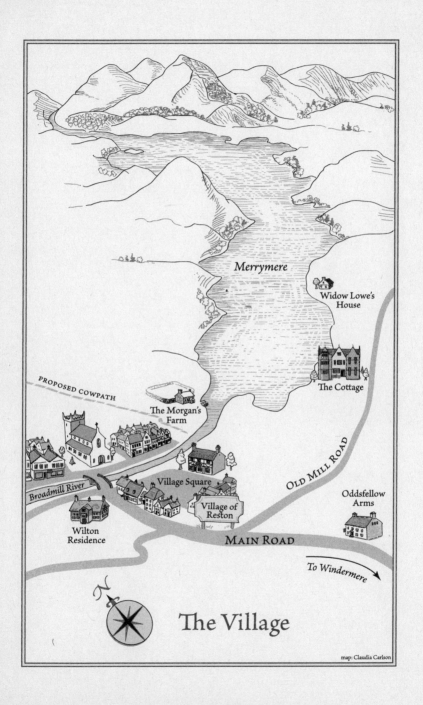

Merrymere

Widow Lowe's
House

The Cottage

PROPOSED COWPATH

The Morgan's
Farm

OLD MILL ROAD

Broadmill River

Village Square

Oddsfellow
Arms

Village of
Reston

Wilton
Residence

MAIN ROAD

To Windermere

N

The Village

map: Claudia Carlson

Prologue

L ONG ago, before England was cut up with pavement or bisected by railways, there existed in the county of Lancashire a small village called Reston that never bothered anyone. Oh, of course its residents knew of the greater world and participated—paid those taxes and fought those wars that greater men told them to. They kept their eye on the periodicals for the latest fashions and dances. But of far greater concern to the village of Reston was how the trout were running that year, when the summer squash would be ready for picking, and whether the village council would vote to allow the creation of a cow path across the Morgans' farm, mere miles from the village proper.

Reston sat on a small river connecting two small lakes, wedged delightfully in the valley of remarkable fells and mountains. We will concern ourselves with the easternmost lake, called Merrymere. It was not like the grand bodies of water that attracted most of the tourists, but it did provide most of the scenery and sport for the locals, as well as the occasional sightseer who became lost and bypassed larger venues to the south like Windermere or Coniston Water.

The people of Reston amused themselves in much the same manner as other villages, earned their living in much the same manner, prayed, danced, lived, loved . . . all of those things that make people people. Their biggest gossip concerned the public assemblies, and their biggest fears were those people for whom they had yet to be introduced. Everyone in Reston was pleasant, polite, and above all, socially correct.

All except one.

They said he was a war hero—others thought perhaps he was an enemy soldier, cowardly hiding from his losses in the middle of their happy valley. Some thought him romantic, a lost soul—others merely a beast. But everyone learned after their first encounter to stay far away from old widow Lowe's house, for her nephew, the man who inherited, was certain to send them running back to the safety of the village.

It was whispered that he had dreams. Terrible dreams of blood and water, salt and gunpowder that haunted him, had him crying out in his sleep—mournful noises that carried over the lake, the sound of the damned being ferried to hell.

But, as vexing as they found his presence, their British souls refused to bow to their fears and be undone. So the people of Reston went about their lives, ignoring the far side of the lake they called Merrymere and its sole inhabitant. And he ignored them. Reston rose, ate, worked, talked, took tea, danced, and slept, all while keeping in the periphery of their mind the danger, the monster, that lurked mere miles away.

One

Lady Jane Cummings, only daughter of the Duke of Rayne, second cousin twice removed of the Prince Regent (or was it three times?), and most sought-after ginger-haired—but unfreckled—dance partner of the Ton, was in trouble.

And it was all Phillippa Benning's fault.

Or Phillippa Worth, as Jane supposed she must become accustomed to calling her recently reclaimed friend. But how long would that friendship last if Phillippa persisted in causing Jane such distress as to commit social blunders was undetermined.

For you see, Lady Jane had missed a step.

She could be mistaken for a statue in that moment, standing stock-still in the center of Phillippa's great ballroom, which was festooned in bridal drapery, white silk bowers running between massive bouquets of summer roses in every color. Dancers swirled around her, as colorful as the flowers, stepping with mirth and verve in time to the music, while Lady Jane's attention was caught and held by the alarmingly familiar shock of hair she saw at the other end of the row, lazily scanning the dancers from the sidelines. Everyone who was anyone was celebrating Phillippa's recent conversion from Benning to Worth, i.e., her marriage. And being as this was London, and it was the Ton, and Phillippa being, well, Phillippa, she must have invited the entire catalogue of Debrett's to her wedding celebration. Oh, but how could she have invited *him*?

Jane was jolted out of her shock when a twirling debutante, doing her best with the tricky steps of the quadrille, bumped into her frozen form. Murmured apologies set off a ripple of whispers that Lady Jane, of all people, had taken a misstep when dancing. Jane quickly rejoined her partner, falling into the steps with a hurried but well-practiced ease.

"Is everything all right?" Lord Turnbridge asked in his reedy, if earnest, voice.

"Of course, my lord." She smiled prettily at him, causing his face to take on a decidedly berry shade. "I was simply . . . struck by the decorations on the fireplace mantel. Mrs. Worth has outdone herself."

Jane turned her eyes toward the far end of the room, where the gold and white silk-draped fireplace stood and where she last saw that blazing shock of hair, that tall, languid form. But this time, no such sight was presented. She turned her head back around, scanning the crowd behind Lord Turnbridge fervently, but to no avail. Drat it all, where had he gone?

Lucky for Lady Jane's sanity and Lord Turnbridge's ego, the music ended then, and she need no longer subject her dance partner to such inattentiveness. Instead, she smiled sweetly at him as he escorted her to the side of the room. Annoyingly, Lord Turnbridge escorted her very slowly. Once there, he bowed tediously low—it was all Jane could do not to tap her foot with impatience. But finally he rose, and Jane performed the most perfunctory of curtsies before he turned away to find his next partner, and presumably, allowing Jane to be found by hers.

That is, if she had wanted to be found.

As quick as grace and the crush of people would allow, Jane

moved through the crowd, ducking and weaving the flow of traffic like a fish in a current.

She couldn't have imagined him, could she? Oh please, let her be suffering delusions and she imagined Jason. He couldn't be in London. He just couldn't. It had only been six weeks since she came out of mourning and back into society—maybe two months . . . but now . . .

Jane ducked into a corridor that she hoped led to Phillippa's outrageously pink drawing room—really, if Jane and Phillippa had been speaking to each other at the time of her redecoration, Jane would have seriously attempted to steer Phillippa into a few more varied shades. It was in the Pink Room, however, that desserts were being served. There, overly plump matrons would be devouring sweets with a speed that would distress their laces come tomorrow, and where Jane knew no sane eligible man would go. (Those men who did cross the threshold of a room that pink quickly scampered away, either because of a lack of young female attention or the fervent enthusiasm of their mothers.) But alas, a left turn, and another left, and Jane quickly found herself nowhere near the Pink Room. Backtracking, Jane lifted a curtain she thought led to the hallway.

Suffice to say, it didn't.

"Jane!" Phillippa Worth (née Benning) cried, as she tore her lips away from those of her husband, who was kind enough to use his height to block her from view as she readjusted some clothing that had gone suspiciously awry. "Whatever are you doing?"

"I'm looking for a place to hide!" Jane whispered furiously, placing her hands on her hips.

"I apologize, Lady Jane," Marcus Worth said in his even, affable drawl, "but as you see, this alcove is occupied."

Jane shot him a rueful glance to which Marcus only smiled. "You've been married all of twelve hours. You can't wait another two until your wedding banquet is over?" Jane snorted at Phillippa.

Phillippa looked up at her husband and he down at her, his easy grin apparently infectious.

"No."

"Don't suppose we can."

"Well you've got to," Jane replied, "because I am in a dreadful spot, and it's all your fault!"

"Why?" Phillippa looked immediately concerned. "What have you done now?"

"I've done nothing," Jane scoffed, "'tis your doing, and I demand that you fix it!"

"Me?" Phillippa replied, outraged. Then looking to Marcus: "Darling, you can't let her . . ."

"My dearest wife," Marcus interrupted, then, grinning, added, "I just love saying that. Ah—anyway," he continued, at said dearest wife's look, "if there is one thing I've learned during our brief courtship, it's not to get in between the two of you when you squabble."

Phillippa looked like she was about to teach her new husband a very keen lesson about disagreeing with one's wife, but Jane had no time for such a segue. "How could you invite him?"

"Invite who?" Phillippa replied, immediately snapping back to the pertinent conversation.

"Jason!" Jane whispered in a rush and watched a slight look of confusion mar Phillippa's brow.

"Jason? You mean your—" at Jane's nod, Phillippa expostulated. "But I didn't. I didn't even know he was in Town—I would have added him to the guest list had I known, but—"

"You would have *added* him?" Jane exclaimed.

"Well of course—he is, after all, a Marquis—" Phillippa replied blithely, but Jane threw up her hands.

"Did it never occur to you that I might not wish to see him?"

"So sorry," Phillippa snipped, "I haven't kept up with your preferences—next time I'll plan my wedding celebration around *your* likes and dislikes, shall I?"

Before the conversation could further devolve into a spitting match, Marcus Worth luckily (and intelligently) intervened.

"Dearest," he said, putting a gentle hand on his wife's arm before turning to her assailant. "Lady Jane—I take it you feel the need to make an expedient exit?" She nodded, and so he continued, "Did your father attend with you this evening?"

Jane shook her head. "He was feeling a little tired. Lady Charlbury was good enough to act as my chaperone this evening."

Even Phillippa raised her brows at that—Lady Charlbury was an interesting paradox: a widow of middle years, she ruled society through her friendships with the Lady Patronesses, but it was of late more and more difficult to get her to respond positively to an invitation. They had both been lucky enough to attend her fete earlier this season, but to have her attend Phillippa's—!

"She's an old friend of my father's," Jane replied with only the slightest of braggadocio.

"Well, then my darling wife will go and tell her you had a headache, and we sent you home in our carriage," Marcus said, forcing the conversation back onto its original track, "and I will show Lady Jane the back way to the door."

Phillippa, nodded, agreeing to this scheme—in no small part, Jane was certain, because it afforded her the opportunity to be seen conversing with Lady Charlbury—who was impressive even by Phillippa's standards.

Phillippa leaned in and gave her husband a not-so-quick peck on the lips. Then, once Jane stopped cringing, Marcus offered her his arm and led her out of the alcove and in the opposite direction of the flow of human traffic.

Marcus Worth neatly ducked and weaved his way through the crowd, managing to blend himself into the throng so much so that not a soul stopped him or wished him well or smiled in acknowledgment. Considering this was *his* wedding banquet, it was an astonishing feat. One that must have served him well in his covert role with the Home Office. It was rumored he would be knighted for his services to the Crown, and no matter how much the public cajoled, Phillippa would not divulge specifics of said service. Which, of course, made the gossip all the more rampant.

But Jane was privy to the truth. She had witnessed Marcus and his brother Byrne in acts of heroics usually reserved for sensational novels.

"Turn here," Marcus's whisper interrupted her musings as he abruptly turned down an underlit servants' corridor.

It took Jane's eyes a moment to adjust, but when she did, she followed Marcus Worth's abominably long stride toward the kitchens.

"Right this way, Lady Jane," Marcus Worth said solicitously, carefully stooped in the low corridor—Phillippa had met and married perhaps the tallest man in London, outside of the circus. Lady Jane was just a hair shorter than the average female—and so to keep up with his leisurely stride, she was reduced to trotting.

Once in the kitchens, so rife with activity no one noticed the new master of the house and the daughter of a Duke wandering through, Marcus, after a quick word with one of the servants, guided her into a different corridor.

"This will take us to the butler's pantry, which is right beside the front door," Marcus informed her.

"Phillippa keeps her silver next to the front door?" Jane questioned. "Does she wish to invite burglary?"

But Marcus simply laughed at her snide remark. "No, the silver is kept in safer stores—we call it the butler's pantry because it keeps the butler, who has a habit of lying down in between answering the door."

Considering Marcus and Phillippa had been married mere hours, it was on the tip of Jane's tongue to ask not only how he became so familiar with the workings of this household, but also with all its secret corridors. But Jane found it prudent to keep her mouth shut, especially since they had just breached the hidden door to the butler's pantry.

There was indeed a lack of silver, and in its stead a comfortable chair and blankets for either a terribly indulged or greatly beloved family retainer. A book on the chair completed the tableau, and Jane was tempted to peek at the title, but that would have necessitated moving, and the space was too tight for such allowances.

"Right through this door," Marcus pointed in front of them, "and left out of the house. I believe you'll find a carriage waiting to convey you home at the top of the drive."

"Mr. Worth"—Jane smiled at him—"you are a terribly useful sort."

Marcus, it seemed, decided to take that as a compliment, for after a moment he inclined his head with a smile.

"I am very glad Phillippa married you," she said, patting his arm, "and do hope you survive it."

At that, Marcus Worth threw back his head and barked with laughter. He opened the door in front of him and escorted her out of the butler's pantry.

And since he was laughing, Jane simply had to join in. And so, as they laughed, and came into the candlelight of the main foyer, they perhaps were less than attentive to who else could be in that general vicinity.

So the fist to Marcus's jaw came as a bit of a surprise.

Not that it actually connected. Marcus had alarmingly quick reflexes, and his extra height allowed him to narrowly avoid his attacker's reach. Jane smothered a scream, as Marcus caught the hands of his attacker and pinned them mercilessly behind his back. Then, attracting far too much attention from the festivities' attendants down the hall, he shoved him face-first against the door to the butler's pantry.

"For heaven's sake, Jason," Jane cried, as he squirmed beneath Marcus Worth's iron grip, his right cheek pressed against the wainscoting, "have you gone completely mad?"

"I take it this is the man you were so keen to avoid?" Marcus drawled.

"Yes—Mr. Worth, I'm so sor—"

"Oh shut it, Jane!" Jason spat out of the side of his mouth. Then, to Marcus, "Now, who are you, and what the devil were you doing in that closet with my sister?"

Two

"HAVE you become a raving lunatic while abroad?" Jane crossed the foyer of Rayne House in Grosvenor Square in a huff, her voice echoing against the cold marble and gilt-painted moldings. Jason followed her in, after slamming his hat and cloak in the waiting hands of the very old and very austere butler.

"Actually, I'm beginning to believe I'm the only sane person left in this family," he retorted.

Jane's head snapped up from the aggravating task of unknotting her cloak's strings, two circles of angry color flooding her cheeks. "You take that back," she gritted out between locked teeth.

But Jason merely approached her in three long strides. "I specifically told you to stay at the castle! When I came back, *together* we would decide what was best to do next."

"When you came back?" Jane screeched. "I waited a whole bloody year, and you didn't come back! You expected me to sit in that drafty, crumbling castle while you gallivanted about with your friends? No, thank you."

Jason had the grace to turn slightly pink under his freckling. "I wasn't *gallivanting*; I had a great deal of research to do. If Mother had been alive, she'd have understood."

Only the fact that her fingers were tied up in her cloak strings kept Jane from smacking her brother. "Mother might have," she said stiffly, "but Father did *not*."

It had been only the three of them, after the funeral, over a year ago now. Their mother, the round-faced, worrying, practical, adored Duchess of Rayne, had passed after a sudden illness and a prolonged suffering. It had been her heart, the doctors had decided. The nervous spasms she had claimed whenever she was overwrought had turned out to be true, and had taken the Duchess away from her family far too soon.

They had made the short trip into the countryside to Crow Castle, the Duke of Rayne's ancestral estate, when she had first fallen ill. It was called such not only for the great black birds that graced the Rayne crest but also for the crows that had taken nest in the north tower sometime in the fourteenth century. There, in the dark, hard earth of the spring, the body of the Duchess was laid to rest, next to the bodies of the previous Dukes and Duchesses, in rigid lines of crumbling stone. The mound of dirt that covered her mother was too black, Jane had thought, the marble of her headstone too new. How could her mother be here, in the midst of this cold, still cemetery? Her mother fluttered, she fussed . . . she did not quietly lie in the ancient ground. She moved! She talked!

Jane had barely begun to process the loss of her mother—barely had time to dye her wardrobe an inky midnight for the year of mourning she was embarking upon—when Jason announced he intended to complete his grand tour of Europe . . . immediately.

"You can't leave now!" Jane had cried, wrapping the old wool shawl tighter about her shoulders. The castle had long been drafty, so even in the temperate breeze of the southern counties, there was always a large collection of wraps kept in stock.

"I have to," Jason had replied, as he organized papers from his desk into thick leather folders. Behind him, his valet was directing a small army of footmen as they packed up the finest linen shirts and silk cravats that could be found on Bond Street, along with every color of riding jacket, dinner jacket, and greatcoat. Jason had been going through a slightly foppish phase. He would discover Brummell's definition of dress while abroad. "You know I'm going to present a paper when I return to the Historical Society."

Admittance to the Historical Society—or as it was known by its full name, the Society of Historical Art and Architecture of the Known World—was Jason's true dream. Unfortunately, it also tended to serve as his best excuse.

"It's history; it can wait!" Jane had replied.

"My subject is the damage done to medieval architecture on the Continent during Boney's last campaign; I need to take an inventory while it's still fresh—before anyone else does. Charles and Nevill are already in Bruges—"

"Ah yes, Charles and Nevill." Jane arched a brow as she repeated the names of Jason's two greatest friends—and partners in mischief. She let the sarcasm drip like honey. "You'll get *so* much work done with them by your side."

When Jason showed a modicum of intelligence and did not rise to her bait, Jane crossed the room and placed her hand gently on his arm, stilling his movements.

"Please, Jase," she said, her voice soft in its honesty, "I don't want to be here alone. It's so strange without—"

"You won't be alone. Father is here," Jason countered.

Jane sighed and spoke the truth that had prickled at the back of her conscience. "Father is not well."

Jason looked into his sister's eyes, then looked over his shoulder, giving his man a curt nod. The efficient valet clapped his hands once and led the bevy of footmen out the door.

"Father is fine," Jason said once they were alone.

"He is not, and you know it," Jane replied quietly. Jason was contemplative for a moment, and his silence assured her that he knew she had the right of it, even if he wasn't yet willing to admit it.

"He's . . . he's simply in mourning. His mind will right itself," he finally said. But Jane knew better.

The Duke of Rayne was a proud man—proud most of his two

children but also proud of his strong mind. He could calculate to the fiftieth decimal the numerical pi without pen and paper. He could name every bird that flew past his window, its common English name and its Latin scientific counterpart. But lately, occasionally, he had begun to forget things. The name of Crow Castle's housekeeper, who had been in service to the family since before Jane's birth. That England was no longer at war with France. The children could have blamed the grief, the loss of the man's wife . . . if only these little slips hadn't started before the Duchess's death. And since they arrived at Crow Castle, they had only gotten worse.

"At least let's go to London—have a physician examine him—" Jane reasoned, but a flash of anger crossed Jason's face, cutting off her argument.

"No!" he retorted vehemently. "You think Father would want anyone to *know* about his . . . lapses?" Jason went back to clearing his desk of papers, violently shoving them into their folders. "A little respite from the city is just what he needs. I daresay he had enough of the dramatics surrounding your debut season to wear out anyone's brain."

Tears stung Jane's eyes as she felt her cheeks go red. "That's not fair." Jason looked up and immediately went back to his sister's side, contrite.

"I'm sorry," he said, putting his arm around her shoulders. "I shouldn't have said that. But Jane, you can't go to London anyway— the family of the Duke of Rayne mourns at the family seat. It's the way it's always been done."

"The *family*—that includes you." Jane sniffed.

"I'll be back in no time," he promised, chuffing his sister on the shoulder. "And when I get back, if father's . . . problem is still unresolved, *then* you and I shall figure out what's to be done. But until then, you must stay here and look after him." Jason took her by the shoulders, looked her dead in the eye, like he used to when they were children and he had to elicit a promise from her to not tell their governess about the frog on her chair. "Jane—it's you and me. We're in this together."

And so she'd nodded and acquiesced and waved her brother good-bye at the castle gate the next morning. And waited.

And waited.

It was not long before Jason's letters home became cursory. It was not long after that that they became nonexistent.

This didn't bother Jane much—she knew her brother. He may have claimed, even intended, to be abroad with some nobler purpose, but the delights of the Continent would forever outweigh its virtues. Besides, her letters to him were being received (or at least, were not being returned as undeliverable), so she knew he was healthy enough to pay for a penny a page. No, it didn't bother Jane—in much the same way that oversalted meat does not bother: it annoys, but it does not require global conflict. We all grieve in our own way, she thought charitably. He would be home soon.

He promised.

In fact, Jane—however lonely she refused to acknowledge she was—was of the opinion that her brother's absence was unnoted by the rest of the house. After all, if the lifelong staff voiced an issue, they certainly didn't do so to her. And her father—his grief for his wife was still so profound, it overtook any disappointment in his son. Nay, he did not notice Jason's absence.

Or so she thought.

One morning, Jane came down the stairs of the castle, wrapping her shawl firmly over her shoulders. It was past Christmas now, and raining. Through the summer and autumn, people would call with condolences—their tenants, their neighbors. But since the winter came, everyone stayed in on their own. Whatever comfort they had in the solitude of the country was lost on Jane. She yearned to go to London for the Little Season, to see people, to be seen, and not be left alone here, forgotten. But thoughts like that she pushed aside—it was selfish to indulge in misery. Especially when she had her father to keep her company, and her him. But when she settled down to break-fast that morning, her father had not joined her.

Worried, she searched and found him at the open front door, awaiting the footman he'd sent for the post.

"Jason must send us a letter soon, my dear," he'd said, his breath a sharp slice of frost in the freezing rain that soaked the Duke and the Oriental rug in the foyer.

"It's only been a few weeks since the last one," Jane soothed. "Truly, you can't expect him to write every day." Even though Jane herself had been hoping for a bit more frequency. "Come away from the door, it's wet and awful out."

"It's been five weeks. Five!" the Duke countered, and Jane was surprised that he had been counting.

"The post is never regular in this weather—" she rationalized, but was cut off by a curt shake of the head.

"I mandated he write once a week, dearest. If he intends to try for a first once he goes to Oxford, his grades at Eton must be impeccable! I need constant reports from him, from his teachers—"

Her father continued, but for a moment, Jane could hear no sound. The world had gone quiet.

He thinks Jason a boy, off at school, she realized with shock. *And he thinks me . . .*

"Jane will be off to school all too soon, darling," the Duke was saying, "and I will despise not being able to influence my children's education."

That was the moment Jane realized her father's condition was worse than they'd feared.

But as Jane recounted the story to Jason in the main drawing room of the London house, all he did was remove himself to the sideboard and pour out two glasses of brandy.

When he handed one to Jane, she responded with a quiet, "Ladies don't drink brandy."

"Which precludes you, how?" was Jason's reply. Then, after seating himself in the wing chair to the right of the fire, he downed his brandy in one quick gulp.

Jane gave her glass a discreet sip and managed to hide her ensuing shock at its fire.

"I stopped at the club before I came out to the Benning Ball, searching for you—by the by, what on earth were you doing at Phillippa Benning's party? I thought you hated each other."

"You've been away a long time," Jane replied tersely. "Things change."

Jason waved away her ire, continuing with his initial line of thought. "At the club, the first thing I was asked was not, 'How was the Continent?' or 'Did you enjoy your time abroad?'" He held the empty glass up to the fire, watching the light glint across the facets. Her brother's best effort of nonchalance. "It was, 'How does your father?'"

Jane stilled in her movements. "A perfectly natural question," she hedged, "to ask after the Duke."

"You aren't understanding me, Jane. It was the first question *everyone* asked me."

And with that, Jane drained the rest of the brandy.

"You shouldn't have come to London." Jason cursed, sitting up straight in his chair. "Father is a proud man. Do you think he wants the dukedom tarnished by the rumor that his mind is going? He's second cousin twice removed to the King!"

"I thought it was thrice removed," Jane interrupted.

"It doesn't matter! A mad King, a mad Duke—people will think the whole bloodline corrupt!"

"Father is not mad!" Jane said hotly, coming to stand. "Besides, what would you have me *do*, Jason?"

"Don't pretend like you didn't jump at the first chance to come back for the Season—a year of mourning Mother, and at the chiming of the church bell, Lady Jane of Society Fame runs back to Town."

"We were practically alone at the castle!" she shot back. "The servants, they have every other Sunday off, and I was frightened. If he's having a good day, it's fine, but there have been more and more bad days, and . . . I couldn't do it, I couldn't be the only one there."

"Why? Has Father grown violent? Is he a danger to himself or others?" Jason asked, suddenly alarmed.

"No," Jane admitted and was pleased by the relief she read on her brother's face. "But he's more . . . confused, more often."

Jason was quiet for a moment. Then, "What did the doctor say?"

Jane sighed. "They say many things. And nothing. They blame age, they blame his bloodlines, they—"

"They?" he interjected, alarmed. "How many has he seen?"

She ignored that, saying, "But what they all say is that it's getting worse, and he needs constant care."

Jason looked thoughtful a minute. "Then we shall procure constant care."

Jane exhaled her relief, let her body slump for a moment—unrestrained by proper posture for the first time all evening. All year, perhaps. Finally, Jason understood. He would take some of this awful weight from her shoulders.

"Send out a letter to the agencies tomorrow," Jason was saying, "Hire whomever you need, but make certain they are discreet and can travel."

"Travel?" Jane's posture snapped back into attention.

"You'll take Father back to the castle, of course," Jason dictated blithely. "This time you'll have sufficient help and can . . ." However, Jane did not hear the rest, simply because her mind swam colors in front of her at the staggering quantity of error her brother had managed to incorporate into his speech.

"Jason," Jane said very clearly, holding on to composure with whatever strength she had left after the long night, "I am not going back to the castle."

"What, you think to flit around London, dangling after a Marquis or two?" Jason answered wryly, as Jane felt her face turn hot. "Didn't think I'd been in Town long enough to hear about that one, did you? Your little wager to win the hand of that fripperish Broughton?"

Jane had to admit the wager she made with Phillippa Benning to see who could catch the newly returned to Town Lord Broughton a month or so ago was one of her more ludicrous follies. But then, she had been newly returned to Town herself, and eager to throw herself back into the game that she had been forced to abandon the year before. But something had shifted—either the merry chase had lost its merriment, or Jane had lost a bit of hers. For some reason, running about Town, striving for the most sought-after man and the most sought-after invitation didn't hold the interest it once did.

The engagement of such pursuits proved empty . . . and proved to Jane just how much things had changed. The thrill was gone.

"That has no bearing on why I do not wish to go back to the castle." Jane responded to her brother's query with a superior sniff.

"Why?" Jason asked suspiciously. "What trouble did you cause there?"

"I didn't cause any." She sighed but did not elaborate further. Because . . .

Because . . . It was the silliest thing. It was weakness on her part, and she would refuse to admit it to Jason, but—the castle was where their mother had been ill. It was where she was buried. And Jane had borne it—the constant edge to her thoughts, walking down a corridor and catching a glimpse of the hall where her mother had stumbled . . . the bed where her mother had perspired through the sheets . . . but now that she had been away, the idea of going back was unbearable.

But she'd be damned if she ever told her brother that. Because she knew he would laugh.

"Whatever mischief you got into at the castle—" Jason began, but Jane cut him off.

"Hear me, Jason Cummings. I am not going back to the castle."

"And did you not hear me when I said that Father cannot be seen on the streets of London? Especially with a caretaker, being coddled as if a child. I suspect that is why you held back from hiring someone so far—fear for father's pride."

"The scales have tipped, Brother. I now fear far more for his health and safety."

Jason brooded for a moment. Rubbed his hand against his chin— so much like their father, however much he did not realize it, Jane thought.

Jason's head came up. "The Cottage is a mere three miles from Reston," he said.

"The Cottage? Reston—Jason, you can't mean to retire us to the Lake District!" Jane expostulated.

"Why not? Dr. Lawford is eminently respected, and his practice is very near the Cottage's grounds. Father will have the benefit of the outdoors—"

"His constitution is not in question," Jane retorted. Then, with more whine in her voice than she liked, "It's . . . *the Cottage*, Jase. In the Lake District. You would *exile* us to the north?"

"Your objection to the castle has forced my hand. Reston will be nearby, the good Dr. Lawford at hand—we would be within a half a day's ride to Manchester or York, if more drastic action is necessary."

"There are half a dozen other estates we could go to—" she argued.

"None so plausibly. We used to go to the Cottage every summer. Well, it's summer now. No one would blink an eye at you going," Jason rationalized, much too neatly, damn him. "A little rustication. Besides, the rules were always more relaxed there—"

"For you, perhaps," Jane grumbled.

"And," Jason continued, ignoring her, "Father always loved going to the lake. It will make him happy."

And Jane knew her brother had her. Her father did always love going to the Cottage. It had been part of her mother's dowry and very much her mother's house, but the Duke was never less an aristocrat and never more a man than when he was on the lake.

Yes, Jason knew he had Jane. But Jason didn't know that Jane had him in turn.

"You're incorrect on one major point, Jason." Jane rose, sliding gracefully to the sideboard and replacing her long-empty glass on its polished surface. "You said no one would blink an eye at my going to the lake."

"And so they shan't," Jason replied. "Half the Ton will abandon Town within the next month for the sweeter country air; you simply traveled a bit earlier." Jason's eyebrow shot up. "I know you, Jane—you will not get out of your obligations that way—I was not gone from the country so long that I am wrong about that."

Jane came to lean over her brother as he leaned back in his chair, stretching his legs out, all too comfortable in his superiority.

"No," Jane smirked, "your mistake was merely singular." At her brother's confused look, Jane bared her teeth in a feline smile. "I'm certain you meant to say *we*."

Three

"THE Cottage? Minnie, are you sure?"

Victoria Wilton paused at the bank of the Broadmill River, one hand hiking up her skirts from getting wet, the other looped around the base of a particularly stubborn sprig of mint. It grew wild on the riverbank that cut through the small park of the Wiltons' residence, and she needed the whole thing for the mint jelly she and Mother were intent on setting up for preserves this afternoon. But suddenly all her attention was given to the Wiltons' stout housekeeper, Minnie.

"Yes, miss," the housekeeper replied, her hands fluttering over her thick muslin apron in excitement. "The butcher had it directly from the Cottage's housekeeper—she said she was roused in the middle of last night by a rider with the missive. The rider told her he had been paid at double his normal rate to get here quick." Minnie raised her eyebrows at this lavish display of coin.

But it was not the money spent that made Victoria's heart move as a hummingbird's wing. "Goodness, that must mean they intend to be here soon." Victoria dropped her skirts and ran her hand over her blonde locks. She had just started to wear her hair up last year, and in the warmth of the sun found no small comfort in having it off her neck—but somehow she found herself yearning to twist her curls around her fingers like she did as a child when nervous.

Instead, she concentrated on her next inquiry, and keeping very, very still.

"Perhaps the Duke has decided to rent the Cottage out for the summer?"

But Minnie shook her head. "Nay, Miss Victoria. The housekeeper said the missive came straight from Lady Jane's hand! It is the family that comes for the summer at last!"

Lady Jane! Oh, Victoria had not seen Lady Jane in ages—not since she was almost thirteen and Lady Jane fifteen. She had been utterly refined then, but surely Lady Jane was the most elegant creature now, what with her impeccable schooling and fine Town fashions and London soirees—goodness, Victoria herself had never even been as far away as Manchester, and . . . oh, what would she think of Victoria's hair? Surely its simple country style was not at all the thing . . .

"The Duke and his daughter, come to rusticate at the Cottage," Victoria breathed. Finally, something worth talking about in Reston!

"Nay, miss," Minnie began, causing Victoria's mouth to fall open in confusion.

"But you just said—"

"Yes, miss, but I meant to say—the family is coming. The *whole* family."

But . . . but that meant . . .

Jason.

The mint was forgotten—thrown ruthlessly to the ground as Victoria picked up her now-soaking skirts—far above the ankle, terribly unladylike, Minnie thought—and began to run toward the house.

"Michael, Joshua!" Victoria cried out to her two younger brothers, playing cups and bowls beneath the large apple tree by the house, "Go and fetch Mother back from the rector's! Now!"

The boys (used to being scolded by their elder sister but rarely with such panic) were shocked out of their game and into action. They sprinted toward the gate to the road, but Michael's dirty hand had barely touched the latch before the gate was swung open from the outside.

"Good afternoon, Dr. Berridge," the boys said, clambering to a halt and giving the most cursory of bows before scrambling past him and through the gate toward the village.

"What on earth . . ." Dr. Andrew Berridge said to the retreating forms of the boys and turned back to the Wiltons' garden, only to see Miss Victoria Wilton sprinting toward him as if her skirts were on fire.

"Oh, Dr. Berridge!" Victoria came to a halt, curtsied with the same ingrained good manners that her brothers displayed, and then smiled up at him. Dr. Berridge—Andrew, as he had told her once to call him but she never had the nerve to do so—had only come to Reston within the past year to join Dr. Lawford's practice, but in that short time he had become quite a good friend to her father. Initially, Sir Wilton had been suspicious of having two doctors in their village, thinking that this was a sign the town would grow out of proportion to its unique quaintness. But upon being assured by Dr. Lawford that he intended to retire and merely wished to introduce his replacement into Reston life as kindly as possible, Sir Wilton took to the new Dr. Berridge like a long-lost brother. The young doctor was twenty years Sir Wilton's junior, but they had both studied at the same university, and Father enjoyed talking about his years at school so much, Dr. Berridge found himself invited to dinner almost thrice weekly. And since Victoria often found herself seated next to him, they, too, had struck up an enjoyable friendship.

"Miss Victoria, whatever is the matter?" Dr. Berridge said, concern overflowing his voice. "Is someone injured? Let me fetch my bag—"

"Oh, no, nothing like that—the boys are off to bring back Mother from the church," she said breathlessly, her face warmly flushed with exertion. Behind her, Minnie had caught up to her young mistress, breathing even heavier.

"Minnie, you, too?" Dr. Berridge inquired, his eyebrow reaching new heights of suspicion. "What has the Wilton household running like lunatics?"

"Minnie, we need to find my pin money—I'm so sorry, Doctor, I expect you've come to accompany my father on his daily walk," Victoria apologized.

"Never mind that—would someone please tell me what is wrong? Why are the boys to fetch Lady Wilton?"

Dr. Berridge—Andrew—grasped her hand with his, concern emanating from his frame. Suddenly Victoria realized that her breathless countenance had shocked the always calm and good-natured doctor into intense worry. She laughed then and squeezed his hand reassuringly.

"The most wonderful news! Jason has come back to Reston, and I desperately need a new gown!" And with that, her eyes alight with pleasure, Victoria half skipped, half ran back to the house, leaving a stunned Dr. Berridge, and a still-breathless Minnie in her wake.

Dr. Berridge looked down at the small bunch of wildflowers he carried in his hand. "Minnie," he said, startling the poor housekeeper to attention, "would you please be so good as to tell me who this Jason is?"

Four

JANE had always found blackmail to be remarkably useful. It allowed her to attain what she needed with very little effort on her part and generally, no harm to either party.

Oh, she wasn't cruel about it—she had no use for other people's money, took no joy in taking someone low. However, when the ends required it, Jane found the means justified.

Jason would likely contradict her philosophy, saying that, as Jane's perennial blackmail victim, she most certainly did take a perverse joy in making him bend to her will.

It could be true, Jane thought smugly. But she would never admit it. Because if Jane was going to be stuck on this wretched journey all the way out to the Lake District, where not a soul worth knowing lived at the height of the Season, she would be damned if she would lack for company.

Jane leaned forward in her seat, nudging back the heavy carriage window curtains with her hand. There, trotting along in a jubilant style that belied its rider's humor, was Jason's great golden steed Midas. And on his back—a glum Jason.

That should teach him the dangers of leaving her alone in a place where he stored his belongings, she thought triumphantly.

Of course, three days ago he had not been nearly so compliant.

Jane had been at her escritoire at their house in London, writing her regrets to all of the hostesses she was obliged to disappoint. She felt keenly for all of them, but most especially when writing her note to Phillippa. Their friendship was of such an odd construction, it could be easily categorized into phases. Best of friends when they met at school—when Jane was still scrawny. Then the year she turned thirteen, she had come back to school fully formed and intoxicated by its power, and everything turned. Now, after years and personal tragedy on both ends, adulthood made them see each other as people again.

Funny thing, growing up.

If only Jason would join her.

"I wrote those when I was sixteen!" Jason had said, the veins in his neck sticking out like the roots of a tree as he loomed over her desk, trying his best to be threatening. Jane simply smiled and turned back to her correspondence.

It was taking much longer than Jason liked to hire a qualified nursemaid, pack up the London house, and leave for the Cottage, and so he took the opportunity to whine, once again, about the method his sister employed in forcing him to accompany them.

"Yes, I can tell," Jane replied calmly. "Your hand and syntax drip of juvenile feeling."

"Damn it, Jane, those are my letters; you have no right to them!" he grumbled.

Jane would have answered this argument, but she already had, repeatedly, over the past three days. Jason knew that if he hadn't wanted the letters he wrote when he was sixteen to be discovered, he should not have left them in his quarters at the castle, stuck between the pages of a book on Tudor-era architectural jointure, which was wrapped in oilcloth and hidden beneath the floorboards . . . where anyone could find them.

Especially a restless, lonely sister with (as her mother had once lovingly described her) no talent for anything other than mischief.

"Come, come, Jason," Jane tried for her most light and reasonable voice. "If I recall, you enjoyed your youth at the Cottage very much. Surely you would like to see it again."

Jason grunted in reply.

"Besides," she continued with a sly smile, "I also believe that the intended recipient of those letters is in Reston. Perhaps you'll chance to see her again."

Never in her life did Jane think she would see a ghost—but that is exactly the shade Jason turned.

"No," he croaked, his voice like dry paper. "You can't know."

"No?" she replied, all innocence. "Are you sure? I was certain you wrote them to Penelope Wilton. I know, I know, you addressed them merely to 'P,' but you described her golden hair and her beauty mark rather profusely. Although I have to categorize the paragraphs about her backside as adolescent fantasy—I hope you know by now that human beings aren't meant to bend in the ways you described."

"AAAARRRGGHHH!" Jason let out, causing Jane's quill to blot horribly on her missive to Phillippa. "Jane—please, I am reduced to begging. Please, please, please . . . allow me to forego this trip. If I stay, you and Father could leave immediately—there would be no need to close up the house. And I could work on my paper to present to the Historical Society. I promise, I would visit often—write more so. Can't you see it would be for the best? You know what to do for Father—I would be useless to him."

He was kneeling in front of her, prostrating himself before her mercy. Jane looked into her brother's face. They shared the deep inky brown eyes and red hair of their mother, but otherwise Jason was so like their father: his jaw set, his aristocratic nose long and stubborn. His face and frame still had some of its boyish narrowness, but an extra layer of flesh had been added by his wine- and food-laden European excursion. All it did was make him seem younger than his four and twenty years. And, as he knelt before Jane, completely and wholly vulnerable, she felt her resolve crumble. Slightly.

"Oh, Jason," she said, placing a consoling hand on his shoulder, "I did not take into account how difficult the journey would be for you. Of course you should stay in London."

Jason's face broke out into the most beatific grin. Goodness, the thought struck her, he could be very charming when he wished. "You are terribly understanding—absolutely cracking, Sis." He leaped up, kissed the top of her head, and waltzed toward the door. "Charles and Nevill are waiting at the club for me—I shall tell them the news."

"Wonderful," Jane replied. "I'll just send your letters off to the print shop while you're out."

Jason stilled by the door. Turned, ever so slowly, on his heel, coming back to face Jane.

"Oh, don't look at me like that. Think of it this way. You've always wanted to be published."

Jason froze, his once-ghostly countenance turning red.

"It's you and me, Jase," Jane echoed. "We're in this together."

Jane smiled at the memory of his murderous stare, as well as the defeated scowl he wore on his face now, riding alongside the carriage.

On their way to exile.

Letting the curtain go, she leaned back against the plush velvet seat, rocking gently with the sway of the well-sprung carriage. Her father was ensconced comfortably next to her. At least, he was as comfortable for the long journey to the Lake District as Jane and the newly hired nurses could make him—blankets in case he was cold, a flask of water in case he became hot. There was a leather medical case sitting across from the Duke, filled with sedatives and smelling salts alike.

The Duke was having a good day. His expression had lightened immediately upon being told Jason had come home—and when he learned of their intentions of traveling to the Lake District, he was positively delighted. The Cottage had always been one of his favorite places.

"I used to joke with your mother, that if she had been a mythical banshee, I would have at least *considered* marrying her—if only because of the Cottage," the Duke commented as the carriage rollicked along.

Yes, the Duke was having a very good day. His mind was with him, and had been consistently for a few days now. Jane had to squash down the foolish hope that always sprang to her breast when her father seemed himself for a good stretch of time. No doctor had ever offered her any hope.

"Why would you have mistaken her for a banshee, Father?" Jane yawned, setting up the joke she had heard a hundred times before. "Her Irish complexion?"

"Nay—she could not sing a note." Her father threw back his head in laughter, arousing the newly hired head nurse, Nancy Newton (earning her the unfortunately unforgettable alliteration of New Nurse Nancy by the London house's staff) from her doze.

"Oh, I'm so sorry, my lady!" she said with a start, her hand pressing into the starched white nurse's apron. Nancy was one of those people who defined roles in life by what was worn. A lady wore her gowns, a thief wore his rags, and a nurse, whether traveling or in the home, wore her starched and pinned apron.

And despite her nickname, New Nurse Nancy was not new to the profession. Of middle age, gray creeping into her neatly braided and coiled hair, Nancy had impressed Jane with nothing so much as the length of her references. It was only two names, but both patients were men of pride and gentility, both of whom were her patients for over a decade apiece.

"I worked at a foundling hospital before that, your ladyship," Nancy had said with the forthright nature Jane had come to know since hiring her, "but I discovered I had more to give older patients than babes."

Nancy was intelligent, practical, and kind to the Duke. She had enough experience with the peerage to not be too in awe of them to help them be human. And she led the other two nurses hired to act as assistants with the practical skills of a field commander. In short, she was perfect.

Except . . . she did snore.

Which she did, after she gave the Duke a quick once-over and settled quickly back to snoozing.

The Duke watched New Nurse Nancy carefully, and at the moment that she was well and truly asleep, he took his daughter's hand.

"I want you to know," he began, banked emotion in his voice, "I am very happy to be going back to the lake. I do not wish you to worry on that score." He looked into Jane's eyes, the steady hazel intelligence that Jane had always known from him. "I have missed it. And I am glad to get to see it . . . one last time."

And as the Duke settled into his seat and followed Nancy's lead and set to snoring, Jane was struck dumb by her father's awareness of his situation. And his acceptance of it. According to some doctors, the time would come when he would not even be aware enough to know he was ill.

Jane did not know which would be worse.

As the carriage swayed back and forth, and the countryside rolled past, Jane wished she could sleep, like her carriage mates. Traveling was exhausting, but Jane had never taken to sleeping in a carriage. Reading was nearly as impossible, as it caused headaches in the enclosed space. Unfortunately, this left Jane with nothing for company but her own thoughts.

She hated leaving London. She hated leaving her friends, new-found and old; she hated leaving the parties—a wonderful distraction for her hurried and overwhelmed mind—and she hated taking her father away from the best possible medical care.

Although, she thought glumly, Jason was right on that score: Father would despise being seen by all his peers while ill. And Dr. Lawford was a respectable caretaker. How many times had he treated the Cummings family's fevers and pains in how many summers? *And* they had New Nurse Nancy.

But Jane could not help but feel as if she were being taken prisoner . . . or perhaps returning to indentured servitude. It wasn't fair, she thought, as she allowed herself a little sulk.

Or at least, she had intended to sulk. To rail against the injustice of being taken out of the cream of society at the height of her popularity, forced on her by a lost old man and a dunderheaded young one. But then, over the course of the journey, days spent rambling down familiar roads with two snoring companions, something strange occurred.

It started with the gnarled oak tree, the one that sat a few miles outside of Stafford, on the North Road. The Beast, she had called it as a child. The massive growth that rose from the ground like a boil on the earth, the moss that covered its black hide a faded green, blending the Beast into the grass it sat upon. Its leaves fell like wisps of hair on a bald man's head, and the Beast was so tall and so thick that when Jane was little and of a frightfully macabre mind, she was certain it would eat passersby and force them to live in its knotted innards. But then, Jane's mother, seeing that her daughter cowered whenever they passed the tree, whispered in the child's ear that the tree wasn't about to devour them as they trotted by in the barouche. Nay, the gnarled old tree was in fact the manor house of the Fairy Lord—and instead of holding her breath as they passed, she should wave hello, and the fairies would lift the limbs of the tree, and it would wave back.

So tentatively, Jane had waved. And then, an equally tentative breeze floated along the air, nudging the Beast's limbs into motion. Jane shrieked with delight, waving enthusiastically now, and with the wind coming up, the tree waved just as enthusiastically back.

Every year after, even when she was long past the age of believing in Fairy Lords, she would wave to the Beast, taking a childish delight in its rumpled visage as it waved back, or didn't, on the whims of the breeze.

And so it was only natural that now, as the carriage rolled past, Jane raised her hand and gave the smallest of waves. But the surprise was how her heart lifted to see those ancient limbs lift on the wind, cheering her on her journey.

The farther north they ventured, the colder it became, even in summer. Jane was outfitted for the journey, but New Nurse Nancy was not, and Jane found herself lending the good lady a very expen-

sive champagne-colored wrap. Jane didn't give the thing a second
thought, until the Duke eyed it. "It's the exact color of the sunrise on
the water at Merrymere," he said.

So it was, and Jane found herself picking the hue out of her
memory.

Then there was the signpost at the village of Palfrey, which had
been knocked by a passing lorry twenty years ago and never righted.
It simply leaned, pleasantly defying the principles of gravity.

The posting inn at Stockport had always boasted the most delicious honey rolls, and when they stopped to change horses, why, it
was only natural that Jane would find herself rooting around in her
reticule for the penny necessary to purchase such a treat.

Each of these, markers on a journey done over and over.

By the time the carriage of the Duke of Rayne passed the Bridge-
downe Fell, where if one sat up very tall, they could see the first glimpse
of the blue waters of Merrymere, the lake the Cottage was situated
upon, Jane was sitting so high in her seat, she bumped her head on
the window frame of the carriage door.

"Looking at the water?" Jason yawned from his perch aboard
Midas. "I thought you weren't excited by going back to Reston."

"I'm not excited," she countered. "But I must have something to
do—these two snore too loudly for me to hope for sleep."

Jason harrumphed, but he could not fool his ever-watchful sister.
He was sitting suspiciously high in his seat, too.

It was not long before they breached the trees and came into full view
of the lake, called Merrymere after its crescent shape: someone a very
long time ago thought it looked like a smile. Jason had pointed out
on more than one occasion in his mournful youth that it could also
be seen as a frown, and could have been called Sorrowmere, but their
mother had been horrified. Sorrow did not suit Merrymere, the village of Reston, or the Cottage. It was a place of absolute joy to the
Duchess: the calm, cool waters, lapping against the shore in lazy
licks, sparkling like diamonds in the sun. A sky of pure blue turned

the water into its mirror, with the occasional pleasure boat or fishing dinghy cutting its oars through the water the only sound made by man in a cool summer suspended in time.

At least, that's how Jane's mother would have described it.

The Cottage sat a mere hundred yards from the lake's edge. It was, admittedly, a ridiculous name for any structure that contained twenty-six bedrooms, three parlors, a ballroom, a sunroom, and a full library, but out of all the Duke's establishments, it had certainly the most home comforts. A sandstone and brick structure, Jane tried to remember if there was an ounce of marble in the place. Likely not—her mother made all of her improvements to the house with an eye toward the rustic.

They were at the door before they knew it. Greeted by servants, many of whom were newly hired within the last week to fill out a mostly retired staff. Their belongings unloaded, their clothes changed, luncheon laid out and eaten—a blur of everyday activities to prepare the family for what was to come. Once the trays were taken away, Jane pulled Jason to the drawing room.

And waited.

"What are we waiting for?" Jason asked, after about three minutes of watching his sister stare out the window.

"The onslaught."

Jason's head perked up. "What onslaught?"

And then they saw it, in the distance, at the same time. A coach, cresting the hill in the drive up to the Cottage.

"Are we expecting visitors?" Jason asked.

Jane shot her brother a look as if he were a very, very young child. "No, we are not expecting."

"Then who could it be?"

"I would wager it's Sir Wilton—he's the head of the local gentry. Oh, and the carriage coming up right behind? That is probably either Mr. Morgan, Mr. Cutler, or Dr. Lawford. Although Dr. Lawford is likely to be attending to his business and not likely to make a social call in the middle of the day. Besides, he'd be on horseback."

"Are we to be invaded?" Jason replied, alarmed.

"Of course. We haven't been at the Cottage in five years, Jase. The whole village must be rampant with curiosity."

"Surely they would give us time to . . . settle in?"

Jane snorted. "Not in Reston."

Jason took a long look at what was now a line of carriages coming their way. "Well, I think that's my cue. Ta, Sis."

And with a perfunctory kiss to Jane's head, he spun on his heel and went for the door.

"Where do you think you're going?"

"I haven't the foggiest."

"You mean to leave me alone with them?"

"Precisely."

"But you can't! Father has gone to rest, and . . . gentlemen make their calls to each other before the families do," she pleaded.

"That only applies when *introducing* families," Jason countered, a smile spreading across his face. "And we've known everyone in the village since well before you ran naked through the square that time when you were five."

"I told you never to bring that up," Jane responded hotly.

"And while you wager that those carriages carry Sir Wilton, Mr. Morgan, or Mr. Cutler, I would wager that they carry Lady Wilton and her daughters, Mrs. Morgan and her children, and Mrs. Cutler's vast progeny."

"You still can't leave me to receive the entire village of Reston by myself!" Jane screeched. (She hated it when she screeched. It sounded so . . . screechy.)

But to said screechiness, Jason did not respond. He simply went to the door and, with a wink, stepped through.

Leaving Jane alone, just as the front door knocker echoed through the first floor.

Jane allowed herself one moment of hot anger before composing herself for her incoming guests. God help her, if it took her the rest of her life, she would make Jason rue this day. Taking her and Father out of London, only to abandon her (again!) to his own pleasures.

She would make Jason pay.

Five

"I'D wager my sister is plotting my demise about now," Jason said aloud to no one in particular.

The portly man behind the long chipped and scarred wooden bar looked up from wiping the remains of ale out of dirty glasses. With a lift of the hand from Jason, he flipped one over and poured him what could almost be described as a pint, before turning back to his wiping with the expected enthusiasm.

The Oddsfellow Arms was located a spare few miles from the Cottage, but it might as well have been a few hundred. And for Jason, that was its appeal.

He'd discovered this tavern—in the opposite direction from Reston—during his last visit to the Cottage, at nineteen. Before that, he had frequented the Horse and Pull or the Peacock's Feather in the village, like all gentlemen with aspirations to a rowdy nature. He'd even once been talked into going to the Bronze Cat, in Ambleside, which had a reputation for its barmaids—namely, that its barmaids had reputations—which was utterly alluring to a randy seventeen-year-old whose largest body part at the time was his Adam's apple.

But no one—absolutely no one—came to the Oddsfellow Arms.

It had no cozy hearth fire, no place to change horses. It had no barmaids with reputations . . . in fact, its only worker, other than the portly man behind the bar, Mr. Johnston, was his wife, Mrs. Johnston, a woman determinedly sour-faced and surprisingly good at cooking. Its location was neither in the village nor out of it—neither way station nor stop for the mail carrier. No one came here—no one bothered. It was only frequented by fellows who wished to be alone—which is exactly what the young Marquis of Vessey, Jason Cummings, wanted. For, you see, misery was quickly filling his frame, and he felt the need to replace it with something else.

How did he get roped into traveling to the wilds of the Lake District? Why couldn't he stand up to his sister? He was the elder of them! Nearly four and twenty, and always bowing to Jane's whims. He barely escaped the last time, and now—now he was back, saddled with more family than a nearly four and twenty-year-old gentleman should be responsible for, and blackmailed into exile, away from his friends to boot.

Responsibility. The very thought left him in shreds. Wasn't it the prerogative of being young to do as you wish? Experience the world? And yet here he was—silently agreeing to the makings of his misery.

He truly believed he did the right thing by insisting they remove Father from Town. Whether or not Jane had exaggerated his symptoms (and, indeed, Jason had seen little to support her fears that the Duke's forgetfulness had progressed into something worse), he knew that if it were the case, the Duke would be ashamed to be seen by his friends as anything other than himself. The Duke was proud—and so was his son.

Jason was mildly surprised to find his glass empty so quickly, but barely had his hand lifted before Johnston had it refilled.

"Excellent service, my man," Jason spoke with a salute. "It reminds me of a little establishment on the streets of Copenhagen—" But the man turned away, back pulling a draft for the only other customer in the place—a plainly dressed man with a blank expression and a cane, who slurped his ale over a plate of kippers and eggs.

Jason shrugged this slight off—people didn't come to the Oddsfellow Arms for conversation—and returned to his original train of thought. What had it been, again?

Oh, yes.

He was glad of one thing, he mused, as a smile pulled up the corners of his mouth. That removing his father from London had the added effect of removing Jane from the Ton. Jason loved his sister, he did—but during her first season, unleashing her on Society was like giving a cat catnip. And to find her running around London, basically unsupervised . . .

A shudder racked his body. No good could have possibly come from it.

Oh, for heaven's sake. His glass was empty again.

The Oddsfellow Arms pints surely must be shorter than pints on the Continent. Why, when he was abroad, he never drank this quickly. Did he? Well, he certainly didn't feel as if he had downed two whole drinks. As well as being short, he determined darkly, his drinks were watered down.

A black feeling arose in Jason's breast. He was the Marquis of Vessey, son and heir to the Duke of Rayne. Did Johnston mean to bilk him? Or did he think he was such a green boy that he couldn't handle his liquor? Well, he would see about that.

"Johnston!" Jason barked, putting on his most autocratic tone. "The ale is weak," he announced to the room at large. "Bring me the whiskey."

The next few hours were fairly predicable, as hours spent in taverns are. The owner and brewmaster, back set up by the accusation of weak ale, brought out his best whiskey for the young lord, high on his perch. Or at least, he brought out his best-looking whiskey bottle. Johnston realized quickly that the young lord was not well versed in the language of spirits, and as such, would believe that the higher the price and more elaborate the bottle, the higher the quality of its contents.

The sole other patron ate his eggs slowly. The front door opened and closed twice—once to let the cat out and once to admit another customer, equally quiet, equally anonymous, but much faster with his eggs.

Johnston wiped glasses.

And Lord Jason Cummings, Marquis of Vessey, became deeply inebriated.

Oh, of course his mind did not register this inebriation, certain of his superior handling of drink. In fact, his mind was convinced he was not merely sober but remarkably observant and eloquently clever, thinking such thoughts as: *Would the universe look different if the earth were oblong, instead of spherical?* And, *I don't care what Charles and Nevill say; I think Miss Austen's work very agreeable.* And, the idea that made him snicker aloud, *I'd bet that Mrs. Johnston's face wouldn't be nearly so sour if someone took her for a decent tumble.*

He was snickering in the direction of said lady as he watched her cross to take the long-suffering plate of eggs from the man with the cane at the back table. So her form wasn't young—it was still female. Or he assumed it was; she and her husband had taken on oddly similar rotund frames over their marriage. But she still moved well, and he wasn't picky—he assumed she had all the parts that would make a tumble worthwhile, Jason thought as his drooping gaze followed her back to the kitchen doors.

It was unfortunate that his wandering eyes had been noted by other pairs, however—most notably, Mr. Johnston's.

Jason's attention returned to his glass. "Johnston!" he signaled, rapping his knuckle on the scarred wood. But that good—and laconic—man did not come as called. Instead, he walked away!

From a Marquis!

He was nearly four and twenty, and Jason had never been treated thusly. Jason stood up off his chair, the floor moving unkindly beneath his feet. Damn floors.

"Oy—Johnston!" he called, the floor moving again, and this time taking his feet with him. Happily, he did not fall to the floor. Unhappily, he more or less fell *into* the gentleman with the cane, who, having left his coin on the table, was headed for the tavern's front door.

"Oy!" he repeated, steadying himself. Clever though drink made him, apparently it robbed him of his vocabulary.

"Steady, lad," the gent said, and with an annoyingly strong arm wedged Jason firmly against the bar—a solid object in a surprisingly fluid world. Jason raised his bleary eyes to the piercing gaze of the stranger and saw pity.

Pity.

Before he knew it, Jason had lurched himself away from the bar and followed the caned stranger out of the Oddsfellow Arms and into its small, muddy courtyard, where that gentleman was hobbling his way toward a plain black curricle.

"Oy!" Jason cried, his vocabulary still oddly short, causing the man to pause, sparing a glance over his shoulder.

"I . . ." Jason began, not at all certain of what would come next from his mouth, "am nearly four and twenty!"

The stranger raised a winged black brow. "Congratulations?" he drawled.

"Which means I am no *lad*."

"Ah." The stranger turned fully, resting his weight on his cane, which sank another inch into the mud. "My apologies."

The stranger bowed stiffly, a small jerk of his shoulders—which in the sober light of, well, sobriety, Jason would remember as easily caused by a stiff leg and a sinking cane, but under the current circumstances, he knew in his veins it to be a bow of derision.

That—combined with the earlier look of pity—burst something inside of Jason. Maybe it was the headache from travel, maybe it was the realization that he was shackled into a position of responsibility. Maybe it was the fact that at that very moment, his house was being invaded by townsfolk eager to gawk at their lives. Maybe it was the fact that Johnston had first watered down his ale and then purposefully ignored him when all he was doing was admiring his wife's form—something no one had likely done in nigh on a decade. Maybe it was that this stranger wrote him off just as easily.

But at that moment, Jason really wanted to fight.

Which was new, as Jason had never been in a fight. He didn't even take boxing. He preferred the clean distance of a good fencing match. But his hands found themselves in white-knuckled fists, his head ducked with a murderous glare.

"You ... you fucking *cripple*," Jason spat, "how dare you dismiss me?"

Once again, the stranger turned. "For someone of nearly four and twenty," he remarked coldly, "you seem to lack the life experience necessary for the amount of drink that you consumed. Go home, *sir*, and grow up."

Red, blinding rage took his sight. He knew his feet were moving, and he knew his shoulders to be hunched down, ready to act as battering ram to his opponent, cripple or no.

Later, he would remember a surprisingly quick blur of movement as the man stepped to one side.

And then that the man had been standing directly in front of the curricle.

Then the white light and crunch of impact as his head hit the carriage door.

And fortunately, that is all he would remember.

"Nicely done, sir, if I may proffer that 'ere compliment."

Byrne Worth gave a deep sigh as he gazed dispassionately down at the young idiot who had charged him with no skill and less aim. "Thank you, Dobbs," he replied, looking up to the coachman's seat. "Tell me, do you think the wheels will clear his body?"

"Oh come now, sir. Don't tell me you're gonna leave 'im here. In the mud?"

Byrne gave his valet, driver, cook, and body man a rare half smirk. "It's where he landed."

And he landed faceup, luckily, for Byrne did not know if he had the wherewithal to flip him over. His leg injury was acquired over a year ago, and in that time he learned that while he was able to move his own weight with occasional silver-handled, mahogany assistance, he was useless at moving much more than that.

"Mr. Worth, least make sure the lad is breathin'," Dobbs admonished in no uncertain terms.

"When did you become a humanitarian?" Byrne questioned.

"When murder became a hanging offense," the smaller man countered, then honked with laughter at his own good joke.

"He charged me, you realize. No seat in the county would convict." But still, Byrne struggled to bend down far enough to check the steady rise and fall of the lad's chest. But damn was his leg hurting him today. He was regretting that attempt at a morning ride—but he needed the air, the distraction.

Dobbs was far more nimble, jumping down from the coachman's seat with the grace of a small woodland rodent—a squirrel or hedgehog. Assuming hedgehogs could jump. Byrne didn't know. He landed with a splat, mud flying in all directions, but mostly on Byrne's trousers.

Any other gentleman would have laid some short words at Dobbs's door. But the fact that Dobbs did not say a word, or offer a hand, and let Byrne come to a standing position on his own, was what earned him a few lengths of slack. Dobbs knew his employer's pride and determination.

"He's breathing," Byrne replied, fighting his breath back to steady. "In fact, I think he's snoring."

Dobbs knelt to examine the body, prodding his fingers into the lanky lad's fleshy side, over the ridges of his skull, through the ginger hair, his fingers coming up clean of blood. Dobbs had always been thorough at triage in the field.

Then he began running those nimble fingers into and out of the lad's pockets, emerging with the customarily expensive trinkets of the Town gentleman.

He had always been thorough at that, too.

"Dobbs . . ." Byrne said, warning in his voice.

The little man returned his reproachful look. "I'm merely looking for a card, a scrap of paper with his name." As he said this, he pulled a silver card holder from the lad's breast pocket. Opening it, he pulled out a pristine white card, squinting to read it. "Mar . . . Mark . . ."

Byrne plucked the card from his hand. "Marquis of Vessey," he read, flipping the now-smudged card back onto the lad's prone form.

"A Marquis?" Dobbs's eyes nearly popped out of his head. "Blimey." Then he proceeded to attempt to heft the lad –er, *Marquis*, onto his shoulder.

"What on earth are you doing?"

"I'm not leaving a Marquis in the mud of a coach yard," Dobbs replied, struggling to get the weight of an over-tall, slightly paunchy Marquis balanced against his side.

"Why ever not?"

"You saw the contents of his pockets! This one's easy pickings for any rabble-rouser, not just highwaymen."

"Where do you propose to take him?" Byrne asked. "Not my house—what if someone comes looking for him? I'll not be responsible for kidnapping a Marquis." A drunken, annoying one at that.

"Who'll come looking for him? There're none named Vessey that lives round here," Dobbs argued, finally getting the lad somewhat on his feet.

"Do you see a coach or a horse?" Byrne countered, knowing full well the courtyard was empty except for his carriage. "That means he walked here and must be staying locally with friends. *They* shall come looking for him." Byrne's mouth pressed into a line, deciding on what action to take. "We should inform the Johnstons, let them put him up in the private dining room."

Dobbs merely snickered and stumbled forward with his load. "You see the way this one was looking at the lady of the house? Johnston will likely put him right back where we found him. *If* the lad has friends, the Johnstons will point them in your direction, and they'll come *thanking* you." Dobbs stopped, took a steadying breath. Then he looked Byrne dead in the eyes with the spaniel-like expression that had swayed Byrne into hiring him in the first place, all those years ago. "Come on, sir. We've all been young and stupid. Have a heart."

Byrne sighed and gave his body man and the mud-covered weight that he carried against his side a long, appraising look.

"Fine," he finally said, turning again to step into the carriage. He pulled himself up onto the step, then shot a glance over his shoulder. "But you get to clean the mud off these seats."

Six

I T was approximately five minutes after Jason left that Jane's anger had been choked down far enough to allow her to receive guests.

It was nearly seven o'clock in the evening when the last guest left them to their supper and allowed Jane's anger to burst back again.

It was exactly three in the morning when Jane's anger turned to worry.

Finally, Jason came stumbling into the breakfast room at ten o'clock, as the servants were just finishing clearing away the remains of a mostly uneaten buffet, looking as if he had been trampled by His Majesty's mounted regiment. When she saw him, Jane—in deference to her lack of sleep and frazzled mind and having gone over every iteration of what could possibly have occurred to her only brother in the hours since they last saw each other—lost any composure she might have had claim to.

She started crying.

"Where have you been?" she wailed, an alarming amount of liquid streaming from her eyes and nose. Jason looked at her, shock in his bloodshot eyes. Then, any sentimentality left his face as it resumed its affectedly casual sneer.

"Cease caterwauling, woman, I'm fine," Jason said, as he gingerly dumped himself into a chair. "Coffee, please," he requested of the footman who came and placed a napkin on his lap.

Jane took a moment to recover. A few deep, calming breaths turned her pale complexion back to its normal shade. As she did, she looked over her brother. He was dirty, and grungy, and missing a sock, but otherwise, he seemed to be whole. No jagged cuts or bloodstains slashed his clothing. As he sat down, he even removed some articles from his pockets and laid them aside, his gold pocket watch and silver card case among them.

"You weren't robbed," Jane said, her voice clear, a small sniff the only trace of her slight hysterics.

"Of course I wasn't robbed—this is Reston," he shot her a look of naked disbelief. Then, "Don't look at me like that. You have no idea what I've been through."

And that is when Jane stood up, walked round to her brother, balled her hand up into a sadly undersized fist, and walloped him on the shoulder.

"Ow!" he said, rubbing the offended shoulder tenderly.

"You have no idea what I've been through, you idiot," Jane replied. "The Wiltons, the Morgans, the Cutlers! Oh my God, the Cutlers!"

Indeed, Lady Jane had certainly spent the better part of yesterday enduring the trials of Hercules. The speed and order of the onslaught had been ruthless. The Wiltons, as suspected, were the first family ushered in the door. Only, instead of two daughters, Lady Wilton only brought one.

"Penelope was married a few years back, my dear. How kind of you to ask after her. She lives in Manchester, her husband a solicitor. She has two little girls, one just a babe still," Lady Wilton said, all in one great string of breath. "I'll write her that you inquired. She'll be so touched. But la! Penelope was your brother's childhood companion. You were greater friends with my Victoria all those years ago. Isn't she looking well! And all grown up, the both of you."

Jane had thought Victoria had grown up very nicely, and granted, her mother made it difficult for either of them to get a word in edgewise, but so far, her conversation did not resemble that of the annoying girl who had shadowed her for entire summers.

That is, until Victoria said, "Speaking of your brother, I . . . I understand he has come to stay as well? How is Ja—er, the Marquis?"

No, Victoria hadn't changed one bit.

But before Jane could reply, she was regaled with every bit of gossip from the last five years within a fifty-mile radius. How the village was lobbying the Morgans to allow a cattle bypass road to be plowed through their land. That the widow Lowe had passed, quite peacefully, in her sleep, leaving her house to a nephew—an unsociable fellow, says he's up from London but never comes to any of the assemblies or society meetings. That Dr. Lawford had taken on a new partner in his practice. And oh! How the Fredericksons' boy ran off with the Crandells' girl—everyone was in such an uproar because she had only just turned fifteen.

"I swear to you, Lady Jane, it's the most scandalous thing to have happened in Reston since you ran round the square naked as a jaybird when you were but five!" Lady Wilton laughed. Jane forced herself to smile serenely. She hated that story and only had a vague recollection of actually doing it. But she knew that in Reston, it was the first thing anyone ever said about her. She could have all the Town polish in the world; it wouldn't matter. Here, she would always be five and naked.

The Wiltons didn't visit for so long. They had the good grace to leave after a prescribed half hour, issuing a pointed invitation for her *and* Jason to make a call. Not so of Mrs. Morgan and her two young daughters. They *had* been in the following carriage, coming up the drive, and once the Wiltons left, felt free to succeed them in conversation. Mr. Morgan was a gentleman farmer and had one of the largest farms in the area, and as such, Jane learned from Mrs. Morgan the vagaries of the weather of the past five years and its effect on the crops, and of course, a great deal more detail about that cattle bypass road, and whether or not it was a good idea. "Well, I just don't know what to do—I daresay Mr. Morgan is as fired up about it as your mother was that time you ran through the village square naked."

After that, the Lennoxes and the Vespers invaded. Then—Mrs. Cutler, with her *seven* children, all under the age of ten, entered the house. While the young ones ran about, nearly destroying a few of her mother's very favorite smoked glass vases, Mrs. Cutler would sigh and remark that it was lucky they had recently moved from the village proper to a small stretch of land on the outskirts. It would give the children somewhere to run. "Oh, children can get rambunctious, as I'm sure you know—we were all five and running around naked once."

For every question she was asked about Town, Jane received a dozen essays on what life had been like in Reston. Someone would ask her if her dress was watered silk, and before she could answer, she would get a list of various young ladies' wardrobes for the summer. If someone asked her about the safety of London for a young woman such as herself, she would immediately be told of the rash of highwayman robberies that had occurred over the winter and spring. And of course, anytime she tried to act as hostess, with the grace and discretion generations of bloodlines and decades of education imbued her with, someone with a twinkle in their eye and too pointed a memory for their own good would bring up the time she was five and . . .

There really was no hope for it.

She was invited, and expected, to return calls to everyone. To host a dinner, or, she shuddered at the thought, a ball. And so, by the time that last person finally left her in peace, all Jane wanted to do was scream.

"But of course I couldn't, because it would upset Father greatly," Jane told her brother, who was too struck to even look her in the eye. And she was particularly difficult to avoid, as she had, in the course of her speech, come to lean over him. "You are lucky that Nancy already took him out for his morning stroll, and he hasn't seen you in this state."

Jason had the grace to look chagrined, but only long enough until he could cover the lower half of his face with the coffee cup.

"What did you do to get you into this state, anyway?" Jane asked.

"... ihadapintdownthub," was the mumbled reply, as Jason took a great gulp of the black liquid.

"I beg your pardon?" Jane asked archly.

"I said, I . . . had a pint—or two—down at the pub. The Oddsfellow Arms."

Jane blinked at him.

"That's all? You went to the Oddsfellow Arms for a pint."

Jason nodded, cupping the coffee to him, paying suspiciously close attention to it.

"And it took you till morning to drink it?" Jane continued drily.

Jason looked up at his hovering sister, peevish. "No, I . . . I might have had more than one. I'm not allowed to have a drink now? Is that one of your confining house rules?"

Jane took a deep, calming breath. "Believe it or not, Jase, I didn't drag you all the way out to Reston to *confine* you. You insisted on dragging me." A long look held between brother and sister, and Jane finally sat down in the chair next to Jason. She allowed a cup of tea to be placed in front of her—not the best tea, mind, but the Cottage's stores had not had much time to be stocked with their preferences. She breathed in its soothing vapors, slowing her pulse, cooling her head.

God, but she was tired.

"So you were at the Oddsfellow Arms? You put up there for the night?" she asked finally, all the fight leaving her exhausted body.

Apparently all the fight had left Jason, too, as he answered plainly, without rancor or guile, "No. Fellow patron took me home. I slept on old widow Lowe's sofa."

Jane shot her brother the arched brows of her surprise.

"Widow Lowe's house? Why on earth were you there?"

Jason shrugged. "That's where the fellow lived. Honestly, Jane, I don't remember much—just that I have a splitting head."

"The nephew? The one who inherited widow Lowe's house when she died?"

"God, Jane—probably, I just don't know."

"The one everyone says is a disagreeable hermit?"

Jason stood up from the table on a great, labored sigh and proceeded to down the last of his coffee. "Sounds like him—look," he said as he exited the breakfast room, forcing Jane to trot after him for the rest of the story, "I remember having a few more than I ought—then I went out of the pub, saw their carriage, and I must have asked for a ride home, but I was woken up this morning on that horrid sofa by a man who can only be described as grouchy, throwing my boots at me."

"Well, did you at least get his name?" Jane persisted.

Jason stopped at the base of the stairs, turned on his sister. "Why do you care about a disagreeable hermit? What sort of mischief are you up to now?"

"Not mischief—*manners*," Jane countered with a superior glare. "Because of your drunken foolishness, I now have to thank the disagreeable hermit for being so agreeable to you."

And so, when Jason simply snorted at his sister's attempts at manners and tripped his way up the stairs, intent upon sleeping Town hours, Jane turned in a huff and went to the kitchen to arrange a basket.

Then she went to the drawing room—where she sat at her mother's escritoire, intending to write the disagreeable hermit a short note, and send it off with a footman. After all, a disagreeable hermit would likely rather be sent thanks than receive people. A consideration she herself had not been paid yesterday by the good people of Reston.

At that moment, Jane glanced up at the window looking out on the drive. Lo and behold, in the distance, there was the glint of movement—horses' hooves and carriage wheels. Stage two of the genteel invasion.

A decision was made. In that moment, Jane could not blame her brother for his escape the previous day. Because she was about to do the same thing.

"Thank you," she said to the waiting footman, who was holding the basket of Cook's best scones, preserves, and a rounder of meat, waiting only for the deposit of the note. "You may leave that with me; I shall deliver it myself."

And so, that was how Lady Jane Cummings decided to discreetly use the kitchen door, exit down the path in the woods that ran next to the lakefront, and stroll.

She breathed in the mint air; allowed her skirts to rumple a bit with the mud of the mile-long path; let the sounds of the clear, cool water pushing with lazy waves soothe her distracted mind. Then she gathered up her best Lady Jane of Society Fame smile, straightened her back, and emerged into the sunny clearing where the widow Lowe's house stood.

And she came upon, much to her surprise, Mr. Byrne Worth.

Stark naked.

Seven

"MR. . . . Mr. Worth!" Jane exclaimed, turning a most uncharacteristic scarlet before maidenly modesty won out over maidenly curiosity, and she averted her eyes. But the image was already burned into her brain.

Byrne Worth stood in waist-high water, clothing nowhere in sight. Jane's experience with the male form was limited to swimming with her brother as children and the Greek statuary populating the British Museum, and Mr. Worth's torso was *far* more reminiscent of the latter. The summer sun beat down on his shoulders, reflecting the light like a god. Pale as marble, he obviously hadn't spent a great deal of time in the sun, but planes and hollows and molded flesh bespoke of a lifetime of health and hard work. Some of that health had escaped him, she knew—they had met before, in London, and he had looked weaker then. But it seemed that in the intervening weeks, some muscle had been added to his frame.

Heavens, she had to stop thinking about this. Maybe it was time to venture her voice again.

"Mr. Worth—I don't know if you remember me . . . Lady Jane

Cummings, I'm, ah—a friend of Phillippa Benning." She paused, waiting. Then, "We met last month in London?"

"I remember you, my lady," Byrne's voice grunted, and much closer to her than she had anticipated. She chanced a peek out of the corner of her eye—he was standing on the shore now, thankfully wearing dark breeches, wet through and clinging to his legs. She watched as he picked up a silver-handled cane on the shore and rested his weight against it. "But I did not think you and Mrs. Benning particularly friendly."

"Hmm?" Jane responded, distracted, averting her eyes once again. "Oh. Ah, we—Phillippa and I, well . . . perhaps we're learning to be friends again. And it's Mrs. Worth. She is your brother's wife now, I'm sure you know."

"Hmm," was the only reply. She could hear his stuttered gait crunch on the grass as he approached her.

Then his voice came again, this time from directly behind her, making her jump. "You may turn around now, Lady Jane. I promise your modesty will remain intact."

That did cause Jane to turn, rise to the challenge of his words. She looked him straight in the eye, her voice cool and impassive. "Perhaps I was being considerate of *your* modesty." She smiled, but did note thankfully that he was fumbling with the buttons of a thin lawn shirt.

"How could I forget such wit?" Mr. Worth replied, done with the buttons. He leaned heavily on his cane as he edged his way past her and toward the small house that edged the lake. "Why would you think I should not remember you?" he called over his shoulder.

She took that as the cue to follow, and did so. "We met under rather extraordinary circumstances, if you recall."

Extraordinary, indeed. They had been thrown into each other's company when Byrne Worth had accompanied his brother Marcus on the chase for a (now thankfully deceased) enemy of the Crown. Lady Jane had come into the picture at the Hampshire Racing Party, when Byrne's brother Marcus had taken a bullet to the shoulder, and Marcus's now-wife Phillippa had reluctantly turned to Lady Jane for help. It had been the most shocking and exciting thing to happen to

Lady Jane . . . ever. And it was the beginning of repairing Jane and Phillippa's friendship. And of course—there had been Byrne . . .

"Extraordinary?" Byrne asked as he approached the little house's door. Turning, he leaned against the doorframe. "Is that your word for it?"

"I realize that gunfights and intrigue may be quite common for you, but it was out of place for me."

He acknowledged that with a shrug. A very small one. But then he returned to his standoffish demeanor. "Doesn't explain why you are on my lake, however."

Jane cocked her head to the side, confused. "But I am not on your lake."

A black wing of an eyebrow lifted. "My front lawn, then. Did Marcus and Phillippa send you? Checking up on me, are they? You can tell them I am fine. Well, even. Superb!"

Jane wrinkled her nose in annoyance. Dry wit was one thing—sarcasm quite another.

As he turned his back (roped with muscle through the thin shirt, she noted) to her, swinging open the door to widow Lowe's little house, Jane crossed her arms over her chest and repeated, "I am not on your lake, Mr. Worth." She continued archly, "Nor your front lawn. In fact, you are on mine."

He turned. And if Jane had not been subjected to his terseness for the whole of this remarkably awkward (for her, at least) conversation, she would have mistaken the lilt that came into his voice for amusement.

"Indeed, Lady Jane? I'm fairly certain it was I who inherited this house from my great-aunt Lowe, not you. Truly, I saw the deed myself."

"Obviously you did not read it fully," she countered. Turning, she pointed to the west, where down the lake's shoreline sat the Cottage, proud and warm in the late-morning sun. "I live down there—at the Cottage—and my family owns all of the land on this side of Merrymere. Your house used to be a playhouse for my great-grandmother when she was a little girl."

He looked at her curiously. "I'm living in your great-grandmother's playhouse?" At her nod, he leaned forward just a hair. "Then how did it come into Aunt Lowe's possession?"

"Apparently—ah—" Jane could feel her ears pink, "your aunt Lowe was—later in life—a, er, *friend* of my grandfather."

Mr. Worth looked at her for a short moment, his ice blue eyes piercing at her skin, causing more than just her ears to pink. Then, holding her gaze, he exhaled a laugh. "Aunt Lowe—I would never have guessed the old broad had it in her."

"Indeed," Jane smiled . . . for the first time that day, she realized. Possibly for the first time since arriving at the lake. "Ah—in any case, he gifted the house to the widow Lowe. But he couldn't gift the land it sat upon—can't break up the family property, or some such thing. So, if you looked at the deed to the house, you would see that the house itself is all you own." She shrugged. "The rest is ours."

"So, every time I leave my house, I'm trespassing on your land," he concluded.

"Only until you come to the Mill Road," she replied pertly. "And my family is more than willing to overlook some trespassing to allow you to move more freely. Especially considering your kindness to my brother last night."

If she expected him to acknowledge having taken care of her inebriated brother the previous evening—to acknowledge having even *met* Jason, Jane was to be disappointed. Instead, Byrne moved his gaze from her eyes, down her body, to her hand.

"Is that for me?" he asked.

Oh goodness! The basket she'd had made—she had forgotten she was even holding it. "Yes!" she replied and quickly held it out to him. "A small token of thanks, for my brother, even though he was too pained in the head this morning to think of it." He just kept looking at her, and so she continued talking. "And also a way of saying welcome to the neighborhood, since even though I have just arrived, I've been here far longer, really. We used to spend every summer here. My mother loved it, but she died recently—however, she would have insisted on a basket . . ." Jane stopped there—just shy, she was sure, of fully rambling.

"I've received welcome baskets like that, Lady Jane," Byrne replied, finally turning from her and crossing the threshold into his house. "They usually contain more probing questions than they do jams and jellies."

Jane had to acknowledge his astute assessment of the village's curiosity. But neither did she want him thinking that such curiosity would be applied to her. No matter how curious she actually was.

"Yes—I myself have just recently arrived and endured such a welcoming. At least you receive a stock of jams and jellies in the bargain," she said into the house, careful to keep herself just this side of the threshold. But that didn't mean she couldn't peek in.

She remembered the widow Lowe's house as being fascinating when she was young. She would run over here, the knees of her dress muddy, her hands sticky from tree sap, and come up to widow Lowe and beg for sweets. Widow Lowe would let her only onto the porch until she had wiped her hands of the sap—everything in the house was to be maintained pristinely. Oh, widow Lowe would act put out by her visits—such a dirty child! How could she be the Duchess's daughter?—but Jane knew she secretly enjoyed her presence. The older woman had a suspicious supply of lemon cakes with tea, which was Jane's favorite.

Only when she passed widow Lowe's standard of cleanliness was she admitted to the house proper. It was filled with bric-a-brac, tiny figurines, enamel flower candlesticks . . . all silly, cheap, beloved. And nothing like what was found in any of the Duke of Rayne's homes. Jane had been young here, and fascinated.

But some of those things—the limestone carved fish that sat on the end table, the lace runners across the end tables—were strangely missing.

"Would have thought you'd relish the attention," Byrne grumbled, breaking into her thoughts.

Her eyes narrowed. What an unearned presumption! He thought

he knew her? Jane shot him an icy look, suddenly letting go of any politeness, since apparently, he had done the same. "Tell me," she said in her coolest tones, "if I were as recalcitrant as you, do you think I could avoid the onslaught of human curiosity?"

Byrne paused in his movements. "I suppose not," he said, contrition in his voice. Jane continued to watch him, a slightly disapproving frown on her face, as he took a cloth from a nearby chair and began rubbing the excess lake water from his hair. It was longer than the fashion, she noted. It curled about his ears in a way that suggested his valet was remiss in keeping it trim. When he was done, he threw the towel about his neck and over his shoulders. Catching her eyes on him, Byrne gave a quick lift of a brow.

"Should we try again?" he asked. At her nod, continuing, "Lady Jane, what a marvelous surprise. Lovely to see you."

"And you as well," she played along with a curtsy. Jane shook her head to suppress a laugh. This was certainly one of the oddest conversations she had ever taken part in. "I came to thank you for your kindness to my brother."

"It was nothing, my lady. Your brother is an idiot; I'm sure it happens all the time."

Jane had no response for that.

Byrne, for his part, obviously felt the awkwardness of his last comment as well, because he looked about him for a moment, hoping his eyes would fall on something that could remedy the situation, before turning abruptly to the far back of the house, to the kitchens, basket in one had, cane in the other.

"Er . . ." Jane fought to fill the void. "What happened to the stone fish?"

He shot a look back at her. "What stone fish?" he called out, using his cane to bang something—a tin—down from a high shelf.

"The one that used to sit on the sideboard. And the lace runners on the table? And the shepherd figurines?" She still stayed outside the door to the house, very careful to keep nonchalance in her voice.

Byrne frowned very slightly as he pried open the tin. "Ah. Those are gone."

"Why? They were willed to someone else, I suppose?" Jane asked idly. Her eyes fell on the far table and smiled slightly. "But you still have the enamel flower candlesticks." Before he could answer, though, a hot breeze rustled through the open window of the kitchen and pushed its way through the small rooms to the door. "Is that—" Jane took a deep breath, "is that the jasmine tea?"

"Yes," Byrne replied, surprised. "Part of the inheritance. Aunt Lowe has a surprising collection of—"

"Oh, I know! She collected teas. From far and away, and she would dole them out on special occasions. She used to allow me the jasmine on my birthday. No one in the county has teas like hers."

"Well, in that case, would you join me for a cup?" Byrne asked. Jane's eyes flew to his face. "Join you?"

"I'm trying to drink it all before it goes bad. The Darjeeling was past use, I'm afraid, but the gunpowder tea and the jasmine have survived thus far." He shrugged, and answering her unasked question, "And yes, I can prepare a pot of tea. Come inside." He swung the kettle out over the fire. "I promise I won't charge you with trespassing."

She really shouldn't. No matter how much time she had passed in this little house in its former life, it was now the dwelling of a gentleman. A dripping, coatless bachelor gentleman.

But . . .

But this was the first conversation she'd had since arriving at Merrymere that didn't include either her issuing a death sentence for her brother or the time when she was five and chased that dog naked through the village square. It may be strange, speaking more than plainly with a half-naked and wet man, but it was also strangely comforting. Someone who didn't know her as a child, only the person she was now.

Oh, she should say no. She should excuse herself, thank him for assisting Jason again, and be on her way. Run into him in Reston and smile and chat politely. Hold herself aloft—encouraging his friendship would surely set tongues wagging, and the last thing she wanted was to invite speculation onto her house. No matter how much he seemed to make an effort for that friendship.

But . . .

But the old Jane would have done it. The Jane before the Duchess's death and the Duke's illness would have been happy to flirt her way into a gentleman's front parlor. She would have laughed and smiled, and hang anyone who spoke against her. And as much as Jane now looked back and saw that version of herself as foolish, there was a part of her that wished she could be that careless and happy again.

She would say no. It was decided. She had the politely refusing smile set on her face, the posture of the repentant. But then . . .

The breeze came again, a hint of jasmine tea leaves floating in the air. And suddenly, Jane was homesick for something she had forgotten. For a time before she knew how to flirt and before her face and figure set men afire. Back when she was scrawny and awkward and muddy and sticky and freckled and filled with the joy of being young and at widow Lowe's door, hoping for lemon cakes with her jasmine tea.

She saw him smile as she raised her foot to cross the threshold, watched him start and turn as the kettle he had set on the kitchen fire began to whistle.

Tea. It was hot as blazes, and she was going to sit in the widow Lowe's parlor and take tea. With, of all the people in all the world, Mr. Byrne Worth.

"My lady!" A voice came from behind her. Turning, Jane saw a young lad—one of the gardener's assistants, she recognized—tumble out the wooded path, and head for her.

"My lady," the boy said, after a few quick breaths, "I was sent to fetch you—your father . . . the Marquis said—"

Jane could feel the blood drain from her face. Something must have happened with her father. Another episode? Please, nothing serious. Please.

She glanced over her shoulder, into the house and met his eyes.

He was resting his weight against the kitchen doorframe, arms crossed nonchalantly over his chest. He held her gaze, those strange bright blue eyes, razor-sharp in their assessment. But there was something else she saw there, other than intelligence and stone.

He nodded once, simply. And that's all she needed.

With the young lad in her wake, she sped into the wooded path and back to the Cottage. Back to her life.

And away from him.

Byrne took the whistling water off the heat, placing it to the side, allowing it to cool, allowing the silence to engulf him. He was alone again. As he had designed and desired.

He was not good for people. He had long since recognized that fact, and his self-destructive ways were only worse when allowed full rein in the masses. It was the reason he moved all the way up here from London when he inherited.

That was almost a year ago. Initially, he came up here, intending to allow himself to go to the devil. He knew he couldn't do it in front of his family, his brothers. They loved him so much it began to hurt. So he would allow himself to fade into his vices, his demons, away from anyone who knew of or about him.

But he hadn't been able to—not entirely. Some little part of his mind resisted, insisting that he come back to the fore.

That same part of his mind won over his body—but that body still resisted being around people. He didn't trust himself with them.

But that little part of his mind whispered now, *How nice to see a familiar face.*

She's not that familiar, Byrne countered.

But at least she knew you—not like the others in town, who have only the worst opinion of you and stay away.

"They have the worst opinion of me because that's what I gave them," Byrne argued, somewhat surprisingly, out loud. "And they stay away because that's what I wanted."

Do you still want it?

Byrne looked around his little cottage. Its rooms still pristinely his aunt's—minus a few ornaments and lace, but her crochet work lined the arms of the sofa, her watercolor paintings hung on the walls. But for a moment, when the red-haired inquisition came, flushed scarlet at his wet figure and still proceeded to follow him to the house, defiant of decorum . . . the still little house had felt alive, woken from its long winter. And it had felt warm.

It was nice to have someone to talk to, other than Dobbs.

And Byrne had to acknowledge that was true. They *had* talked surprisingly pleasantly. He hadn't growled or swiped at her. He hadn't wanted to.

But even if he found it pleasant, even if he was struck more than ever by the stillness of his life, he knew the minute he allowed himself to enter into the world again, the minute he went back to London, the minute he let *anyone* in, he would only end up destroying whatever little pieces of himself he had managed to rebuild.

He poured out the hot water into the pot of tea. Waited for it to steep. He didn't even want it now. His body was invigorated by the swim and chilled by the air. His leg throbbed, the dull ache that was now his constant companion. He looked out the window, through the overgrown vines at the window frames, to the water beyond.

It was going to be a lovely day. The kind of day that invited brisk afternoon rides and meeting friends for picnics on the water.

And, as always, Byrne would spend it here, in this little house. Alone.

Lady Jane arrived back at the Cottage expecting pandemonium. Jason met her at the door, pacing back and forth in a dressing gown and bare feet.

"Jane!" he said, looking deeply relieved to see her and terribly annoyed to have been waiting so long. "I was trying to kick off to sleep, I came down to the library for something to read, and that's where he is, and I didn't . . . I couldn't . . ."

"It's all right," she said, turning quickly down the corridor that led to the library, Jason at her heels.

"Jane—He didn't recognize me," Jason said, his voice breaking like it did when he was a child. He cleared his throat to get it under control.

It was the first time Jason had seen one of her father's spells—and it seemed to truly shake him. Jane reached out and smoothed the lapels of Jason's dressing gown. Then she smoothed her own hair and threw open the doors to the library.

She was prepared for the worst but was surprised to find her father sitting comfortably in one of the large velvet chairs by the fire, reading a sheaf of papers, with a pot of tea by his side.

"Ah! My dears, there you are. Did you know we have a half-finished sailing skiff in the carriage house? I commissioned it when you were still a babe, Jase, and only now just found the work order. Apparently, the carpenter I hired died unexpectedly and left us with only the spine of a sailing vessel and the rest of its makings." He smiled up at them now, his eyes clear and strong. "What do you say, Jason—want to try your hand at woodworking this summer?"

It was as if there was nothing wrong—they had simply come to the lake for a few months of leisure. But for the small pile of jumbled papers next to the library's great desk, signs of a previous agitation, Jane spied as she sat in the matching velvet chair opposite their father.

"Father," Jane ventured cautiously. "May I see?" She held her hand out and, with a jovial smile, took the antique work order he handed over. She glanced at the pages and then back at her father. He was beaming at her, looking as if he had not a care in the world.

"Now, my dear," the Duke reached out and took his daughter's free hand in his. "You're looking very lovely today. The northern climate has always agreed with you."

Jane smiled prettily at the compliment—truth be told, the northern climate had always agreed with her. But it had also very much agreed with her mother. And Jane didn't know whom her father thought he was speaking to. She chanced a look over to the door, where Jason stood, his mouth a hard line, his pallor unaccountably white.

Their father had just recognized Jason, which boded well. Jane had hope she had been called home for no reason.

"Are you having tea?" she asked, a smile on her face.

"Certainly, my dear, certainly," her father said. "It is, after all, teatime."

Jane felt her smile falter; a tiny crack fractured her hope. It was not yet noon.

She sought her brother's eyes again and found them confused, then embarrassed. He looked down at his shoes, contemplating. The Duke smiled, uncomprehending.

But before Jane could say anything, New Nurse Nancy entered the room, bearing a tray of medicines, a harried footman close on her heels.

"Ah, milady," Nancy said in her brisk but kind way. "Come to join your father for tea?"

"Yes, Nancy, I think we could both use a spot," Jane said, her voice steady but cold. "The Duke was alone when I came in?" The question of Nancy's whereabouts, and why she would have left their father alone during a spell hung in the air.

It was answered when Nancy looked to Jason, surprise apparent on her face.

Ah, Jane thought. She had left their father with Jason while she went to collect her medicines. And Jason had abandoned him to pace the hallway.

But Nancy, true to her professionalism, simply said, "I'm sorry, ma'am. It will not happen again."

This tension did not go unnoticed by the Duke. He withdrew his hand from Jane's and began to nervously pick at his wrist, playing with the cuff of his sleeve. A sign of agitation, one Jane had come to know and take heed to.

"What's going on?" the Duke asked. "Are you mad at me?"

"No, Father!" Jane said, impulsively reaching for him. But he recoiled from her touch. "We should have tea—would you like me to pour?"

A look of confusion crossed his face, childlike, fleeting, but there. His eyes came to rest on the tea tray, and it soothed him. He turned his gaze to Jane, and she could see it was no longer happy, but at least it was calm. That is, until Jason shifted his weight to his other leg, the small flash of movement catching the Duke's eye.

"Who is that man?" the Duke asked, fear in his voice. "Who are you, sir?"

Jason looked shocked, unable to answer. He and Jane could only watch as the Duke rose out of his seat and backed away from Jason, as if confronted by an attacker. "What's going on? What's happening? Who is that man?"

"Now, sir, calm down, if you please," Nancy began, moving to him in slow, easy steps. "We'll take a little drink, and you'll feel much better." But the Duke must have felt that the world was closing in on him, because he began to back away from Nancy, too. Nancy, whom he had laughed with and told old stories to during the long days in the carriage up to the lake. He could see none but his own fear. And that's when he broke into a run.

He didn't get very far, only turning and taking a few steps. He was stopped by the great crash and thunder of overturning the tea tray, the piping hot tea spilling out over his hands, which were out to brace his fall.

Eight

THE afternoon was a blur. Nancy scooped up the Duke, helping him to the settee, as he cried like a child in pain. She managed to calm him down enough to take a sip of water, laced kindly with laudanum. The skin on his hands was angry and raw, but the laudanum took away some of the pain and his agitation, as Jane sent their fastest groom out to Reston to bring back Dr. Lawford.

Jane then took the immobile Jason out of the room, leaving their father to Nancy's ministrations. They sat in the drawing room, where that morning Jane had been writing letters, when she saw carriages begin to pull up the drive and decided to go out. A small tray of cards was on a table, evidence of their butler's tact in telling all who tried to call that morning that the family was unavailable. She would have to return those calls, Jane thought vaguely.

They waited now, together, for Dr. Lawford to arrive. Jason had quickly changed into a clean set of clothes, but his face still bore the exhaustion of his misspent evening. However, he was wide awake.

"This is what he's like now?" Jason asked, breaking the silence, his voice drawn.

"This is what it's like now," Jane confirmed, her tone even.

Jason was quiet again, his gaze constant on the window.

"How many doctors did he see in London?" Jason asked.

"All of them." Jane sighed. "They said there's nothing they can do."

"We'll see what Dr. Lawford has to say," Jason said resolutely, his chin once again stubborn, his posture once again young and defiant.

Jane didn't hold much hope that a country doctor would have anything more to say than dozens of London's finest, but she let Jason hold on to hope. She had been through every thought and feeling he was having right now, and she merely had to wait for him to catch up.

But surprisingly, it was not Dr. Lawford who would be proffering his newest opinion—it was an alarmingly young man named Dr. Andrew Berridge.

Dr. Berridge, for all his youth, presented himself as entirely knowledgeable. He salved and bound the Duke's hands and then took a good hour examining him head to toe, Nancy hovering the whole while, seeing that the Duke remained calm and comfortable during the examination.

It was all Jane could do to sit still in the drawing room, waiting for the tall, kind-looking doctor to come and speak with them—and all she could do to get Jason to stay put, and not run out of the house, as she could see he was itching to do.

Finally, a footman admitted Dr. Berridge to the drawing room, and Jane rang for tea. She doubted any of them would drink it, but she rang all the same.

"Your father—apart from his hands," Dr. Berridge began, as soon as the maid who brought the tea stepped away, "is fit, in terms of his body. His muscles are strong and his eyesight clear."

As both Jane and Jason remained silent at this news, Dr. Berridge took it as his cue to continue. "But it is not the body that concerns you."

Jane nodded, and Jason began pacing, framed against the windows in the bright afternoon sun. The doctor's eyes followed her brother's movements but then returned to her steady gaze.

Jane cleared her throat and related to the young doctor the whole of the story. How their father's memory had become faulty, but not alarmingly so—easily attributed to age and a life well lived. But then after their mother's death, it became, to her eyes, much worse.

"And you, my lord?" Dr. Berridge asked, stopping Jason in his pacing. "After your mother's passing, did you notice this degeneration?"

Jason crossed his arms over his chest and leaned against the window, his movements as careful and cold as his words. "I agree with my sister's evaluation."

The young doctor held Jason's gaze for a moment, seeming to assess him. But the moment passed, and he returned his attention to the matter at hand. "I took the opportunity to confer with your nurse. She is remarkably knowledgeable. She attributed this latest lapse to perhaps the stress of travel having caught up with your father finally. Would you say that his—"

"Spells," Jane supplied.

"—spells are brought on by situations of increased anxiety?"

"Sometimes," Jane replied. "But it seems he can have a spell when he is calm as well."

"This is all bloody well and good, sir," Jason interjected, "but is there anything you can actually *do* for the man?"

Jane blushed at her brother's harsh words but couldn't bring herself to admonish him. She had once felt that frustration. She often still did.

Dr. Berridge obviously had some experience with a family's anxiety. His voice softened away from the clinical. "I am sorry. I have little experience with these matters." He paused briefly, considering his words. "I do have a school friend who now works in a sanitarium in Manchester . . ."

"My father does *not* belong in a sanitarium," Jason interrupted, and Jane shook her head vehemently. More than one doctor in London had made that suggestion, and Jane had quit their service immediately.

"I did not intend to suggest such a thing." Dr. Berridge held up his hands, peacemaking. "My colleague has told me of patients with memory problems that have had improvements with the implementation of routines and patterns." He ventured all this kindly, but Jason spat out a bark of laughter.

"Routines? Patterns?" He rubbed his temples. "My father is a world-class poet, scientist. His mind sharper than your scalpel. Wordsworth himself once praised my father's descriptions of Merrymere's peaks and shores. And you think he can gain his mind through . . . *repetition*?" He sent his sister a smirk of superiority. "Jane, have you ever heard the like?"

"No, I haven't," Jane replied quietly. "And that's something at least, isn't it?" She eyed her brother, who swung his look of disgust from her to the doctor. "My father will be fine," he said, conviction in his voice if not his heart. "Without your patterns."

And he let the slam of the door echo behind him.

"I'm sorry about my brother," Jane said smoothly, with her best charmingly exasperated smile. It failed to reach her eyes.

Dr. Berridge waved it aside. "He's young. Younger than the village led me to believe."

"He's four and twenty," Jane supplied absently, earning a surprised glance from her guest. "Could you . . ." She hesitated. "Could you write your friend in Manchester about his methods?"

"Certainly, my lady," Dr. Berridge replied. "I'm very curious about their effects as well."

"You have to understand, the other doctors I've spoken with—they either write my father's condition down to his age, or they want to keep him bedridden with laudanum—or they want to prod his skull with needles, drain the fire from his head. And I couldn't—"

Dr. Berridge nodded. "Your father is of an age where memory fades—even if his own difficulties outpace what is considered normal. But this is a time of great learning—you were right to cast off the medieval."

When Jane inquired about his medical training and learned the man came from hospitals in Cambridge and then London, she could not help but ask, "How did a man of your liberal mind end up in Reston?"

This earned a quick smile from the young doctor. "It is a bit of an adjustment, I must admit. But when working at those large hospitals, I discovered a desire to know my patients—not just as bodies but as people. When Dr. Lawford offered the position, I accepted."

Jane rose, and Dr. Berridge followed suit. She walked with him to the door of the drawing room, pausing with her hand on the knob. "I do ask—that is, I would greatly appreciate—if you, in your letter to your friend in Manchester, kept your patient anonymous?" She looked up at him hopefully, and he gave a quick bow in response. "Of course, my lady. A doctor cannot practice without keeping his patient's confidence. And that includes," he added, before she could think of it, "keeping said confidence from the village as well."

Having greatly relieved her mind, Jane led the doctor to the front door, when she offered her hand.

"I do not wish to offer false hope, my lady. Your father is ill and will likely become more so," he said, his hand releasing hers.

She simply smiled at him as he took his leave. Once the door closed, Jane took a moment to herself, leaning her back up against the wall and closing her eyes, letting air into her lungs.

"Mooning over him already, are you?" Jason called from the top of the great staircase.

He sat there like a child exiled, Jane thought, even as her eyes narrowed at his spiteful words.

"You always did like a pretty face," he continued blithely, "even better if it's a bit below your station. What was it—the music tutor, correct? When you were fourteen?"

"What is it that annoys you, Jase? The fact that he's a man of good looks, or one of talent and training?" If he was going to poke at her, she would twist the knife in his vulnerable spots—and Jason always regretted his lack of accomplishment.

"No matter," he retorted. "You shall have to commit his talents to memory. We're going back to London."

"You want to move Father. Again?" Jane sighed. "Didn't you hear what the doctor said? About the difficulties of travel contributing to his confusion?" She mounted the stairs and slowly climbed, measuring her words with every step. "Repeating the journey would be far from helpful."

"I don't care," Jason grunted, petulant.

"Well, I know you care about the gossip having us reappear back in Town would stir up."

"I thought you wanted to go back to Town. I thought you hated it here," Jason replied. "I thought you wanted Father near to better doctors and you nearer your friends, dancing the night away."

Jane thought for a moment about London. About all the medically minded men who had sat with their wigs and their instruments and frustrated her to the point of crying. She thought about the people she had left behind, not friends, really, save a few, but people that she would have to smile at and flatter, laugh and dance with, flounce about and be vivacious, sharpened, catty, daring, witty Lady Jane Cummings for.

Then she thought about all the people who called on her yesterday, all of them recalling her escapades at age five, all of them hoping she would return those calls, long, tedious hours spent in long, tedious but ultimately kind company. Then she thought about the doctor—his practice provincial, but his mind not. And then, unaccountably, her mind flashed to that morning, to the oddest of conversations had with a half-dressed man by a lake, and for a few rare moments, she was herself, her carefree, younger self.

And all of it, all of who she was expected to be, drained her.

She dropped herself to the stairs next to her brother. And sat there.

"When Mother died, and you headed off for adventure," she said in a whisper, "I thought the worst of it was being left by myself. But then Father began to . . . deteriorate, and I discovered I was wrong. The most frightening thing was realizing I was the one in charge."

Jason regarded her queerly. "What do you mean?"

"I'm exhausted, Jason," she said.

"God, so am I," he replied. "I still haven't slept yet."

"I'm exhausted by being alone. By shouldering the weight of this family alone." She looked him dead in the eye, forced him to meet her gaze. "If we go back to London, you would disappear into your pack of friends altogether. But you don't get to avoid this anymore."

"Avoid what?" Jason asked, and Jane could feel her heart break a little, as she walked past him on her way to lie down. He simply had no idea.

Your life, she thought silently, leaving her bewildered and angry brother behind.

In her room, which had not been redecorated since her childish love of sunny yellow had waned, Jane went to her bed and sat. She felt the unconventional day drip down her spine like syrup from a tree. Jane had almost fallen asleep sitting upright when a soft knock sounded at her door.

"Yes?" she responded, admitting a young maid to the room.

"Pardon me, milady," the girl spoke in the sharp regional tones and looked to be about fifteen. "This just came for you." She hefted a small paper-wrapped box, placed it on the bed next to Jane, and excused herself.

Jane's curiosity won out over her tiredness, and she slowly picked open the wrappings, revealing a large tin.

Of tea.

Widow Lowe's tea—and Jane's favorite. She pulled open the tin, releasing the vibrant smells of earthy jasmine leaves, and spicy sweetness, and finding inside a small note.

Lady Jane,

Since you shared my late aunt's love of this blend, I hope you will accept it as a gift. My taste for tea is sadly crude, and I know she would have wanted someone who appreciates it to enjoy it. Thank you for allowing me to trespass on your property—

Yours, etc.

Mr. Byrne Worth.

P.S. The jam is fantastic.

Jane was surprised to feel her heart race and her eye give way to a small tear at the corner. Until that moment, when all the strength had been sapped from her, she did not realize just how much she needed to be touched by a little kindness.

And maybe a friend.

The next day it rained. And the day after. The heavy droplets of water hitting the surface of the lake reflected Jane's mood—at once laden with disturbance, with the dark alone, but also washing her clean. Jane sat with New Nurse Nancy and laid out a schedule of routines for her father in anticipation of Dr. Berridge's friend's advice. Breakfast, exercise, luncheon, nap, tea, on into the evening . . .

Jane didn't know what Jason did during these days. He was not in the house during the day, but he was not coming home drunk at night. He was silent, and in Jane's experience, when Jason was silent, he was letting his mind stew on something. Jane gave him his space.

The next day dawned bright and clear, and Jane clear-eyed with it. It was, in fact, rather warmer than usual—so much so that Jane felt justified in leaving off her wool shawl as she gathered her bonnet and gloves in the Cottage's main hall.

"Where are you going?" Jason asked, coming out of the breakfast room. He had his riding boots on, his own sturdy leather gloves in his hand.

"Father is off for his walk with Nancy, and I'm going into Reston," she replied, as she tied her bonnet under her chin. "I've a number of purchases to make and calls to return. The weather forbade me from making the journey until now." She let her gaze meet his. "Would you care to come with me?"

She wanted to say that he should come with her, that he in fact owed more calls than she, since he had refused to be in when people came to the Cottage, but she bit her tongue. Her mother would have nagged—she would have cried, cajoled, and shamed Jason into reluctantly accompanying her to call on Lady Wilton and the rector and his wife and all the important things a lady of quality did in the country. She would have shamed the Duke as well, but his show of reluctance would be just that—a show. By the time they set out in the carriage, he would be whistling.

However, just now, Jane held her breath and kept her counsel. For Jason seemed to actually consider the notion.

Finally, he shrugged. "I'll ride alongside you. I was heading into the village in any case."

"Oh?"

"Yes, I need to speak with the blacksmith—he hasn't been out to see to the horses yet; we've been here five days already."

"Did you send a stable lad out to engage him?" Jason shook his head, and Jane shrugged. "Likely why. Father would always make certain to send for the labor men as soon as we arrived."

Jason looked confused for a moment. "It's not just . . . taken care of? The butler doesn't do it?"

"Not unless they deem it necessary. And if they don't, not unless you request it," Jane replied. "Do the horses require attention, and it was missed?"

"No—I just thought . . . that the blacksmith always came. Whether it was necessary or not."

"Father sees the intelligence in giving work to the village."

Jason looked momentarily chagrined. A lifetime at school and idleness had made him inept at the practicalities, Jane thought, and now it was coming to the fore. But whatever he felt, he tamped it down.

Jane smiled and offered him her arm. "Shall we go?"

Jane could not recall the first time she saw the village of Reston. It was too ingrained on her consciousness—the way the high street curved with the Broadmill River that ran alongside it; the way the milliner's sign was painted in red lettering, with curlicues on the ends of the words, turning into ribbons; the village square at the end of the row, the four large oak trees anchoring its corners, and the site of her infamy at five years of age.

It would never change. Sometimes the thought gave her solace. But only sometimes.

Jane and Jason parted ways at the blacksmith's. She made certain to tell him her itinerary—that she was to spend time at six or seven of Reston's finer establishments before visiting the Wiltons on the outskirts, and then possibly the rector.

He hummed his acknowledgment.

Jane let the carriage pull up in front of the print shop, where inside she spoke with the proprietor, Mr. Davies, about replenishing her family's stock of embossed card, as well as ink.

"We've some lovely fire-red ink in," said Mr. Davies. "Your mother was always one to go for the unusual." Jane smiled in acknowledgment and purchased the fire-red ink, unable to tell Mr. Davies that she had no intention of writing in anything other than black.

While there, she met with Mrs. Cutler, who along with her seven children had lost the race to the Cottage front door a few days ago. Luckily, the children were left at home. Mr. Cutler was a solicitor, the village's legal expert—he was the one advising the town council on the question of the Morgans' cow path. His wife was very proud of his position as a man of learning and the status it afforded her in town. She could go on for hours about his accomplishments.

It was a very stimulating conversation.

By the time she left Mrs. Cutler to examine a selection of paper for her husband's business writings, word of Lady Jane Cummings's carriage having been spotted in the village had spread, allowing for every shopkeeper to display his best goods, and every lady to put on her best lace collar. She stopped at the bookshop, directly next door to and connected with Mr. Davies's print shop. He must be doing well enough if he can operate two spaces, Jane mused. She followed that stop with the milliner's. Even though she had more clothes than she could ever wear, she stopped at the dressmaker's, ordered a few yards of cambric for a day dress. It would be good to have something that she could walk through the woods in, or around the lake, she told Mrs. Hill, the shop's proprietor. Funny, it used to be Mrs. Thornton's shop—but she had retired, and her daughter had taken it over.

Maybe some things did change, Jane thought.

And everywhere she went, she spoke with any number of people who came up to greet her.

She met with the Gaineses by the town square, the Pages at another shop, and followed her father's example of stimulating the local economy by purchasing a number of candles, just arrived from Town, which were advertised as promising much better reading light.

She greeted Big Jim the blacksmith as he walked along the street with another gentleman, headed for the Horse and Pull tavern. He blushed a little awkwardly and bowed, remarking that, "Miss . . . er, Lady Jane. You look so grown up!" It caused Jane to smile, thankful that he did not mention any dogs or naked running.

Her intention was to spend a little money in every shop on the high street, and she almost managed it. But try as she might, Jane could think of absolutely no reason to go into the cooperage. Maybe she should purchase a barrel and give it to Mr. Worth—the mischievous voice popped into her head. Give him something to bathe in other than the freezing lake.

A small smile spread to her lips, and she was forced to lie and tell the Pages that she was smiling over joy at hearing their sheep had been impregnated at an alarming rate that spring.

By the time she left for the Wiltons, it was almost noon, and Jane had enjoyed a thoroughly exhausting morning. She was actually looking forward to her next stop—but only, she told herself, as she would be permitted to enjoy it sitting down.

Jane was not surprised to find that she was not the only visitor— indeed, Lady Wilton often had any number of the town's ladies at her beck and call. And knowing that Lady Jane could not possibly come through town without calling on the Wiltons—well, that must have sent the genteel population scrambling. But one particular guest surprised her.

"Dr. Berridge!" she exclaimed upon seeing him in the formal receiving parlor, where Lady Wilton sat next to Mrs. Morgan—she of the cow path—and several other ladies, including young Miss Victoria.

"You've been introduced?" Lady Wilton asked, her voice suspiciously without suspicion.

"Yes, the doctor was kind enough to come to the house when, ah, my father injured his hands," Jane replied. It was easier to tell a limited version of the truth, she knew.

"Oh, dear," Lady Wilton tutted. "My dear doctor, why did you not tell us the Duke had sustained an injury? We would have sent a basket! The good doctor does not yet realize," she said to Lady Jane, "that we take care of our own here."

Dr. Berridge smiled politely. "It is not my place to tell of people's infirmities. Lady Jane, you're looking splendid," he changed the subject neatly. "Rosy cheeked—you must have walked the length of the whole village."

"Twice, I think," Jane replied, as she was handed a cup of tea. Not quite the exotic blend she had come to enjoy over the past few days, but it would do. "I had a great deal of shopping to do and hospitality to return. And it's so warm out. Quite invigorating."

"Yes, it is unusually sunny," Mrs. Morgan murmured into her tea.

"Shopping!" Victoria piped up. "What did you purchase? There is a length of cambric in Mrs. Hill's shop that would look divine with your hair."

"If it's the lavender, then I believe I bought it." Jane smiled. "You have quite the eye, Miss Victoria."

Victoria blushed prettily at the compliment, and, Jane observed, Dr. Berridge smiled very proudly toward Victoria, too.

Interesting, Jane thought to herself.

Lady Wilton and Mrs. Morgan expounded at length on the fluctuating cost of fabrics in the village, and how Sir Wilton blamed the whole thing on the end of the war and a sudden influx of foreign goods from the Continent and the Americas. "Suddenly, everything that was expensive is cheap, and vice versa—or so says my Sir Wilton," Lady Wilton expostulated, to the murmured agreement of all the other ladies present. "You watch, he claims, we'll be invaded by more and more people, and suddenly our little lake will be overrun with pleasure boaters!" she cried, as if pleasure boaters brought with them the four horses of the apocalypse. Oddly, at that moment, Lady Jane caught the gaze of Victoria—who rolled her eyes and gave a small smile. Which prompted a similar smile from Jane.

Maybe Victoria Wilton wasn't so annoying after all.

"So, Lady Jane!" Lady Wilton addressed her most honored guest. "Who did you see in town?"

And so Jane found herself narrating her morning adventures through the shops and streets of Reston.

"I would not be surprised if I met with everyone in the county today," Jane finished, helping herself to a mouthful of tea.

"Everyone except for that awful Mr. Worth," Mrs. Morgan replied.

Jane nearly spat out her tea.

"Awful?" Jane asked, after she managed to swallow. "What makes you say that?"

This simple question set off such a flurry of flushed faces and fast words that Jane could not discern what was being said for several seconds.

"Atrocious man!"

"Barreled me down in the street once, last winter, do you remember?"

"Repugnant—never even came to one of the assemblies!"

"Excuse me—" Jane interrupted. "But are we speaking about the same Mr. Worth? Mr. Byrne Worth? Widow Lowe's nephew?"

All eyes rounded to Jane. "Do you mean," Lady Wilton said incredulously, "that you've been *introduced*?"

"Of course," Jane replied, her astonishment apparent. "And not only here, but we met in London." Where Mr. Worth performed heroic acts to protect Crown and Country, she thought, but kept that part to herself. "His brother married a friend of mine just a few weeks past."

"Are you saying that Mr. Worth was recently in London?" Victoria asked, when all the other ladies lost their voices.

"Yes. Just this summer, in fact."

"But it's impossible!" Mrs. Morgan sputtered, near to tears. "He couldn't have been to Town!"

"For heaven's sake, why?"

"Because," Lady Wilton replied, nearly apoplectic, "he's the highwayman, of course!"

Nine

"You'll have to excuse my mother," Victoria said as she gathered hats and shawls for guests as they took their leave.

"Victoria, what on earth did she mean—Mr. Worth is the highwayman. What utter nonsense," Jane replied as she slowly tied her ribbons under her chin. "And what highwayman?"

"I'm surprised you have not yet been told, Lady Jane," Dr. Berridge said from behind her. "There has been a rash of robberies—both of coaches on the road and of local businesses in the nearby towns."

"The tack shop in Ambleside lost *two* saddles," Victoria added, with a bit too much gothic glee. "Reston was attacked in the winter— Dr. Lawford's offices were burgled, and the next night, Mr. Davies's shop was ransacked!"

"But it is the main roads into the district that have taken the brunt of the thief's . . . er, talent," Dr. Berridge said.

"Father has even made us start to lock our doors," Victoria added.

"That is all very tragic, and I will be certain to add a few night watchmen to the Cottage's staff," Jane replied stiffly, "but what makes this whole town think the perpetrator is Mr. Worth?"

"It's an issue of timing. The highwayman has been operating in this area for nearly a year now, which coincides almost exactly with when Mr. Worth came to stay." Dr. Berridge shrugged, stating simple facts.

Victoria, however, was not bound by simple facts. "And no one—absolutely no one—likes him. He was unconscionably rude to Mama when he first arrived, and she traveled all the way to the widow Lowe's house with a welcome basket." Victoria sniffed.

Jane remembered what Mr. Worth had said about welcome baskets—and how they came more with questions than jam. And if Lady Wilton was the deliverer, Jane was not surprised that he was left with that impression.

"And when he does come to the village, which he himself rarely does, he never says hello to anyone in the street," Victoria continued. "He *growled* at the rector's wife just this past Christmas, when she tried to ask if he was coming to services."

"Circumstantial evidence at best," Dr. Berridge replied.

"My dear doctor—medical school *and* the law? How accomplished you must be," Victoria said pertly, eliciting a grin from her admirer. "And what makes something circumstantial but its circumstances?"

"If you were to ask Mr. Cutler, he would say that circumstances matter very little in the face of facts."

"But in the absence of facts, you cannot blame those with a mind to gossip for relying on circumstance to invent them," Victoria countered, her hand on Dr. Berridge's arm and smiling winningly at him.

And earning a smile from Jane. Victoria may not know it, but she was flirting with the doctor. Delightfully. No wonder the man was so taken.

Victoria led both Dr. Berridge and Lady Jane through the door and into the afternoon sunshine. Impressed not only by Victoria's flirtation but by the intelligence it portrayed, Jane decided to be impulsive and invite her old playmate to come to the Cottage for tea in a few days.

"I'm afraid that day is my mother's knitting circle at tea. Impossible to cancel."

All the better, Jane thought. "Well, if she can excuse you, please come."

Victoria smiled, but then hesitated. "We haven't seen much of your brother this visit."

Oh dear. Jane watched the doctor's expression carefully as she gave a noncommittal, "Hmm. Yes, he's been reacquainting himself with the countryside."

Victoria's face betrayed a flicker of disappointment, but to give credit to her restraint, she did not continue the line of questioning. Waving good-bye at the gate, Jane allowed Dr. Berridge to escort her across the Wiltons' small park to her carriage.

"Dr. Berridge," Jane began, "I find I like you. So, might I be impertinent for a moment?"

The young doctor glanced over at her, then replied, "I should be honored, my lady."

"How is it you have not yet fixed your interest with Victoria?"

The young doctor blushed, but that was his only visible reaction. His response was equally measured, his voice pitched low. "Likely because she has not taken notice of my interest."

"That cannot be true," Jane answered in equally low tones. "She obviously likes you a great deal."

"Miss Victoria is of such good nature, she likes everyone a great deal," Dr. Berridge responded. "Whether or not they are worthy of her affections."

"Including my brother," Jane inferred.

"I . . . I beg your pardon, ma'am, I did not mean to imply . . ." the doctor stammered, but Jane patted his arm.

"It's quite all right. Miss Victoria, I remember, had a rather strong fascination with Jason growing up," Jane said circumspectly. "I fear it has not been squelched." She regarded the doctor a moment. "I am certain you have nothing to fear from my brother. Victoria is not a stupid girl; surely she will see your worth."

But the doctor shook his head. "You will have to allow me to make my own assessment, madam." He paused briefly, then with an embarrassed stutter added, "As much as I appreciate an honest conversation, might we change the subject?"

Jane smiled kindly. "Of course. I actually have another topic I would like your opinion on."

"Mr. Worth?" the doctor guessed.

"Heavens," Jane drawled flatly. "Was my interest that obvious?"

"Only in so much as your bewilderment. As to whether or not he is the highwayman that everyone suspects he is . . ." He shrugged. "It is possible, I suppose."

"Even with his leg? You must know he cannot walk without a cane."

"Yes—an injury he says he sustained in the war."

"So then you've met him," Jane cried. "So you must see that he could not be the highwayman. He has no reason."

"I have not met him." They were walking incredibly slowly to the carriage, slowing almost to a stop. "But," Dr. Berridge continued, "my partner, Dr. Lawford, has. And his report was of a man as friendly as a mauled bear, and he's done little to change that opinion of him in the village."

Jane waved off this assessment. "Did Dr. Lawford examine him?"

"When he first came to the village, last year. And against Mr. Worth's will. He reported that Mr. Worth said my partner could take his advice for swimming as exercise and . . . well, do something very impolite." He grinned impishly. "So, yes, to answer your first question—it's likely his injury would preclude his being the highwayman. But try telling that to the village, when he's given such a . . . colorful first impression."

At that, Dr. Berridge escorted her the last few steps, tipped his hat, and handed Lady Jane up into her carriage. Which was good—she had been given much to stew on and required solitude to do it.

So it was just too bad that she found herself with company in her carriage.

"There I was trotting through town, stopping here and there, and suddenly, Midas throws a shoe. So I go back and leave him at the black-smith's," Jason drawled, lazily grazing his whip against his leg, "who had already left for the pub, after getting such a generous commission from the Marquis of Vessey, lazy bastard. So, Midas is being shod by his ap-prentice, and I'm thinking, how lucky it was my sister was kind enough to tell me her schedule today, and that I might catch a ride back to the Cottage with her." He nodded his cynical gaze toward Dr. Berridge, who walked down the lane back into the village.

"You two seemed cozy." Jason smirked, all his apparent worries about his sister's taste in men and mischief seemingly justified. "So," he said cheerfully, "how was your afternoon?"

Two days of rain, and being kept indoors, with nothing to do but play hand after hand of solitaire and stare at the quickly emptying basket of jams and breads that Lady Jane had brought him, had made Byrne a touch, one might say, disgruntled. By the time the sky cleared that morning, he was practically delighted to throw himself in the lake for his morning swim. For once he did not grimace in the cold . . . for once he did not complain about the pain in his leg. He simply let his lungs expand and contract, his arms cut through the water, joyous in being able to go outside.

He felt so blissfully good, his blood pumping so clean, that upon emerging from the water, he briefly considered going for a ride—then remembered that Dobbs had taken the rig into Reston first thing, to replenish their stocks. Chances were, he would meet up with his friend, Big Jim the blacksmith, and grab a pint before heading back. Byrne didn't expect to see him before sundown.

He just hoped Dobbs remembered the supplies.

Since he had finished his swim and could not countenance being indoors another moment, there was very little left but to take a walk. He dressed in comfortable trousers, a shirt and coat, looking for all the world like a northern farmhand, not a military man with a noto-rious past that he'd rather forget.

As he hobbled nimbly to the door and grabbed the silver-handled cane that rested there (anachronous with the farmer image, but necessary), his eyes again came to rest on the near-empty basket, sitting on the side table, its jams and jellies depleted, a testament either to the Cottage's culinary skills or his and Dobbs's lack. Likely both.

Lady Jane—Byrne couldn't account for seeing her here. Much like his silver cane with his farmer's wardrobe, it was completely anachronistic.

And how he must seem to her! He knew his appearance had changed. He was healthier, stronger. But more wary.

And somehow, she appeared changed as well. In London, she was beyond citified. The epitome of the Ton's sense of style and worth. He remembered the first time he saw her, very clearly.

It had been a few months ago, at the Hampshires' Racing Party. Byrne's brother Marcus had dragged him there—Marcus had suspicions that turned out to be well-founded that a malicious presence they had encountered (and fought, and provoked) in the war had found his way into London society—and Byrne had reluctantly, angrily accompanied him in his hunt.

He was not well then. His leg ached, and he'd fought the urge constantly to give in to his weakness and abate that pain. Sometimes the weakness won. But that day, he was fighting especially hard. After a long few hours in a carriage, with none but his preoccupied brother for company, which had been preceded by a few *days* in a carriage, Byrne . . . well, suffice to say, he was a little worse for wear.

The Hampshire Racing Party was a house party, lasting a weekend. He remembered being inured to the festivities—his need to get through the next five minutes outweighing his need to get through the whole party.

He had been watching the racing. Watching the horses thunder past on the oval dirt track Lord Hampshire had ruined his grounds with, having just had a fight with Marcus, leaving him in a decidedly brown study, staring out into the field.

He'd wanted to dull it all so badly. The night before, he'd managed to abstain from taking a few drops, just a few, of the precious vial of laudanum he'd brought with him. He'd needed to make it last, he told himself. He wouldn't be able to just use it whenever it pleased him. And so, in fact, he had abstained ever since coming to London.

But he was so tired. He was supposed to be keeping his eyes open for anything suspicious—he had used this very skill to serve the Crown in the war, so this was second nature to him—but he was sweating about the collar, the sun making him want to shrink away. The track was loud, and the crowd around him, yelling, urging their favorites on, lambasting the horses that beat them. All he wanted was a tiny bit of respite. A moment where he didn't have to feel this way.

And then, as he closed his eyes, to find the blackness he sought there not at all reassuring, he opened them again, and they came to rest on a young woman strolling casually with an older gentleman.

Bright red hair. There was no other way to describe it—not ginger, not auburn, not a strawberry blonde, none of those softer, more socially accepted colors. Bright red, and shining. She wore a hat, of course—it was far too sunny for any lady of quality to be without some protection—but it was a smart little thing, obviously the first stare of fashion, and did nothing to hide that glorious color.

But it wasn't her hair or her endlessly stylish clothes or the gentleman with her that captured his attention. It wasn't even her beauty, which was undeniable, but he had seen beautiful women before. Hell, there were a few dozen within fifty feet of him.

Nay, it was the tightness at the corners of her mouth. Even from a distance he could read the strain under her polished perfection, her shoulders just a hair too straight, her eyes just a fraction too weary. She couldn't be more than nineteen, he thought, and sheltered by her wealth and privilege. What could she possibly know of life to make her that distressed by it? Likely some folly of the heart, he grunted dismissively.

And as she turned away down the lane with her escort, Byrne turned her from his mind, which was still keenly aware of certain needs, but oddly, they had lessened. He let himself believe he was winning the fight that day.

That was the first of several times he would see Lady Jane that weekend—although it took a moment of discreet inquiry to discover that was who she was. Lady Jane of Society Fame. The polished, perfect daughter of a Duke, a leader of the Ton. To think that a mere month later, she would be tramping through the woods, basket in hand, like a character from a German fairy tale . . . the contrast boggled his mind.

Except . . . she'd still worn that tension about her mouth, her shoulders. In fact, it seemed exacerbated. The only thing that seemed to melt it—beyond the shock of seeing him in the water—was when he brought down that tin of tea.

That, more than anything, was the reason he sent it to her.

Is it? It wasn't because you were hoping she would call again?

Byrne put that little voice—the one that felt the need to point out how quiet he found his life—correction, how quiet he had *designed* his life—to rest. No—if he had wanted her to call, he would have kept the tin, he told himself. She would have been more likely to visit with the prospect of her favorite tea in stock.

Still . . . he thought, his hand on the knob of his porch door, maybe he ought to return the empty basket to her.

It would be a neighborly gesture.

Byrne rolled his eyes at that thought, and—leaving the basket where it was—strolled out into the sunshine.

Not three seconds later, he turned back and grabbed it.

He decided to stroll a bit on his way to the Cottage. There were a dozen paths to explore. The fashion for walking was born and bred in this part of the country: wild untamed lands, nestling the rugged earth under the vastest of skies. Climb high enough in the peaks, and you feel like you could shake God's hand—or so Dobbs had told him. Byrne had not yet ventured to the highest height, his cane still forcing him within limits. Before his leg, before the war, he would have run up and down, twice a day, to be the first to see the sun in the morning and the last to bid it farewell at night.

He missed who he used to be.

But, he thought, pushing himself out of a fugue—he was having a good day. He had gotten to swim, to push his blood and body. He could not let mourning the loss of his younger, stupider self interfere with that.

He may not have his former mobility, but he was getting a great deal better, he had to admit, as he hobbled his way over a rocky bit of path toward a moss-covered cove of trees, where a stream trickled over well-worn stones in the afternoon sunlight. He lowered himself to sit on a smoothly flattened stone, a bench for resting, provided by Mother Nature. A moment of reverie, allowed and taken.

Of course, he heard her footsteps before she spoke.

"I wonder if you would have been able to navigate this path before you began taking morning swims?" The pert question came from behind him.

Her voice wasn't really lyrical—there was too much alto, too much rasp and rumble to its tones—but it was unmistakably Lady Jane's.

She hadn't meant to head toward Mr. Worth's house—truly she hadn't. In fact, she studiously avoided the lakeside path that took her directly to his home. But, in need of a little breathing room for reflection, she had not even entered the Cottage, instead informing her brother—whose presence had sucked up all room for thought in the carriage—that she was going to take the air, in an attempt to work up an appetite for supper. She was very pleased that Jason had simply grunted his assent and gone into the house.

Jane instead chose the path that took her through the woods—the rocky pine forests that fractured the afternoon sun into stage spotlights—falling gracefully on that tree trunk, that large stone, that babbling brook. No, she had no intention of seeing Mr. Byrne Worth today.

Even though he took up the better part of her thoughts.

Fate found him sitting at one of her favorite spots, on the large, smooth stone by the small creek. And yet, fate could not stop her from asking impertinent questions.

"I wonder if you would have been able to navigate this path before you began taking morning swims?" she called out, a small smile coming unbidden to her face.

He didn't even turn around to respond. "Do you now?" he called out, which Jane took as leave to approach.

"Yes," she replied, as she reached the sitting stone after nimbly traversing the cobbled ground. She caught his eye, and he nodded for her to sit. "I also wonder what someone who had apparently rejected Dr. Lawford's advice to use swimming to strengthen his wounded limb would be doing in the waters of Merrymere."

Jane saw the corner of his mouth twitch. "Did you have a nice day in the village, Lady Jane?"

It was exhausting. "It was lovely," she said brightly. "Do you ever go into the village, Mr. Worth?"

"Not often."

"Then how did you know I was there today?"

"Because it's been raining the past two days—and you're suddenly full of gossip." Before she could open her mouth to retort, he continued, "*And* this is gossip you would have mentioned when we last saw each other, had you known it then."

Jane smiled, tipping her head back to catch a few slices of sunlight across her face. "Well done, Mr. Worth. No wonder you were so valuable to King and Country."

She wondered if he would deny it. She wondered if he would ask her how she knew. No one had told her, of course. That would be a breach of the nation's secrets. But having been thrown into the company of Mr. Worth and his brother Marcus under extraordinary circumstances, she managed to discern it.

It didn't help that Phillippa—Marcus's now-wife—was one of the worst secret keepers in the country, as Jane knew from experience.

"Am I meant to wonder what you speak of?" Byrne asked, his voice flat and foreboding.

"That you are the Blue Raven, of course?" Jane replied.

The Blue Raven. The infamous English spy, whose exploits made the front pages of the *Times* during the war, and whose identity had been held secret since then.

But the events of a month ago—the exposure and destruction of the Blue Raven's archenemy by Byrne and his brother Marcus—had incited speculation anew. Marcus had refused to acknowledge the rumors. Up here . . . Jane doubted anyone had even heard them. Including Byrne.

"I really am going to murder Marcus one day for thinking up that ridiculous name," Byrne grumbled, keeping his eyes on the stream. Then he asked, "Are you enjoying the tea?"

"Very much," she breathed, her demeanor melting just a bit at the thought of his present. She lowered her eyes demurely. "Indeed, one of the most thoughtful gifts I've received."

He blushed at that—something Jane didn't think the man who had climbed naked out of the lake in front of her was capable of. She nudged the basket at her feet with her boot.

"Are you having a picnic?"

"What? Oh—no," he replied once he saw what she indicated. "I was, er, going to return it to you. Without the contents, of course."

"Unnecessary—especially considering I purchased a dozen woven baskets in the village today."

"And likely paid too much for them," he countered. "They see your carriage, and they mark up the prices, I'd wager."

Jane's eyebrow went up. "I hadn't thought of that. And here I thought I was spurring the local economy."

Silence descended for a moment as they both stared out over the trickling water.

"In any case—here's your basket." He turned his cane over and used its silver handle to hook the article in question and dropped it neatly in her lap.

"You are rather adept with that thing," Jane remarked.

Byrne regarded his cane, began rolling it between the palms of his hands, its spinning handle catching the light with every quarter turn, like the brightest flickering candle. "It's been my constant companion for . . . well over a year now. One would expect me to be adept at it."

"I only wonder as you seem eager to give it up," she replied, earning a surprised glance from her companion. Finally. She managed to pull a little bit of emotion out of his quietly even state.

"Now, who told you that?" he replied.

"You did. By going swimming in the first place. Especially after you—how did he put it? Told the doctor to 'do something extremely impolite' with his advice." She smiled. "It speaks to your intentions. Poor cane. It shall have to go friendless."

Byrne Worth, however, did not have the grace to look chagrined. He merely took a politician's posture, saying, "Perhaps I simply like to swim. And awaited a more temperate time of year to do it."

"Indeed. You waited just until the eels were at full size."

"I have been swimming for weeks now; I have yet to run into any eels," he answered.

"More good you." She wrinkled her nose in distaste. "I remember very clearly seeing their long slithering bodies when Jason taught me to swim as a child."

"Have you not gone swimming in the lake since you were a child?" he asked, and when she shook her head in the negative, he commented, "What a waste of a perfectly good lake."

"I'm also wondering," Jane continued, as she bit down a smile, "why someone who was so rude as to *growl* at the rector's wife this past Christmas was kind enough to take care of my inebriated brother."

At that he shrugged. "I cannot countenance my momentary lapse in judgment."

"Growling at the rector's wife?"

He shook his head. "Helping your brother. Terribly unlike me."

She laughed aloud at that. "Misguided charity aside, I find it odd that someone who is belatedly taking the town doctor's advice and being kind to strangers is held in such distaste that the whole village of Reston thinks him to be the highwayman that's robbing travelers blind."

And with that, Byrne was silenced. Well, more silenced than his normally reticent self, but this time, Jane was sure, it was out of pure shock.

"Is that what they think of me?" he asked once he regained his voice. She nodded solemnly. "Well, it explains a great deal."

"Such as . . ." she prodded.

"Such as," he hemmed, "how no one will look me in the eye in town. Or at the Oddsfellow Arms."

"I doubt growling at the rector's wife helps."

"She was attempting to physically pull me into the church," Byrne replied. "She stole my cane, certain a little religion would save me."

"What about being rude to Lady Wilton when she brought you a basket, much like this one?" Jane countered.

Byrne simply shot her a look so cynical and beleaguered, it explained the entire occurrence in a glance.

"It occurs to me that you are suffering from a rather extreme case of first impressions," Jane replied.

"And what would you know of it?"

"Oh, I know that Reston is particularly enamored of them. I cannot tell you how many times I've been reminded this past week that I ran through the town square naked when I was five years old." She paused, idly traced an indentation in the rock between them. "It seems that I'll always be that little girl in this town. Or else, I'm expected to be my mother," she finished a little sadly.

She waited for him to say something. Some banal phrase that meant nothing beyond politeness and the invitation to feed his morbid curiosity. It never came. Instead, he kept still but leaned infinitesimally closer to her, his large, warm frame a comfortable presence. She leaned into it, allowing herself to be soothed by his gruff silence, his commiseration, and not tutting sympathy.

She leaned close enough that her arm grazed his, the sensation of touch shocking her out of the reverie with electric contact.

"But," she said too brightly, covering her reaction to his touch, "I take comfort in the fact that your case is worse than mine."

"Oh?" he asked, leaning his body back to its original position.

Then, taking a breath, she ventured forth on the idea that had just occurred to her—one that by even the most lenient judges would be considered rash, impulsive, but one that could not be denied. "Yes, while I can easily endure my lot in life as a naked child or lady of quality, you have been effectively shunned from all society. If you want to get back into their graces and make them forget you are a growling hermit, we are going to have to do something drastic."

"I am *not* going to tell them who I was during the war," he said, his whole body stiffening.

"I wasn't about to suggest it," Jane replied without hesitation. "Granted, it would turn their opinions around immediately, but then I doubt you would ever have *any* privacy whatsoever. Tourists would drive by your little house. All the men wanting to claim you as friend, and all the women . . ." She trailed off, turning slightly pink.

". . . And all the women . . . ?" he prompted.

"Well . . . the Blue Raven does have a, er, reputation with women."

Byrne looked Jane up and down as she squirmed in her seat. Oh Lord, what made her mention such a thing?

"It is also possible," he slowly drawled, no doubt enjoying her discomfort, "that the information would further convince the townsfolk that I am adept at thievery."

She looked up, surprised. "I hadn't thought of that."

"That's because you still consider what I did during the war honorable," he said darkly.

Byrne shifted in his seat then, turning his whole body to look at her, forcing her to meet his eye. She tried to remain unruffled, but . . .

Byrne Worth had very blue eyes. Ice blue eyes.

"Three questions, Lady Jane."

"Hmm?" she asked, then snapping her back to the present conversation, she flushed slightly, and nodded for him to continue.

"First of all: What makes you think I wish to reform myself in the eyes of the town? I may like being left alone."

"Then why do you take account when you can't get anyone to look you in the eye?" she countered and felt the small triumph of his shrug of acknowledgment.

"All right then. Number two: What is this drastic measure you're proposing?"

She smiled, her best mischievous smile. "Prove you're not the high-wayman, of course."

"And I would accomplish that by . . ."

"By catching the real one," she finished matter-of-factly. She could tell he was amused by her suggestion, but underneath she could also see bewilderment. Why, she did not know—it made perfectly good sense to her.

"This leads me to my third and final question." Byrne paused here, either for emphasis or to collect his rapidly unwinding thoughts. "What do you mean, 'we'?"

"Mr. Worth," she began, assuming her best lecture posture, learned at the elbow of Mrs. Humphrey in Mrs. Humphrey's school for Elegant Ladies—and a fiercer lecturer there never was seen. "I understand you are renowned for your prowess at subterfuge, but I also know that during those times, you worked with a partner, who is currently in London. Given my lifelong knowledge of the locals, I would prove an ideal substitute."

Byrne leaned back against the stone, retreating from their banter into his hardened, achingly polite shell again.

"Trying to reform me? Take care of me? I don't need to be cod-dled by a woman," he remarked gruffly, his mouth, which had been so near a smile, pressed down at the corners.

"Good, because I have no intention of coddling another man," she retorted.

He raised one black-winged brow at that. "Jane, you must have a thousand other things you could be doing."

She caught her breath at her name. It was the first time in their acquaintance he had dropped the formality of her title. "Correction: I have a thousand other things I *have* to do. I would welcome a respite from them." She met his eyes again, once more disturbed by their in-tense color. "But my question is, what else do *you* have to do?"

He didn't answer. And so Jane rose, taking her basket in one hand and her skirts in the other.

"I'll give you a day or two. Surely, the infamous Blue Raven can in that time come up with a few plans as to how to proceed in finding this local scourge and routing him? I would be desolated if that wasn't the case."

Again he didn't answer, and so Jane, after an awkward moment of waiting, gave a short curtsy and navigated the rocky ground to head back to the main path, leaving Byrne to his thoughts.

"Lady Jane," he called out to her, once she reached the path. She turned, expecting him to ask what time to arrive at the Cottage or whatnot. Instead he asked, "Did you really run around the town square naked when you were five?"

Jane felt herself blush again, and Byrne obviously took that for an affirmative answer.

Then he smiled at her.

Later that summer, when the atmosphere was beginning to dip into autumn, Jane would be able to look back and pinpoint this moment in time—the moment of Byrne Worth's lascivious, delicious grin—as the moment that the earth hit a bump and the winds changed their course . . . and the great northern heat wave of 1816 began.

Ten

UNSEEN in the last decade, unheard of in this century, the heat wave that encompassed the north of England and half of Scotland had the following effects on the small town of Reston:

The insect population rose by the billions, seemingly overnight.

Shirtsleeves suddenly became remarkably fashionable.

Mrs. Hill ran out of cotton fabric, in all its incarnations, within three days.

Mrs. Hill also ran out of fans, wicking, and ribbons for bonnets—the sun being unkind to the snow-pale ladies of the north.

Farmers contemplated shearing their flocks weeks ahead of schedule, to give the sheep some much-needed relief.

The Wilton boys took up swimming.

This last is mentioned not because the Wilton sons were unschooled in the art of swimming—they had been taught long ago. It is mentioned because Michael and Joshua Wilton, ages nine and seven respectively, had developed a reputation in Reston as the worst rascals of their generation. They ruled a motley group of children (including several of the Cutlers' brood and one of the Morgans' girls—the only

female in their ranks) who ran around the village in their breeches and
shirts, covered in dirt most of the time—their smudged, thieving fin-
gerprints the only sign that an apple had been taken or the Cutlers'
picket fence had been broken apart to act as swords in a game of
knights and ladies. The Wilton boys were viewed as youthful exuber-
ants, who, considering their parentage and Michael's unending charm,
were generally tolerated, and considering their handprints, generally
caught and reprimanded.

Taking up swimming kept them unusually clean.

"Michael! Joshua!" Minnie, the Wiltons' housekeeper, cried out
from the kitchen door. "Did either of you take the cold roast from the
larder?"

"No!" the boys cried back in unison from their station by the
riverbank.

Minnie looked at the boys suspiciously for a moment. But in the
absence of any tangible proof, she could not prosecute the offenders,
so she turned with one last wary glance back into the house.

"I dare you to jump in the river," Michael said to Joshua once
Minnie left.

"That's easy," Joshua spat out the reed he was chewing and prepared to jump. He wasn't wearing shoes or stockings, just his breeches
and shirt—both of which had seen the inside of the river several times
that day.

"No!" Michael replied, his impish grin turning devilish. "I dare
you to jump in the river . . . from *there*."

Joshua looked up to where Michael was pointing. It was the large
tree that grew tall and high along the bank, its strong limbs stretching
out over the water to the deeper, dredged center, where the current
ran quick. Joshua's face took on a slightly fearful aspect, but he
tamped it down before his brother saw it and called him a baby. And
he wasn't a baby. After all, it wasn't his fault he was the youngest!

"All the way out?" Joshua asked bravely.

"All the way out." Michael nodded, brushing his sandy blond hair
out of his eyes. Joshua, for his part, swallowed manfully and began
his ascent into the tree.

Michael watched as his brother reached the branch he'd pointed to and scooted himself out to its farthest point, to where it began to fracture into smaller branches and bowed under a seven-year-old's weight. Joshua shot his brother a satisfied grin (since his two front teeth fell out, his smile had become remarkably wide and charming).

"All right—here I go!"

Joshua looked down into the water below him running fast in the center of the river. It was deep enough, right?

"*One . . .*"

He let go with his hands, still holding fast with his legs. The cold pit in his stomach had him wishing he hadn't eaten the roast earlier.

"*Two . . .*"

Michael kept his eyes glued to his brother, digging his bare toes into the grass in anticipation.

"*Three!*"

"Joshua! What are you doing?" The outraged voice came from the garden gate. Joshua and Michael both snapped their heads up and around. Joshua's balance—already precarious, gave out at this moment, and he wobbled and bobbled, and of course, as is predictable, fell.

"Joshua!" Penelope Wilton cried as she ran from the garden gate to the river, her youngest girl in her arms and the toddler running behind on her short legs, crying, "Mommy!" and laughing across the garden.

The splash in the river alerted the house, and out came Victoria, dressed in her best afternoon dress, gloves, and bonnet. Michael, if he hadn't had his eyes glued to the river, would have groaned. Now Victoria was going to come and yell at them and call the doctor and have them wrapped up in blankets.

Luckily, at that moment, Joshua's head popped up from under the water, and he moved his arms with youthful enthusiasm, if not studied practice, and swam his way to shore.

"Joshua Lawrence Wilton!" Victoria cried as she reached the great oak tree. "You scared me half to death. Get out of that water now!"

"It's all right, Vicky," Joshua said, and he pulled himself out on the bank. "I'm fine. And *that*"—he pointed to the tree branch he fell off of—"was great fun."

"I'm next," Michael said and made for the tree.

"No!" Victoria said with authority, grabbing Michael by his wet, dirty collar and ruining her last pair of gloves in the process.

"You're too scared anyway," Joshua returned with a grin.

"Am not! I can do what you did—I can do stuff ten times more daring!" Michael shot back.

"No one is doing anything daring!" Victoria scolded. "Now, into the kitchen with both of you." She pointed. "Go. And, Joshua, do not go upstairs in those wet clothes."

"Heavens, Vicky, you did a passable imitation of Mother just then," Penelope said from behind Victoria.

"Penelope!" Victoria started, shocked. "Whatever are you doing here?"

"I told Father we were coming. Didn't he tell you?" Penelope smiled, as her two-year-old, Ginny, finally caught up to them.

"Aunt Vicky!" Ginny said, and held up her grubby hands to be picked up.

"Father sent for you?" Victoria said while tactfully avoiding the child's dirty hands. Any other time she would have loved to pick up her niece and tickle her behind her ears, but she was wearing her very best day gown, the one she had just had made a few weeks ago—the weight of its calico a little stifling in the heat, but still lovely.

"No," Penelope replied with a musical little trill of a laugh. "My darling Brandon spoke with a friend of his, who said this heat was going to stay, and he decided I should take the girls here. It's far too hot in Manchester for little girls."

Penelope's husband, Mr. Brandon, although a solicitor, was great friends with the town's scientific society. If he said the heat was going to stay, he had the right of it.

"But it's hot here, too," Victoria countered, trying not to sound unwelcoming.

"Yes, but here at least you have the hope of a passing breeze on the water. In Manchester . . . well, I won't even begin to tell you how horrid city life can be." Penelope smiled and adjusted the baby in her arms. "Here, Vicky, can you take her? I must find Mother and let her know we've arrived."

Before Victoria knew it, she was holding the sprawling baby girl in her arms, one whose inherent adorability belied her potential for ruining Victoria's gown. "Mother—oof"—Victoria adjusted the baby in her arms—"Mother is preparing for her knitting circle; the ladies will be over shortly."

"Is that why you're all dressed up, then?" Penelope smiled. "I must say I do like this blue on you. Is it new?"

"Nu-uh!" Michael piped up, Joshua still standing beside him, picking at his brother's sleeve. "She's going to tea. At the Cottage!"

Victoria felt herself pink about her ears at Penelope's astonished gaze.

"The Cottage!" Penelope gasped. "Well, of course Mother wrote me and said it had been opened, but how wonderful that Lady Jane invited you. I remember you used to quite follow after her and annoy her as a child."

"And now she follows after the Marquis!" Joshua added, causing fits of giggles from his brother.

"Jason is here as well?" Penelope asked, her periwinkle blue eyes alight with pleasure.

She used to look like that when Jason came around five years ago, Victoria thought darkly. Jason and Penelope had spent several summers in each other's pockets, of course, but that one summer, five years ago, something shifted. That summer they were never without each other. They walked out every day, ran through the village like children, took the Morgans' dinghy out to the center of Merrymere and drifted for hours—all while Victoria could only watch wistfully, as her sister stole the one love of Victoria's young life. After Jason left to go back to university, Mother had cried for days when she realized no offer was forthcoming, far longer than Penelope had spent in tears. No wonder Mother had neglected to mention Jason's presence at the lake in her letters to her eldest daughter.

Penelope flitted out her hair, which was worn far too long and lovely for a married woman, and placed her hands on her waist, which was far too narrow for a mother of two. And then she smiled that dazzling Penelope smile that was only highlighted by the little birthmark at the corner of her eye, and made men weak at the knees for miles around.

And Victoria felt her heart sink.

And then she felt something sticky and wet, just above that heart.

For of course, the baby had chosen that moment to spit up the remainder of her lunch.

Victoria Wilton then realized she had absolutely no luck at all.

Jane read the note from Victoria Wilton begging off their tea with annoyance. Well, really. If she was going to cry off, she should have done so much earlier. Not that Jane was looking forward to the tea with Victoria Wilton, oh no. Only that . . . well, it was terribly hot, and Jason had locked himself in the library with his books—on architecture, Jane supposed—and Jane and her father had played hand after hand of whist until he was taken up by Nurse Nancy for his afternoon lie down, and Jane . . . well, she had nobody to complain about the heat with. Nobody to discuss the annoyance of three petticoats and wool stockings with. Complaining was what made the unbearable bearable, her mother had once said.

Her mother.

Jane wandered through the conservatory, where she had had the tea laid, and paused at the bay of windows that looked out onto the lake.

On a day like today, the Duchess would have complained endlessly about the heat. She would have also begun the day by commenting to everyone, from the lowest scullery maid to her oldest friend in a letter, that the day was hot. Nothing unkind about it, just simple fact. The day was hot.

When Jane had been younger, fourteen or fifteen and feeling very grown-up and far more worldly than her parents, her mother's conversation was a constant source of embarrassment, as it consisted chiefly of visual observations in the present and repeating to other individuals the last conversation she'd had. So, if Jane were to be looking out over the lake, as she was now, and observing a flock of geese, her mother would be compelled to say, "Look, a flock of geese." Even though, plainly, no such comment was needed. Then, when her father approached, her mother would say, "Look darling, geese on the lake, I was just telling our daughter."

"Hmm," her father would say.

Or her mother would remark upon the lack of jam in the pantry to her father, who would then admit to having had the last over tea. Her mother would feel it necessary to hunt down her daughter—whether she be in the barn or in the chair next to her father, and tattle that there was no more jam because her father had eaten it all over tea. Whether she wanted jam or not.

Normally, one wouldn't think this a flaw unconquerable. Certainly, someone has to play narrator to life, even if she only managed to remark on things that everyone else had already seen and felt no pressing desire to vocalize. But unfortunately, her mother was gifted with a voice that had gone nasal with age and was prone to shrieking when excited, whether by fireworks, a field mouse, or a lack of jam.

Jane never expected to miss her mother's nasal tone or remarks about jam and geese. But in that moment, looking out over the lake, her clothes sticking to her back in the heat, she did. She could see her mother's shoulders slump in exasperation and then square in determination, and the echo of her feet on the floor as she went to find someone, anyone, to tell the latest news in her shrill voice—the hottest day of the decade! How unbearable! But the fact that Jane was unequivocally alone in this big house weighed so tremendously on her heart that the prospect of a hot day and no one to complain about it made her want to cry.

But she wouldn't. Her tears had been shed. And no one—not her addled father nor her absent brother—had any use for them.

Instead, she would square her shoulders and push the sadness aside. And find something, anything, to distract her.

Byrne was in his kitchen when he felt the movement on the almost nonexistent breeze. The winding fury of someone beating a path to his door. He hobbled over to his cane, gingerly bearing weight on his bad leg. The cane was both his strength and his vulnerability now—he could move very well with it and use it as a weapon in a pinch.

He silently maneuvered his way around floral upholstered furniture and remaining knickknacks to the front door of the house, where he waited.

Would the movement pass him by? Was it simply a passing deer or waterfowl, wandering across his path? No, it was more direct than that, more focused. A female force, marching right up to his door.

He heard the light, deliberate steps on the porch, could hear the hand rise through the air. Byrne wrenched open the door and stared directly into the deep brown eyes of Lady Jane.

"Well, I told you I'd give you a few days," she said immediately upon his opening the door.

There was a moment, so slight Byrne could not count its passing, that those eyes held him rooted to the ground.

"Beg pardon?" Byrne said, after regaining his own ground.

Her cheeks were flushed under her straw bonnet. Her eyes sparked with purpose, her voice and posture determined. This was not the contemplative, deductive woman who sat with him by a creek a few afternoons ago. Nay, hers was a body that was straining for action. That wanted to jump at the bit and leap into something headlong. And it sent his blood pumping.

"The highwayman?" she replied, stepping inside the house with no preamble.

"You just crossed the property line," he remarked wryly.

"Yes, well, I want to see what the plans are that you came up with." She began inspecting various cluttered surfaces, rifling through meaningless papers. "Did you spend any time coming up with a plan?"

She paused as she ran a finger over the table, leaving a stripe in the dust. She wrinkled her nose at him, then, in a motion that could only be described as prissy, flitted the dust off her fingers.

"On how to catch a highwayman?" Byrne asked drily.

"No, on how to drain the lake and catch all the fish—of course on how to catch the highwayman," Jane snitted, her mood unlike any that Byrne had ever seen. It was impatient and fractious. She practically vibrated with energy.

He consciously held himself still, lazy, hoping to let his body language influence hers. "As a matter of fact, I did," he drawled.

Point of fact, he hadn't stopped thinking about it. When she initially proposed the idea, he had scoffed. The entire walk home he thought of every reason to reject it: It wasn't his place. It was inherently dangerous; he was meant to be recuperating, living a quiet life. Lady Jane should be nowhere near a highwayman—and she was far too eager to see such an occurrence.

But, he'd thought, as he walked back to his front door—if he *were* to stake out this highwayman, he would first want to learn where he had been making his robberies—exact locations, and every one of them. Chances are he would avoid thieving too close to his actual home, so as to not draw attention to himself. What was the man taking? If 'twas only banknotes and coin, it would be less traceable than if he were taking jewels off ladies' necks. He would need a means of pawning those goods . . . Byrne would have to acquire a list of everything that had been taken, exactly, down to the last farthing.

By the time he had entered his home and collapsed on the fragile-looking but surprisingly sturdy settee, he was mulling over how to go about following the highwayman's routes.

"Dobbs!" he'd called out, and that good man emerged from the kitchen, carrying a tray of bread and meat, complemented mightily by the bottle of whisky at its side.

"Thought you might like to eat on the veranda this evenin'," Dobbs said, bypassing Byrne and moving to the small porch out the front door. "It's turning warm, might be nice to be outside."

"Dobbs, do you know anything about the highwayman?" Byrne called out, not moving from his chair. He heard Dobbs setting down the tray and rustling with the flower-patterned china.

"Not much beyond what everyone in the village says," Dobbs said as he reemerged.

"Then you know that people seem to have the opinion that I am the man in question."

"Now that you mention it"—Dobbs had the grace to look sheepish—"it might have come up once or twice."

Byrne sat forward, began rolling his cane between his hands, a habit he'd developed while he was thinking. Dobbs waited patiently for Byrne to fill the silence.

"If I asked you to find out where the attacks have taken place, do you think you could do it?"

"I could ask around . . ." Dobbs conceded with a smile, but his eyes remained wary. "Am I going to like what you're plotting, sir?"

"Probably not," Byrne replied.

And for the next two days, as the temperature of the northern counties rose exponentially, as the lilies bloomed faster and larger than ever and the frogs croaked late into the night, Byrne plotted and planned.

Then he waited for Lady Jane.

But now that she stood before him, rifling through his belongings, he was oddly nervous. Not that the course he had decided on would be met with disapproval or sarcasm, no. But some twitching schoolboy energy, a need to impress, overtook him.

He watched her bend over to look at the bottom shelf of a case of books—and suddenly, his thoughts did not belong to a schoolboy anymore.

"Well, where are they?" she asked, standing up straight and drawing Byrne's attention back to her flushed face.

"Hmm?"

"The plans!" she cried, her frustration belied only by a small laugh. Even she could see she was acting slightly at odds with the calm, intel-

ligent demeanor she usually presented. She crossed the small room
and came to stand directly in front of him, holding out her hand. "Let
me see them. Now . . . please."

Byrne considered her for a moment, her sparkling eyes and high
color, the smart little straw hat that shielded her face but would do
nothing to protect her slim shoulders and arms from the sun. He
could see freckles rising just from her walk through the woods.

"Do you have a shawl?" Byrne asked.

"No," she replied, somewhat taken aback. "It's hotter than a frying
pan; a shawl would be almost as unbearable as these petticoats."

Byrne held his tongue in check, sheer force of will keeping him
from giving voice to his thoughts.

"And since a shawl is able to be left off, I have done so," she concluded with a sniff. Her hand was still outstretched, still waiting for
him to hand her some kind of paper, some agenda, something organized and double-checked. He grinned.

"Then you're lucky I have a fondness for freckles." He took her
outstretched hand in his and pulled her out the door.

Jane discerned very quickly where they were going, having walked
these trails and wooded paths hundreds of times in her youth. But
since Byrne seemed intent on his direction and strong in his steps
(with the help of his cane, of course), Jane let him guide her up the
smallest of the steep fells to the east of Merrymere.

They made the long climb in silence—and the weather did not
assist. About halfway up, Jane could tell Byrne was beginning to
falter, but he persevered. And Jane gripped his hand all the tighter.

Once they reached the crest of the fell, Jane allowed herself to
glory in the view.

Breathtaking. Up this high, the wind blew away the heat and left
only the glory of the vast landscape around them. They could see
all of Merrymere and the connected lake beyond it. If they turned
south and squinted in the afternoon sun, they could see the waters of

Windermere. They could see Reston, its various rooftops nestled against the full foliage of ancient oaks, and the Broadmill River, with small crafts floating on it, some flat, bearing goods, some simply holding men looking for a few fish. They could see the roads running into the country, the farms, and the sheep and milking shorthorn cows that bunched in herds along the sides of the fells. They could see everywhere.

"The first incident occurred over the winter," he said, letting go of her hand to point to the south of Merrymere and Reston. "It was down past the valley, on the main road from Windermere. Plenty of visitors from that direction—but not in the middle of January. They ended up robbing the mail, because it was the only coach to come that way."

"Where did you learn all this?" Jane asked.

"I have a friend who helped me discover the locations of some of the robberies."

"How did your friend come by the information?"

"I have determined never to ask that question."

"Sir Wilton is the local magistrate. Did he go to him?" Jane's brow wrinkled. "And if your friend told you the locations, how do you know the mail was the only coach—"

"I only have the information he gave me. Everything beyond that is conjecture," Byrne replied. "I have a theory, if you'd allow me to elaborate."

"Oh, my apologies," she said, immediately contrite. "Please continue."

"Now"—he smirked at her—"there was another robbery, in March. Still cold, but the weather was turning. That one was on the road leaving Windermere, and farther away."

"But Mrs. Wilton said"—Jane blushed, but continued—"she said that the robberies were practically in town. In Reston." Noting that he was looking at her again, in that way of his, she held up her hands. "Again, my apologies."

"No, you're correct. In April and May there were three robberies, each farther north, closer to Reston." Byrne squinted into the western sun and pointed to direct Jane's sight. She inched closer to him, peering down the length of his arm. "There were none in July—" he continued, and Jane started, forcing his eyes to hers.

And his eyes were alarmingly close to hers.

"Ah . . . none in July?" Jane asked. "While you were in London?" She could feel a small hum of excitement. "That's highly inconvenient, isn't it?"

"Very," Byrne concurred, returning his gaze to the horizon. "It could be considered proof of my perfidy by the more suspecting."

"Idiotic people," Jane breathed, shaking her head.

"Yes, well, it's those idiots we are attempting to impress," he replied.

"But I could tell them—"

"No. What we have to do is deal with the here and now. So," he said as he moved to a jut of rock and leaned against it. "Those three in April and May were each successively closer to Reston. And back in January, there was a break-in on the high street."

"Dr. Lawford's, and then Mr. Davies's shop was ransacked," Jane supplied, "according to Victoria Wilton." She watched as he chewed over that knowledge. "It means they must be local, doesn't it? That they first stole from the town proper?" she inquired softly.

"It is possible that the storefront robberies are not connected," Byrne argued, his face shuttered. "A different methodology and all that. But I do believe the thieves to be local." He looked at her then. "They are getting more comfortable, more bold." His eyes narrowed as he squinted into the distance. Jane could practically see the cogs in his brain turning. "The first occasion, in the winter, was out of desperation. The second, in March, was a test to see if they could do this properly. Then, the better they get at their robberies, the more comfortable they feel closer to town. There were another two in early August, the last a mere week before your storied arrival."

Jane moved to lean against the rock beside Byrne, its cool surface a pleasant sensation in the sun and wind. She didn't even allow herself to think about the grunge to which she was exposing the back of her day dress. She was too intrigued by the expression on Byrne's face. When he was speaking about the robberies, his voice was direct, impassioned; color came to his face, and his focus—when she wasn't constantly interrupting him—was unparalleled.

He was born for this. The hunt . . . it was in his blood.

"One thing is for certain," he was saying, "the man, or men, who do this . . . it's homegrown. It's someone who lives here, or in Windermere at most."

"Because the attacks are so regular and becoming so close to town?"

He nodded, an approval of her assessment. "Maybe they discovered it's easier to blend into the background in the village, or they are so much closer to home, it cuts down the amount of time they are exposed between the robbery and reaching safety."

"But they are also more likely to be recognized," Jane countered, and Byrne held up a finger, ready to counter.

"They know the town; they know the carriages. They know who to rob and who not to. Those who travel to the north to view the country, staying only a few days . . . those carriages—"

"Are the ones that have been taken," Jane concluded. "So no one would be able to recognize voice or stance or . . . or anything, really." She sighed. "This spying business is more detailed than I anticipated."

"It does take some getting used to," Byrne agreed drily.

They stood there for some minutes, letting the air cool them and the view stir them. It wasn't something that she thought about often while in London, but the north . . . oh it was beautiful country. And standing on top of the world was the most peaceful Jane had felt since . . . since three days ago at the creek. And before that, a brief moment of calm while contemplating having tea in widow Lowe's house. He was recalcitrant, and according to the village, a criminal hermit, but Jane was more content in Byrne Worth's presence than she had been in . . .

In years.

"What do we do next?" Jane asked after a few moments.

"We?" Byrne replied.

"Yes, we," Jane replied with a little laugh. "I trust you do not have some underlying prejudice against working with a woman."

"None at all," Byrne replied, "so long as said woman is willing to acknowledge her limitations."

Jane's eyebrow perked up. "Which are?"

"Research," Byrne replied. "Not action. Anything that said woman wants to or thinks she can find out through conversation with towns-folk, I am more than willing to accept her help. The moment she decides to take a rented carriage up and down the Windermere road late at night in the hopes of being robbed, any partnership would be dissolved."

"What kind of idiot would do such a—" but Jane stopped when she saw the serious expression on Byrne's face. "Those terms are acceptable." But he held his face in the same still, unsmiling manner, still bored his eyes into hers, until she could do nothing but laugh. "I have no intention of endangering myself. But I can talk sweet to Sir Wilton and find out what specifically was stolen." She smiled at him. "You can't believe what's been said in the village—according to them, everything from family pets to the crown jewels was taken."

"All right," Byrne conceded. "And once we have that information, I'll ride down to Manchester, see if things have been sold down there."

"Yes, but why wait that long to take any action?" Jane asked and was rewarded with a curious glance. "In the meantime, you should go into Reston and introduce yourself to the villagers."

"What kind of idiot would do such a—" he started to say, but he clammed up when he saw the expression on Jane's face. The one that matched his from mere moments ago.

"How are you to identify someone if you don't know what they look like—or stand like, or speak like? And," she added, before he could comment, "even if you catch the highwayman, you still need to undo your first, disastrous impression with the townspeople."

He scoffed. Harrumphed, even. "I don't see the advantage to walking around town tipping my hat to ladies who won't respond. I've tried that."

Jane sighed. "At the very least, you should come to the public dance next week. They can't keep you out."

"Neither can I dance," he held up his cane.

"No, but you can converse, and that will go a long way." The wind whipped a stray tendril of hair across her eyes and mouth, getting trapped in her lips. Before her hand could wipe the wisp back into order, Byrne's hand was there, placing it where it belonged.

Electricity coursed through her body at his touch. But she held still as he wound the tendril back around her ear.

And then, just as suddenly as his fingers had moved, caressed—they stopped. Dropped to his side, finished. As if they had never erred from the proper in the first place.

Jane kept her breath steady and looked at the watch chained to her shirtwaist. Time was slipping past. "I'm sorry, I must go—" she began regretfully, but he held up his hand.

"Your time is not your own. I'm impressed you managed to find an hour to spare."

An hour stolen, Jane thought. But she would not give it back. He held out his hand to her, and this time she took it willingly, took its warmth and strength, and let him escort her back down the fell, back to the lake.

Back to her life.

The dream began the same.

He could feel the blistering pain rip across his flesh, resting there, incubating in his blood. The fire surrounded him, the orange heat and smoke clouding his vision, the weakened floor beneath his feet bowing, creaking under his loping weight. The dead man's body rested on the floor beside him, chewed up in seconds by the fire. Consumed, gone. Lost to memory and forever banished. But still the fire enveloped him.

He could move. The cane that bore the impression of his grip no longer filled his hands—there was instead, an intricately carved silver pistol. It was leveled at the spot where the body had fallen and disappeared into smoke and ash.

He had to get out. He went to the door—met heat and blaze. Went to the window, and stared down into a bottomless pit on the outside. No way out.

He felt the panic set in, felt the hopelessness of his situation. There was no escape. Better to sit. To let the heat and fire take him and . . .

And he heard a voice.

A throaty, rich alto; a laugh that filled his senses like cinnamon. He caught a scent on the air . . . honeysuckle. He turned and saw the fire reflected in a pair of eyes so dark, they melted into obsidian.

"Come with me," she said, the fire warming her lightly freckled skin but not touching her. Not consuming her, the way it consumed him. She held out her hand, pulled him to her, and took his fever inside herself, laying her mouth on his and breathing in life.

And suddenly, they were outside, they were safe, and all that blazed was the sight of her pale skin in the starlight, and he could feel grass beneath his naked feet, beneath his knees as he pulled her gently down with him. Under her back where the dew made her skin slick and fine. The cool night air enveloped them as heat possessed him anew, and he took a breath and laid his lips to her throat and devoured, a trail of fire lit from him across her body, down, down, gloriously down, until—

Byrne awoke suddenly, breathing hard. He was still in his bed, still in his little house on the perpetually cheerful lake. It was pitch-dark, no moon to lend him light, the only sounds crickets, harmonized by the house's creaking.

Normally the dream had him awake with terror, but not this time. No, the dream had morphed, changed, become something new and intriguing. Jane had infiltrated, her cinnamon scent stale in the air, like leftover spiced tea. He shouldn't be surprised, but he was. She had wormed her way into his daytime thoughts; his unconscious was simply catching up. Maybe if he were to try to coax himself back to sleep, he could continue with it, pick up at the heavenly spot where he left off.

But his entire body was awake, on fire, bursting with need. His muscles taut, his cock hard, and for the first time in ages, his leg, whose wound endured a perpetual dull throb on good days, felt like it could run from here to town and back. There would be no more sleep tonight; that he knew. Damn it all.

He stood up from the bed and grabbed his cane. He walked out into the dark world stark naked and plunged himself into the lake. Its cool comfort was a sad replacement for cinnamon and fire.

Eleven

It was an unequivocal truth of Jane's life that the minute she needed to find something, it would find itself hopelessly lost. Jane, being uncommonly organized, decided to blame this particular failing on variables outside of her control, such as the people she happened to be living with.

"Jason, where on earth did you put my pale blue gloves?" Jane said as she barged into the Cottage's library. Jason had been holed up here for days, crossing paths with Jane and their father only over mealtimes and then retreating back to the library. Likely he was concocting some paper for the Historical Society and would ride off to present it as soon as possible, but at least he was still here now, Jane thought. And considering his hibernation-like tendencies, Jane had to admit it was unlikely he had done anything with her gloves, but he was the last person left to ask and therefore the most likely suspect.

"I left them on the settee in the drawing room. Did you move them?" she asked, not breaking her stride as she moved about the room, looking over and under various stacks.

"Why on earth would I move your gloves? You're always losing things," Jason grumbled, not looking up from his writing.

"I am not, and take that back," Jane replied, affronted.

"Go without," Jason shrugged, "far too hot for gloves, in any case."

She huffed in disbelief. "I cannot go into town without gloves, and the pale blue are the only ones that match this ensemble." Not wholly true—a pair of white gloves would work just as well . . . but when else could a girl be so particular but with her wardrobe? She moved to his desk and began rifling through the papers there.

"I say! Can you . . . not disturb what I'm doing?" Jason asked, grabbing at the piece of correspondence Jane had just picked up, which she held conveniently out of his long reach.

"Whom are you corresponding with? More love letters?" Jane held the paper just out of his grasp, as Jason futilely swiped for it. "I hear Penelope Wilton is back in town."

Jason suddenly froze. "Penelope Wilton?" he asked, slowly lowering his arm.

"Hmm." Jane replied as she perused the letter in her hand. "Well, Penelope Brandon now, of course." A small frown marred her brow. "Why are you writing to Crow Castle's steward?"

Jason sighed. "Because I cannot make heads or tails of these account books." He pointed to the desk, where lay stacked a pile of ledgers and papers a foot high. "Nor can I with the account books for the estates in Surrey, Brighton, and the house in London. I was always hopeless with numbers."

Jane ran her hand over the account books, their leather bindings smartly cracked, their pages well thumbed. She checked Jason's fingers—they were indeed stained with ink. He had been working on these for a while.

"You have gone over the accounts?"

Jason looked at her askance. "Of course I have. Father hasn't cracked a book in more than a year, and the stewards have been sending reports every quarter that haven't been taken into the account books . . . what do you think I've been doing in here for the past week?"

Jane shrugged sheepishly. "Paper on the architecture of the northern pub?"

But Jason just snatched the letter back from Jane and set about folding and sealing it. "Anyway, I've asked Crow Castle's steward to clarify some of the questions I had about the accounts."

Jane couldn't help it. She felt the well of a tear come to her eye as she smiled down at her brother.

Jason rolled his eyes at his sister. "Oh for God's sake, don't look at me like that."

"I am sorry," she sniffled, "I'm just so pleased."

"If you're going to get all weepy, go do it elsewhere, would you— you're getting water stains all over the columns." Jason stood and straightened his coat, ran a hand through his shock of hair.

"I have an idea," she said brightly. "Why not invite the stewards of Crow Castle and the London properties to come up and teach you about their accounting methods?" She looked hopefully at her brother, who seemed to mull over the notion, but then he ultimately rejected it with a shrug.

"Probably unnecessary," Jason grunted.

"You're quite right," Jane replied, even as she made up her mind to the contrary. "I am going into town. I can post your letter for you."

"Actually"—Jason blushed—"I thought I might go with you . . . maybe make calls with you as well."

"Really?" Jane asked archly. "Any call in particular? Penelope Wilton, perhaps?"

"Penelope Brandon, now," Jason replied but still pulled on his cuffs nervously. He shot Jane a too-charming smile as he placed the steward's letter in her hand. "I will let you pay for the post on this, though. Much obliged."

As Jason veritably strutted to the library door, Jane was bemused enough to smile. That is, of course, until she saw a hint of pale blue kid sticking out from underneath the foot-high pile of account books.

"You *did* have my gloves! I knew it!"

It was one thing to try to flatter Sir Wilton into divulging the details of the highwayman robberies, Jane thought as she slumped ever so slightly back against the Wiltons' brocade sofa. It was quite another to do so while watching Victoria Wilton make a cake of herself over Jason.

They were all gathered in the Wiltons' westernmost parlor, which stayed cool until the hot afternoon hours beat the sun into the windows. Jane, Jason, Penelope, Victoria, and Sir Wilton, with the two young boys, Joshua and Michael, running in and out at their leisure, Penelope's babes being taken into town. Lady Wilton was out with the housekeeper, purchasing that week's meals, and felt the need to show off her granddaughters to everyone from the butcher to the blacksmith to the rector. If Jane and Jason did not have the wherewithal to leave before that good lady came back, she was certain they would be prevailed upon to stay for luncheon, which must be avoided at all costs. Not only would it disturb their father's schedule to not have his daughter present at the meal, but Lady Wilton had a penchant for hardy fare, which made her daughters' slim figures all the more admirable—they must have stayed that way through sheer force of will.

So there they were, Jane, Jason, Penelope, Victoria, and Sir Wilton, all seated in a pleasant circle, all politely saying "No thank you" as the Wiltons' young maid brought in a tea tray, and Victoria valiantly tried to ply the assembled party. Conversation tended to flow something like this:

Jane would say, "Sir Wilton, Reston seems to have flourished in the time we've been away. Surely, as one of the leading men in the county, you've had a hand in that."

Sir Wilton's face would become mottled with color as his chest puffed out, straining the brass buttons of his waistcoat. "Oh, yes indeed, we've flourished," he said, his eyes narrowing. "*Tourists* have begun to take note of us as more quaint than Ambleside. I'd rather they'd have kept their rabble—why it's practically a metropolis now; they laid cobblestones down their high street, can you imagine? Reston's earthen streets are far more friendly to the local livestock—and if the Morgans ever allow for the construction of that cow path—"

And then, from Jane's other side, Jason would feel the need to interject his opinion. "Actually, Sir Wilton, cobblestones add a level of authenticity to a town's history, I've always found. Indeed, when my friends and I were in Copenhagen, we found townsfolk who told us that their great-great-grandfathers laid the stones."

To which Victoria, her hands full of tea tray and her eyes full of wistful admiration, said, "Oh, my lord, that sounds fascinating. To be walking on history!"

At which Penelope would cry, "Oh leave off, my lord—did they also tell you that for a *very* nominal fee, they would pry up a cobblestone for you to take home with you?"

Jason barked with laughter. "You mean like that old peddler—"

"Who tried to sell us tickets to the traveling circus!" Penelope answered.

"That had traveled through the week before!" Jason finished, and the two would dissolve into giggles like the youths they were remembering themselves to be.

The dejected expression evident on Victoria's face pulled at Jane's heartstrings. Or it would have, if she had heartstrings.

Oh, that is not true, Jane thought. Of course she had heartstrings. And Victoria's predicament was just the kind of thing to tug them on an average day. But today Jane was on a mission. And so, after about three or so circuitous conversational loops, all ending in Jason and Penelope laughing over some adolescent memory, Jane decided enough was enough.

"Goodness! Sir Wilton, with the development of the area beyond the rural, I imagine that an unsavory element has come creeping in?" Jane asked, trying to turn the conversation back to what was important.

"Of course! Goodness, child, didn't you hear me about the cobblestones?" Sir Wilton replied.

"I think, Father," Victoria piped up, "that Lady Jane is referring to the highwayman."

Jane caught Victoria's eye, saw that young lady's conspiratorial intention, and immediately resolved to act on her heartstrings the next time they tugged.

"The highwayman! He's been a complete nuisance!" Sir Wilton cried, his face turning russet, as Penelope nodded.

"We've heard tale of him as far away as Manchester."

"Have you?" Jason asked, his attention undivided from anything Penelope said.

"Oh yes! They say he has plagued the Lake District. He strikes day and night—and he's taken horses, monies—half the jewels in England!"

"If he's taken half the jewels in England, I am surprised that Manchester is the farthest his story has reached," Jane said, doing the best to keep the sarcasm out of her voice. She saw Penelope's mouth pinch a little at the comment, but Jane turned her attention to Sir Wilton before she could react further. "Surely you can tell us what was taken, in truth."

"Well, er, yes," the older man prevaricated. "But why do you wish to know?"

"Perhaps if we knew the extent of the highwayman's deeds, we would not be so quick to put his actions to legend."

Sir Wilton seemed to consider that notion, glancing back at his book room across the hall from the sitting room.

"Besides, sir," Jane pressed, "if the man is able to be so successful, partially on his reputation, if that reputation were not earned, perhaps . . ."

But she was not allowed to continue with the thought. At that moment, Lady Wilton and Minnie the housekeeper burst through the door, Minnie laden with bags from the butcher and the grocer, Lady Wilton laden with news.

"Well, I have just seen what I never expected to see in my many days!" Lady Wilton cried as she entered, fanning herself vigorously, the heat of the day less the concern than the affectation of the overwrought.

"My lord," Lady Wilton curtsied to greet Jason, somewhat stiffly, her eyes shifting to Penelope. But if Penelope was willing to accept Jason's friendship with ease, her mother would have to as well.

"Mama, where are the girls?" Penelope asked, standing to greet her mother.

"Bridget has them, darling," Lady Wilton replied as she removed her bonnet.

Bridget being the nursemaid, Jane surmised, knowing full well that Lady Wilton would have gone out in the village showing off her grandchildren with only the fullest complement of servants she could manage.

"The lazy girl fell behind—I simply had to rush back here and tell you all the news!" Lady Wilton exclaimed. Once she had everyone's eyes, she intoned dramatically, "Mr. Worth was in the village."

Met by blank stares from many, only Victoria and Sir Wilton gave the response that was desired. A gasp of shock and a "Goodness!" fell from her daughter's lips.

"Walking up the high street! He even tipped his hat to me! Well, I never!"

Jane gave a secret smile, while Penelope questioned her mother. "I don't understand, Mama. What is the significance of a tip of the hat?"

This comment launched Lady Wilton into a sputtering recounting of her opinions about Mr. Worth, which Jane sat through patiently.

"I will say," Jason added once Lady Wilton had taken a crumpet, which stopped her speaking, "that my interactions with the man have been less than friendly."

Jane shot her brother a dark look, from which he looked sheepishly away. "Well, it was," he grumbled under his breath. Jane would have kicked his ankle if it could have gone unnoticed.

"If he is such a bad character, why haven't you run him out of town, Papa?" Penelope asked.

Sir Wilton turned, if possible, a more ruddy shade of red, as his eyes narrowed angrily. "Well, we will—once, that is, we have evidence enough to catch the slippery—"

But he was not fated to continue on his rambling, because at that moment, a heartfelt shriek emanated from the kitchens.

"Milady!" Minnie cried as she ran into the sitting room. "The boys have gone mad, they have!"

"What have they done now?" Sir Wilton grumbled, while Lady Wilton took on an expression of abject horror.

"Gracious! What trouble are those poor boys being led into now? The Morgans' daughter has been a terrible influence on Michael and Joshua, my lord," she said by way of explanation to Jason.

"They've felled a sapling and are riding it down the river!" Minnie cried, and rushed back to the kitchen, no doubt to view the melee from her window there.

Everyone was on their feet in a trice. "Don't worry, Penelope, Lady Wilton, we'll catch them before they get past town," Jason replied, his gallantry apparently not at all rusted from disuse.

The crowd bustled toward the kitchens, and from there, to the back gardens and the river beyond. Jane made certain she was at the back of the group, sidestepping neatly from the sitting room into the book room, with none the wiser.

Sir Wilton's ledger of all his magisterial duties had to be here somewhere, Jane thought, as she surveyed the tumbling piles of paper that a country gentleman produces. However, this was certainly more paper than the average country gentleman produced, wasn't it? Sir Wilton's book room was covered in piles of paper, packets, and boxes of bric-a-brac that was disorganized to the point of absurdity. And somewhere in this mess was the information she required. All she would have to do is find the proper ledger, borrow it, and copy out the passages relating to the highwayman. And given the state of this room, she doubted a volume would be missed for a day or so.

Conscious that she had little time, Jane danced her way around a pile of newspapers on the floor to examine a waist-high pile of books—but they turned out to be a rather extensive collection of lurid novels.

"You won't find it there," Victoria Wilton said from the doorway. Her voice was pitched at a conspiratorial whisper, but it still made Jane jump in surprise.

"Why . . . Victoria, I was just—er, I wondered if I could borrow this novel!" she said, picking the top one from the pile.

"You can't have run through the Cottage's library already," Victoria replied with a knowing look as she discreetly closed the door. "And I can't imagine"—she glanced at the title—"*Vice Amply Rewarded* is your cup of tea."

"Good heavens!" Jane gasped, dropping the book like a stone. They both looked at it, sitting innocently on the floor. "Why on earth is *that* in your father's book room?"

"They are evidence—I believe Mr. Fredrickson received them accidentally in a shipment, and he turned them over immediately. Now there is a hunt for a smuggler of vice in the Ambleside publishing shops." Victoria shrugged, placing the book back on its innocuous pile.

"Has no one been arrested yet?" Jane asked, but Victoria simply shrugged, as if to say the chances of having actually caught anyone were fairly nil.

"Well, he certainly shouldn't have them around children!" Jane admonished.

"True—but no one ever comes in here but Father. But enough of that—you are far more interested in another case, I imagine."

Jane could only smile. "When did you become so intelligent?"

"Around the time you became so highly polished," Victoria retorted smartly. "What are you looking for, Lady Jane, and how can I assist you?"

Jane looked into Victoria's shining and eager face, ripe for mischief. It was the same face that had followed her around like a puppy for all those summers past, desperate for attention and intrigue and friendship. But now there was something different about her. Or perhaps Jane was just happy to have a coconspirator.

"I was hoping to borrow your father's magistrate ledger. I assume he keeps one, and he keeps it in here—I would bring it back, unharmed, no one the wiser," Jane said, her voice pitched low.

"He does keep one, or possibly several . . . and he does keep it in here," Victoria replied and began scanning the shelves with a frown.

Jane hesitated a moment. As handy as Victoria's assistance could prove to be, surely her father would not appreciate her prying through his things. She would hate to get the girl in trouble, not to mention jeopardize her entire endeavor, if discovered. "Are you sure you do not wish to join the others? The young boys might need your help, after all."

A flicker of concern crossed Victoria's young face, but she buried it under a blush. "No, they'll be fine. After all, the Marquis and Penelope . . . I'm certain they have it under control."

Jane turned from the shelves and bit her lip. "Victoria, I have to ask . . . you seem to have become a very lovely young lady. And to put it bluntly, my brother is an idiot. I don't understand—"

"Why I'm in love with him?"

Jane paled, but kept her face schooled into friendly concern and nodded. Love? Oh dear.

Victoria smiled wistfully. "Do you remember the summer when I was nine or ten? You were about twelve, and we still ran around together, with skinned knees and holes in our stockings?"

Jane nodded, easily able to recall the summer before she went back to Mrs. Humphrey's School for Elegant Ladies, and nature turned her from the freckled, skinny thing she was into an elegant lady of society. The summer after, she would come back to Reston and be far too grown-up to climb trees for apples or for little playmates like Victoria.

"Well, one day, when you were having tea with widow Lowe, I was in town, and fetching some items for Mother, and was nearly mowed down by an ox cart. I was quite all right," she hastened to add, "but I fell and bloodied my nose."

Victoria's eyes misted a little at the memory, and Jane could not help but leave off her search for the ledger and listen. "My sister and the Marquis happened along—and he gave me what must have been his best handkerchief. The softest linen, shot through with silver thread and his initials, can you imagine? It was the loveliest thing I'd ever seen, and he thought only of stopping the blood from my nose."

Jane hadn't the heart to tell her that all of their ordinary handkerchiefs had their initials in silver thread—their better linens were shot with gold. Added to that, Jason had an absentminded, casual attitude about his belongings . . . but Victoria did not need to know that now.

"Then, as Penelope was so squeamish around any injury, he sat and *stayed* with me, while she ran for the doctor. He told me jokes. And that's when I fell in love with him."

Jane sighed. The one moment her brother showed true chivalry, he entrapped a poor young girl's heart with it.

"My eye turned black for a week after," Victoria continued, lost in her memory.

"I remember that," Jane replied. "You refused any visitors—I only learned of it when I saw you in church."

Victoria nodded, "But Jas—er, the Marquis came anyway. Not to see me specifically of course, but he ducked his head in twice that week and said I was looking well." She laughed. "Can you imagine? He thought I looked well, even with my eye."

"But that was years ago," Jane ventured carefully, deliberately returning her eyes to the shelves.

"I know, but he is just so wonderful"—Jane held in a snort at that—"that my love has not diminished. Indeed, in your family's long absence, it has increased."

Oh good God. Jane knew Victoria had an unrequited crush on Jason—and considering the lack of dashing young men in Reston, it was only to be expected that a Marquis would excite interest in a young girl's heart. (Indeed, Jane had seen the Morgans' daughters, no older than thirteen, mooning after Jason as he strolled through town. 'Twas enough to turn one's stomach.) But this was so much worse than Jane had ever imagined. And to think that poor Dr. Berridge was as mad for Victoria as Victoria seemed to be for Jason!

"Oh—oh this will not do!" Victoria said from behind her father's desk, unknowingly echoing Jane's own thoughts.

"What is it?" Jane asked, turning around.

"This," Victoria said, pulling a book the size of a Guttenberg Bible out from under the desk and landing it on the surface with a thud, "I believe is the ledger you seek."

"Oh dear. I'll never be able to sneak that out of your house," Jane said, vexed.

"He kept it down there, as a footrest, I think." Victoria lifted the heavy cover and opened the book to a random page.

Twelfth of March 1805—Mr. Cloper reports the loss of three sheep. Discovered his neighbor Mr. Frederickson had three new sheep. The sheep were unmarked, Mr. F— had copy of the bill of sale. No charges against Mr. F were filed.

This had to be the record of every complaint brought before the magistrate since Sir Wilton's appointment, Jane thought, bemusedly. "No wonder it's so large," she murmured.

"Indeed," Victoria agreed.

Sir Wilton, it seemed, wrote everything down—whether or not he took down the correct information and what he did with it was a different matter entirely.

Jane glanced up at the doors, but apparently Michael and Joshua had managed to get much farther down the river than anticipated, because the house was silent. She reached over and flipped the pages up more than a decade, scanning the tight handwriting for what she hoped to see.

Fifteenth of January 1816—the Mail was attacked by Unknown Person or Persons on the Windermere road. Valuables taken in the amount of 11 pounds 6 in notes and coin, one small gold ladies' ring with black stone, two pocket watches, one silver, one tin, two shoe buckles. Unknown Person or Persons being pursued in earnest—

Jane did not need to read further. "This is exactly what I need."

Victoria shot Jane a mischievous look. "Are you hunting highwaymen?"

Jane chose not to answer, as she feared revealing too much. And to Victoria's credit, she did not await an answer before saying, "Well, you cannot sneak the ledger out in your reticule, obviously."

"And I can't sit here waiting for your parents to discover us while I copy out the necessary text."

"But I could," Victoria offered. "I can copy out the pages easily—well, much easier than you."

"You could?" Jane asked.

"Of course—I'll do it tonight. Just tell me what you need."

"Anything having to do with the highwayman—go back as far as you remember him being a, er, problem," Jane said excitedly. "And come to tea tomorrow and bring them to me."

"A conspiracy! Oh this will be such fun!" Victoria clapped her hands.

Jane had to smile at Victoria's youthful glee. Hopefully these reports would fill out Byrne's sketchy reports with far more detail. Perhaps therein lay the clue to what they needed to track the highwayman and catch him where he lay . . .

"But . . . oh, I will not be able to come to tea tomorrow," Victoria's face fell. "The public assembly is on the day after, and tomorrow my sister and I are to be overcome with preparations."

Jane's brow furrowed.

"The assemblies are monthly, regular as clockwork. You cannot tell me you are not already prepared," she pouted unprettily. She was hoping to be able to present Byrne with the information as early as possible, surprise him with her cleverness.

But Victoria's shoulders set. "The assembly is the only party for weeks and for miles. Everyone is attending. Especially since—"

"Especially since the Duke of Rayne's family will attend." Jane nodded with understanding. Of course the assembly would be an event of great pressure for the Wiltons. People would invade the town from far and wide—much to Sir Wilton's chagrin. Victoria would be expected to show to great advantage, hoping to catch the eye of the local gentlemen, while Victoria would want to look her best for Jason. And Lady Wilton would no doubt apply the pressure thick. And here Jane was, irked that she wouldn't get her pages in an expedient fashion.

"Would it be possible for you to bring them to the assembly?" Jane asked, her tone smoother and kinder. Determined to ask, not dictate. And it was a successful tactic, because Victoria's shoulders relaxed.

"Of course," she replied, "I'll be able to copy them out to—"

But at that moment, the door to the book room burst open, thrown wide by the wet and sopping figures of Michael and Joshua Wilton.

"Vicky!" Joshua cried. "You should have seen us—the Marquis and Penelope and Papa and Mama all chased us, but we lost them all by the bend!"

Michael nodded, shaking water all over the floor like a pup. "You won't believe what fun we had!"

Twelve

THE Reston Assemblies took place on the third Monday of every month, in the aptly named Assembly Hall located on the main square of the village. When she had been a child, Jane had hated the assemblies. Her mother always made her wear something spotless and white, and Jane would never succeed in keeping it that way, and the Duchess was always sparkling, chatting—and there was nothing more loathsome to a child than to see one's parent having a marvelous time when you were not.

The only part that had been tolerable was being able to dance. No matter when or where, or forced into a dress that would inevitably have punch spilled on it by the end of the evening, Jane relished the chance to dance. That feeling had never changed, but as she became fashionable, her other opinions about assemblies did.

Now, Jane thought, as she flitted from one group of villagers to the next, giving happy compliments to the revelers and dancing her way across the floor, she was truly in her element. Everyone from the gentry of the Lake District to the town blacksmith was there. Mrs. Humphrey's and London had taught her how to glide through a room with ease, her dance instructors at school had marveled at how quickly she picked up the steps and how cheerfully she went through them. She thrived in a merry atmosphere and made it seem as if she had not a care in the world—which had the effect of taking away others' cares, too.

The night was warm, as had been every night that week, and the doors of the Assembly Hall were thrown wide to allow summer breezes to waft through from the grassy town square—and hopefully keep too many young ladies from smacking their neighbors accidentally with their fans. For the room was quite crowded. The spectacle of aristocracy combined with the truly lovely season had brought out every matron with daughters, gentleman farmer, busybody, eager young lover, traveler, bookshop clerk, and smiling young miss within the county.

And Jane chatted and flirted with them all. This is truly where Jane shone brightest. Something she had learned watching her mother, however reluctantly—how to be the crown jewel of any room. Jane moved from group to group. She complimented Mrs. Hill on her shop's latest success—a silk printed fan that, due to the heat, had flown off the shelves—Jane had spied several of them on the wrists of young ladies tonight. She moved to Mr. and Mrs. Cutler and made certain to listen intently as that good man held forth on the minutiae of the last town council meeting (a subject made all the more interesting by Mr. Cutler's glass of punch, or three). She laughed with Mr. Davies, promising she had written a letter in the fire-red ink (she hadn't) and imparted to a young couple traveling on their honeymoon her particular favorite walks along the tarns and fells. It was as if some key had been turned, and Lady Jane became the very soul of the festivities.

In truth, Jane was feeling rather high. She was enjoying herself, more so than she had since coming to the lake. There was nothing like a party to remind a person that the world was larger than their own frustration. Music moved her feet, making her smile, her russet silk flattered her pallor, and her mother's diamond earbobs brushed cool against her warm, soft skin, making her feel sensuous and alive.

There was cause for worry, to be sure. Jane expected Byrne to come through the doors at any moment, and she had to find a few spare moments for Victoria Wilton, who was as much in demand as a dancer as she, but why should she let those things diminish her enjoyment right now?

"I must admit, these assemblies have never been so full—nor so full of life," Dr. Berridge commented, as he took Jane through an easy turn on the dance floor.

Jane grinned at her partner. "I imagine they are rather thin in the colder months," she replied.

"Not so many as this, certainly, but I discovered that a surprising number of people can be found attending during the winter—everyone standing close together, shivering, attempting to share body heat and keep warm."

Jane laughed again, her natural laugh—not the false humor she kept on her face most days.

"You are remarkably happy this evening," Dr. Berridge could not help but comment.

"I very much enjoy dancing. Especially with a competent partner," Jane replied honestly.

"I had the benefit of sharing my sister's lessons—I trust I am competent enough?"

"Indeed, Doctor. You are doing very well."

"As is your father, I see," Dr. Berridge commented, when they came together again, his voice low enough to not reach any prying ears.

Jane glanced over to where her father sat, near the cool breeze of the open windows. It had been a monumental decision whether or not to have their father attend tonight. Jane had gone back and forth on the subject, debating in her head for hours, and driving Jason mad with the ever-changing results. However, New Nurse Nancy had been quick to remind them that the letter they received from Dr. Berridge's colleague had said stimulation in familiar surroundings might be good for his mind. Since the Duke had attended the Reston Assemblies for more than thirty years, they decided to chance it. And indeed, the Duke seemed to be doing rather well. He tapped his foot in time to the music, smoked a pipe. He even greeted several gentlemen by name—and if he got any of them wrong, it was doubtful he, as a peer of the realm, would be corrected. Nurse Nancy was close at hand always. Jane and Jason were constantly on guard. But it seemed possible that tonight would be a true success.

"He is," Jane replied. "Indeed, I hate to admit that my brother is right in anything, but he may have been right to have us come to the lake."

Jane watched as Dr. Berridge slid his gaze over to where Jason stood, chatting with Penelope and Lady Wilton. He was animated in his conversation, relaxing into the festivities. Of course, he refused to let Jane see that, so when she caught his eye, he had to wrestle his expression back to snobbish boredom.

Jane glanced back at the young doctor, whose mouth had become set in a grim line. But his expression quickly changed to a smile when he caught Jane looking at him. Poor Doctor, Jane thought, knowing he must feel displaced in the Wiltons' affection. Since her and Jason's arrival, Lady Wilton was courting their favor and leaving the feelings of the poor doctor aside. Jane doubted it would be so devastating, if only Victoria would glance his way.

But alas, Victoria's attention, when it was not on her dance partner, was on Jason, of course. Jane didn't know if she had even once smiled at the lovesick doctor today.

Well, Jane would rectify that.

The music ended shortly thereafter, and Jane took Dr. Berridge's arm as he escorted her to the side of the floor. If one were truthful, she escorted him.

"I say, my lady, you seem determined to . . . well, leave the floor," Dr. Berridge commented as she pulled on his arm. "Eager for your next partner?"

"Not at all," Jane smiled but kept her pace steady and her eye on where Victoria was being escorted—luckily, by the punch bowl, at the opposite end of the room from her mother and sister. "I am eager for yours."

Dr. Berridge looked up then. And saw where Jane was leading him. "My . . . my lady, I am certain that Miss Wilton has her choice of dance partners."

"And I am certain you must be among them. Come"—she tugged—"I'm simply parched."

They arrived at the punch bowl at almost the exact same moment as Victoria and her dance partner, a jolly, mustachioed gentleman whom Jane did not recognize.

Jane greeted Victoria with a kiss on the cheek. "I'm terribly sorry I haven't been able to make my way over to you," Victoria said with a happy flush. "It's rather mad here, isn't it?"

"Indeed," Jane agreed, and stepped to one side, allowing Victoria to give a neat curtsy to Dr. Berridge, who bowed over her hand.

The mustachioed gentleman cleared his throat, his chest puffing out in anticipation.

"Oh!" Victoria cried, her mouth falling into an apologetic smile, "Lady Jane, Dr. Berridge, allow me to introduce Mr. Brandon, my sister Penelope's husband."

Mr. Brandon bowed deeply, his face coming up flush with the effort. "Lady Cummings, Doctor, a pleasure to meet you both—indeed, Vicky here has told me about both of you at length."

Jane could feel the shock and pleasure radiating off of Dr. Berridge. Victoria blushed prettily, as Mr. Brandon ribbed her. "Well, you do, my girl. You go on for hours. I just arrived yesterday, and I haven't managed a conversation with my wife because this one keeps a running commentary on the virtues of her friends, new and old."

He gave a hearty chuckle, and Jane decided at that moment to like Mr. Brandon immensely. Having an older brother herself, she recognized good-natured funning. However, Victoria was turning an unforeseen shade of red—perhaps it was time to rescue her.

"What is the news from Manchester, Mr. Brandon?" Jane said with a smile. "We've been cloistered here for a fortnight, and I swear, England could have been taken over by the French, and we wouldn't know it."

Mr. Brandon laughed. "Too true. But that's half the joy in such a place." He then proceeded to go on at length about any news or information that might have been of interest to Jane and Dr. Berridge. Only when Brandon touched on a lecture he attended at the college, commanding Dr. Berridge's attention, did Jane finally manage to have a short word with Victoria.

Victoria, of course, was already a step ahead of her.

"It has been terribly hectic at my home, but I managed to finish last night," she whispered as she pressed a small packet into Jane's hand. "I still have ink on my fingers, under my gloves." She giggled.

"I cannot thank you enough," Jane whispered back as she stuffed the papers into her reticule.

"There were fewer entries than I expected," Victoria ventured.

Which was exactly what Jane suspected, but she merely smiled. She nodded to the men, steeped in conversation.

"Mr. Brandon seems very nice."

"Yes, I heartily approve of my sister's choice in husband." She raised her voice just enough to be overheard, "No matter *how annoying* he tries to be."

"I promise I'm not trying to be annoying," Mr. Brandon answered back. "If I was trying to be annoying, I would tell Dr. Berridge about how when your sister first brought me home, you poured your custard on me."

Victoria's mouth dropped open. "That was an accident!"

"Yes, and heaven save me from any more accidents."

"Heaven save me from any more brothers-in-law!" Victoria grinned back at him.

Jane shot Dr. Berridge a very decided look. This was his moment.

Luckily, he did not disappoint. "I'll save you, Miss Wilton. Would you do me the honor of the next dance?"

"Happily, Dr. Berridge." Victoria gracefully placed her hand in his outstretched one and took the floor. She was the epitome of a poised young lady, until she stuck her tongue out at Mr. Brandon as she passed.

Jane and Mr. Brandon stood for a moment, watching the young couple as the first strains of a waltz began.

"My sister-in-law thinks very highly of you," Mr. Brandon commented.

"And she thinks very highly of you," Jane replied, much to his surprise.

"You think so?"

"Of course. The two of you remind me of myself and my brother." Or how they used to be, Jane thought with a hint of sadness. Would they ever be that way again? There were hints of it from time to time . . . if only Jason did not disappoint her. She caught Brandon's concerned look and smiled pertly, nodding to where her brother stood next to Penelope.

"I must admit, I adore my wife," Brandon said, his color rising simply from looking in her direction, "but to have her come from a family I adore as well was an unforeseen benefit."

"Never had a sister?"

"No, sadly. Had I known they were so much fun to tease, I would have acquired one much sooner."

"We are useful in that regard," Jane joked and then took Mr. Brandon's arm. "Come, Mr. Brandon, I'll introduce you to my brother, and you can ask him all the ways to best torture little sisters."

The music was a popular minuet, and Victoria found herself humming along to the tune as Dr. Berridge—Andrew—led her neatly about the floor. These few minutes were a welcome respite from her family. Her mother had been so terribly motherlike for the past few days, making certain she knew to dance with which gentlemen, ordering the maid to clean her gown again, readying the house for Mr. Brandon's visit. The dance itself was little better, as Lady Wilton kept a steady tally of all the positive aspects of the evening alongside the negative.

One of the positive or negative aspects that her mother had not listed in her ear was watching Jason dance attendance on Penelope.

Victoria wasn't certain about her mother's feelings about Jason. On the one hand, she was being welcoming, obviously not wanting to undo their family's connection with his. On the other, she made no effort to display her available daughter (Victoria) to him. It was a missed opportunity, in Victoria's opinion. And Lady Wilton was not one to miss opportunities.

"You've left the dance floor," Dr. Berridge said low into her ear as he took her through another turn. "And here I had been assured that my dancing was wholly competent."

She blushed, coming back to herself. "It is," she smiled up at him. "In fact, I was thinking of how welcome a respite it is to dance with you."

"Really?" His eyebrow went up, a dark blond arch that bespoke a mischief he rarely showed.

"Of course!" she laughed. "My family has the tendency to over-whelm . . . and now that my sister and her husband and children are here . . ." she trailed off, under his constant, warm gaze. "You have not come to the house in days; I am certain my father is likely to expire for lack of conversation."

"I had some business in Windermere; it took me away," Dr. Ber-ridge explained. He looked down at her, his eyes piercing, probing. Victoria felt a strange prickling down her spine when she met his look; a strange warmth spread across her cheeks.

"And you?" he asked, his voice barely a thrum. "Have you man-aged to find conversation without me?"

She felt his hand at the small of her back and the slight movement of his thumb. "Some," she swallowed, her mouth inexplicably dry. "Lady Jane has . . . visited, and Mr. Brandon never misses an oppor-tunity to . . . ah, set my back up."

"Good." He smiled, adopting a playful, jovial tone. "I should hate to think you lonely."

True, she hadn't been lonely—how can one be lonely surrounded by so many people? But Victoria had to admit, the house had missed his calming presence. Everyone was loose nerves, everything was both terribly important and too trivial. And it all needed taking care of.

However, at that moment, with Dr. Berridge's—nay, Andrew's—hand and gaze holding hers, she couldn't remember what a single one of those things were.

Thank goodness he didn't require any answers of her, because Victoria was in no position to give them. The oddity of her feelings was certainly just the heat of the room. Her awareness of his proximity . . . that was simply the effect of the dance.

"Dr. Berridge," she said breathlessly, "we are friends, are we not?"

He let out a short gust of air, never taking his eyes from hers. "Yes, Victoria. We are friends." A note of sad detachment had crept into his voice. A loss.

But before Victoria could even pay it heed, the music came to an abrupt and unscheduled halt.

A murmur flew through the crowd, and the sea of revelers parted.

"Oh my goodness," Victoria breathed, when she managed to spy what had captured everyone's attention.

If Jane had expected any outbursts or dramatics from her brother when she introduced Mr. Brandon to Jason, she was to be disappointed. Not even a flicker of surprise crossed his face. Jason merely bowed neatly, and Mr. Brandon returned the gesture. They chatted a few moments about Manchester and its architectural history—about which Mr. Brandon knew sadly little—never once touching on Penelope and Jason's shared adolescence.

She was tapping her feet in time to the music, letting her attention drift just a little. Dr. Berridge seemed to be doing very well with Victoria on the dance floor—she was a very warm pink, and she fit easily into his arms. Jane watched with reckless hope as Dr. Berridge stepped infinitesimally closer to Victoria, leaning in—and whether they were aware of it or not, skirting the bounds of propriety.

"Still staring at your darling doctor?" Jason breathed at her side. Mr. Brandon and Penelope had turned their attention to Lady Wilton's long recitation of dietary instructions for children, i.e., whether or not warm stew was appropriate for a toddler, and Jason had apparently (and wisely, in Jane's opinion) turned his attention elsewhere.

However, he had turned it to his sister. Which could only prove annoying, she thought as she held back an eye roll.

"He acquits himself rather well on the floor, don't you find? Especially for a country doctor." She gave her brother a poisonous look.

Jason grumbled slightly. While Jane had taken to her dancing lessons with verve and joy, Jason never had. In point of fact, he had only stood up four times this entire evening, and that was only for reels—the only dance he was confident he could do.

"Well, your wiles may not work on him this time," Jason said with a smirk. "The poor man seems to have eyes for none but his partner."

"Victoria?" Jane replied, shocked that Jason had managed to see what others (Victoria in particular) could not. "Whatever makes you say that?"

"You're not the only member of this family with intuition."

But the only one who can use it properly, Jane thought, but kept it to herself.

"It's the way he looks at her—the way he's holding her," Jason said, his face turning a bit red. "I don't actually have to explain this, do I?"

Jane shook her head at her brother, relieving him of the necessity of conversation with any emotional content.

But, it did make Jane's mind wander—and yearn, perhaps, for what she didn't have. When was the last time someone had pulled her a hair too close on the dance floor, she thought, suddenly a smidgeon peevish. When was the last time someone slid a step closer than he should have been? Not that she had any desire for anyone here to do those things—but the excitement of grazing fingers, of a long stare across the room . . .

The electricity to be borne from a simple touch. She had danced and flirted in London during her first season, so youthful and naive—and then again this past season, trying to recapture some of that golden innocence and joy. But never once since coming back into Society had she felt *touched*.

She wanted anticipation. She wanted that moment when you forgot to breathe and were swept away by the possibility of what was to come.

That was when the music stopped.

That was when she saw him.

Byrne Worth stood at the far end of the hall, the black night framing his darkly clad form, making his pale face and shockingly white neckcloth seem disembodied, monstrous, a vision out of a gothic horror novel. Some of the ladies actually gasped at the sight.

No wonder he was cast the villain by this town.

His icy blue eyes roamed the room and met with nary a returning gaze. Everyone ducked their vision, or chose at the moment to find a fascinating bit of wainscoting to examine. Everyone, that is, except for Jane.

When his eyes latched on to hers, Jane did not avoid his gaze like the others. She held it clearly, happily. But at the same time, Jane was struck by the sensation that she was unable to look away.

He looked dangerous.

He looked nervous.

The voices began to buzz and hum around them, but Jane's gaze was anchored on Byrne.

"What on earth—" Lady Wilton commented under her breath.

"Is that him—Mr. Worth?" Penelope whispered to vigorous, angry nodding by her mother.

"Who's Mr. Worth?" Mr. Brandon asked.

"I told you about him—the one Mother thinks is the highwayman," Penelope answered.

"Not just me—the entire town *knows* he is the culprit." Lady Wilton sniffed. "He has thwarted your father far too long. He will not stand for him being among decent folk. How dare he think—"

As Lady Wilton grew her head of steam, Jane pulled her brother to her side. "Jason, you need to go over and greet Mr. Worth," she said in a rushed undertone.

"Why on earth would I do that?" Jason scoffed. "He's not exactly welcome."

"Three reasons," Jane said, her voice deadly serious. "First of all,

you are the Duke of Rayne's son. You *lead*. Secondly, he deserves
thanks for taking you in when you needed it. You did," she added,
before he could protest.

"And third?" Jason asked as he heaved a reluctant sigh.

"And third, if you do not act as a peer should and make him welcome, there will be a public lynching at this assembly. Lady Wilton is
right on that score—they will not stand for someone they view as a
dangerous outsider being here."

Jason glanced up and noticed the growing ire of the townsfolk.
Mr. Cutler and Sir Wilton were nearest the doors, and in general
were, as leading gentlemen of the town, the first to greet newcomers.
But neither had moved. Indeed, Mr. Cutler had a terribly ruddy anger
about him, as if a few too many cups of punch and a heightened sense
of authority would soon prove to be an explosive combination. He
was whispering something in Sir Wilton's ear, whose complexion
soon matched Cutler's. And by their line of vision, any explosion to
come would be directed at Byrne Worth.

"You owe me," Jason muttered.

"If you do this properly, the entire town will owe you."

Jason straightened his coat and his shoulders. And then, with the
dignity taught only at the finest schools and handed down through
generations of aristocratic intermarriage, Jason crossed the room and
came to stand in front of Byrne Worth. And gave a short bow.

The entire assembly hall watched as the Marquis extended his
hand to the highwayman. They waited, unblinking, as the latter
transferred his cane, his ever-present weapon, to his other hand. And
then they shook.

Jane was not in a position to overhear any words that had been
exchanged, but Jason grinned with good humor and slapped Byrne
on the back in that way that was adopted long ago as a friendly yet
masculine sign of acceptance. Those simple gestures—the handshake,
the slap on the shoulder—had the ability to end wars.

And tonight was no different, if on a slightly smaller scale. It was
as if all the tension that held the Assembly Hall in stasis leaked out
the windows. The music began again, the dancing began anew. Mr.

Cutler's anger cooled into befuddlement and then a shrug, as another glass of punch fell into his hands.

Jane let out a breath she hadn't known she was holding. Sir Wilton's mouth was set in a hard, disapproving line, and a few people looked taken aback, but most everyone else returned to their revelry uninterrupted.

Because no one was about to cut a Marquis for his associations. Not in London. And certainly not in Reston.

"Lady Jane!" Victoria squeaked as she trotted to her side from the dance floor, Dr. Berridge not far behind. "Did you see what your brother has just done?"

"I did," Jane replied. "What is your opinion, Doctor?"

"I think it's good to see Mr. Worth out, but I find it interesting he came at all," Dr. Berridge said. "He's never come to an assembly—at least not so long as I've been here. And he's not exactly welcomed."

"But don't you see?" Victoria said, her face flushed with awe. "That's what makes what the Marquis did so very brave. He stood up and welcomed him, making it so everyone else would have to as well." She gave a worshipful sigh. "That's what makes him wonderful."

Oh dear. Dr. Berridge stiffened, unable to hide the dejected expression on his face. It seemed that any headway he had made during the last dance was to be undone by Jason's simple gesture toward Byrne. It almost made Jane sorry she had forced Jason to do it.

Almost.

Because when she looked over at Byrne, something strange occurred. A flutter of nervousness in the pit of her stomach. The nerves under the surface of her skin began to awaken—sleepy, lazy things, too long dormant. A small hitch in her breath, the anticipation of possibility—all that she had mourned the loss of, suddenly, slowly, coming back to her—alive and active and . . .

Touched.

Byrne knew this was a mistake. He was more nervous than he let on—more nervous than he had been in a long time. His expression may have been grim and uncaring, but to the careful eye, one would see his posture was that of a man ready to flee. An instinct borne of stepping into enemy territory a thousand times before.

Dobbs had been commanded to stay with the horses, just in case a hasty exit was required. He could sense the tension in the room, the hatred and dismissal vibrating off the ladies and gentlemen of Reston—those versed well enough in local gossip to be certain of the absolute truth dispensed there. Oh yes, this had been a mistake. Just like the leisurely walk through the village two days ago had been a mistake. But two days ago, all he had to do to escape was walk a straight line. Here, he would have to turn around—a cowardly act. But one, given a crowd's ability to turn quickly into a mob, he was ready to do.

Until, that is, he found her eyes.

Sinking into the warm brown of Lady Jane's gaze, Byrne found himself still, tethered to her as a ship to its anchor. No, there would be no turning around.

The murmurs gathered around him, growing in pitch and anger. He would wait them out. Civility would win out, wouldn't it? All the same, Byrne gauged the men nearest to him—who was most likely to come at him, who could possibly be of assistance.

Just as he was making the grim realization that there were very few men he could count on for said assistance, assistance came from the most unlikely of quarters.

"Mr. Worth—pleasure to see you again," Jane's brother Jason, the Marquis last seen waking up in a pool of his own drool on Byrne's settee, said loud enough to reach the ears of all who wished to listen. He bowed smartly and then extended his hand—a northern custom, the handshake, and its use in this instance very intelligent. The boy had read the room, apparently.

"I hope you appreciate this," Jason said through gritted teeth, as he pulled Byrne close and slapped him on the back. "My sister insists a mob would claim you if I didn't."

Ah. Apparently it had been Jane who read the room, not her

brother. Pity—Byrne almost shifted his low opinion of the man, and instead found it, and his high opinion of his sister, confirmed.

"A mob might be an exaggeration. But not by much."

"Then consider this as payment on any debt I may or may not owe you." Jason smirked, his voice still low. "Being welcomed by the Marquis of Vessey goes a long way with these country folk. Perhaps you'll survive the night for it."

"As you once survived the night with my assistance?" Byrne drawled evenly. He caught sight of the younger man's mouth tighten out of the corner of his eye.

"It . . . it was your duty as a tenant and a fellow gentleman," Jason replied, "to offer me shelter."

"As it is your duty as a fellow gentleman to welcome me here— not an averaging of debts," Byrne countered. Jason bowed to him then, and Byrne reciprocated. "Oh, and I'm not your tenant," he added. "You should check the terms of your grandfather's will."

And with that, Byrne, leaning gently on his cane, moved forward into the crowd.

Pulled by warm brown eyes, toward his destination.

She looked marvelous tonight, he couldn't help but think. But he tamped it down—he was not here to oblige his fancy for pretty girls, no matter how pretty they happened to be, nor how focused his fancy. He was here to attempt to correct the village's impression of him—one of the crucial steps in Lady Jane's plan to rehabilitate him in the eyes of the town.

Although, why you agreed to this plan may have something to do with just how marvelous Lady Jane looks tonight, don't you think?

He frowned at his own runaway thoughts, determined to ignore them.

The rust-colored dress set her hair afire, and the sparkle in the large teardrop diamonds at her ears; it matches the sparkle in the depth of those brown eyes and her smile, wide and welcoming . . .

Stop it! A distracting line of thought was one thing, he surmised, but he refused to be accused of romantically sensational description.

Rust-colored dress, sparkling eyes, indeed. She looked beautiful. Which was a constant for Jane, he reminded himself. No need to be so . . . *syrupy* about the matter.

"I have to say, sir, that is not a terribly welcoming expression," Jane said, her seductive alto far more welcoming than the look on his face, apparently.

He almost rolled his eyes. *Seductive alto.* He must be going soft in the head. But instead, he schooled his frown into a blandly neutral smile as he bowed to the good lady.

"I apologize, Lady Jane. I had no intention to approach you scowling."

"Never mind." She smiled at him. "You're without it so rarely, I doubt I would recognize you otherwise."

He acknowledged the truth of that with a smirk, his posture relaxing into something resembling ease.

"May I introduce Miss Victoria Wilton, and Dr. Berridge? I believe you already know Lady Wilton," Jane announced to the group.

Lady Wilton's mouth hung open, but in the presence of Lady Jane was able to do little more than give a shallow dip and a mumbled greeting. Victoria, however, did her mother better, and after a lovely curtsy, greeted the Notorious Hermit/Suspected Highwayman, saying, "How do you do? I'm so pleased to meet one of Lady Jane's London friends."

Byrne saw the conspiratorial look pass between Jane and Victoria and Jane's subsequent smirk at Lady Wilton's further drop of jaw. Good Lord, it must have unhinged, at this rate. At Jane's raised brow, Byrne determined he must play along.

"More of a Reston friend than London now," Byrne replied, bowing smartly over Victoria's hand. "After all, we've been acquainted here almost as long as we had in London."

"Victoria!" Lady Wilton cried, her jaw having finally found its way back to its proper place. "I must speak with you—*now*." And with that, Victoria was dragged away by her mother, who swept up Penelope and Mr. Brandon in her wake and took them a solid number of steps away.

Byrne looked to Jane, who gave the smallest shrug of her slim, white shoulders. That left Dr. Berridge—and all eyes were upon him.

Thankfully, Dr. Berridge had more manners than his hoped-for mother-in-law.

"Mr. Worth, how'd you do? I apologize for not having made my way out to your little house as of yet—I'm a recent arrival myself."

"The new doctor—yes, you ah, joined the community a few months back," Byrne replied, as he assessed the man who stood before him. Tall, fair of face, sufficient to have the tongues of town wagging when he arrived—and wagging loud enough to reach even Byrne's ears. There was an openness about the young doctor's demeanor, an honesty. As if he'd listen to all sides before making a judgment. Might be useful.

If only he wasn't a doctor.

"Might I ask you about your injury?" Dr. Berridge asked, professional curiosity radiating from his frame. Then, remembering himself, the doctor's face turned plum. "I realize this is not the place for such inquiry," he spoke in a rush, "and I know you've met with my colleague, Dr. Lawford, but I have some experience with wounds sustained in the war—bayonet and the like—and there are many therapies to strengthen the muscles—"

"I thank you, sir. Some other time, perhaps," Byrne said evenly. He paused, before grudgingly adding, "And it was a bullet. Not a bayonet."

Dr. Berridge nodded, and then, eager for some other subject, allowed his eyes to roam the room.

"Lady Jane, if you'll excuse me, I think I should like to visit with your father."

Jane's head whipped around, finding the doctor's line of vision. A familiar older gentleman, the one Jane had been walking with the first day he saw her at the Hampshire Racing Party, Byrne realized. The Duke of Rayne sat with a pipe in hand, his foot tapping to the music. A stout and starched middle-aged woman sat next to him, tapping, too.

To Byrne's eye, the Duke of Rayne looked healthy enough, so his acquaintance with the young doctor might not be of a professional nature. But if not, then why, when Dr. Berridge took his leave of Jane and made his way over to the Duke, did the two of them seem such friends?

"You'll have to forgive Dr. Berridge," Jane said, drawing Byrne's attention back to her. "He's just nervous. I'm afraid you have acquired a patina of infamy. But I think he might be a good friend to have."

Byrne looked down at Jane—his height was not as great as his brother Marcus's, but it still gave him a worthwhile vantage, peering down into the Lady Jane's open, mischievous face. Peering down her rather low-cut dress, the mounds of soft white flesh rising . . . no, he told himself, and forced his gaze back to her eyes.

"So," he said, "I have arrived at the assembly."

"And made quite an impression," she replied.

"What do I do now to curry the village's favor?"

She smiled. "You can dance with me."

His neutral smile faltered. "I am afraid that is one thing I cannot do," he replied, tapping her lightly on the foot with the end of his cane. She looked down, and caught the glint of silver in his hand, her face falling.

"Oh," she breathed, a decided sadness in her voice.

"You're disappointed," he observed.

"I know you told me before that you could not dance, but I had hoped—"

"That I was being modest?" Byrne asked. "I'm afraid not. Walking is becoming easier, but I fear pivots and turns will cause me to disgrace myself. And my partner."

She gave that artless shrug of hers, accepting this latest change of plans and adjusting to it. "It was part of my plan to have you seen dancing with me and several others." She looked aside for a moment. "And truth be told, I like nothing better than dancing."

"Nothing better?" he asked, a winged brow cocking up.

"To spin to the music, to step in time—to be a tiny piece of clockwork in the whole of the movement. It's marvelous," Jane sighed.

She said it with such reverence, such passion, that he could see it was of the plainest fact. Her eyes followed the dancers on the floor merrily, her body swayed to the music just barely, making it a part of her, as if the melody was her blood and the harmony her breath. She didn't just like it . . . she loved it.

"I think it good to be passionate about something," she said matter-of-factly.

"Yes," he agreed. Truthfully, he was so swept up in her feeling that he would have likely agreed with her if she said she thought calico cats made for a good luncheon.

"Do you have anything like that?" she asked innocently. "Anything that you find wholly transformative?"

A thousand thoughts ran through his mind. Yes. He found things transformative. Automatically, he thought of his weakness: he had found opium transformative—getting lost in the smoke and slow, steady thrum of his blood had set his mind to flight . . . but it had been hell wrestling it back to the ground. But then his mind fell on more earthly delights. The transformative power of a woman to a man—falling into the warmth they held, that turned a man to a beast and a beast to a god. Hell, sometimes, not even the whole woman was needed. Just the soft skin hiding in her bodice, the rise and fall of a graceful shoulder in an adorable shrug, standing close enough to count the faint freckles that dusted her cheekbones . . .

"Swimming," he blurted suddenly. "I . . . I find swimming very transformative."

"Swimming," she repeated. "With the eels."

"I told you, the eels leave me be. And yes, swimming. Slicing through the water, moving weightlessly across the lake. I can get lost in it. I don't often get lost." He smiled down into her eyes. And God knows, he could do with a swim right now. A very cold swim.

"Well," she breathed. "Since we cannot dance and we cannot swim at the moment, do you have any suggestions?"

Byrne glanced about the room. "You could introduce me to your father," he ventured.

Jane's mouth turned down at the corners. "I, ah . . . I think we should make a round about the room, don't you agree? I'll introduce you to everyone, and we can guess what color their faces will turn."

Knowing that it was in his best interest to do so, Byrne did agree. And he focused on the task of making himself agreeable. A difficult challenge, indeed—which was just the thing to take his thoughts away from a nice cold swim.

They were quite the spectacle, Jane realized. The Duke's daughter and the highwayman, greeting the village in their best dress. They moved in a circle of the hall, nodding or bowing to everyone they met with. A sort of strange receiving line formed, made up of the cautious, the curious, and occasionally the politely hostile citizens of the county. Sometimes there was a small bit of conversation to be had; most of the time there wasn't. Since Byrne had Lady Jane on his arm, no one could possibly cut him, but what was that old adage? If looks could kill . . .

Jane held her breath the first few times someone looked askance at Byrne, but then she realized, she had to allow air into her lungs eventually, else perish of the heat on the spot.

But it was not the people who showed their contempt that surprised Jane. No, it was the people who welcomed him that widened her eyes.

The rector's wife, one of the victims of Byrne's so-called cruelty, had taken his hand in both of hers and made a point of introducing her sixteen-year-old son. The son, of course, was a bit too unformed still to smooth over his shocked silence, but his mother smiled gracefully and inquired after widow Lowe's house.

Dr. Lawford met Byrne courteously, if a little coolly. He had greater restraint than his youthful protégé and held back from inquiring about the state of his leg.

And Mrs. Hill, the proprietor of the dressmaker shop in the village, pumped his hand like a water well—even though it was impossible that he would ever become a client.

Maybe they were simply fascinated by the idea of standing next to someone who could be a criminal, maybe they actually believed him misunderstood, innocent of the gossip—or maybe they shook his hand to gain favor with Jane. But for those few that did, they made the hard stares and whispered words from the Sir Wiltons and the Mr. Cutlers tolerable.

But even then, there was only so much one person could take. Jane watched as the corners of Byrne's mouth, the points of his eyes, grew tighter and tighter with each person they encountered. He was tired, she realized. Hot, tired, closed in this space. Being out of practice with common niceties must have made an assembly such as this akin to climbing a mountain with a wounded leg.

"Mr. Worth, I find I could use some air," Jane whispered when they had at last completed a whole circle. She had skillfully managed to avoid introductions to her father, skipping the corner where he sat, instead leading Byrne to another standing group. Jane knew she hadn't the capacity to handle those two parts of her life mixing just now. How to explain one to the other? So best to leave them alone for the moment and leave herself shiny and whole for each.

Byrne shot her a glance out of the corner of his eye. "I should be happy to escort you," he replied gratefully.

They moved out the front doors. The Assembly Hall had no terrace, or balustrade, or gardens where young couples could stroll slowly. But it did face the village square, a green expanse of lawn with tall, strong oaks that provided shade during the day, and for the revelers, a little privacy that night. The party had spilled out to the square, laughter and conversation filling the sweet summer air. Shadows moved on the lawn, ladies' gowns catching on the grass and twigs, and gentlemen pressing them back into the trees. Farther beyond, the coachmen had abandoned their posts and raucously enjoyed a bit of ale and company, doing lively drunken steps to the music that floated out from the hall.

"This should do," Byrne said, as they came to an unoccupied tree. "Are you sure your reputation will survive being alone out here with me?"

"We're hardly alone," Jane pointed out, "and I think my reputation will survive being out here with you just as well as yours will having been in there with me." She smiled at him, took a deep breath of the night air, let it fill her lungs, her body relaxing as she let it go. "Whether you yourself would survive it in there was a possibility open to debate, however."

He acknowledged the truth of that with a soft snort. "It was touch and go for a moment."

They let the silence stand then . . . not uneasily, just taking a moment to breathe in time, to listen to the noises around them. How pleasant, Jane thought, to be silent for a few moments. Normally noise overtook her life—normally she sought it, finding silence solitary and confining—suffocating. But how pleasant to be silent with someone.

That's when they heard the twitching in the shrubbery beyond, the mischievous giggle of young boys, out of bed far later than they were allowed. What they were saying Jane could not make out, but Byrne—gracious, she could see him listening. He didn't move his head or shift his gaze, but she saw his eyes narrow, his scowl return.

"Now!" was the one word she made out, right before she saw two small figures pop out of the shrubbery, pitching two red orbs into the air at speed, and letting them fly.

Oh no.

In the barest second before impact, Jane tried to duck, tried to shift out of the way. But it was too late. She hunched down, shielded her eyes . . .

And glimpsed the lighting-quick flash of Mr. Worth's hands as he intercepted the projectiles.

"Gor!" Jane heard Michael Wilton say—there was no hiding now, he stood straight up from the bushes in shock. "He caught 'em!"

"He *must* be the highwayman," his little brother Joshua lisped, in complete awe. Then Byrne turned his head, his body, by spare degrees, just enough to eye the boys. His brow shot up fractionally. And if Jane hadn't known better, she would swear she heard him growl.

"Run!" Michael yelled, and he and Joshua made quick work of

beating a path back to the Wiltons' house, nothing but a trail of dust left behind them.

Byrne straightened and turned back to her. "Apple?" he asked, proffering one of the orbs. Unable to do or think or say anything else, she took it. "Rather solid," he commented, as he took a bite. "And sweet. When I was young, we found the rotted ones better for throwing—they explode upon impact, make a fine mess. These would brain you before they ruined your clothes."

"You caught them," Jane said, finally finding her voice beneath her pounding heart.

"Yes," he replied.

"You *caught* them," she repeated.

"For heaven's sake, madam—I could hear the boys rustling in the shrubbery . . . and having been a boy myself, I had a feeling mischief was afoot." He leaned down, hopping a bit as he grabbed the cane that must have fallen to the ground when he released it to pluck fruit from the sky, Jane thought wryly.

"I do have some skills left," he grumbled.

"But how . . ." she began again, only to have him shake his head.

"I would never expose any tricks of the trade," he replied, and happily took another bite of his apple.

"I should march inside and tell Sir Wilton," Jane remarked, turning the apple over in her hand. "He has the audacity to despise you, but those are his sons, and the biggest mischief makers this village has seen since . . ."

"Since . . . ?" he prodded curiously, as he took another bite.

"Since me." She smiled sheepishly.

His eyes lit with wicked curiosity. "Now, aside from running naked through this very square when you were five, what kind of mischief did you manage in your youth?" he asked, a wry twist transforming his face in the sliver of moonlight. No longer the beast that frightened children or the stone-faced gentleman that made polite conversation with the rector's wife. Nay, that little smile, that spark in his eyes . . . He looked like a devil, she thought . . . but not the demonic, nasty kind, with sharpened teeth and pointy tails . . . nay, he looked like the devil that will offer you a sweet, play you music . . . and lead you into temptation.

If possible, her heart began to beat even faster.

"Oh, the usual," she replied, her voice a mask of gaiety and light. "Mud pies. Stealing eggs from the Morgans' chicken coop. Moving old Mr. Frederickson's fishing dinghy from the lakeshore to the top of a fell . . . while he was asleep in it."

If anything, Byrne's smile became more devilish. "Now, how on earth did you do that?"

"I would never expose a secret of the trade, sir," she replied primly.

He laughed aloud, a rusty sound, deep and fitful. But real. Jane was so startled by it, she felt the need to take a look around the square, finding none of the partygoers as interested in his laughter as she—just as they had been unresponsive to the apple throwing. Everyone was in their own world, discussing their own lives, creating their own secrets.

"A mischief maker," Byrne repeated through his laughter. "No wonder you're so eager to run after a robber."

Jane stuttered, "But . . . no, I . . ."

"Jane," Byrne said, looking her dead in the eye, his voice strangely seductive. "Eat your apple."

So she did, taking a small bite, enjoying the tartness of its flesh. "I should still tell the Wiltons about the boys' behavior. Or at least Victoria. The parents may not believe me, but Victoria would try to set the boys to right."

Byrne regarded her at a distance. "Miss Victoria seems a good friend to you."

"She is," Jane replied. Yes. Victoria, for all her foolishness about Jason, was a surprisingly good friend. Especially considering how Jane had abhorred her in the past.

"Good. I should think you could use some friends," he remarked.

"Don't be silly, I have dozens of friends," she replied offhandedly, taking another bite.

"Lady Jane Cummings has dozens of friends," he countered. "I sometimes wonder if Jane has any."

Her head snapped up, swallowing hard the bit of apple in her mouth. She stared into his face, for once open, unguarded. But it was Jane who felt exposed. Because . . . how did he know?

Unwilling to follow that course of conversation, Jane cast about for a new one. And she remembered half her reason for coming tonight.

"Not only has Victoria been a good friend, she's been a useful one! Here," she said, handing him her bitten apple as she needed both hands to fish in her reticule and draw out the small packet of papers Victoria had given her earlier that evening. At his quizzical expression, she told him what they were.

"And you should have seen his office—I'm surprised we managed to find this," she finished, breathless.

"Well, if Sir Wilton didn't suspect me before, he will now," Byrne drawled, and he leaned close to her, peering down into the papers she held in her hands. "I'll know the exact details of every crime."

The spare moonlight did little to illuminate Victoria's tight handwriting—which was why Byrne had to stand so close, she reasoned.

"I haven't read them yet," Jane replied, her mouth surprisingly dry, "and I very much wish to. Might I review them tonight and bring them by tomorrow?"

She looked up into his eyes. He was shoulder to shoulder with her, close enough that she could feel the warmth of his frame, but it was the heat in his gaze that set her cheeks burning.

They held there together in their own silence, both waiting for what would happen next.

She could do it, she realized. All she had to do was lean in a fraction, let her gaze drop to his mouth, and he would kiss her. She could feel it. It was such an easy thing. And she knew he wanted it, too.

She wasn't some foolish young thing with a scared heart, nor was she a novice at the business of being made love to. She had been kissed before, she had let men sweep her into corners on warm nights under solitary oak trees.

And oh, she wanted it. The anticipation. That moment when you forgot to breathe, the electricity of being touched.

But . . . a small worry pricked the back of her mind. Those other gentlemen—nothing would change with a kiss. With Byrne, would it change the way they spoke to each other? Would it color every conversation that was to come, every time they ran into each other between their houses, every look? And suddenly, it mattered to Jane.

It mattered, she realized, because he was her friend.

So, even though she craved the connection, more than she had ever craved it before in her life, Jane did not lean that fraction closer. She did not glance down at his perfect, wry mouth. She did not let herself get gloriously swept away.

Instead, she pulled back, ignoring the confusion she saw in his eyes. And Jane remained ridiculously, frustratingly, safely *untouched*.

But not for long.

Because at that moment, a pair of revelers, male and female, tripped merrily across the square, headed for their corner.

"Do you remember which one it was?" Jane heard Jason say, the laugh in his voice apparent and all too infrequent.

"I think it's that one," the lyrical voice that could only be Penelope Wilton replied.

They weren't merely headed for their corner. They were headed for their tree.

Jane met Byrne's eyes. If Jason found them, he was likely to burst like a volcano.

Byrne obviously surmised the same thing and judged the easiest recourse. Quickly he grabbed her hand, and together they stumbled to the bushes recently abandoned by Michael and Joshua, leaped over them, and hid.

And Jane found herself in the most awkward position in her memory, wedged between the disturbing body of Byrne Worth, a surprisingly large stockpile of apples, and peering through the thick shrubbery as she listened to her brother in what had to be one of the worst conversations of his life.

Lord Jason Cummings, Marquis of Vessey, was having a better time than he expected. He was rarely one for dancing and never one for quaint village gatherings, if they could be helped—and yet, here he was, having talked with the puffed-up men of Reston and danced with their country daughters, and he was having a marvelous time. Not even Mr. Worth's aggravating presence dampened the evening.

"It is—this one," he cried, coming to a tall oak at the far corner of the square. From here, the light from the Assembly Hall left them almost completely behind. Him and Penelope.

It was such a giddy thing to be back here, in Reston, with her. He had been gnashing his teeth since Jane had blackmailed him into coming, tearing his hair out trying to deal with long-neglected accounts and bored to tears by it, begging for some kind of distraction from his family . . . his father . . . and then, suddenly, she was here.

And there was still that little mole just below her left eye.

"It was this tree where I kissed you for the first time," Jason said, turning to face a bemused Penelope.

"And did a fine job of it," she complimented.

Jason saw his opening—and he would be damned if he let it pass. "I have a feeling I can do better than fine now," he growled (at least he hoped it came off as a growl) and grabbed her about the waist.

"Sir, I—"

"Let's find out."

"My lord, n—"

He placed his mouth on hers, pressed, pulled, teased.

And got nothing in return, except for a firm hand on his chest, pushing him back.

He straightened and looked into a face that had lost its smile.

"I am married," she said sternly.

"I know."

"You met my husband; you spoke with him."

"Yes, and he's a very amiable chap, but, Pen—don't you miss us? The thrill of it?" he took a step toward her and watched as she took a wary step back. "I'm here now, you're here now." He shot her his crooked grin, the one that had earned her kiss five years ago. "Let's have some fun."

Penelope looked over Jason, then matched his eye. But what he saw there was not the sparkling mischief that he remembered from their childhood. Nor was it the starry gaze that she had every time she looked at him that long-ago summer. Instead, she looked at him steadily, her expression neither judging nor engaged.

"You haven't changed at all," she finally said. "Have you, Jason?"

It should have warmed him to hear his name on her tongue, under this tree, but it did not. She spoke with admonishment, as if to a child, which caused him to respond as one. "I certainly hope not," Jason replied, squaring his shoulders proudly.

"You recall well that summer we spent together?" she asked.

"And all the ones before." An easy grin spread across his face. "But especially that one."

"And would you take the memory of those lovely days from me?"

He regarded her quizzically, and she continued. "My husband is in there." She nodded to the lights and music of the assembly hall. "And I love him so dearly." She sighed, the smile on her face apparent in her voice. "When you pulled me out here, he was torturing Victoria into dancing with him, and before that, he was telling everyone who would listen that his daughters would only be allowed to marry princes."

She laughed then, one that made the heat of shame begin to flood Jason's cheeks.

"That summer," she continued, "the one you and I finally spent together—all flushed and fumbling, our hearts open to each other . . . when it ended, I despaired. Absolutely wretched to be around, my mother would tell you. But out of those explorations, those idle hours, my heart became prepared to meet Brandon."

Penelope turned her body to him then—no longer the lithe young frame of a girl at seventeen but that of a woman. Still trim and young, but she had borne children, and putting her body to its purpose had lent her a woman's gravity. "I would not trade our summer together for anything."

"Nor would I," Jason found himself saying, his own voice surprisingly thick.

"But with every leer, every propositioning word you make now, you taint those memories. It strips me of an hour or two of the past. Do you understand?" Penelope asked.

Jason did understand and was ashamed of it. He felt the blood drain from his face, utter embarrassment leaving him stern and white. He looked down at his shoes, at the grass, anywhere but at her.

Penelope took pity on him then, extended her hand: the northern offer of friendship and a modicum of absolution for Jason.

He did not take it.

Slowly, she withdrew her hand. "I may not be the girl you remember, and you not the boy I recall, but I had wished to go on as friends, my lord."

Jason set his mouth in a grim line and gave Penelope a curt bow. "Of course, Mrs. Brandon."

Penelope looked at him once more, dead in the eye, and Jason saw exactly what she was thinking. She felt *sorry* for him. It was written plain as day on her face. But all she did was curtsy politely, and then she turned and left him alone by that tree, in the dark of night, the only noise the breeze moving the shrubbery . . . while she went into the assembly to join her husband. Her life.

She felt sorry for him? Well, of course she did—he was in a right sorry state. Banished to the country, feeling provincial and rejected by the one person he truly wanted to see here. Jason had never made friends easily, the way Jane did, but he didn't expect to be *pitied* by the only one in the county he counted as one.

He was stuck here. Stuck in this godforsaken outpost of Wordsworth tourism, and all he wanted was to feel like himself again. Not the Duke's son, not his heir, not fettered and weighted with those titles' inherent responsibilities. He wanted loud. He wanted new. Anything to distract from this constant silence.

Well, why not? he thought. Why not kick the dust off this sleepy little town? He may not be able to leave with ease, but that didn't mean he couldn't invite the fun to join him.

Perhaps it was time Charles and Nevill paid the Cottage a visit.

They waited until they heard Jason's retreating footsteps before exhaling. He did not move toward the assembly but rather up the high street . . . likely toward one of the pubs. Maybe he'd escape the village proper and go all the way out to the Oddsfellow Arms . . . if Mr. Johnston would take his business. But Byrne decided if any man ever deserved a drink tonight, it was Jason.

Still crouched low in the bushes, Byrne watched Jane digest everything she had overheard. He had watched her during the whole conversation, watched as at first her eyes had bulged with shock, then as she blushed with embarrassment, and then finally, as she became drawn with sympathy.

She pressed a hand to her heart as her brother faded into shadow, massaging away the phantom pain.

"Oh, Jason," she breathed. "Oh, you fool."

Byrne couldn't think of anything to say to her, did not know how to console a person for her brother's folly.

Although Byrne's own brothers might have some insight.

So instead he placed his hand over hers, tentatively, in a gesture meant to soothe, to calm.

So when she jumped and shrieked, it caught him slightly off guard.

"Oh, I'm so sorry!" she whispered. "I just didn't expect . . ." her voice faded into a giggle. And then it wouldn't stop. A terrible fit of giggles overtook her body and lit her face with mirth.

It shot through his body like a ripple, full of life. This soft laughter, her wide welcoming smile made him want to dive at her, push her into the dirt, scatter the apples . . . they were alone in the shrubbery, after all, they were ignored by the party . . . it was summer, and it was the two of them, under the starry sky . . . it was perfect.

Byrne had wanted women before. And there was a time when the species came rather easily to him. But now . . . his need had never been this focused. He had felt it pull at him since he arrived at the assembly, pull him to her side. There was a moment, earlier, when they had found themselves standing beneath the oak Jason had just abandoned, that Byrne was certain she felt the same pull. But instead she had cut the line and left him floundering.

Like he was floundering now.

"Why are you laughing?" he grunted. "I may not like your brother very much, but it's rather poor sport to laugh at him."

"I'm not!" she protested between her giggles. "I'm laughing because nothing ever changes. I might as well be twelve years old. Jason is still mooning after Penelope, and I'm still getting into scrapes and hiding in the shrubbery." She looked about her, bemused. "*Why* are we still hiding in the shrubbery?"

She turned her smile to him then, her eyes wet with laughter, shining, happy.

She had a leaf in her hair. A smudge of dirt on her elbow. And that pull tugged at his core.

Oh to hell with it. "This is why," he said and took her mouth and kissed her.

It was hard, quick. She gave a small yelp of surprise, quickly muffled into a moan.

And it was thrilling.

He released her before she could protest further. From the shocked look on her face, he suspected she might have.

"Why . . . why did you do that?" she asked in a whisper.

He shrugged. "It was worth the doing," he whispered back. He grinned into the darkness. Hell yes, it was worth the doing.

She could have slapped him. She could have left in a huff; he wouldn't have stopped her. But whatever her delayed reaction would be, they were destined to never know. Because at that moment, a different set of voices approached them—and these, even more interesting than the last.

The shrubbery was proving remarkably useful that night.

"Did you see 'em?" the first voice said, in a rushed whisper. "Gold, diamonds . . ." It was unrecognizable, but clearly from the area by his sharp accent. "Loads of people here—I'm tellin' ye, we could make a fortune on the road out of town."

They were walking quickly, moving past the bushes as they spoke. Byrne tried to see through the vines and twigs, but the season had made them thick with new leaves. Excellent for hiding, not so good for seeing.

Byrne couldn't make out what the other man said, even though he strained to hear. They were too far away now, their voices melding with the hum and bustle of the assembly.

After a moment, Byrne cleared his throat. "Well. Hiding in these bushes is proving more informative than originally thought."

"I should say," she breathed. "Is that what I think it was? The highwayman?"

"Possibly." Byrne chanced to bring his head up, peer over the edge of the bushes, and look in the direction the men had moved, up the path into town. But it was too dark to see anything, too dark to tell.

"You should go after them, capture them!" Jane cried.

"On what charge? Conversing about the traffic the road out of town is going to have tonight? You yourself said we need proof." Byrne stared into the darkness, the black abyss of the long road. "I'm going to follow them."

"I'll come with you," Jane volunteered.

"You absolutely will not," Byrne countered. "What would your father say if both his children left the assembly without him? What would the town?"

The excited color faded from Jane's face. "Oh! You're right of course. I really should get back . . . how long have we been out here?"

"No more than a few minutes," Byrne assured her as they rose to their feet carefully. To his leg it felt like hours. To the rest of him . . . mere seconds.

He watched as Jane gave herself an efficient once-over, checking to make sure that her hair was in place, her dress straight. She rubbed the smudge of dirt off her elbow.

"Did I miss anything?" she asked quickly.

He couldn't resist. Reaching over lightly, Byrne pulled a small leaf from the copper tendrils of hair just behind her ear. "You're perfect," he said.

That made her smile. And because she smiled, and because he felt that pull inching him toward her, telling him to ignore his purpose, Byrne let those be the last words he said to her that evening.

He turned and moved down the high street, letting the darkness fold in around him, becoming little more than a shadow.

Hunting his prey.

He did not look back.

Thirteen

IT cannot be thought surprising, given the events in the shrubbery, that Jane forgot to tell Victoria about her younger brothers' apple-tossing abilities. Therefore, the morning after the assembly, Michael and Joshua Wilton found themselves pleasantly unpunished and therefore able to perpetrate their next adventure.

"What time is it?" Joshua mumbled, as Michael poked and prodded him awake.

"Not yet dawn," Michael whispered. "Hurry up and get dressed. Bridget and Minnie will be up soon, and they'll stop us." He tossed his younger brother his trousers as he pulled on his own. No stockings or shoes—the whole house would hear them; better to go barefoot.

Joshua yawned through the quick minutes it took to get dressed. "But what are we *doing*, Michael?" he asked.

"We are going to stand on the deadhead," he replied with a grin.

Joshua's eyes opened immediately. "The deadhead?" he squeaked.

The deadhead was a massive tree trunk, a log felled decades back and dropped in the middle of Merrymere by enterprising fishermen, stuck into the muck at the bottom. The theory being that a sunken

object would become an attractive place for trout to gather and
hide—and therefore a perfect fishing spot. Local fishermen had sunk
a variety of objects over the years. A bed frame, a wagon with broken
axles . . . all with the hope of attracting more fish. And any sport
fisherman worth their salt would tell you it worked . . . although they
would be hard-pressed to tell you the last time they had successfully
caught a fish at any of those locations.

The deadhead itself was approximately forty feet long, stuck at
an odd angle in the lake floor. It was mostly underwater, but a foot
or so stuck out at the top. It was the absolute ultimate act of derring-
do to stand on the deadhead, and none of their friends had done it
yet. They were all too scared—it was too far out, they said; the water
was too deep.

Truth was—it was too creepy. It gave them all a fright, every time
they rowed by it.

But Michael wasn't scared. No, he and Joshua were going to be
the first to stand upon it, conquer the fear.

But Joshua didn't look so sure.

"Are you sure this is a good idea?" Joshua whined, once they had
snuck out the kitchen door and into the gardens.

"It'll be brilliant," Michael replied. "All we have to do is borrow
Mr. Morgan's dinghy and row it down the river and out onto the
lake."

"But won't he notice his boat's gone?"

"Everyone was at the party last night—they'll be sleeping in,"
Michael argued, secure in his logic. After all, if he'd been eating and
dancing until three in the morning, he would sleep until at least
nine—as would Michael's parents and sisters.

"But what if he doesn't?" Joshua asked again.

"He won't."

"But what if—"

"Don't be such a namby-pamby, Joshua!" Michael cried.

"But . . . it's the deadhead," Joshua replied, coming to a complete
stop.

"You don't want to stand on it? Fine," he said as he crossed his arms. "Then you can be a namby-pamby like everyone else. But I'm not scared. I'm going to go stand on the deadhead, and you can just watch me."

Michael turned and started walking down the riverside, toward the Morgans' farm, where he knew Mr. Morgan kept his dinghy tethered. It was mere seconds before he heard his brother's footsteps catch up to his.

"I'm not scared, too," Joshua said, and trotted alongside his brother, ready to face this next adventure.

❧

Byrne hadn't slept much or well. He hadn't expected to. He had stressed his leg last night, first crouching for so long in the bushes, eavesdropping on everything from lust unrequited to a possible highwayman plot, and then following after the suspects, who, after a half hour of skulking in the shadows, he had found neither hide nor hair of.

There was very little more frustrating than discovering you have been chasing nothing, so Byrne had declined rejoining the assembly and grabbed Dobbs, who had the carriage ready and waiting. He could feel the burn in his thigh beginning, the long night he had in front of him. He needed a hot brandy and a cold compress. He needed to be home, away from people, before he began snapping and growling like a beast.

Oddly though, he realized in the wee hours of the morning, as he massaged the cramping muscles of his leg, it had felt good to be on the chase again. He had been too desperate in London, helping Marcus, to enjoy the skills it took to hide in plain sight, the senses of sight and hearing he had spent years refining. But it felt worthwhile to be using them again. It felt as if, for a few short minutes, he had a purpose again. Even given the frustrations of not knowing if what they'd overheard had anything to do with the highwayman, and the annoyance of losing the men in the darkness, it had felt right.

Jane would crow with triumph when he told her.

And thoughts of Jane automatically turned to thoughts of kissing her. He could chalk up his actions last night as a product of the stars, the summer air, and the gaiety of the other partygoers. The excitement and intensity, the nerves and the relief of having survived the gauntlet of villagers. All were perfectly good excuses for an errant kiss. But Byrne didn't think they held true.

The truth was, he had been headed in this direction for weeks now, since he first offered friendship with a tin of tea. Perhaps even months, since he first saw her standing with her father at the Hampshire Racing Party, proud and sad.

Of course, Byrne didn't know how she would act the day after—if she would play coquette and invite such advances, or bury their memory, acting as if nothing ever happened. He suspected the latter, more's the pity.

He gave up on sleep just past dawn, his leg still a little stiff, but working. He walked out onto the porch and gazed out at the fog-covered lake. The sky was clear, so the sun would burn the mist off quickly, but for now, it seemed as if there was nothing in the world but his house and the water.

Byrne could hear Dobbs whistling in the stables beyond. He would be saddling up to ride into town for fresh bread and eggs—a hearty breakfast for hearty men, he liked to say.

He tested his weight on his leg. A twinge, not enough to keep him from exercise, but if he were being careful, he would wait until the afternoon or tomorrow to dive in. But he didn't want to be careful.

She said she would come by today with the pages from the ledger. He couldn't simply spend the whole morning waiting for her. He wanted to swim, to put everything out of his mind for a short hour, and let his thoughts become clear and calm.

It was just him, the water, and the morning mist as he stripped down to his smalls and dove in.

Joshua and Michael managed to get the dinghy down the river and out onto Merrymere without raising any hue and cry, which Michael took as a good omen. He was going to do it! Nothing could stop him!

The oars sliced through the water cleanly—although with Joshua on one and Michael on the other (and Joshua being markedly smaller than Michael), there was a slight listing to one side that required several course corrections as they made their way out to the deadhead.

It wasn't in the middle of the lake—Michael doubted there was a tree tall enough to go all the way to the bottom of the middle of the lake—it was about a hundred feet offshore, on the eastern side of the lake.

It was sunny and clear by the time they pulled up alongside, Michael reaching out and grabbing the top of the deadhead to steady themselves. Despite the clear day, the deadhead loomed out of the water like a demon from the deep, disappearing into the abyss of muck and water below.

"Ew!" he cried happily. "It's all slimy!"

"That's disgusting—let me touch it!" Joshua stood up, nearly oversetting them in his haste.

"Joshua, sit down. You have to hold the boat steady as I stand up!"

Joshua settled back into his seat, taking control of the oars, as Michael stood in the dinghy, balancing himself on the plank that served as their seat. Once he was upright, slowly, and with infinite care, Michael put one foot out, and placed it on the slimy, moss- and muck-covered top of the deadhead.

"Careful, Michael," Joshua whispered, as Michael transferred his weight to the deadhead, and quickly brought his second foot to join the first.

He put his arms out for balance, and held for three seconds, four, five . . .

"I'm doing it!" he cried in the still morning air. "I'm standing on the deadhead!"

Of course, that was when he fell.

Quickly arcing into a dive, Michael splashed into the cool water, then surfaced several feet away, laughing. He had done it! He had stood on the deadhead!

"The other boys are never going to believe it!" he cried, pushing his wet bangs off his forehead as he treaded water. Minnie was going to yell at him for being all wet, and if Mr. Morgan found out they'd taken his boat, they were about to be skinned alive, but he didn't care, because just then, he was the king of the lake.

"I want to try," Joshua said, leaping out of his seat and balancing himself on the plank seat.

"All right," Michael replied, as he started back toward the deadhead. "Let me get back into the boat first."

But Joshua wasn't listening. He put his foot out, placed it on the deadhead. Then, quickly, too quickly, he brought his other one on—kicking the boat away and setting it adrift.

"Joshua, no!" Michael burbled, but it was too late.

Joshua had stepped on too fast, he hadn't given enough time to balance, and his second foot caught only the edge of the top of the deadhead, and slipped on its slimy surface.

He didn't fall away from the deadhead, like Michael had. Instead, he fell down, and hard, hitting his chin on the log as he went.

Michael didn't know what he did next, didn't know how to move his arms or legs—all he knew was he heard himself screaming as his brother disappeared beneath the surface.

Byrne heard the boy before he saw him. His head surfacing from a stroke, the cry rent the still, cool air around him. He had been swimming for almost an hour, the fog on the water had dissipated, and the sun gleamed off the surface, blinding Byrne as he looked around for the source of the sound.

Then he caught sight of the screaming boy.

"Help! Help me! Joshua!" the boy cried from a hundred, maybe two hundred yards away, near the log that stuck haphazardly out of the water—the one the locals called the deadhead. Several yards away a small dinghy was floating aimlessly.

"Joshua!" the boy yelled again, then burbled as he went underwater.

Byrne put his arms and legs to work. He moved through the water faster than ever, faster than he had ever dared to push his body. Kick, stroke, breathe, kick, stroke, breathe . . .

Finally, he reached the boy's side—apple-tossing Michael Wilton, part of his brain recognized dimly—as he surfaced once more for air, and yelled for his brother. Byrne grabbed him before he went back under.

"What happened?" Byrne cried over Michael's splashes. The child looked wildly about, and finally saw that Byrne was holding him by the shirt collar.

"He hit his head—went under. I told him not to do it!"

Byrne looped Michael's arms around the deadhead, growling, "Stay here!" before he gulped air and dove under.

It was murky beneath the surface. Byrne's eyes stung with the freshwater and algae that clouded his vision. He went down, down deep, the temperature dropping with every inch, using the deadhead to feel his way, climbing down it like a ladder, while he scanned the world around him.

A glint of silver in the distance—a fast-moving school of fish. A flutter below him—a length of seaweed, twined around an arm of the deadhead. His lungs began to burn, and he was about to surface to gulp a breath of air when, suddenly, he saw him.

He was drifting slowly down, his arms raised up as if reaching out for help, his body lifelessly limp. Byrne didn't think about how still he looked, didn't speculate about how long the boy could have been underwater—he laddered down the deadhead as fast as he could, grabbed the boy underneath his arms, and kicked furiously for the surface.

He burst through into the sunlight, gasping for air. The unmoving body of little Joshua Wilton did not. Byrne treaded water as he turned the boy around in his arms, brought his face to his. He shook him, slapped the body lightly, tried to rouse him.

"Joshua. Joshua!" Byrne cried, but to no avail. Joshua remained still.

Dammit. He couldn't do this treading water. He needed to get to land. Byrne glanced at the dinghy, now floating even farther away, then to shore. A quick calculation of time—shore was the better bet.

"Can you swim?" Byrne asked Michael brusquely. Michael, who had been watching wide-eyed since Byrne surfaced, nodded quickly. "Come on!" he said then, and cradling Joshua in his arms, Byrne kicked his way toward shore.

It was agony. His thigh burned every time his leg came down in the water. It burned twice as much when he raised it up again. But he did not allow himself to think about it. He concentrated on the boy, on how to get him breathing again, awake again.

Byrne only glanced back once. Michael swam behind him, not as fast but steady. He was a strong swimmer—which was good, because Byrne doubted he'd be able to swim with both their weight. Finally, after what felt like eons but could only have been a few minutes, they reached land. Byrne collapsed to his knees, dropping Joshua as gently as he could manage on the rocky, muddy shore.

Do not think about your leg; think about the boy. The leg is nothing. There is nothing.

He leaned down, held his ear to the boy's chest. Nothing. No sound, no rise and fall.

"Dammit," he whispered, picking the boy's limp body up again, throwing him against his shoulder.

"What are you doing?" Michael Wilton cried, as he crawled out onshore.

"The water has gotten into his lungs; he cannot breathe," Byrne answered, and then with a great *Thwap!* he slapped Joshua on the back, as if he were burping an oversized baby.

"Come on, boy," he growled, slapping his back again, "come on!"

Another slap, and another . . . Michael was crying now, tiny hiccups of fear and panic as he watched his brother's blue face jostle with each slap . . . and then finally, Byrne felt the body go rigid, and shudder, and a stream of lake water flowed up from Joshua Wilton's lungs, out his mouth, and down Byrne's back.

He laid the boy back down on the muddy earth. He was breathing again, his chest rising and falling—weakly, but it was functioning. His color was returning slightly, but he was still unconscious. Then Byrne saw the bright red blood begin to trickle out of the corner of the child's mouth.

"We need to get your brother inside—a doctor," Byrne said, standing with only a small grimace, taking Joshua into his arms. Byrne looked around, took stock of where they were. And for the first time all morning, he knew he had a bit of luck. Because they were a mere hundred yards away from the only place on Merrymere's shore that could possibly help them now.

"This way," he said, as he led Michael toward the Cottage.

Jane woke up to the sounds of banging and commotion. She sat up in bed, drew back the bed-curtain just in time to see Mary, her lady's maid, opening the door. She did not come bearing firewood (which had been unnecessary for over a week now, the temperature remaining high throughout the evenings) but instead, seeing Lady Jane awake, rushed to the wardrobe and fished out Jane's dressing gown.

"Milady! There's been a terrible accident!" Mary squeaked before she rushed back out into the hall. Jane had no choice but to follow close at the girl's heels.

Her first thought was her father. Something happened in the night, something bad. But he had been sleeping so well since coming here. Nancy said he was very rarely wandering the halls at night now . . . but they passed her father's door, it was still closed, still undisturbed.

Perhaps it was Jason. He had not yet come home by the time she went to bed last night. Jane suspected he had chosen to drown his sorrows over Penelope Brandon somewhere, but what if he had gotten himself injured? What if he had gotten himself killed driving a team, or in a duel, or . . . the highwayman?

Jane quickly shook off that last notion. Goodness, she was becoming as gullible as the locals! Likely Jason had gotten drunk and twisted his ankle or some such thing, Jane thought. Yes, that's it. He's fine, a little battered, but fine.

He had to be fine.

So Jane readied herself to see her drunken brother moaning in pain on the settee in the receiving parlor—but she was not at all prepared for the sight that met her eyes.

Byrne Worth knelt, dripping wet and in his smalls, by the unconscious form of Joshua Wilton, who was also wet, and lying on the settee. Michael Wilton stood in a corner, watching a flurry of Jane's staff bring hot water and pillows and quilts at Nurse Nancy's direction.

"I need that blanket, thank you," Nancy said, as a footman handed her a feather quilt embroidered with silk thread, and ruthlessly stuffed it around the boy. "We need to warm him up, keep him breathing. And give them quilts, too!"

Jane saw a young maid wrap a blanket around the stock-still form of Michael Wilton as she rushed into the room. Someone threw a quilt around Byrne's shoulders just as Jane reached his side.

"What happened?" Jane asked, kneeling at the settee, her eyes raking over the boy.

"He hit his head and fell into the water," Byrne answered softly, his eyes focused and hard, never straying from the boy, "he took a great deal of it into his lungs, and . . . now there's blood in his mouth and . . ." He looked at her then, and Jane saw his face crumple for just a moment, in some emotion Jane could not identify—Pain? Fear? His expression was intense, as if he was reining something in, and unleashing it would be disastrous. But it only flashed for a second, before his mask hardened again, and his eyes refocused on the small child in front of him.

Jane wanted to reach out to him, soothe him in some way, but his entire body vibrated with warning. He was no longer aware she was there, and barely aware of the rest of the room. There was no solace he would accept. Not yet.

Jane spared one last glance for Byrne and then turned to Nancy.

"Has anyone sent for the doctor yet?" she asked.

Nancy shook her head. "They arrived but moments ago," she said, breathless. Then turning to one of the footmen, "Get a horse saddled, and go now!"

"I'll go," Jason's voice came from the hallway.

He was still wearing his formal kit from the night before, cravat long lost and his shirt partially undone, his hair an utter mess—but he was alert and there.

"Jason," Jane asked, trotting to him, "have you even slept yet?"

"No," he admitted, "but I'm not in my cups, and I'm the fastest rider in the house."

"But—"

"Your arguing is wasting time," Jason reasoned, then called out to the footman, "have them saddle Midas—and he better be ready by the time I walk out to the stables—which is now!"

The footman lost all decorum as he broke into a run, almost bumping into Jane and Jason as he careened out of the room and down the hall to the door.

"You must fetch the family, too—the Wiltons," Jane said, pitching her voice low. If a flicker of emotion crossed her brother's face, he swallowed it down in the way of men—or at least, in the way of men this morning.

Jason leaned down and kissed Jane's cheek—something he had not done in years, something that told Jane he knew the seriousness of the situation—and then followed the path of the footman and was out the door.

And now Jane did not know what to do. Nancy hovered over the child, directing maids to fuel the fire, bring more blankets, and she applied smelling salts to a handkerchief.

Byrne did not move from his position by the couch. He knelt there, as if in prayer. But his whole body was a tense live wire, all his energy focused on the boy, watching his chest rise and fall, willing him, un-successfully, to wake up. Jane took a step toward the settee, intending to . . . she did not know what she intended. To help? How? She had no medical training; she couldn't reassure Byrne that way. She prayed that the boy would be all right, fervently and with her whole self, but any assurance she made to him would fall flat. She could do nothing.

It had been over a year since Jane felt this useless. Since she sat by her mother's deathbed, placing cold compresses on her brow, reading books aloud to fill the dreadful silence, only broken by her mother's raspy breaths. Trivial, fruitless things that gave no comfort to either mother or daughter. With her father's illness, Jane had fought, was fighting, striving to understand, to find better treatment, but with her mother . . . there was nothing to be done. Nothing but to sit and wait for the moment when the awful noise of her mother's breathing ceased, at once a relief and a horror.

Jane wrapped her dressing gown about her tighter, her memories too chilly for the overheated room. She was about to turn from the room, go upstairs and quickly change into a gown, something service-able, when she caught a small movement out of the corner of her eye.

Michael, standing by the side of the room, out of everyone's way, wrapped in his blanket, quietly shaking. As lost and as helpless as Jane in that moment.

She crossed the room, knelt by Michael. Normally full of mirth and mischief, his eyes were now uncertain, water streaking his cheeks.

"Michael," Jane began softly, putting her hand on his small back. She expected him to flinch at the touch, to be startled—not to turn immediately into her arms and hold on for dear life. He clutched at her neck, this tiny, fragile child with scraped knees and elbows. His flesh was clammy and he shook, vibrated continually, as if he could not get warm.

"I don't know what to do," he whispered between gulps of breath.

In that moment, Jane swallowed her own feelings of uselessness. There were things to be done. She pulled back, glanced down at Michael's reddened joints.

"We," she said authoritatively, "are going to take care of those scrapes on your knees and elbows." She stood and held out her hand to him, which he took. "And you are going to tell me everything that happened."

She led Michael to the door to the kitchens, letting her eyes fall once more to the settee as she passed, where Nancy tended the boy and Byrne remained motionless by his side.

Waiting.

Seconds ticked into minutes—and every minute that passed, every minute that Joshua remained unconscious, Byrne felt a year of his life drain away.

He had to be all right. This child was in his care, and it was his responsibility to watch over him until the doctor came.

He had to hold on until then.

Seconds ticked into minutes.

He could feel the red, raw edges of pain shooting from his leg up his spine, trying to overtake him. It would eventually; it was so much stronger than him . . . but not yet. Not as long as he concentrated on the boy.

Byrne, as a rule, did not pray. His faith was ambiguous—war made men either believers or atheists, and having been witness to and perpetrator of its atrocities, Byrne leaned toward the latter. Men— good men—and innocent children had fallen to their fates for less than Joshua's sins. No, Byrne did not pray; it would have been use-less. But he devoted his will. He focused on the boy, willing his breath to flow, willing him to stay alive . . .

Seconds ticked into minutes.

God, his leg throbbed.

Jane had been there, he realized dimly. He remembered her eyes, two wells of concern. He couldn't accept her sympathy now, her help. Not yet. It would break him, and he was just barely holding it together. To think, just this morning, he had been reliving their kiss.

It seemed so long ago.

He knew she had gone to the boy, Michael, and left Byrne to Joshua and his will.

Seconds ticked into minutes.

The nurse bustled around him, the servants doing her bidding— all of them waiting, watching. A door opened and closed—he knew it was Jane, returning with Michael. Byrne knew how Michael was feeling, knew that blank shock. Byrne was an older brother, too, and had stood by as his younger brother was hurt. He had been responsible for him; he should have watched him better . . . It had been his fault . . . It was his fault . . .

"Mr. Worth?" Michael's voice came, small and unsure. Byrne chanced a look up.

"I'm really sorry we threw the apples," the boy whispered penitently.

Seconds ticked into minutes.

Byrne nodded dumbly, accepting the apology before turning his focus back to Joshua. Jane took Michael's hand again.

It had cost him to look away. Those red, raw edges of pain were gaining ground. But he had to hold on just a little longer. Had to stay clearheaded until—

"Where is he?" Dr. Berridge demanded as he burst through the drawing room door, followed quickly by Victoria Wilton and Jason.

"My family's following," he heard Victoria say to Jane as the doctor barreled past him and began examining the boy.

Dr. Berridge whispered words to himself, long tangled Latin words that Byrne did not try to understand. For as soon as the doctor had arrived, he scrambled to the other side of the room and let those red, raw edges overflow and take him.

Jane saw the moment Byrne crumpled and collapsed against the wall. Victoria must have seen it, too, and since Michael was now in his sister's care, Victoria gave Jane a nod, releasing her to attend him.

She reached his side quickly, and silently crouched by him. He breathed hard through his teeth, his eyes a dark haze. Byrne's hands clutched at his injured leg—as he was clad only in smalls and a blanket, Jane was able to see the thick, ugly scar that twisted over strained muscle. He rubbed, massaged, but it offered no relief.

His eyes met hers, finally.

He was in a great deal of pain.

"Get me out of here," he pleaded quietly through clenched teeth.

"Can you stand?" she asked. He looked unsure for a moment, but then, resolved, gave a small nod. Jane reached over and grasped his hand, using all her strength to pull him upright. He nearly fell over, though, when he tested his weight on his bad leg, so Jane went under his arm, took his weight, and nimbly helped him hobble to the door.

No one followed—the focus was on Joshua, as was right. Jane maneuvered Byrne across the hall, to the unoccupied library, still littered with Jason's papers and her father's ledgers, but blissfully quiet. She set him down on the long leather sofa, took the blanket from his shoulders and covered him with it. Hard to do when he would not release her hand. Indeed, he clutched, held fast—as if she were the only thing tethering him to the ground.

"Don't leave," he said, as he labored to keep his breathing even.

"I won't," she replied, seating herself on the floor beside the couch, her hand still grasped in his. "It's your leg, is it not?" After his nod, she asked, "Is there anything you can take for the pain? Surely the doctor—"

"No!" he barked, startling her with his fierceness. "I won't take anything—Jane, don't let them give me a drop. Not a single drop."

"But it must be severe—" she argued, only to be met by a growl.

"Don't let them!" his voice had become feral, his eyes bloodshot as he sought her gaze. "Promise me," he demanded softly. Then, squeezing her hand harder, "Promise me!"

"Yes. I promise." Her hand was crushed in his, but she did not speak of it. It was a measly hand, after all, a bruise to be gloved until it faded. A small sacrifice, considering what Byrne had gone through that morning.

"Do you know," she said, keeping her voice as light as she could manage, "that the ladies of Reston are going to inundate you with preserves now?" He looked at her wildly, questioning. But she continued blithely, "There will be no end to the baskets they bring you—I'm afraid you are going to have to practice your most humble manners. You will have to endure at least ten minutes of conversation with everyone who comes to call."

"Why?" he asked, bewildered through his pain.

"Because you saved that boy," she whispered. "You're incredibly brave."

Byrne shook his head tightly, "I didn't save him. He's not safe."

"He will be. The doctor will rouse him," she argued, her heart in her throat. "He *will*, Byrne. Mark my words. And you will simply have to survive being called a hero."

He might have laughed then, Jane was unable to tell. But he gave a short burst of disbelief and continued massaging his leg.

They held silent for a while, listening to the bustle of voices in the hall, as the rest of the Wiltons arrived and poured into the drawing room. The noise died off as they moved out of the hall, leaving Jane alone in the silence with Byrne.

"I was thinking about kissing you again," he said suddenly, softly. It was possible he hadn't known that he spoke aloud.

Jane's breath caught. She could not deny that she had been thinking about something similar, before she was awoken this morning by chaos. But now, it was a remnant of a time before—crisis had suspended the thought, and Jane had no reply.

So instead, she put her head down on the leather sofa, rested it there as she held his hand, and watched Byrne's face wrestle with the pain she would take from him if she could.

And waited for word from beyond the door.

Fourteen

T HERE is no accounting for how time flows in a crisis. It stops and
starts, holds infinite in single moments and blazes through hours.
People hold their breath for news, as the entire world becomes focused on a tiny point.

They had all rushed in—Jason taking Victoria up behind him, and
Dr. Berridge riding fast on his own horse. Sir and Lady Wilton had
readied their carriage, stuffed it with blankets, and followed shortly
thereafter. Victoria had been near to tears, but her parents were
calmer, if no less concerned. Lady Wilton had a mother's concentration, the experience of knowing that little boys got into scrapes, and
that one had to be strong and sober to handle what came next.

Michael told them all the story of how they had come to be out
on the lake—and that perhaps they might need to fetch Mr. Morgan's
dinghy from wherever it had floated. He then explained to all that
Mr. Worth had come to their rescue and swam Joshua to shore and
pounded on his back until he breathed again. Michael was hugged
and scolded in turns by every member of his family. But still they
awaited the doctor's prognosis.

It was quickly discovered by Dr. Berridge that the blood coming from Joshua's mouth was because he had bitten his tongue in his fall. He turned him with haste to his side so he wouldn't swallow any more blood and become ill with it. The tongue would heal, he assured the family. Then Dr. Berridge discovered Joshua had no broken bones, no visible injuries to his skull. It was decided that he remained unconscious due to possibly having a concussion, or "a shaking of the brain," the doctor explained, "and we shall simply have to wait for his mind to right itself."

And there was nothing in the universe like the relief felt when Joshua's mind righted itself enough to allow him to open his eyes, see his mother and sister, and smile weakly. Then he promptly fell back asleep.

The Wiltons and Dr. Berridge voiced a desire to shake Mr. Worth's hand in gratitude . . . and they did so, once they found him in the library. He took their hands but was remarkably recalcitrant, thought Sir Wilton, unable to meet their eye, his movements cold and controlled. Terribly odd behavior, this avoidance of being thanked, this uncaring attitude about whether or not Joshua lived or died. But, Dr. Berridge interjected, the man's oddities aside, he did save their son and should be shown some allowance. The Wiltons grudgingly agreed. Then Lady Wilton spied Dr. Berridge having a short exchange with Mr. Worth, in which the latter man answered the doctor's questions with a gruff and vehement "No!" before he turned away again.

Odd behavior indeed.

Some time later, after Victoria had taken Michael home, it was decided that Joshua was recovered enough to be moved back to his own house. He was a little groggy and complained of a headache, but he was awake now for minutes at a time, and the trip was short enough that Dr. Berridge had no objection.

Byrne's man Dobbs, having heard the commotion in town and finding the widow Lowe's house unoccupied when he returned, put two and two together and came to the Cottage. He took one look at Byrne and fetched him away, despite Lady Jane's protestations.

Nurse Nancy had gone upstairs to attend to the Duke, whom she had left in the care of the second nurse all morning. Jason, having gone almost a full day without sleep, stumbled upstairs to change out of his evening kit and crawl into bed. Two chambermaids set about folding up the blankets and banking the fire in the drawing room, righting the space to what it normally was.

And suddenly it was quiet in the house. The crisis had passed, and Jane was alone in the foyer, in her dressing gown. She looked at the grandfather clock that ticked away merrily in the echoing space. It was barely noon.

What a terrifying, incredible, strange start to the day, she thought wildly, as she turned once, twice, and then decided there was nothing else to be done but go upstairs, change, and find some breakfast.

It goes without saying that over the course of the next week, Jane was proved correct about many things. The first being that it would be quite some time before Byrne would want for jams and jellies in his little house. The second being that he really should have brushed up on his manners.

The pain in his leg dulled over time, but he kept off it as much as possible, not wanting to reinjure himself and endure the agony again. Dr. Berridge came by, and after again suggesting a course of laudanum for the worst of the pain and being rebuffed, insisted that Byrne remain abed (or as Byrne insisted, a-sofa) for the better part of every day. Byrne grumbled at this but complied. Unfortunately, this compliance meant he was in residence whenever anyone stopped in—and it seemed none of the villagers cared whether or not he was in a state to receive.

Mrs. Hill was the first to call, while he was lying on the sofa wearing little more than a shirt and trousers, his leg elevated on cushions. She fluttered kindly, depositing a basket of blackberry preserves and fresh bread in the kitchen, telling him all the while of his incredible bravery in saving that poor boy from drowning. She then proceeded to tut at the old curtains and told him that she was expanding her dress shop to other textile services, including drapery, if he was interested in "sprucing the place up," as she put it.

Mrs. Hill was shortly followed by Mrs. Morgan, who also came with a basket, this time a cold ham from their farm, praised his heroics, and asked if he had any idea where Mr. Morgan's dinghy had floated off to. They had yet to find it, which was surprising, considering the relatively small size of Merrymere. And Mrs. Morgan was elbowed out of the way by Mrs. Cutler. She brought cheese.

It took about a half hour that first day for his small sitting room to fill with townswomen. And soon, Byrne was to discover why. For it was not long after, the entire space tittering and clucking and sipping (someone had found widow Lowe's old tea service and made a pot of one of her exotic teas) that Lady Wilton arrived, bearing the largest basket of fruit—apples from their apple tree—and commanded the attention of the entire room.

"Mr. Worth," she said, her voice filled with a somber hauteur, for the benefit of her audience, "I've come to thank you for your kindness to my son Joshua. He would not be alive today, were it not for you."

The ladies applauded Byrne as Lady Wilton regally took a seat. Then she obligingly took questions from the others, all of whom cried to know how Joshua was faring, what the doctor had recommended for his care, and what was being done to remove the dangerous, offending deadhead from the waters of Merrymere, so it would not tempt other young boys.

Really, it was all he could do to keep from pitching the lot of them out of his house then and there.

Admirably, he held his countenance. But he didn't know how much longer he would be able to endure it. So he pulled his face into a pained expression and whimpered once.

This had the effect of setting many of the women fluttering and making excuses, not realizing that they had overtired poor Mr. Worth. As many of them bustled out, Lady Wilton hung back, making noises about seeing to his comfort. She had begun folding a blanket, and tut-tutting about the old-fashioned state of the house (which Byrne resented—he was a bachelor after all, he was allowed to care little for decorations) before Dobbs entered, bearing a load of wood for the stove. Byrne sent him a signal—although one was hardly needed.

Dobbs had bustled Lady Wilton out the door before she could fluff a single pillow more.

The next day, the men of Reston visited. Their visits were far shorter and less grouped, but still they sat awkwardly in his living room and tried to start conversation. Some asked him about his family in London—and considering he hadn't returned his sister-in-law Mariah's letters in ages, he was fairly certain there was no news of import, and therefore gruff, bare answers were all he had. Mr. Cutler asked Byrne about his service in the military during the war. This was a subject he liked even less, and therefore his answers were shorter and even gruffer.

Byrne did as best he could, but he had never understood the small town's desperate need to know everything about everyone. And somewhere along his travels, he knew he had lost the ability to be engaging and charming—to be a man who could talk of nothing with people unknown to him and do so happily.

Would he ever get it back? He did not know.

The men left shortly thereafter.

The only person he thought he could stand seeing did not come. Jane Cummings remained away. Even as he was visited daily by one of the women from Reston, who fluffed pillows, put tea on, and brought samples of fabric (they had apparently decided between them that Byrne required tending and worked out a schedule, and as long as they held themselves to the sitting room, he managed to stand their curiosity), Jane was not among them.

He didn't blame her for avoiding him. He had shown her the worst of himself, mad with pain, growling and spitting.

The only word he had from her was a letter, carried by a footman from the Cottage, containing a short note saying she had read the copied pages from Sir Wilton's ledger, and enclosed them for his perusal. That was it. No indication that she would visit to discuss the pages, no reason for her avoidance.

She probably pitied him.

The thought turned Byrne's stomach worse than Mrs. Frederickson's blood pudding (which she kindly brought on her scheduled day).

And so it went for over a week: Byrne, keeping his leg aloft, testing its strength daily, enduring with better grace each day the ladies of the town's best, most meddlesome intentions, wondering briefly if he would hear word of Jane.

In spite of all the attention, it was truly one of the most boring, pedantic stretches of time he'd had at the lake.

That is, of course, until the highwayman attacked again.

Lady Jane Cummings was a coward.

There was no other way to paint it. After the dramatic events of the morning over a week ago, she found herself remarkably busy. Or, more to the point, she *made* herself remarkably busy.

She went through every item in the linen closets and trunks, detailed what needed to be mended and what needed to be thrown out. She walked with her father daily. She planned menus for the next month with the cook. She inspected the gardens with the head gardener and decided on new plantings in the south lawn. She went through her pile of books she had brought from London and read seven. She wrote letters to all her friends, sent away for sheet music for a new sonata on the pianoforte, and requested copies of dress plates from all of the publishers she could think of.

She visited Reston and was delighted to see that after a few days of rest, Joshua Wilton was back to his old self, as evidenced by the amount of dirt he and Michael had collected on their clothing.

She played two dozen games of chess with her father in the evenings and lost nineteen of them. Jason either moped around the house, complaining of boredom, or rode out into the country. He took no hand in their father's care, and Jane was distressed to see that he seemed to have lost all interest in mastering the accounts, instead leaving the books in the same disarray in the library, slowly collecting dust—as Jane refused to allow the maids to clean the desk, wanting to keep the books out in the same arrangement Jason had left them in case inspiration struck him as he passed.

In fact, Jane did anything and everything except what she craved most to do—to escape her house, walk down that wooded path by the lakeshore, and visit Byrne Worth.

What would she say to him? She didn't know. What would he say to her? He had saved a child's life, but she had a feeling that he would accept no gratitude from her for it. Would he reject her for having been witness to his weaknesses? It was another weight on her already weighted mind.

But before that morning, there had been that night. When he had kissed her in the bushes, hiding from the assembly beneath the stars. He had just done it. No wavering, no wondering how it would affect their friendship like she had. Just the press of his lips to hers, the brief but electric exchange of breath, the jolt to her heart.

And what had he replied when she asked why? "It was worth the doing." As if random, unplanned kisses were a constant in his line! So, no, Jane had no idea how to look at Byrne and how he would look at her. So she avoided it in the practiced way of polite people everywhere.

That is, until she could avoid it no longer.

It was after dinner, the house gone quiet and the land gone dark, spotted with stars, when the knock came at the door. Jane was in the midst of losing her twentieth game of chess to her father, as Nurse Nancy worked on some stitchery by the window.

"Now who can that be?" her father asked, looking up from the board, slightly dazed by the interruption. "Is it a caller?"

"It's far too late for callers, Father," Jane replied with a quizzical look. She laid down her king (her father had her in six moves anyway) and went to the drawing room door. Peering out, she saw an alarming number of gentlemen being admitted to her foyer.

"It's disgraceful!" cried one man, who removed his hat to reveal the grayed and balding head of Mr. Hale, the steward of Crow Castle.

"Appalling!" agreed the schooled accent of Mr. Thorndike, the man in charge of the London house. Apparently, the stewards had received Jason's letter of inquiry . . . along with Jane's added note inviting them up to stay.

And it seemed they weren't alone.

"Ohoohooh," Nevill, half of the diabolical twosome Charles and Nevill Quincy-Frosham, snickered at the older men. "Did the nasty highwayman scare you?"

"Hee!" giggled his other half. "Did you think he was the bogey-man? Mind you, I should be more aggrieved than you! The man made off with my watch; he only got a valise from you!"

"That valise had all my clothes in it!" Mr. Thorndike retorted, his mustache twitching in anger.

At that, Charles and Nevill gave him a look up and down. "Gent did you a favor, old man," Nevill drawled, sending Charles into a rollicking peal of laughter threatening to take them both down to the floor.

Jane quickly closed the door.

"Nancy," she addressed the nurse quietly, "perhaps it would be best for my father to retire now?"

Nancy nodded and gently took her charge's arm. He looked about in confusion, the noise from the hall agitating him in his evening routine. But Nancy smartly maneuvered him out a door that led to the kitchens, promising a glass of wine before sleep.

Jane took a deep and steadying breath before she emerged out into the hall.

"Did you see when he brandished his rifle!" Nevill was saying, in between snorts of laughter. "Egghead here just about lost his wits!"

"Gentlemen!" Jane called out, immediately stilling the foyer, except for a few residual giggles from Charles, who Jane suspected had imbibed about half a flask's worth of brandy that day on the trip.

"It's a pleasure to see you. Mr. Thorndike and Mr. Hale, of course, I expected, but Charles, Nevill—how do you come to be in this corner of the world?"

"Little Lady Jane!" Nevill cried, his eyes raking her up and down. It had been a number of years since she had seen Jason's cronies. "My, didn't you become all stiff and proper."

She had changed a bit, she supposed, since she last saw them during her London Season, but she could tell in an instant Nevill had not. Still just as facetious and just as drunk. (Obviously, the other half of the brandy flask had been his.)

"You should have expected us!" Charles interjected. "Because we were expected! I mean to say, we were invited!"

Jane shook off Charles's puppylike excitability and tried to remain calm. "Jason invited you?" she asked.

The puppy nodded. Jane tried her best to keep the steam from coming out her ears.

"And we ran into these fellows at the posting inn in Stockport!" Charles continued. "Nevill said since we were all going to the same place, they should ride up the rest of the way in our carriage—which was cracking good of Nevill, don't you think?"

"Yes," Nevill agreed, "and it was all going rather swimmingly, until about an hour outside of this . . . removed place, we ran into some difficulty."

One look at the faces of Mr. Hale and Mr. Thorndike, and Jane could tell the ride had been less than swimming, even before the difficulty. "Did I hear you correctly before?" she asked the two stewards. "You were overset by a highwayman?"

Nevill nodded again, but luckily, Mr. Hale was quicker with his tongue and managed to answer. "Yes, it happened on the road to Windermere. Suddenly, the horses reared up, and the driver rapped on the roof of the carriage. Then a rifle barrel comes through the open window." Mr. Hale shook his head and mopped his rather moist brow. "I beg your pardon, my lady, but do you think I might have a glass of water? It's dreadfully hot."

Jane nodded and ushered the men into the recently abandoned drawing room, where she rang for a tray and some water—and Charles and Nevill found less sober refreshment in the sideboard. As the gentlemen made themselves comfortable, Jane fetched a footman to her and addressed him under her breath.

"I need you to go into the village and wake Sir Wilton, as he is the magistrate," she said. "Tell him what has occurred and bring him here." Then she added, lower, "and dispatch someone to find my brother and bring him home. Immediately."

The footman bowed and scampered off to do his mistress's bidding. Jane allowed herself a moment to glower.

Jason had better have the world's best excuse for inviting Charles and Nevill. He had better have brought them here to perform manual labor or to publish a study on the effects of the northern climate to the uninitiated. But Jane feared that the only reason Charles and Nevill were here was that Jason was desperate to be dragged back down to their level of male stupidity.

And Jane would be damned if she would sit by and allow such a thing to happen.

Jason was found quickly, and nearby. However, as much as Jane wanted to deride him for being drunk in some inn, he was, in fact, perfectly sober and simply out in the stables, discovering he was bored enough to oversee the brushing down of his Midas himself. When Charles and Nevill's carriage was brought in, he rushed back into the house and was met by the murderous stare of his sister.

He was appropriately chagrined. But not before he embraced his friends and was slapped several times on the back in return, while being filled in on their travels.

Then he noticed the stewards—and it was his turn to give a murderous stare to his sister.

"What are Hale and Thorndike doing here?" he growled, once he pulled her aside.

"I invited them."

"I'd ask why, but I fear the answer."

"Because I wanted to help you." She narrowed her eyes. "I'd ask why Charles and Nevill are here, but I, too, fear the answer."

"Because I wanted to annoy you, Jane," Jason sniped. "It couldn't be because I'm lonely and miss my friends . . ."

Jane was about to retort hotly, but for the moment she and Jason would have to remain quietly locked in their battle, as Sir Wilton arrived, and in a perfect lather.

"It has gone too far this time!" he cried, backed up by the frequent nodding of the men he had managed to find at such an hour to bring with him: Mr. Cutler, likely happy to be out of his overcrowded house, two tenant farmers, and the blacksmith Big Jim. Big Jim was likely brought to intimidate should a suspect be captured, as he was overly tall and strong. Although he lost some of his intimidation, standing in the foyer of the Cottage gaping in awe.

"I quite agree," Lady Jane replied over the nodding and gaping. She stepped over to ring for tea. She had a remarkably full house to contend with. "That is why I have consulted with—"

"This time Sir Wilton will not tolerate it!" Mr. Cutler sputtered. "Worth cannot avoid it any longer. We will settle this once and for all!"

Jane's head snapped back to face Mr. Cutler. "What?" she cried, turning to Sir Wilton. "You cannot possibly think Byrne Worth had anything to do with this."

But Sir Wilton remained silent, stewing and grumbling.

"Why?" Jane continued. "Because you dislike him? How can you even dislike him now—considering the great service he has done for your son?"

"Jane—" Jason stepped in to argue but was stopped by her hand.

"Let her speak," Nevill whispered to Jason, but loud enough to annoy Jane. "Your sister's always more fun when her color's up."

Jane refused to dignify that with a response, instead focusing on the here and now—namely, just how high Sir Wilton's color had risen.

"His service, while admirable, has nothing to do with the matter at hand," the now plum-faced gentleman said with a nod from Cutler. "It is the fact that his whereabouts are unaccounted for."

"Have you asked Mr. Worth his whereabouts this evening?"

"No—it was where we were headed next."

Jane tilted her head and regarded her adversary. "My brother's whereabouts were unaccounted for until a few minutes ago. Perhaps he is the highwayman."

"Don't think that's likely, my lady," Charles piped up. "Think we would have recognized Jase, even if we have had a sip or two."

"Or twelve," Jane was certain she heard Mr. Thorndike say under his breath.

"And, madam, the fact of the matter is, Mr. Worth has not been able to verify his whereabouts for *any* of the attacks," Sir Wilton reasoned. "At least, he has not done so to me."

"Madam, if I may," Mr. Hale calmly interjected, and not a moment too soon, because Jane felt her color rising to unparalleled heights, "perhaps it would be best to go and see this Mr. Worth."

All eyes turned to Mr. Hale. "As that one said"—he indicated Charles—"we would have recognized your brother. Perhaps we can identify this Mr. Worth as our attacker." Then carefully, to Jane, "or, rule him out."

Jane eyed Sir Wilton, to see how he took this proposal. It seemed to temper his rapid desire to crucify Mr. Worth, because he remembered proper protocols, grumbling, "Well, yes, of course. You would have to make an identification, Mr. Hale."

"That's all well and good," Nevill argued, "but I would prefer a rest before I make any identifications."

"Yes, I ain't going to go now!" Charles whined. "It's so late, and we just got here . . . and oh, look, tea's arrived," he gestured to the maids who were laying out trays of cold meats and pastries along with pots of steaming tea.

"Well, I ain't going to let the man make a run for it!" Sir Wilton growled. Jane was about to open her mouth, but for once, it was Jason who acted as the voice of reason.

"Come, sir. The man's never made a run for it before. Why should he start now?" Jason argued. The reasonableness in his voice was followed up by a clap on the shoulder. "It is terribly late, and my guests have just arrived. Surely they would like to wash. And you and your men would like a glass of wine—"

"While you take down a report," Jane added quickly. "After all, you must take official reports of the robberies, don't you?"

And thus, any idea of traipsing out into the hot summer night was ruled out, as Sir Wilton, Mr. Cutler, the farmers, Big Jim, the stewards, Charles, and Nevill all tucked into an evening repast.

Jason eyed his sister speculatively as they sat down together.

"What?" she asked, catching his gaze.

"Nothing," he replied. "I was simply unaware of your interest in the law."

"I'm interested in seeing it executed fairly—and even you have to admit that Reston is in a lather to capture the highwayman."

"Understandably, considering the havoc he's wreaked."

"All the more reason for its proper employment," Jane countered in her sweetest tones, "and *not* going off and arresting men without cause." She paused for a moment and considered her brother. "I'm sure Dr. Berridge would agree with me."

It was unfair, really, for her to mention the doctor. But she knew her brother suspected that she had formed an attachment to him—and if he became suspicious for a moment that her true interest was Byrne Worth, well . . .

It would be giving up her secret. The one fragile thing that made the days go by. Even in light of her recent cowardice, her oddly changeable and deepening feelings, she couldn't let Jason know. Not now. Not yet.

"Perhaps I should send him a missive," she continued. "After all, it would be worthwhile to have his medical opinion available tomorrow, especially considering the state of Mr. Worth's injury."

But even with Jane's goading, all Jason did was shrug and say, "Likely a good idea," and head into the drawing room.

"Jason!" she cried, forcing him to turn around before he reached the door. "I was unaware of *your* interest in seeing the law executed fairly."

Jason was thoughtful for a moment, considering his answer. "I may not like the man personally, but I saw what Mr. Worth did for Joshua Wilton, too. Sir Wilton is just under pressure from Ambleside and larger towns to take care of this 'problem,' I imagine. He'll come round."

Jane regarded her brother—her reckless, feckless brother—with something akin to admiration.

"What?" he asked, growing sheepish.

"Nothing," she replied with a smile. Although she did have one last question: "You would defend the man . . . even as it's your friends who were robbed?"

At that, Jason smiled—his reckless, feckless smile. "Are you joking? Charles and Nevill will dine out on this story for a month. It'll be the best thing that happens to them this trip, I'll wager."

Fifteen

THE next morning, a coterie of gentlemen and Lady Jane descended upon Byrne Worth's small house that edged Merrymere.

Needless to say, he was surprised.

He counted no fewer than ten men—recognizing the Marquis of Vessey, Sir Wilton, Dr. Berridge, Mr. Cutler the town solicitor, a few men he guessed were tenant farmers, and the brute force of the local blacksmith. The four men he didn't recognize were divided easily into two camps: the sober and neat, and the rumpled and hungover.

Well, this should be interesting.

"Gentlemen," he called out in greeting from the wrought-iron chair and table he had placed on his front porch. "I'm afraid I would have made more tea had I known to expect you."

He was not dressed for receiving guests. He had recently concluded his morning swim—the first he'd partaken in since his confinement. His breeches were plastered to his thighs, he had on no shoes or shirt—just a towel wrapped around his shoulders. His hair was dripping down in points, wet from the lake, but he ran a quick hand through it. "My lady," he acknowledged, leveraging himself up from his seat and putting his weight on the table as he bowed to Jane.

She curtsied back politely, murmuring, "Please sit, Mr. Worth."

If she or any of the gentlemen were averse to her seeing him in his current state of undress, they did not mention it. They were intent upon a mission, it seemed. Her eyes never left his face as he thankfully took his seat, but he could tell she was wary, watchful. He watched her out of the corner of his eye as he addressed the crowd of gentlemen.

"My lord, Sir Wilton, Doctor," he acknowledged in quick succession. "How can I help you?"

"Oh, don't bother, Jase," one of the hungover bucks said. "I don't recognize him."

"It seems there was another highwayman attack last night, Mr. Worth," Jason explained. "My friends were the victims."

Byrne felt his jaw tighten. "I see," he growled. "And you are here to accuse me?"

"No!" Jane cried, before she went silent again, a blush covering her freckles.

"What Lady Jane means to say is," Jason continued, "Sir Wilton has taken statements from my friends and now asks that they see if you can be identified or effectively ruled out. Correct, Sir Wilton?"

"Humph," was the ambiguous response. "Where were you last evening, Worth?"

"Here," he replied slowly and clearly.

"None with you?"

"My man rode to Manchester the day before last; he should be back sometime today."

"Then you have no alibi."

Byrne felt his temper flare. He tamped it down. "But you have my word."

Sir Wilton indicated the four gentlemen to his left. "Would you be so kind as to let these men look at you?"

Byrne narrowed his vision to look over the four unknown gentlemen who stood in a line, looking him up and down, except the last one, who had already spoken and seemed to be dozing on his feet.

"I'm sorry," the thinner of the sober gentlemen said after a moment, "I cannot tell."

"There, you see?" Jane said quickly. "He's not your man; let him enjoy his tea in peace."

"Hold on a moment, my lady," Sir Wilton countered. "Mr. Hale, you said you could not tell. Explain, please."

"Well, just that, sir. I cannot tell if he is the man who robbed us, or isn't. 'Twas very dark, you see, and the man had his face covered, and commanded we keep our gazes down." He looked to his friend for confirmation. "Mr. Thorndike?"

"Quite," the mustachioed Mr. Thorndike replied. "I had thought I would be able to recognize a voice, but . . . I'm sorry."

"Can we go now?" the nondozing gentleman whined. "It's bloody hot, and I've had far less sleep than I require."

"Excellent suggestion, Charles," Jane said smoothly. "Mr. Worth, if you would excuse us . . ."

"No need, my lady. Thank you for acknowledging my presence and not acting as if I were invisible." His eyebrow went up as he looked over the gentlemen of the party, the one controlled movement he allowed to express his anger. But at least one man did not heed the warning of that black wing.

"Hold a moment," Mr. Cutler said, his voice concerned and paternal. "Mr. Worth, I thought your leg too strained for activity."

Byrne was not used to people knowing his whole history, medical or otherwise, so even though he could trace the source of the information back to the ladies of Reston, it still made him edgy.

"It has been," he replied, his voice a paced warning. "But *I* am too strained to be still a moment longer, and so, resumed my swimming," he answered, his voice as cold as ice. And really, on such a day as this, where the sun threatened to bake them into the earth by noon, one would think these gentlemen would have noticed.

But they didn't.

"Aha!" Sir Wilton cried, following his friend's logic. "If you are well enough to swim, then you are well enough to be seated on a horse last evening."

Byrne would have rolled his eyes if he weren't so intent at staring daggers at the foolish man. And Sir Wilton was inclined to throw caution to the wind and stare right back.

"On the contrary," Dr. Berridge spoke up, dissolving any tension. "I suspect that had Mr. Worth ridden a horse last evening, he would not have felt well enough to swim this morning."

Byrne saw Sir Wilton shift his glare to Dr. Berridge. A crack or two showing in the friendship, Byrne thought with a wicked satisfaction. Hopefully this little betrayal wouldn't ruin the doctor's chances with Miss Victoria, but Byrne still had to be a little grateful for this smattering of common sense.

"Thank you for your time, Mr. Worth," Jason began saying, tugging at Sir Wilton's arm, as the crowd tried its best to disperse.

"All right, Mr. Worth, it seems that the only way to resolve this situation," Sir Wilton said, pulling his arm free of Jason's hand, "is for you to allow a search of your property."

"What?" Jane cried, followed by an "I say!" from the doctor and a surprising, "Yes, let's!" from one of the tenant farmers. Apparently, there had been far too many dramatics without any shattering of china and rummaging for his taste.

"Not on your life," Byrne replied easily, calmly. Too calmly. His hand shook as he rolled his cane between his palms to calm himself.

"You, Sir Wilton, have been in my house just this past week. As have you, Mr. Cutler," Byrne pointed out, to Wilton's consternation.

"Yes, but we weren't *looking* for anything," Sir Wilton argued, but Byrne still shook his head, so he turned to his friend.

"Mr. Cutler, surely you can think of some way . . ."

The solicitor looked bewildered for a moment. Then . . . "My lord," Mr. Cutler turned to Jason, "as he's a tenant of yours, you may give permission."

"Actually, I cannot," Jason replied. "First of all, if he was a tenant, he would be my father's, not mine. And secondly, the house belongs to him; it was willed to him. Its contents are his and his alone." Then, to an astonished Jane, he added, "I looked it up."

"Then let me in, damn you!" Sir Wilton cried to Byrne, coming just short of stepping onto the porch and barreling through.

"Ah ah ah," Byrne wagged a finger at Sir Wilton, "if you step on my porch, you are guilty of trespassing."

"Please," he said, the word coming out of his mouth in a long, slow hiss.

"Why on earth would I ever allow such an invasion?"

"Because I don't want to accuse you anymore!" Sir Wilton cried, sending more than Byrne's eyebrows up with shock. Indeed, Cutler looked as if he had swallowed a rather large insect. "I don't want to have to be the man who arrests the man who saved my son!" He paced back and forth in a regular lather. "What I want is to go to my wife, and the town hall, and the magistrate of Windermere and say that I have concluded beyond a shadow of a doubt that Mr. Worth is not the highwayman. But I cannot do that if you bar me from this house!"

He broke off, breathing hard, all his spleen vented. The reasoned argument struck at the core of the assembled group, Dr. Berridge and Jason looking at the red-faced Wilton with consideration. Even Jane . . .

"Er, Mr. Worth, maybe it would be prudent to allow . . ." Jason began, coughed, and then began again, "That is . . . if you have nothing to hide."

Byrne set his jaw, took a moment. He could let them in. They would probably glance about, check his trunks, his writing table, and then tip their hats and leave. They were very unlikely to find anything. He saw Jane's deep brown eyes, wide and beseeching, intrigued by the idea. He could do it. He could put this whole highwayman thing behind him, be accepted by the town, be left in peace. Unless . . .

Unless one of them thought to look beneath the floorboards.

"I have nothing to hide," he said finally, looking up from his feet, "and if I did, I would not have allowed your wife, Sir Wilton, or the rest of the ladies in town, or the gentlemen, for that matter, to *traipse* through for the past week."

"But a search—" Sir Wilton began, only to be cut off by Byrne's vehemence.

"But nothing, sir! I have been more than accommodating for the past week to the whims of this town, lying down like the most wretched *dog* to win their favor. And I tire of it!" He stood, raising his cane in front of him like a sword, a weapon. "I will not have you or anyone else entering my house! I am done with you all! Begone!"

No one said anything for several moments. Byrne held his gaze steady, his breath forceful but even.

"You will not allow us in?" Sir Wilton asked cautiously.

Byrne pounded his cane on the wooden porch, a terrible and startling bang, cutting off Sir Wilton or any other entreaty.

Wilton's shoulders slumped as he shook his head. "Then you leave me no choice but to still consider you suspect."

So be it, Byrne thought, damned once again to his unhappy station. The crowd seemed no more pleased with the outcome. Jason, Dr. Berridge, Mr. Hale, and Mr. Thorndike all looked aggrieved.

"Are we done, then?" one of the pale and tired young fools asked. "Good, let's go. Jase, you owe us one hell of a game of cards for this."

With the quiet murmur of, "Sorry to intrude on your morning," from one of the gentlemen, the party turned and began to walk up the path by the lakeshore, back to the Cottage, and away from his offensive self. Only Jane lingered for the briefest moment, the disappointment and pity apparent on her face.

Pity. Now she definitely pitied him.

The group disappeared into the trees. And suddenly he was alone.

You fool.

That lingering voice in his head drifted back, washing over him like waves on the shore, stripping back layers of sand. Suddenly the day was too bright, he could not abide the pure life of the sun. He hobbled indoors.

You fool, it repeated, over and over and over. *Go on, then. If Jane pities you, there is no one left to care. Dobbs is in Manchester, your brothers all the way in London. Who's to care if you pull up the floorboards? Who's to care if you allow yourself oblivion? After all, you destroyed all your goodwill in town; why not destroy everything else you've worked so hard to build?*

It began to taunt him, that voice, echoing in his hollow chest.

Do it.

He caught sight of himself in the mirror.

Do it!

He was bereft, stripped bare.

DO IT!

"No!" he yelled to the empty room, banging his cane into the cluttered side table, oversetting no small number of enamel flowered candlesticks. The stupid things shook on delicate wires, bouncing from being jostled—and as he watched those enamel flowers wobble, he began to laugh.

Laughter. First at the assembly, now at porcelain flowers. He had earned back the ability to laugh at his situation. Jane had given that to him. He would never jeopardize it again.

You find this funny? You're in quite the scrape.

"I know," he answered to no one in particular. "And I have no idea how to fix it."

His eyes fell to the packet of papers on his writing desk. The copied pages from the magistrate ledger. He'd read them over twice now, but . . .

Why not start there?

Seemed like enough of an idea. And so Byrne sat down and began to read, again, scouring the pages for what he might have missed.

For what might save him.

It was hours of pure hell before Jane was able to again leave the Cottage. Charles and Nevill were actually the easiest to accommodate, as they simply wanted their beds. Mr. Hale and Mr. Thorndike, having endured the torment of the last few days, were very eager to begin working with Jason, which was the purpose of their traveling so far. But Jason did not plan on accommodating them. Luckily, the Duke was up and about by now and having a good morning, so much so that he monopolized the stewards over a pot of tea in the drawing room, and Jane felt it necessary to help Nancy keep an eye for signs of strain.

Big Jim the blacksmith was due back at his smithy, and the farmers had already taken a morning away from their work, and so they took their leave quickly, but Sir Wilton was of a mind to rant and pace. And he decided the best place to do so was in the library of the Cottage—and incidentally wear a hole in Jane's mother's previously impeccable carpet. Jason, Mr. Cutler, and Dr. Berridge were on hand to calm him. But occasionally, Jane could hear an expletive float across the hall.

"Good heavens, my dear," the Duke asked, after one particularly colorful word rang clear as day from the library, "whatever is going on?"

Jane shot a glance at the stewards. Mr. Hale, being the head of the castle estate, and Mr. Thorndike, being in charge of the London property, both were acquainted with the Duke's deterioration. They wisely held their tongues, as Jane smoothly lied. "Dr. Berridge is in the other room, Father," she said—and at least that part was true. "I believe he is pulling a tooth for one of the footmen."

It was past noon before Dr. Berridge departed, with the much calmer Sir Wilton and Mr. Cutler in tow. Luncheon was then served, the Duke was taken upstairs for his afternoon rest, and the stewards were finally able to lock a nervous but determined Jason in the library with a half dozen ledgers and piles of official ducal correspondence.

The house was silent. All the members occupied.

If Jane didn't run now, she would no doubt be assaulted with demands from the kitchen to accommodate the new guests, or a crisis with the linens, or—she suppressed a shudder—more callers.

She was out the door and on the path to Byrne's house within three seconds.

When she got there, she had gone from relief to annoyance. How could he have acted such a bear that morning? He was reconfirming his status as hermit at the very least, and at the very most, he would be lucky to escape tar and feather from the villagers, who Jane wagered would hear of his recalcitrance inside the hour. Why would he be so cruel? Why wouldn't he, after Sir Wilton's impassioned plea, let them into the house?

What was he hiding?

As she emerged out the other end of the path, her annoyance had turned into curiosity.

And when she climbed onto the porch and knocked on the front door, she was practically rabid.

"What?" he called out, and she threw open the door—terribly dramatic of her, she thought—and took one good solid look at Byrne.

He was sitting at his writing desk, poring over some pages, his eyes never looking up, his hands rolling that cane back and forth as was his habit.

She knew he was aware of her, standing in the doorway. She could feel him listening, waiting for her to make a move. And in that instant, she knew he was hiding something.

"Am I barred from the house, too?" she asked, transforming her voice into a wry, airy confection. "I didn't know, you see, if you had decided that *no* one shall ever enter this house again."

He looked up and smiled—smiled!—at her. "You are always welcome—even though you took little advantage of that fact in the past week. Would you perhaps care for a cup of tea? I'm working my way through the green varieties."

She ignored his jibe and his offer of refreshment. His unnerving, disconcerting smile was a bit harder to ignore, but she suppressed the tiny flutter it caused. She was here for a reason, after all.

"You of course realize you have just destroyed any goodwill you've earned in the past week."

"I am aware," he replied, his eyebrow going up. His gaze followed her as she crossed the room and took a seat on the sofa.

"Sir Wilton has likely already told his wife, and she has likely already told everyone in Reston."

"I am aware, Jane," he repeated, bemusement apparent in his voice.

"And I frankly am shocked that you managed to avoid arrest, if only for being a complete brute!"

"As am I."

She turned to him then. "The only question then," she said, her voice dripping with innocence, "is why?"

"Why what?" he asked, far too calmly for his own good.

"Why you would not allow a search," she replied, veritably lounging on the seat. "Sir Wilton, I thought, made his case very passionately and practically. Why would you not allow him inside?" She leaned in then, letting her voice drop low, seductive. "What are you hiding, Mr. Worth?"

For the first time since she entered, his smile faltered, his jaw became set. "What if I believed deeply in the right to privacy?"

"I find it hard to believe from someone who made his name invading privacy as a spy during the war," she countered easily. "What are you hiding, Byrne?"

He held silent for a moment, his hand stilled on his desk. Then he glanced at the papers.

"Perhaps I was protecting Miss Victoria," he replied.

"Victoria?"

"And by extension, you," he smiled again, relief apparent in his demeanor, as he held up the papers. "The pages she copied. Sir Wilton would not take well to discovering these in this house."

But Jane just shook her head. "They would be looking for stolen property, not papers. I will ask one last time, and then I will leave for good. *What are you hiding?*"

He held her gaze then, regarded her for what felt like a full minute. At first she thought he was trying to stare her down, make her submit to his will. But then she realized he was deciding what to say.

He chose to say nothing. Instead, he stood abruptly and hobbled to the stairs in the small house. One look over his shoulder told her to follow.

He maneuvered the stairs with practiced ease, pivoted at the top. Jane had never been upstairs in widow Lowe's house—and rampant curiosity had her following and finding a small loft, its ceiling low and sloped, the walls unfinished. There was a chair by a small, square window, which was thrown open to abate the stuffiness of the space. In the farthest corner, a wrought-iron bed, unmade—its feather mattress still indented from Byrne's body. A dozen books lay scattered by the bed, under the bed, on the bed. Jane would not be surprised if upon inspection, she found dirty china hidden in the mess.

While Jane silently criticized the lackadaisical life of a bachelor, Byrne went to stand by the wall, where the chimney lay against the house. He took his cane and poked the end through a knothole in a floorboard. A twist and the proper amount of leverage, and the floorboard came up.

Jane approached the space in the floor, her curiosity stronger than her trepidation. Peering down, she saw a black leather satchel.

"Open it," he said calmly.

She reached down and pulled the satchel out. It was stiff, heavy. She could feel the fragility of its contents. She placed it on the floor, knelt in front of it as she unlatched the metal closure, and looked inside.

In velvet-lined compartments sat a dozen empty bottles, except one. She lifted it out. It was half-filled with a yellowish liquid.

"Laudanum," she read the small inscription in the silver cap.

He lifted a brow. "Read the side of the case."

Jane rotated the case. On the side, written in faded gold lettering, was *Dr. F. J. Lawford.*

Her eyes flew to Byrne's face. "Where did you get this?" she asked.

A wry smile twisted his lips.

"I stole it."

Sixteen

"You stole it?"

The case sat between them on the floor. Jane stood, paced, shifted her weight from side to side with nervous incomprehension. Byrne, however, leaned casually against the bricks of the chimney, let his weight settle.

"Why?" Jane asked, her eyes wide.

Byrne reached over, picked the half-filled bottle out of her hands. He turned it over in his hand, momentarily mesmerized by the way the afternoon light caught in the liquid, sunbeams and gold all at once.

"I'm sure by now you've realized the . . . hold this substance has over me," he said quietly as he replaced the bottle in its compartment.

Jane stilled in her agitation, her eyes still on the bag on the floor, as she nodded solemnly.

"But it's Dr. Lawford's bag. How did it get here?" she asked softly. And so he told her.

It had been winter. And winters, as Byrne had come to learn, were not kind in the Lake District. Cold and wet, more effort was expended

keeping the firewood dry than actually collecting it. The lakes and
rivers took on ice, the little fells became capped with snow as early
as October, and the whole of the north blanketed by All Saint's Day.

His superiors at the Home Office were told he had decamped to
Merrymere to rest, to recover. But really, his brothers had forced him to
leave London and all the temptations there that indulged his weakness.
Actually, his elder brother, Graham, had desired him to go to their family's small estate in Kent, but Byrne couldn't take the good intentions of
his sister-in-law, Mariah. He didn't want to subject her to him. He
would be alone. He would conquer his demons, his pain, alone.

It hadn't worked.

By that winter he was practically a ghost. Rabid, wild, and lost, the
pain in his leg never abated, the hollowness of his life all-consuming.
He didn't sleep because his dreams never let him be—he was either
forced to relive seeing his brother lanced through the side by a bayonet, and being powerless to stop it—hell, having been cocky enough
to think nothing like that would ever happen as long as he was with
him—or he was struggling to walk to safety on a beach in France,
blood leaking from a bullet hole in his thigh. Or the time he had seen
a young boy, a dispatcher, having his throat slit in an alley. Or the day
he had found himself in an open field, and shots rang out from the
trees beyond . . .

He wanted so badly to just forget. For a little while.

It was just past New Year's. The little town of Reston still had
garlands over the doorframes, the high street littered with footsteps
in the snow, tamped down by the villagers having traveled to and fro
for the season's festivities. Byrne had been in the village because
Dobbs—ever-present and loyal—had gone to his sister's in Manchester for the holidays, leaving Byrne the unfortunate task of doing
his own shopping and forcing the gruff and recalcitrant man to actually interact with the villagers.

As previously stated, that hadn't gone well, either.

In the winter, night came by early afternoon, and people retired
early, so when Byrne made his way up the street that fateful evening,
it was pitch-black and deserted.

He'd gone into the village for a cord of wood, bought begrudgingly from Mr. Morgan for the price of one stone fish figurine. Byrne had been attempting to hold to his principles then, and not use any of the obscene amounts of money he earned during the war . . . although it is amazing what living through a cold northern winter will do to one's principles. Now he had no such qualms.

The purchase was necessary as Byrne no longer had the strength to split wood by himself—God, he hated being so helpless. He loaded the cord of wood on a sled, and pulled it back toward his horse and cart, left at the blacksmith's for a new shoe. He would have to trade a porcelain figurine for that service. It would have been smarter, more cautious, he supposed in hindsight, to wait for his horse to be reshod and then go fetch his wood. But frustration belies logic, and Byrne just wanted to go home. So, on the high street, sled of wood in tow, Byrne passed Dr. Lawford's residence.

And he stopped. And stared.

It was dark. Even the upper level, where the doctor had his apartments, was blackened. The other shops on the street were closed and shuttered, true, but there were lights in the upper stories, meaning the shopkeepers were at home, likely enjoying a good dinner.

Also meaning that it was far more difficult for them to see out their windows into the darkness and spy him there.

Perhaps the doctor had retired early. Perhaps he had to ride out for a house call. The snow on the street was so packed and muddied, Byrne was unable to distinguish new footprints, if there were any.

His hand was on the doorknob before he realized he had made the decision to enter. It wasn't locked. Who in Reston would feel the need to lock their front door? It stuck a bit, so he had to shoulder his way in, but luckily, the noise went unnoticed.

Did Dr. Lawford have a housekeeper? Byrne didn't know, but the possibility was there. So, using skills long thought dormant, he slunk in the shadows, silent as a breath on the wind. He found the doctor's office easily, and his surgeon's room. He scoured, searched the shelves of all their various bottles and creams. He became more and more desperate, discarding vials to the floor, shuttling papers aside, rummaging drawers. He was a qualified physician, he had to have something, anything Byrne could use to abate the pain in his leg, to let him sleep . . .

Then he found it. The satchel. Held away from the other potions, kept in a drawer in the doctor's desk. He opened it up and saw bottle after bottle of that sweet nectar, and nearly began to cry. He would have drunk from a bottle then and there, if he did not have the one stray thought, that instinctual knowledge that if he did so, he would be found on the floor, whether in minutes or in the morning, and that would be the end of it all. And he had just gotten his hands on what he craved. What he needed.

Byrne gave up on subterfuge then, hobbling to his feet and running as best as he could back to the sled of wood, back to his horse, back to his cottage, and back to his oblivion.

"I didn't even close Dr. Lawford's door," Byrne finished, aware that Jane did not blink or speak, merely watched him as he told his story. "What I took . . . was likely meant to meet the needs of the entire county for a full year." His voice became a bit too raw for his liking, as he said, "I went through it in a matter of months."

"Not all of it," Jane replied softly, her eyes falling to the one half-filled bottle.

"No, not all of it," Byrne conceded. "I want you to know—" He swallowed, then began again. "I want you to know that I haven't used a drop in the months since I came back from London. Not a single drop."

She nodded mutely, then her eyes fell to the bag. "What happened after you took this?"

He shrugged. "I don't remember going back up that street, or how I got home . . . and I don't remember breaking Mrs. Hill's window or Mr. Davies's front door, but I must have, because by the next morning, they were broken, and the town was forming a . . . a *posse* to find the culprit. I didn't know any of this then, of course." His eyes flitted to the bottles in their case. Nay, he didn't remember any of it. He had been in oblivion.

"How did you, er, escape scrutiny?" she asked, and at that, Byrne had to laugh.

"Pure dumb luck," he replied, as his guffaw fell into silence. "The very next evening, the highwayman first attacked. The crimes of the high street were either forgotten or lumped in with the attacks of the weeks to come. By the time they began to suspect me, no one asked me my whereabouts the night of the robberies on Reston High Street."

"More fool them," Jane quipped softly.

"Not Dr. Lawford," Byrne disagreed. "Mere weeks later, Dr. Berridge had come to join his practice, invited obviously to make it so the doctor's offices are never empty."

Jane's gaze remained on the dusty, worn bag, the one bottle that remained half-full. He could not help but look at it, too. The source of all his shame, hidden beneath the floorboards.

"The town is right to suspect me, Jane," he intoned quietly. "They are right to hate me. I did them harm."

"But not the whole of what they accuse you!" she cried.

"I did plenty!" Byrne growled, thrusting himself off the bricks of the chimney and coming forward. "I did enough to earn their hatred, so let them have their hate of me!" He took another step forward, forcing Jane to take a step back, stalking past her to the little chair, where the little window afforded the only air in the room. And after telling his story, he needed the air. "And now that you know it, I'm certain I've done enough to secure your pity, so perhaps it's best if you let me be."

He stood with his back to her, but he was certain that he heard her moving for the stairs, her soft slippers on the floorboards . . . but when she spoke, her voice came from right behind him.

"You think I pity you?" she asked, disbelief dripping from every word. He turned, saw the fire in her eyes, the heat spreading across her cheeks in a flush. "You think I walk over here, that I went round the assembly with you, that I took the trouble to find out about the highwayman—that I spent all this time with you . . . out of *pity*?"

"You must pity me, Jane, because I don't understand the otherwise," he argued. "I don't understand how you can defend me to your

brother and Sir Wilton but can't summon the courage to come and
see me any other time this week. Was I so grotesque, lying ill in your
library?"

"No!" she cried, her eyes flying to his face.

"Then why do you not avail yourself of the way out? I've given
you permission to end your little rehabilitation project and consider
me a lost cause! Hell, I've given you ample reason today."

"You are not a lost cause! And you're not a . . . a *project* to me!"

"Then what am I, Jane? If I'm not a lost cause or a project, you
don't pity me, and won't hate me, then what else is there?"

He held her gaze then, saw the rise and fall of her chest as her
breath came hard and heavy. He felt every nerve in his body come
alive, every sensation pool at the base of his spine, as he repeated . . .

"What else is there?"

He saw it then, in her eyes. The awareness of what he was asking.
The answer.

"Jane," he said again, *"what else is there?"*

The moment fell between them. And then . . .

And then nothing was between them.

It was impossible to tell who kissed whom first. They fell together,
grappling with each other. Byrne's cane clattered to the floor as he
grasped her by her shoulders, his fingers burning through the thin
linen of her day dress. She pressed into him, her arms coming around
his waist, up his back, holding him as close as physically possible.

Oh, this was need. This was what had long been craved, and denied,
even if both parties were unaware of it. Byrne had been starved. For
over a week. Starved for this redheaded girl, starved for freckles, starved
for the feel of those plump lips fastened with his, every sense overwhelmed with her very essence. The feel of her skin, the honeysuckle
smell of her hair . . . It was a drug—but better, cleaner. Stronger. He
moved his hands to gently cup her chin, the base of her neck, angling
her head to allow his tongue entrance—and when he did so, felt her jolt
as if a spark of electricity had surged from him into her.

For her part, Jane felt as if every inch of herself, every pinpoint
where her body touched his, was not enough—it left the other parts

wanting; dreadfully, unhappily untouched. Her hands came up around his neck, fingers threaded through his thick hair—she had to get closer, had to burrow herself into him . . .

And Byrne was more than happy to oblige . . . but his leg was not. He lost his balance, and they stumbled back into the old faded chair. Jane was pulled into Byrne's lap, scattering the open book that rested on its arm, letting it thud to the floor. But Byrne didn't hear it. All he could hear were the little sounds out of Jane's throat—the small catches of breath, the tiniest squeak of wonder when he ripped his mouth away from hers to attend to the soft skin beneath her ear, the delicate, torturous line of her throat . . .

Lost to sensation, it took a moment to realize that Jane had stilled against him. That her arms had drawn back from his shoulders, that those sooty eyelashes had opened and destroyed the cocoon they had wrapped around themselves.

He brought his head up, sought her eyes. She was looking over the top of the chair, still with shock. He turned his head around, followed her gaze.

The bed. She was staring at his bed.

He turned back. This time her eyes caught and held his. And Byrne saw everything. The bewilderment, the fear. Oh, but that warm flush on her cheek was not bewildered or fearful.

"Jane," he said hoarsely, his voice a rumbled whisper. He lightly stroked his hand up and down her back, soothing, wanting to calm her fears, but it seemed to have the opposite effect.

Abruptly, as abruptly as they had come together, Jane sprang away to her feet. For a moment, the only sound in the room was Jane's stuttered, uneven breathing. Then . . .

"I have to go," she said, looking about her for something to anchor her thoughts to. "Thank you," she continued awkwardly, "er, for the, er . . . tea."

And then, one last wide-eyed look, like a bird startled by light, and she was gone. The only thing left of Lady Jane Cummings was the delicate footsteps as they echoed down the stairs. And that honeysuckle, cinnamon scent.

For a moment, Byrne couldn't move.

He was too amazed.

They hadn't even had tea, was all he could think. And then . . . then he started to laugh.

Lady Jane wanted him. *She* wanted *him*. There was no longer any dancing around the feelings they had, no longer would they hedge and skirt back to the edges of their acquaintance.

Because he wouldn't allow it.

Go ahead, he thought, a wicked smile coming across his face. *Go ahead and try to avoid me for a week again, Jane. I dare you.*

Because somehow, someway, the oddest sensation was filling his chest. It was warm and light, and . . . joyous. It was joy.

And he'd be damned if he'd let her fear and cowardice snatch it back again.

Seventeen

THAT night, Jane could not sleep.

She turned over again, kicking at the light sheets that had gotten tangled around her legs. She could blame the weather that seemed to have reached temperatures beyond earthbound—Jane wouldn't be surprised if Merrymere began to steam and boil if this continued. Indeed, the phenomenon was curious even to those beyond the district. Over supper, Mr. Hale had told them that they had met with a man from the scientific academy in London, who was traveling north with the hopes of studying the heat wave.

All well and good, but science could do nothing to rectify the situation at present. Because Jane could not sleep, and she could not blame the heat. Perhaps she could blame her brother, as was her habit and his use. After all, he had brought Charles and Nevill into the house at the most inopportune time. Charles and Nevill seemed to agree that it was inopportune, being relocated to the wilderness, and took advantage of every lull in conversation to complain about their situation.

"But there's nothing to do!" Charles whined.

"I say, Jase, you mean there are *no* women in this town for us?" Nevill asked, as Charles dug into his lamb.

"There are a number of very fine young ladies in Reston," Jane began but was interrupted by a laugh from Charles—affording her a delightful view of half-masticated lamb.

"We ain't talking of fine young ladies, Lady Jane—we're talking about—"

But luckily Charles himself was interrupted by Jason, who cleared his throat remarkably loudly.

"Jane," he said, his face a burnished red, "er, commend the cook for me, please; this lamb is very . . . er, fresh."

"Yes," Jane said, as she shot her brother a withering look, "it was likely just recently slaughtered." *Much like you soon will be.*

Jason, to his credit, looked slightly chagrined.

"Jase, while we're here," Nevill began, "what chance do you think we'll have to run into a poet or two?"

"Poets?" Jason asked, throwing a glance to his sister, who shrugged. "I don't believe Wordsworth or Coleridge are currently in residence."

"Damn! I wanted to give those fellows a piece of my mind. All those tedious hours spent committing their words to memory, just to impress European women—some of whom didn't understand a word we said in any case!" Nevill barked with laughter. "Honestly, did you read *The Excursion*? Never been so bored in my life."

And so it went. Nevill and Charles continued to insult the town and area that was playing host to them, Jason continued to turn red, and Jane continued to see red. Jane knew she came to the lake this summer with no charity in her heart for the district or the town or the Cottage . . . but it was *her* region, *her* town, *her* Cottage! It incensed her beyond reason.

Hale and Thorndike, thankfully, spent the evening acting with grace and charity, and Jane could rely on them for sensible conversation. But Charles and Nevill . . . And Jason sat between the two sets of men, his attention swayed back and forth between his obligations and his amusements. Unfortunately, amusement, by virtue of its volume and mirth, seemed to be winning. He was engaged by Charles and Nevill, laughing at their bad jokes and matching them glass for glass for glass throughout the meal.

They hadn't stopped yet. Jane could hear them from her room, the sounds of their laughter traveling through her open window, as they were in the south garden, trying to play some game that involved throwing horseshoes. The occasional clatter of metal striking metal and the laughter that followed was distracting, and Jane could have blamed her sleeplessness on that, certainly. If only she didn't have a history of being able to sleep through the loudest thunderstorms.

No, the blame for her sleeplessness lay with Jane, and Jane alone. Although that wasn't precisely true. It wasn't her *alone*.

Byrne. Oh, heavens, Byrne Worth. He had rifled through her thoughts and nestled there, the memories of his hand on her back and his lips on her ear . . . keeping her too bloody warm for sleep!

What had prompted her actions that afternoon? Why had she even felt so compelled to go over to his house? She could have, should have, left well enough alone—and not dug into his secrets.

But . . . but he had let her in anyway. And in turn, she completely lost control over herself. Nay, truth be told, she had completely lost control, full stop.

It was happening again. That feeling of being . . . *untouched* had welled within her, strong and deep. Just the memory of the afternoon . . . of being near him, and being near him made her so very aware of the space between them.

Jane was ill equipped to handle such a man as Byrne Worth. Normally with men, they would meet in a glittering London ballroom, and she would flirt and play the coquette, and she was always, always in control. But here, at the lake, with Byrne . . . she didn't play.

She didn't flirt.

She didn't even *wish* to flirt. She had let all pretense fall away, almost from the very beginning.

She just wanted to be near him, with him.

Touched.

That, of course, meant she would have to stay as far away from Byrne Worth as possible.

If only he would get out of her head and leave her in peace to sleep!

But still his low grumble of a voice, cynical and vulnerable, whispered over her skin: *What else is there?*

She knew—theoretically—there was so much more. And today, in that little attic, lost to sensation—that delicious, surprisingly powerful want that coursed through her body—she had been so very tempted to let herself discover the more.

And then she had seen the bed.

Oh! It was too bloody hot for thoughts like this!

Jane ruthlessly kicked back her covers, freed herself from the mattress, and found her feet. She stalked to the open windows, letting the slight breeze come to her.

It wasn't terribly soothing.

Instead, Jane sought comfort in the soft lapping sound of the lake against the shore, the tranquillity of rhythm. It was probably nice and cool in the water. She wouldn't have to go in very far, not being a strong swimmer, but maybe wading in would quiet her thoughts and calm her body enough to let her sleep . . .

Jane listened closely . . . she could no longer hear the raucous laughter of her brother and his friends. They must have given up on the pitch and gone back inside to cards and drink and food . . .

No one would see. No one would know. And maybe she could achieve some peace, Jane thought, as she turned away from the window, grabbed her wrapper, and silently moved to her door.

That night, Byrne Worth couldn't sleep. And for once, it was not the pain in his leg keeping him awake.

He sat out on his small porch, the same position he had taken that morning when the entourage from the Cottage had come to call. But this time, he was at peace. Even better, he was planning.

Planning how to break down Lady Jane's defenses, plotting how to seduce—*seduce!*—the daughter of a Duke.

A year ago—hell, three months ago—if someone were to tell him that he would be considering seducing a woman, let alone one of such esteem as Lady Jane, he would have laughed in their face. But here he was, and somehow, he was in it. For the first time in a very, very long time, Byrne wanted something. Something real, something warm. And his intention was to get it.

But this would take time and strategy. Of course, Byrne was very, very good at strategy.

He looked up at the stars, then back to the Cottage in the distance, a few rooms that still had candles blazing, and sound carrying over the water, telling him that some of the gentlemen were carousing till all hours. He had the advantage of proximity. The advantage that he knew she liked him. But he knew he had frightened her that afternoon.

And he had to rectify that.

Another disadvantage was her family. Her brother was not likely to be his champion. And his friends seemed no kinder. Byrne knew little about her father, but if he was anything like her brother . . .

It was little wonder she had done her best to not introduce him.

While Byrne pondered the positives and negatives that would allow him to burrow deep into Lady Jane's heart, he saw an interesting sight. Out the front doors of the Cottage, heading down toward the lake, was a female figure wrapped in white.

He sat up in his chair. His eyes were good, but it was still a distance away . . . If he hadn't already known that Jane was the only lady in residence at the Cottage, he would have still known it was her. The light from the front door momentarily caught the red braid that streamed down her back, as she snuck out the door.

Well, this was an interesting opportunity. He watched her tiptoe lightly across the dewy lawn and hesitate at the edge of the water. His eyebrows went up as she dropped her wrapper on the shore and edged her toes into the water.

A Very Interesting Opportunity. Byrne quickly did the math. It would take him approximately fifteen minutes to walk over there with the disadvantage of his cane, and by then, she would be gone. But that time was halved if he swam . . . and it would give him the element of surprise . . .

A smile spread across Byrne's face. He was never one to pass up an interesting opportunity.

As Jane slid her toes into the water, one thought and one thought alone overwhelmed her:

This lake was *cold*.

Arctic, frigid. The heat of the past few weeks had done nothing to mitigate its icy temperature. Maybe she should go inside. Maybe this idea to float away her frustrations was not quite sound. After all, there were eels . . .

But what had she to return to? Tousled sheets and a sleepless night? Might as well try something different. Something new. After all, Byrne swam in this ridiculously frozen lake every day.

The unrelenting thought of Byrne Worth brought a flush to her cheeks. But it didn't stay confined to her face, instead spreading down through her whole body in the oddest and most uncomfortable manner.

It must be quelled before it got entirely out of hand, she thought briefly, as she summoned all of her courage and ran into the water, submerging herself before she could change her mind.

Cold. Cold cold cold cold cold. But as she brought her head back above water, she began to relax. The shock of the initial impact was over, and her overheated skin began to enjoy the sensation of the hotter air breezing over her drenched self, her legs twining with the thin material of her nightdress as it danced about her under the surface.

She was standing in the water, about chest deep, feeling safe enough this far out. She glanced back at the Cottage. Candles still blazed in the dining and drawing rooms, and surely she was far enough away that no one would see her. So, quickly, she removed the ribbon at the end of her long braid and shook her hair out. Then, lazily, she leaned back, let her legs rise, and began to float.

Her hair spread out in a cloud beneath her head, listing with the rhythm of the water, choosing its own way. She moved her arms languidly, kicked occasionally, lifting her eyes to the stars. The night sky, so huge and overwhelming, made her feel tiny and insignificant. Which was a relief. She was so used to her actions being marked and scrutinized, to feel for once that she was unnoticed in the vastness of the world made her feel . . . free. To do anything.

Above the water, her nightdress clung to every hollow, every peak. The air cooled its fibers, causing the tips of her breasts to tighten and pucker with the sensation. Beneath the surface, the gown drifted and floated, pulling her down with its weight.

What if she went without it?

Suddenly Jane was overcome with the wicked idea. After all, who in the whole vast sky would notice? Or care?

She placed her feet on the mucky bottom of the lake floor, and glanced again at the Cottage. There was nothing to stop her. No one to scandalize. Oh, it had been so long since she had scandalized anyone. Well, proper adult Lady Jane was going to take a page from the Jane of her adolescence. And then, with a mischievous smile, one meant only for herself, she slipped beneath the surface and out of her gown.

She came up with the smile still on her face, raised her arms, free of the heavy, wet material. And then she heard it. A low, anguished, decidedly masculine groan. From behind her, in the lake.

"I wish you hadn't done that," Byrne growled, only his head and shoulders above the surface, a silent predator in the water, his eyes as black as the sky above them.

Jane found her scream silenced when he grabbed her shoulders and covered her mouth with a kiss.

Well, it was either kiss her or shove her underwater, and Byrne doubted she would take kindly to the latter.

But, damn, if he drowned now, he would drown happy. It was the most difficult thing of his life to keep his hands above her shoulders, above the level of the water. Because his fevered imagination knew what awaited underneath. If he just let his fingers drift down, he would graze the tips of perfection, then let his hands fall to her waist, her ass, pulling her full naked self up against him, and . . .

Thank God he'd decided it prudent to leave his trousers on.

Instead of torturing himself thinking of the parts that weren't touching, Byrne concentrated on the parts that were. His hand resting gently against the cool, clean skin of her neck, the other lost in the thick morass of her wet hair. And her lips. She'd been shocked at first, of course, frightened and then forced to swallow a scream. But he could tell the moment she realized who it was that was kissing her. She didn't relax, no. Nor did she fight him. Instead, her lips took on a kind of fire, a gasping nervous awareness that shot from her body through his, making him harder than stone, even in the ridiculously cold waters of Merrymere.

She inched back, barely, opened her mouth to catch her breath. And Byrne, former soldier that he was, took advantage of her tactical mistake, slipping his tongue inside her mouth. And dancing.

He didn't know how she'd react. He didn't care. For once, he was not thinking five steps ahead in their dance, trying to decipher her next move. But what he did not expect was to have her press that luscious, slick, very naked body against his own.

The minute her chest pressed against his, Byrne was certain this was hell. Oh, he had stood among the bleak ruins of a battlefield, sat stupefied in dens of iniquity, even fought his enemy while everything around him burned, but never had he been so tortured than by this girl and the feel of her skin against his.

But it was when her soft body fell against a certain . . . rigidity about him, that her eyes flew open. She remembered herself. And she pulled away.

Away as in fifteen feet away. She ducked underwater and did not surface until she was so far out of arm's reach, Byrne had to chuckle. Just a little.

"Jane," he drawled, but he was cut off with a vehement shushing.

"My brother and his friends are still awake," she stage-whispered, gesticulating toward the Cottage, where indeed, if he listened closely, Byrne could hear the echoes of male laughter and clinking glasses.

"Well, I think you'll have to come closer if you want to whisper." Byrne grinned, but Jane, only her nose and eyes visible above the water, shook her head, adamant. Byrne felt his face fall; he glided in the water, slowly closing the gap between them. "I did not intend to scare you. I won't hurt you."

"It is not that," she replied, her voice a quaver of nervousness as she backed away as he advanced. "It's . . . it's just, I think I felt an eel."

He threw back his head in laughter then. Goodness, this laughing was becoming a chronic condition.

"Shhh!" Jane said, throwing a look up to the house before pushing a splash of water toward him. It fell several feet short.

"That wasn't an eel, Jane." He grinned at her, enjoyed watching her wary, doelike gaze peer out from just above the surface of the water. Who'd have thought Lady Jane Cummings would be such a shy thing? "Your body responded to me," he explained matter-of-factly, "and mine responded to you."

"I'm aware of the mechanics of attraction, thank you," she snapped, obviously hoping to cut him off before he went further.

"So you admit it, then?" his face split into a wide, predatory smile.

"Admit what?"

"That you're attracted to me." He knew triumph when she splashed him again. He slid silkily through the water, like a crocodile on the Nile, advancing on the unsuspecting. "It's completely natural; you shouldn't be ashamed," he continued blithely.

"Yes, well, regardless," she muttered, her skin turning pink in the moonlight, as she stepped backward, "you stay over there . . . and I'll stay over here."

"Why?" he asked.

"Because I'm naked!" she hissed and then ducked underwater,

only her eyes above the water level, darting back to the Cottage when one of the lights was put out in the room on the ground floor, followed by raucous male laughter.

She turned back to him. "Why are you here?"

He answered soberly, "I saw you going into the water. And I didn't know if you would have the courage to call on me again, or if I would be barred from your house if I came to call on you, and I wanted to talk to you." Then he sighed, frustrated. "But I can't talk to you while you're all the way over there, and I'm all the way over here."

"I believe we've covered the reasons I'm not coming any closer to you," Jane answered pertly.

"This is ridiculous," he replied, exasperated. "I feel like I'm yelling down the length of a dining table for you to pass the salt." He glanced around, his eyes falling on a pool of white cloth floating like foam about twenty feet away. He swam for it, Jane's eyes burning into his back as he did so. He picked up the nightdress, the finest of linens made heavy by water, and swam back. When he got close enough to do so, he tossed it to Jane, the dress landing near her shoulder with a hearty splat.

It wouldn't do any good. The linen was so thin, and being wet made it practically transparent. But if she felt safer with it on, if she felt as if that barest of materials was going to protect her like armor and allow Byrne to get within whispering distance, who was he to mention its uselessness?

He watched as Jane slipped the gown over her head, the skin of her shoulders luminous with the faint glow of the still-lit candles from the house and the stronger light of the nearly full moon. When she turned around, she had struggled the material on and stood in the shoulder-deep water, as prim and demure as a nun in church.

Byrne slowly advanced. She didn't retreat. When he got about four feet from her, just out of arm's reach, she held up her hand.

"That's close enough," she whispered.

"Indeed," he replied. Not only was he now close enough to hear her at the pitch she wished to speak, but if he got any closer right now, he'd be too intoxicated by her to say what he came here to say.

But before he could summon his speech, Jane spoke first.

"Why do you think you'd be barred from my house?"

He blinked twice and then shrugged. "Your brother dislikes me. You might balk at entertaining the notorious highwayman in your drawing room."

"That's ridiculous," she replied, as she began to tread water. He circled her, and she circled with him. Dancing with him in the water.

"As ridiculous as it might seem . . . there are any number of a hundred things that made me think I would not be welcome in your home."

Jane stuttered a moment, then whispered back, "You are welcome in my home, Byrne . . ."

He watched her closely. "But . . ."

"But . . ." she conceded, "we have a half dozen guests, half of which I didn't know about, and people calling all the time, and ever since my mother died, my father has been . . . particular."

Byrne thought for a moment that she might go on about her father, how he would disapprove of an untitled gentleman such as himself for his daughter, but she simply shrugged and whispered, more to herself than to him, "Maybe I don't like being in my home."

He nodded solemnly and fought the urge to frame her face in his hands and pull her to him, give her comfort. Instead he held back, far too aware of what she was feeling.

"I couldn't stand to be around my family either," he replied quietly. At her curious look, he went on. "Right after the war ended. Right after a bullet went through my leg." She didn't jolt at his direct speech. Instead, she continued their circling, their dance, but moved infinitesimally closer to him.

"They loved me, petted me, tried to make me well again," he continued, then grimaced. "I couldn't stand it."

"Why?"

"Because I didn't fit anymore. My brothers, Marcus and Graham, they were so bloody normal, except for how worried they were about me. They kept wanting me to be the old version of myself."

"But you weren't," she finished for him.

"And therefore, home wasn't really home anymore."

"What did you do?" she whispered, her voice no more than breath on the water.

"I ran as soon as I was able. First, to places that for a few coins would let me forget. I let myself get lost. Then, when I ran out of money and energy, I came up here." He looked at her. "I don't recommend going to the first places I mentioned. And I know you feel trapped by your family and guests now . . . But if you ever need to run, you can run to me."

She nodded. Then, whether she was aware of it or not, her circling moved her closer to him again. Byrne could have reached out and touched her easily. But he didn't. Not yet.

"Why . . ." She swallowed, looking up at him with those drowning eyes, black in the darkness of the night. "Then why did you think I would be a coward and not come to see you?"

He stepped toward her deliberately now. "Because I scared you. And I'm sorry. But I'm not sorry for what caused it." He gently, quietly reached out and found her hand underwater, grasped it, and tugged her forward. He played with the edges of her sleeve, as he said what he came here to say.

"I wanted everyone in Reston to be afraid of me. So they'd stay away. Until you. I don't want you to be afraid of me."

He paused; his breath caught. The moonlight caught her eyes, he was close enough now to see their reflection, and she didn't pull away. In fact, she brought her other hand to meet his elbow, pulling herself even closer.

"What do you want, then?" she asked, raising her eyes to his face, her gaze dropping just for a moment to his lips. So his dropped to hers. And suddenly, he was entranced by the way her tooth snagged that full bottom lip.

"You want . . ." she prodded again, her gaze unmoving, as her tongue darted out for a moment.

"I want . . . to be your friend," he breathed, lowering his head slowly, painfully slowly, to meet hers.

"You are," she replied in a whisper. He was so close now, he could feel the linen of her nightdress dance across his body under the water.

"Good," he sighed, then grinned. "I always wanted a friend with freckles."

"I don't have freckles," she replied. She tried to be sharp, but instead all he heard was the whisper of a challenge.

"I beg to differ," he responded. "Here's one." He laid his lips against her cheek, where her freckles glowed against her moonlit skin. "Here's another." He kissed the corner of her eye, felt the thick lashes fall blissfully. "Another one." It was just on the end of her nose, making her giggle against her will. And then, "This one's my favorite." He let his lips dance just above her lip.

This was not the quick, hard kiss he had given to silence her. The grappling, surprising need from his loft. This kiss was seduction.

Byrne used to be good at this. The number might have been exaggerated by rumor and innuendo, but the Blue Raven's reputation as a lover had been earned—and no small source of pride for Byrne. However, over a year and a half now of being utterly wretched and lost to pain and unhappiness, his skills were just rusty enough to have his heartbeat quicken in nervousness.

But he felt clean now, real. Better than he had in months. In over a year. And Jane deserved a good deal of the credit.

Hell, she deserved to be rewarded.

He deepened the kiss as he let his fingers dance over the dampened neckline of her nightdress, stuck to her skin like glue. Gently, ever so gently, he peeled it back, exposing the elegant line of her collarbone to his touch. His other hand tangled with fabric underwater as he clasped her waist, pulling her closer.

Jane leaned into him, letting her arms come up and wind around his neck, her hands threading through his hair. Her feet came off the lake floor, and he lifted her as if she was weightless, and the sheer linen of her gown danced up around her waist, and she pressed her full length up against his.

Byrne smiled against her lips.

"What are you smiling about?" she whispered against him.

"Oh, nothing," he whispered back, "I simply guessed correctly."

"Ah . . . about what?" she asked, her head falling back in bliss as he let his mouth drift to the delightful line of her collarbone that his fingers had so carelessly abandoned.

"That your nightdress would prove practically worthless." And with that, he let his hands find her buttocks and lifted her higher against him.

Jane sucked in her breath. His hands were on her bare ass, pressing her most intimate parts into his arousal. And in the most natural way, to gain balance, her legs opened and began to twine around his.

Byrne couldn't believe the water wasn't boiling around them. The strength of Jane's slim thighs pressed into his flanks, holding on tight. The soft flesh she gave him access to. He let his hand drift to her cleft, and she squeaked sharply, pulling herself closer to him. Her lips found his again and ignited fire.

He did all he could to hold himself back, to keep from overwhelming her with his need . . . but, God, when she let go of what she was supposed to be and indulged in sensation, she was . . . *undeniable*. She demanded, teased with her mouth, her breasts rubbed against his chest, the wet material of her dress doing absolutely nothing to disguise their hardened peaks.

He was drunk. Drunk on Jane and grasping for purchase, and there was nothing, *nothing* better in the world, as he prayed that he had the strength to hold out and not embarrass himself when suddenly, he found himself underwater.

They had toppled with a splash, and underneath the smooth black surface, he lost her. She had broken away from him, left him reaching out unsuccessfully for the barest hint of a linen nightdress dancing underwater.

He surfaced with a great gasp, sputtering for air. He whipped his head around and found the frightened, deeply aroused gaze of Jane, her own breathing deep and unsteady.

"You see," she said, shivering slightly, "I'm not afraid of you."

He reached out to touch her, but she swam back, out of his grasp.

"I'm afraid of me."

Eighteen

For a moment, the only sound was Jane's own unsteady breath, and it seemed to hang in eternity. Byrne looked at her, his ice blue eyes darkened by desire in the moonlight. Her body was still vibrating from his touch . . .

"You're afraid of yourself?" Byrne repeated, confusion coloring his voice. "I don't understand. I thought . . . today in my loft . . ."

He didn't understand? How could he not *understand*? Jane gave a great burst of disbelieving laughter. "Good Lord, Byrne." She shook her head. "Do you think I . . . I *plaster* myself against every man I meet with while swimming naked at midnight?"

He shot her a quizzical look, then his face broke into that devilish grin. "Well, considering I doubt you have ever met with another man while swimming naked at midnight, I'd have to wager that yes, you do plaster yourself against every one you've met."

She laughed, a rich, throaty sound. "Well, fair point."

Byrne laughed, too, and took advantage of her distraction to come close to her again, to stand before her.

"Foolish girl," he murmured softly. "You stayed away, thinking that by ignoring me you could ignore your feelings." He shook his head. "It won't work—I don't stall as easily as that. And neither do you."

But when he reached out and cupped her jaw gently in his hand, she could not let the moment hold.

"We're going away," she blurted out, and felt his caress still on her jaw.

After a beat, he asked quietly, "When?"

"Soon enough, I expect." She shrugged. "This is a summer residence for my family; we have never stayed at Merrymere very long into autumn." She paused, met his gaze. "And already it is the end of August."

He withdrew his hand from her then, let the water fill the space between them. Then, slowly, calmly, he nodded. "So this . . . is just a summer idyll for you. When the weather changes, you go back south, to your grand life. To the next dance, with the next Earl or Marquis whose family name matches yours."

She nodded, her eyes never leaving his face. "But that doesn't make our"—she searched for the appropriate euphemism—"friendship any less . . ."

"Any less what?" he asked, taking another step closer. "Reckless?"

"Important," she supplied softly, and watched his eyes change from fire laced with anger to shock at her honesty. "Now do you understand? You ask me to be your friend, but we both know it's more than that. And I cannot keep you, Byrne. Come the end of summer, I'd have to give you back."

Time held still between them again, and Jane held her breath as Byrne took in everything she had told him. Their relationship would be short-lived. Her life was crammed and complicated.

And for one frightening, frozen second, Jane thought he would swim away. Simply stiffen his spine, bow over her hand, and leave, and she would never see him again. It would be the right thing, of course. A man like Byrne would never be content with just the crumbs of her life.

But instead, he took her hand and brought it to his lips, reverently.

"Jane," he said, his thumbs toying over the soft skin of her palm, "I have long since determined to live my life day by day. You speak of weeks from now as if they arrive tomorrow. But now, here and *now*, Jane, what do you want?"

Jane didn't know whether to flush with pleasure or go numb with fear. His lips played over her hand, and he gave her that look—that deeply wicked, laughing look—and all she could think was . . .

I want you.

Oh dear. Oh dear oh dear oh dear. Was it any wonder that she was afraid of herself?

But . . . God help her, she didn't have the strength to swim away.

After all, she reasoned, didn't she deserve to have a little fun this summer? Not a great deal, not so much that she lost all sense—and virtue—but didn't she deserve to have one thing that made her happy?

Her voice was annoyingly timid when she rasped, "You'll make no demands?"

"What you want is what I want," he replied soberly. "What you would want to do . . . or not do . . . is up to you."

She leaned up and kissed him then, light and leading. He pulled her closer to him, teased her lower lip with his teeth.

"However, I reserve the right to try to persuade you." He grinned between kisses, nipping at her, making her drunk with his smile. "Not that you'd need much persuasion, I think," he added, only to be answered by an outraged gasp and a splash of water to the face.

"Yes, well, we can guess at what you'd like to persuade me to do," she said smartly.

"Teach you to swim properly, of course," he answered, all mock innocence. "Why? What did you think I'd try to persuade you to do?" Then, lasciviously: "What idea did you have floating in that wicked mind?"

That just earned him another splash of cold water to the face. So, playfully, he splashed her back.

She shrieked and giggled. And there, under the stars, in a lake called Merrymere in the quiet county of Lancashire, Lady Jane Cummings and Mr. Byrne Worth engaged for some minutes in that most indecorous of activities, the splash fight.

Completely unaware of the attention they attracted.

Jason needed some air.

It had been several weeks since he had last seen Charles and Nevill, and he had forgotten just how much stamina night after night of drinking required. Strange, he never really thought much of it before.

Although before, he would sleep away the afternoon and not have to rise early in the morning to begin the process of going over the duchy's accounts with his pair of stewards. Although perhaps he could put it off, as at least one of them was proving to be as merry as his friends. Jason doubted Mr. Thorndike would be up at the appointed hour, as he was still in the dining room drunkenly discussing the finer point of throwing horseshoes with Nevill. Indeed, when they had taken the man out to the pitch his father had put in the back gardens years ago for their mother's annual summer ball, Thorndike had nearly turned apoplectic with glee. Then he had proceeded to cheer himself to victory so loudly, Jason had to be the one to shush them, lest they wake the whole household.

Shushing his guests. Had he really become such a stick-in-the-mud?

Apparently he had, because when he managed to usher the party back inside to the dining room, he had been the one to hint at ending the festivities. To no avail, of course. Nevill tended to think any time more than two people were together, it was a party and must last as long as possible. Charles, meanwhile, had removed to the drawing room to look for a deck of cards and had passed out on the settee.

And so, while Nevill and Mr. Thorndike discovered they were absolute best of long-lost friends, Jason had stepped out on the balcony to take the air.

At first, he had seen nothing but the stars in the sky. The moon was strong, but it did not detract from the veritable ocean of swirling stars, the Milky Way like a brushstroke on the inky background of the sky. A bare moment of peace in a disturbingly loud evening.

A bare moment of peace interrupted by the sound of a splash. Then another, then another.

Jason glanced down. At first, he didn't see anything in the water. It was too dark out there, and too bright by the Cottage. Then he caught sight of a strip of white in the water.

And then a flash of red hair.

Was that . . . ?

Jason leaned over the railing of the balcony.

It couldn't be. It just couldn't be Jane. She didn't swim. Hadn't since he taught her as a child.

But that was her laugh. And there was someone in the water with her. Someone male, someone with dark hair . . .

And *that*, he thought as he narrowed his eyes, was Mr. Worth.

Suddenly, a great deal became clear to Jason. Such as where Jane took her walks in the afternoons. Why she was so adamant that he shake hands with Mr. Worth at the assembly. Not to subvert any violence, oh no . . .

And why Jane argued so vehemently for Mr. Worth's innocence just last evening. She convinced Sir Wilton to hold his lynch mob back, to protect her secret lover.

And her interest in the good Dr. Berridge? The scales fell from his eyes, as he realized that any interest was a fiction, one she used cunningly to divert Jason's attention from the real object of her dogged pursuit.

Jason felt vaguely ill, watching his sister from afar as she splashed and flirted and played. The brandy he had been sipping all evening was going to return on him if that blackguard got one inch closer to Jane . . .

When Mr. Worth caught Jane up, and she shrieked with laughter as he lowered his face to hers, Jason couldn't stand it anymore. He ducked behind a convenient potted shrubbery, breathing hard through his nose as he willed himself not to retch. That was his *sister*. Sisters weren't supposed to make moany noises while kissing a . . . a . . . *highwayman* in the water. And certainly brothers were not meant to hear it. Jason pressed his hands over his ears, but it did nothing to quiet his imagination, and a shudder of revulsion raced down his spine.

Oh, the indignity of the situation! Here he was, crouched behind a potted shrubbery, trying not to listen to his sister have a liaison with a man of such low character he had quit London only to have an entire village against him. Jason had the presence of mind to wonder briefly why Mr. Worth had quit London, but that thought was interrupted by a larger, louder, angrier thought. Jane was a hypocrite.

She had been running around with Mr. Worth, having her fun, but she had been appalled that he'd gone out to a tavern when they first arrived, and she was angry as a cat that he'd invited Charles and Nevill. Never mind that Jason himself was beginning to rethink having his friends to stay; it was the principle of the thing!

In the house, Jason could hear Nevill and Thorndike laughing again. In the water, the splashing and (ugh) giggling had resumed. It seemed everyone was having a jolly time except Jason himself. Oh, their father would lose his mind if he ever discovered Jane was dallying with . . .

A sharp pang of bleakness came over him.

His father had already lost his mind.

And Jason knew, in that moment, that there truly was nothing more terrifying than realizing he was the one in charge.

He should run out there right now, run into the water and put a stop to her foolishness before someone should see, or before—God forbid—circumstances progressed too far. And Jason had just enough alcohol in his system to do it.

But he was also just sober enough to realize that such behavior would only cause Jane to become insufferable. She always had to have her way, and if he called her out on this relationship, he would have to hold her under lock and key to keep her from making further mischief.

He realized that the splashing was lighter but also somehow closer. Jane must be wading her way toward shore. He chanced a peek over the top of the shrubbery. Yes, Mr. Worth had disappeared, and she was coming toward land. He ducked down again quickly, thinking that his only chance to remain undiscovered was to stay still. He waited in the shadows and soon enough was treated to a flash of white as Jane swiftly and silently ran up the steps and into the house. The look on her face . . .

Well it was only a flash, and Jason was halfway inebriated, but he could have sworn that Jane looked . . . blissful. Happy in a way he hadn't seen on his sister's features in over a year.

Or his own.

But he shook off maudlin thoughts as he stood, stretching his stiff legs, and assessed the situation at hand. Jane could not be allowed to continue her dalliance with this man. But long experience taught him he couldn't force her to his will. He could send her away . . . but that would upset Father, and besides, he needed to keep his eye on her.

So perhaps it was time he made some mischief of his own.

And Jason knew exactly where to start.

It was luncheon, and Victoria was about to tear her hair out.

She couldn't call her father for help—oh, no, he was out, having met with Mr. Cutler and needing to discuss—again—the implications of Mr. Worth's behavior the previous morning. Her mother, on the other hand, had no need to spread such gossip. She had spent all day yesterday doing just that, dragging Victoria along with her to every house, every shop. Today, Lady Wilton had taken Penelope and the girls (Mr. Brandon having gone back to Manchester to attend to his business) to Mrs. Hill's to purchase some new material for the children's dresses—because Michael and Joshua had decided to use the laundry hanging on the line as rope to swing from the tree into the river. These clothes included the girls' Sunday church garments.

It seemed that Joshua's near-death experience had done little to temper the boys' enthusiasm for mayhem. In fact, he was quite annoyingly recovered. Right now, they had Victoria's sewing box and were spread out in the drawing room, rifling its contents, throwing whatever they didn't need onto the floor, where various pins, buttons, and bobbins of thread bounced and scattered under tables and sofas.

"What are you doing?" Victoria cried, coming upon the scene of the crime.

The two criminals looked up from their work, innocent as angels.

"We need thread," Michael said.

Victoria glanced down at the half dozen spools of thread that had rolled to various corners of the room.

A hand came to her temples. "Why?" she asked.

"We want to go fishing," Michael answered.

"And we need thread the color of water, so the fish won't see it!" Joshua added gleefully, then going back to the contents of her sewing box. "But you only have blue and green, not blue-green, like water is."

"Maybe if we tied the two together?" Michael suggested to his brother. And suddenly, Victoria couldn't take it anymore. This was the first moment in two weeks that the house was almost empty. The first time that she was not tripping over Penelope or her nieces, no matter how much she adored them, or any of the accoutrement that seemed to accompany babies. The first time she was not forced to sit and listen to her mother, nor had anyone come to call that she wished to speak to. It had been ages since Jane had come to visit or issued an invitation to the Cottage . . .

Andrew stopped by occasionally, but she didn't know what she had done, because he no longer spoke to her; he simply spoke with her father, monitored Joshua's improvement, and left. Maybe he had found a young lady to court, and that would be *horrible*, because she couldn't think of anyone of age to court in Reston, so he'd have to travel to Windermere or Ambleside—and then when would they see him?

Oh no. What if he was courting Sylvia Prescott from Derwett, a widow who had to be at least thirty? Victoria had nothing in common with Sylvia, and she would never be able to have a conversation with her. If she couldn't have a conversation with the woman Andrew married, how was she supposed to remain his friend?

And unfortunately, all of this misery and discontent became focused on her sewing box and its plunderers.

"That's it!" Victoria yelled. "Get out! Get out of this house right now!"

"But . . . Vicky," Joshua sputtered, only to be tugged by his brother toward the garden doors. At least one of them, it seemed, knew what they had been doing was wrong.

"Get out, get out, get out!" she shrieked and chased them through the room, and out the garden doors. Once they were gone, she took a deep breath and let the silence envelop her.

But there was no peace in it. Instead, she found only regret for her burst of temper. Her eyes fell over the mess of the drawing room. They were just boys, for heaven's sake, who wanted to go fishing. What she should do is go upstairs, lie down, and think of a way to apologize to Michael and Joshua. She just needed a moment of calm and quiet, she thought as she crossed the room, and she would regain her . . .

But Victoria was not fated to finish the thought. Just then, her foot landed on a spool of thread. She slid, and with a surprised yelp, she landed flat on her back, taking down an end table with her.

"Ow," Victoria groaned from the carpet.

"I say!" came a rumbled voice from the doorway. "What on earth happened here? Miss Victoria?"

"Dr. Berridge." Victoria sighed, as that man came into view above her.

"Victoria, are you all right?" he asked, his face etched with concern. She felt his hand dart beneath her curls, gently feeling the back of her head for injury.

"Michael and Joshua . . . my sewing box . . . I slipped. On thread," she said, as his fingers caressed her scalp.

"Lucky you landed on the carpet," he said softly. "Where are Bridget and Minnie?"

"Bridget went to the shop with my mother and sister. Minnie is in the garden, I think," Victoria ventured.

"Your head feels fine. You might have a bit of a goose egg later." His steady, kind eyes met hers. "Can you stand?"

She nodded, and he helped her to sit up. Then, gently, he took her arms and took most of her weight as he helped her stand. Which was lucky, as her ankle decided to not be so accommodating.

"Oh!" she cried, as she fell against him completely.

His arm went around her immediately. It was shocking how warm it was in his embrace. He maneuvered her to the settee, practically carrying her, as if she weighed no more than dust.

"Your ankle, I take it?" he asked, kneeling before her, his demeanor swift and professional. She nodded, blinking back tears. His face softened seeing hers, and he started to say something but ducked his head, quickly turning his attention back to her foot. Gingerly, he lifted it in his hand.

"May I?" he asked, indicating her boot. "It will be easier to examine the injury, if I, ah, remove . . ." his voice trailed off as his cheeks took on a surprising flush for one who examined the human body daily. Victoria froze.

Oh no. He wished to take off her shoe.

Victoria was rather on the petite side, small of frame, short in height, but for some reason, she thought, embarrassed, she had inherited the feet of a duck. Flat and long, wide and ugly. Why, the boot maker had to have a size cut just for her! So, knowing his eyes were on her, she shook her head violently.

"Why?" he asked, his voice holding nothing more than doctorly concern. "Miss Victoria, I promise you I mean nothing untoward . . ."

"It's not that," she said quickly. In fact, having her ankle rest gently against his hand was . . . pleasant. "Surely you . . . you must see . . ." But he just cocked his head to the side, listening patiently. "My feet are too big," Victoria came out with it, averting her eyes to the cushions on the settee, wishing her agony over, wishing she hadn't tripped, wishing Dr. Berridge—Andrew—wasn't now privy to her embarrassing trait.

But . . . when she chanced a look back at him, he was smiling and shaking his head, and pulling out the laces of her boot.

"Don't be ridiculous, Victoria," he grinned at her. "Your feet are perfect."

And suddenly Victoria felt a little wobbly.

He removed the boot with the utmost care, his fingers dancing over the silk stocking at her ankle, then just below and just above it. Victoria could not, for the life of her, take her eyes off his hands. They moved with such gentleness and grace. They seemed to leave a trail of sensation on her skin, a line of golden pinpricks wherever they touched.

Until he gently turned her foot and those golden pinpricks became a sharp line of pain. Victoria immediately stiffened, and sucked in her breath.

"That's painful, I take it?" he asked, immediately returning her foot to a more comfortable position.

"Yes," she replied softly. And then her eyes locked with his. And the strangest thing happened.

She got lost. So lost, in fact, that she momentarily forgot why they were still in the drawing room, him with his hand on her unshod foot, the articles of her sewing box strewn across the carpet and under chairs . . .

"It's my fault," she blurted, and the sounds and circumstances of the room rushed back to life around her. "I lost my temper," she explained sheepishly.

His eyes stayed on hers, unnervingly intense. But his hands continued the examination of her foot (she could daresay he lingered), patiently awaiting further elucidation.

And so she began to ramble an explanation of the events just before he arrived, how Michael and Joshua's mischief seemed to be unending, and how she had overreacted. "After all," she admitted, "all they wanted to do was fish."

"I'm afraid I have to disagree with you," Andrew said, once her story was told. "Those young rascals only thought of their own pleasure, and because of their selfishness, you have injured yourself. You merely gave them a preemptive scolding." His eyes flashed with some emotion Victoria couldn't identify. "And when they come out from their hiding place, I'll give them another scolding myself."

But before Victoria could object or ask him why he would involve himself in such a way, he stood and brushed off the knees of his trousers.

"I can detect no sprain," he announced. "I think it's a simple twist, and would ask you to tread lightly for a few days."

"Tread lightly?" Victoria asked, startled. "But that's ridiculous, I cannot be bedridden!"

She tried to stand, but the doctor pressed gently on her shoulder to push her back onto the sofa. Then he took the seat next to her.

"I'm not asking you to be bedridden, but perhaps taking it easier, being still."

"I can't . . . but who . . . there's too much to do!" she sputtered, but she was quieted by his hand on her shoulder.

"Let someone look after you for once," he persisted with a smile, that hand finding its way to a slightly mussed golden curl and pushing it back behind her ear. "Instead of the other way around."

But Victoria wasn't really listening. Because she had become pointedly aware of just how *close* Andrew was sitting to her. And just how dark his eyes were, although they had those strange flecks of gold that seemed to dance with light. When did she first notice that? When did she stop breathing evenly?

"Victoria," Andrew was saying, his voice low and enticing, "I have long . . . that is to say, I . . ."

Before Andrew could continue his sentence—or Victoria could begin to guess what he meant to say, footsteps sounded in the foyer.

"Hello?" a male voice called out. "Your door is wide open, I do not—"

And then Jason Cummings, Marquis of Vessey, appeared in the drawing room doorway.

"Miss Victoria, what luck!" he made a cursory bow and entered the room. "Good afternoon, Doctor." He greeted Andrew with an outstretched hand.

Habit had Victoria jumping to her feet to greet Jason with the necessary curtsy, but she was stayed by a hand on her shoulder.

"You'll forgive Miss Victoria for not rising," Dr. Berridge said stiffly, as he rose and took Jason's hand. "She's just badly injured her ankle."

"Badly?" Jason asked.

"Badly?" Victoria replied at the same time. "But you said it was only twisted slightly."

The doctor turned a bit ruddy of face but didn't argue with Victoria's statement.

"Oh, then I am much relieved, Miss Victoria," Jason said, as Victoria indicated for him to sit. He did, taking the chair opposite, while the doctor reseated himself next to Victoria on the sofa. Jason looked around the room, not seeming to notice the mess. "May I inquire, are your parents at home?"

"No," Victoria answered. "My father is meeting on business, and my mother and sister are shopping."

"No matter," Jason smiled. That ridiculously charming smile. "I came to speak with you in any case."

Victoria's stomach dropped. "Me?" she squeaked. Not Penelope? She wanted to exclaim in delight, but thankfully kept her mouth shut.

"Yes. I'm afraid I have to ask you a terribly large favor. And thank goodness your foot only suffered a slight twist, as you say. Else I would feel too guilty to prevail upon you."

"Oh, don't feel guilty!" Victoria replied, utterly flustered. "I . . . I would be pleased to help you in any way I can."

Jason's smile returned. "I come on an errand from my sister. She's decided to give a ball . . ."

"Oh, how wonderful!" Victoria cried. "Andr—uh, Dr. Berridge, imagine, I've never been to a proper ball." She frowned, uncertain. "And therefore I don't know how I can be of use."

"It will be quite simple!" Jason assured her. "She just needs an assistant and immediately thought of you. You know everyone in the area to invite, all of the vendors to purchase from . . . I'm certain there is a great amount of detail that goes into planning a ball, but I simply haven't a clue. It's best to just let us men show up, eh, Berridge?"

"Quite," Dr. Berridge ground out, his jaw set tight.

"In any case, it would require you to spend a great deal of your time up at the Cottage—almost every minute with my sister up until the ball."

"With Lady Jane," Victoria repeated dumbly. "And . . . and you?"

He shrugged. "Of course, I'll be around the house. But I fear I ask too much of you . . ." he let his voice trail off, concern etched across his face.

"Oh no!" Victoria answered, excitement rocketing through her like lightning. "I would be honored to assist."

"But your injury," Jason pointed out.

"It's not so bad," Victoria said, turning to Dr. Berridge, her eyes shining with excitement. "Isn't that right, Doctor?"

Victoria looked up at Dr. Berridge. Jason watched Dr. Berridge. And Dr. Berridge suddenly had a decision to make.

Shortly thereafter, Jason took his leave, mounted his horse, and rode off.

Mere minutes later, Dr. Berridge walked calmly out of the Wiltons' residence. And after he passed Lady Wilton and Mrs. Brandon on their way back into the house, he calmly and coolly kicked the unfortunate fence post that happened to be closest when he heard Victoria cry out:

"Mother! I have the most incredible news! I've been asked to help with a ball!"

Nineteen

JASON felt he had a right to be ridiculously proud of his own inge-
nuity. Not only had he secured a babysitter for Jane, he had de-
vised an activity that incited such anxiety in his sister, it would keep
her far too busy in the coming weeks for her to have time to dally
with Worth.

When Jane had first discovered that she was to throw a ball, having been informed by Victoria when she arrived the next morning—
with sheaves of paper detailing who to invite, their individual
directions, and a variety of themes, as she and her mother had stayed
up very late brainstorming ideas—Jane's immediate reaction was
horror. She excused herself from Victoria and dragged Jason into the
library, where the two stewards awaited his attention.

One look from Jane, and the stewards took their leave.

"We are giving a ball?" Jane asked incredulously.

"Well, yes," Jason replied, working very hard to keep his voice
pure and innocent. "It was your idea."

"How was it my idea?" Jane managed to say, after a few outraged
squeaks.

"You have expressed several times that the village expects us to act as our parents have in the past," Jason argued. "You made me hire Big Jim the blacksmith, and you purchase unnecessary red ink from Mr. Davies . . ."

"So?"

"So—Mother threw a ball at the end of every summer. It was highly anticipated by the town," he explained. And this was true, although what he said next might have been closer to illusion than reality. "Perhaps I overheard some villagers discussing the possibility of a ball, and . . . didn't feel I could disappoint them."

As Jane chewed over Jason's explanation, he couldn't help but feel slightly guilty. He was shamelessly playing on his sister's expectations of herself and her memories of their mother. But it was necessary. If it kept her busy . . .

"But I cannot throw a party!" Jane sputtered. "Jason, remember the last time . . ."

Jason did, his sister's disastrous dinner party right before her debut. He suppressed a shudder. "We can go tell Miss Victoria it was all a misunderstanding, that there won't be a ball," he offered, knowing full well that Victoria, with stars in her eyes and her foot wrapped in a bandage, would be a creature too pathetic for Jane to crush.

"No," Jane sighed. "If she has informed her mother—and I suspect she has—the entire town would be disappointed by such a misunderstanding. You are right. We should have a ball . . . but with all of our guests and, er, things, how on earth do you expect me to organize such an event in only two weeks?"

"Actually . . . one," Jason replied.

"*One?*" Jane cried and swatted her brother on the arm.

"Ten days more like . . . ow, Jane, stop it!"

"It's impossible!"

"Weekend after this," Jason said, in between dodging her lethal swats. "And then . . . we will leave for the south shortly after—I'm afraid it cannot be any later."

Jane stilled. "We—we could stay longer. Father . . ." she hedged, but Jason just shook his head.

"You want to freeze our toes off up here when the weather finally breaks and fall descends in earnest? Ask Nurse Nancy—Father's health would not benefit." Jason sighed as he placed a hand on his sister's fallen shoulder. "I knew it was a terribly short amount of time to plan a ball, which is why I begged the assistance of Miss Victoria. And your sanity should thank me."

"Why?" she asked spitefully.

"That I did not request the assistance of her mother."

Now Jason smiled, watching his sister and Victoria in the drawing room as they compiled a checklist of things to do—among them, inspect and polish the silver and locate extra settings if they hadn't enough—knowing Jane was fully occupied and would be for quite some time. His friends were still abed, his father enjoying the unseasonably warm air by taking his walk with Nurse Nancy; perhaps he could tempt Hale and Thorndike into putting off work another day for a ride.

Being in charge wasn't so difficult, he mused. No idea why he'd spent so long avoiding it.

Jason was right about one thing. At least Lady Wilton wasn't here. Jane had absolutely no idea how Victoria had dissuaded her mother from offering her services, but she appreciated that much from the girl. The rest, however . . .

Bleakness swept over Jane like a black cloud on a sunny day. She had hoped to spend the afternoon at Byrne's. Once her father had returned from his walk and lain down for his afternoon nap, she had planned to surprise him with a picnic on the peak. She had packed an entirely new basket with jams and bread and even a bottle of wine. All she wanted to do was pick up her skirts and run out of the room. Run to Byrne.

She had awoken with a purpose, a rhythm to follow—but Lord help her, she found herself designing her day around when she would be able to see him, and how long she could sneak away to her secret life.

To her secret self.

But now, with Victoria prattling on about linens and who to invite from the neighboring towns, Jane's anxiety level rose to a fever pitch.

Because not only was Jane to be denied time away from home today, she was going to have to spend the entire afternoon—the entire week—planning a party.

It was enough to make one break out in hives.

Jane adored attending parties. But throwing one? The last time Jane had successfully thrown a party, she was twelve and broke into the headmistress's office at Mrs. Humphrey's School for Elegant Ladies, and had an impromptu tea party in the middle of the night.

And even that had been on a dare.

Her mother had once, *once* allowed Jane to participate in the planning of a dinner party before her debut Season. To this day, no one in the family ever mentioned the ghastly event, but the end result had the Duchess and Jane spending the next day in separate rooms, each in tears.

"Now, what do you think of a harvest theme?" Victoria was saying, pulling out some sketches of cornucopias and pumpkins. "I know it's not quite harvest time yet, but almost . . ." She trailed off, seeing Jane's disinterest. "Or what about a water theme?" she tried again brightly.

"A water theme?" Jane replied dazedly.

"Yes!" Victoria cried, pulling out another elaborate sketch. "Waterfalls and, er, mermaids . . ."

"Why do we need a theme at all?" Jane asked as she stood and began to pace. "It's not London, Victoria. It's *Reston*. A ball itself should be enough to stun these country folk into awe."

Silence fell in the room, as Jane immediately regretted her words. Victoria delicately put aside the papers.

"You're correct, of course. You know far more about balls than I do," Victoria said quietly. "It's simply that, in all the books, the balls always have some sort of theme."

If Jane had a whip, she would have struck it across her own back in self-flagellation. "I'm sorry, Victoria, I should not have spoken so—"

"No, you're absolutely right, perhaps simpler is better—" But Jane cut her off.

"I'm . . . I'm just wretched."

"Wretched?" she asked, confused.

"Worried," Jane corrected.

"About the ball?" Victoria asked, and Jane let her believe that assumption. "You have nothing to worry about!" she cried, a determined smile on her lips. "I may not have any experience in the matter, but I have a feeling everyone within the county will turn out for it. Certainly there is still the highwayman to contend with, but I don't think that would keep people away."

Highwayman.

"Yes," Jane thought in a rush. "The highwayman is indeed at the forefront of my mind, as . . . as Mr. Worth and I were supposed to take that information you copied for us and put it to use this afternoon!"

"Oh my! How?" Victoria asked.

"Er . . ." before Jane could go into detail, she was spared from having to do so by the bleary-eyed arrival of Charles and Nevill, fresh from their noontime breakfast and already bored to tears.

"Lady Jane," Nevill said, yawning as he bowed in greeting. "And Miss, uh . . ."

"Wilton. Victoria Wilton," that lady supplied, as she curtsied.

Charles and Nevill nodded in greeting, before Nevill turned to Jane. "Do you happen to have bowls? Or any fishing tackle? Or *anything* to do?"

"Miss Victoria and I were just planning a ball that I am supposed to throw. Will that suffice?" Jane answered archly.

"Depends," Nevill's eyebrow went up. "Is it anytime soon?"

"Ten days," Victoria piped up.

"Not much time." A furrow knitted Charles's brow. "Have you ordered the musicians yet? If not, Nevill and I know of a great octet, heard them play on the way up from York . . ."

"And you'll need to have the molding retouched in the ballroom,"

Nevill said, picking up Victoria's papers. "You should add that to this list."

Jane blinked twice. "Nevill, may I ask—have you planned an event like this before?"

"Nah," Nevill replied. "But Charles and I have seen our mother go through the whole thing for each for our seven elder sisters' debut parties."

"We could likely plan a ball with one hand tied behind each back," Charles piped up, grinning.

"And a glass of whiskey in the other."

"Could you help us?" Victoria asked before Jane could say anything. "I'm simply hopeless, and Jane . . ."

"I'm simply hopeless, too," Jane added, to be met by an astonished look from Charles.

"Lady Jane, I've never thought you'd be hopeless at anything," he said with a crooked smile, as he reached for the tea cakes that had been laid out as refreshment for Jane and Victoria.

"Quite right," Nevill agreed. "But if *you* need *us* to pick out table linens, I suppose anything is possible. By the by, if I were you, I would rent tablecloths of Egyptian cotton. It truly makes a difference."

It was terribly strange, but as they sat there, Nevill lounging with his leg over the arm of the chair and Charles chewing on a tea cake with his mouth open, Jane was struck with a deep sense of gratitude.

They were Charles and Nevill, for God's sake. And yet here they were, seemingly sober, engaged, on their best behavior.

Funny, she had never thought of her brother's friends as . . . useful.

"Now," Charles was saying to a rapt Victoria, "what this party needs is a *theme.*"

When Charles and Nevill were inspired, it was a sight to behold.

It was not long before long lists had been assembled, and the housekeeper dispatched to organize the counting and cleaning of all the silver and crystal, the text for an invitation composed, and footmen set about repairing the moldings of the ballroom. A household cleaning schedule was drawn up, and the cook ordered to create a sample menu for all four members of the party planning committee to taste the next day.

If Jane feared that Charles and Nevill would lapse into their more dissolute selves and attempt any foolishness with Victoria, a quick word in Nevill's ear about Victoria's relative poverty and her father's ability to have them deported to an Australian work colony kept them the very keenest of gentlemen in her presence.

The four of them discussed and planned over luncheon, and by the time Jane's father was just lying down for his nap, Jane was able to bid Victoria farewell for the day.

Charles and Nevill were set on going into Reston to take a look at Mr. Davies's card stock inventory in his print shop and having the invitations engraved posthaste.

"And Jason is such a dodger, going off riding without us!" Charles grumbled toward the locked door of the library as he put on his hat. "Certain you won't join us, Jane?" Then he blushed and stammered. "Um, I mean Lady Jane."

"Jane is fine." She smiled at him. "And the two of you will ride faster without me."

Once they left, she stood in the silent foyer for a moment. Jason was occupied, her father resting, and her guests involved.

Circumstances such as these would not last long, she knew. And she had a hundred little things to do for the ball (Nevill had left her with a list). She would be best served to employ this brief lull industriously.

Which is exactly what she intended to do.

"You know, I do feel somewhat guilty," Jane said, as she took another sip of her wine from a tin cup and nibbled on her biscuit.

"Whatever for?" Byrne asked, propped up on one shoulder as he spooned another serving of that ridiculously delicious blackberry jam on his bread.

"Because I told Victoria we were going to investigate the

highwayman—not have a picnic," Jane replied. "And instead we lounge here. Too comfortable for our own good."

"I can think of several ways we can be far more comfortable." He wiggled his eyebrow, only to be swatted by Jane. "I meant we could not be seated on a mess of rocks!"

They had climbed up the fell again to enjoy the spectacular landscape as they picnicked in the late-afternoon sun. It was still unseasonably and unnaturally warm for the north, but Byrne could feel the bite of autumn in the air, the change that was coming.

When Jane would go away.

All it did, he told himself, was change the timetable of his plans. He wanted Jane, and he would get her. But keeping her, providing for her for life . . . that was another story entirely. One he and she would both likely come to regret. Better certainly to enjoy their friendship now, and grow strong with it, than . . .

Than to fall hopelessly.

But he shook off that melancholy thought and instead concentrated on the conversation at hand.

"Speak for yourself—I, on the other hand, fully intended to work toward our goal of ensnaring the highwayman."

"You did?" she asked, her eyes brightening.

In answer, Byrne produced from his breast pocket the pages Victoria had copied so diligently. "Yes, I was going to come up here, and retrace our highwayman's steps, this time with our new information. That is, until you distracted me with such temptations as wine and jam."

"Oh well, my distractions and I apologize," she replied pertly, dusting off her skirts and beginning to gather up the detritus of the picnic. "We'll go if you need solitude for your thoughts."

He looked at her, then down at the half-empty basket—and gave a deep, labored sigh. "Well," he said, pulling her back down beside him on the blanket, "since you're already here, the two of you might as well stay."

She landed with a satisfying thump, falling back into his arms. "You just want the scones and jams to stay." She smiled at him.

"Speaking of . . ." Byrne said, and he levered up and kissed the corner of her mouth, catching the small bit of jam that had been resting there, tempting him for the last minute. She eagerly latched on to him, deepened the kiss. He could taste the wine on her breath, mixed with the jam, the summer breeze, and the cinnamon scent that was all Jane. But before he could get too lost in the sense that life was as sweet as what he tasted, Jane broke away, nicked the pages from his hand, and made a show of studying them while strenuously ignoring him.

"So—what do we know now that we didn't know before?" she asked, holding back a wicked smile.

That you tempt me like the devil.

"That what was stolen was far less than rumor has described," Byrne said.

"But we suspected that," Jane argued, turning over the pages in her hand.

"Monetarily. In terms of quantity it was far more," Byrne countered.

"Where did you discern that?" she asked, scanning the pages furiously.

He pointed to one of the pages. "Here—no, wait . . . here. Where it notes that a whole trunk was taken."

His finger hit the paragraph he sought. It was an annoyingly short entry, as were all the entries regarding the highwayman.

"Highwayman attacked private hired carriage on main road to Reston. Assailant thieved items from the victims' persons, including one large banded trunk, which also contained some monies and jewelry."

Jane read the paragraph with a scrunched nose. "Don't highwaymen usually take the trunks and things?"

"No, actually—they usually take what they can carry on their horse and make a quick getaway. Hence jewels and pocket change. If they are stealing whole trunks, it means two things—they are novices who don't know what they are looking for, and they live close enough to town to hide their goods. Else the trunk would have been found, scattered after being ransacked."

"You keep saying 'they,'" Jane noted. "You believe there to be more than one person?"

"We know that from overhearing the conversation at the assembly." Byrne narrowed his eyes, sat up straight, and looked into the distance, to the road leading into Reston.

"Do you know, I am amazed that these fellows haven't yet been caught. Their actions are reckless and sloppy. Taking the mail in the dead of winter? And no one followed their horses' tracks in the snow? And what about when the attack started moving closer to town? Post a few watchmen on the main roads in and out of town and voilà!" He slammed his fist into his hand. "They're caught."

Jane glanced at him from under her lashes. "Voilà?" she asked.

"It's French," he replied defensively.

"I know. I just never expected the word 'voilà' to drop from your lips."

"I can do lots of unexpected things with my lips." He grinned at her and was rewarded with watching her turn the most uncommon shade of pink.

"You shouldn't do that," Jane replied primly.

"Do what?" he asked innocently, as she turned an even deeper shade of red.

"Try to . . . unsettle me."

"And yet," he leaned down and kissed her, reverently, "unsettling the unflappable Lady Jane is one of life's little joys."

"Well," she replied, a little breathless, "you shouldn't change the subject."

"True. What were we talking about again?"

"Why the thieves haven't been caught yet," she said, sitting up, forcing him to do the same. She shuffled the pages in her hands.

"I suppose that they have benefited from Sir Wilton's lack of organization," she said, looking over the papers. "I expected there to be more information here. He didn't write down anything about what the victims saw . . ."

"True. I received more structured information from Dobbs, who was merely collecting off rumor. Sir Wilton has no record of witness statements. Or descriptions of the attackers," he agreed.

"I'm sure he took them; after all, I watched Mr. Cutler interview Mr. Hale and Mr. Thorndike, and Charles and Nevill, when they sobered up a bit. But you should see his book room," Jane added. "Sir Wilton's—not Charles and Nevill's. It's completely piled with evidence and notes from old and unresolved cases. I was surprised Victoria and I managed to find this ledger."

"So, if he has more notes anywhere, it's doubtful even he could find them?" Byrne surmised, as Jane nodded. "Do you realize that this highwayman escapade has been bungled from the very beginning? Instead of investigating the attacks, it seems like the town is simply waiting for the next one and hoping they get lucky enough to catch someone—me, hopefully—in the act."

Jane regarded him then, as she asked, "What would you do? If you were the magistrate in charge?"

Byrne looked out over the vista and pointed to the mouth of the town. "Post men at checkpoints—here, and then about a mile farther up, and another two miles beyond that. I'd ask Windermere to do the same, maybe the town on Coniston Water. Then I'd take an inventory of the stolen goods—down to every last boot, not just the jewels and money, and send men out to Manchester and York—and maybe even Edinburgh—and search the local pawnbrokers for the goods.

"I'd then take a good hard look at the men in town—which ones are living beyond their means? Which ones have a sweetheart who has a new locket or bonnet that she shouldn't be able to afford?" He started talking with his hands now, as he didn't have his cane to roll back and forth between his palms—it was beside him on the ground. "And then I would cross-reference the dates of the robberies with where those men were—which shouldn't be too difficult to discern, as Sir Wilton's wife is the biggest gossip in the village. Were these men in or out of town? Do they have people who can account for their whereabouts?"

He stopped then, the visions he had—the checkpoints posted along the main roads—he could see them there, in the distant valley, in the fading afternoon sun. As real as day.

"And if we hadn't caught the highwaymen then"—Byrne shrugged—"or at the very least deterred them from practicing their arts in this area of the county, then I'll be hanged myself."

Byrne looked up to find that Jane was smiling bemusedly at him. "That seems to be a great deal of work."

"It's the work that should have been done. The steps that should have been taken before this escalated out of control. I've thought about . . ."

He paused, vaguely embarrassed by his own notion.

"Thought about what?" Jane asked, after a moment.

"Thought about offering Sir Wilton my services. As an assistant to the magistrate, or officer, or whatnot."

"*After* you catch the highwayman, of course."

He grinned wryly. "Doubt he'd be open to it before."

"I think it a fine idea," Jane replied. "I think Reston could use you."

It was funny, but it had been a very long time since Byrne had felt himself needed. That he was proud of what he could contribute.

That he felt the call of purpose, not duty.

"You do?" he asked, unsure.

"Of course. I would vote for you." Jane wrinkled her nose. "That is—if I were permitted, which I don't think I would be. Nevertheless," she said with a smile, "I would force Jason to vote for you."

"I don't think that is necessary, as I doubt a vote would be involved." Byrne laughed, and brushed an errant strand of red hair back behind her ear. "But I thank you for your support."

He kissed her then and felt the want course from her into him. The delicious heat of the delicate skin of her throat, the way she fell into him . . .

It was some minutes later when Jane broke away, breathless.

"What time is it?" she asked, soft and befuddled.

"Ah." Truth be told, they were both a little breathless. "Five minutes to tea," he replied, checking his pocket watch.

"I have to go!" she cried, her mouth an open circle of shock. "How did it get so late?" she grumbled, as she began to throw tin cups and napkins into the basket. "I cannot miss tea."

"Why?" he asked, indicating the remains of a scone. "After all, you've already eaten."

She stopped, caught his gaze, and opened her mouth a few times, as if deciding what to say. Then she looked down, resumed her gathering. "I have guests," she replied. "And they're expecting me."

"Let your brother entertain them for an afternoon," Byrne suggested, taking her hand and tugging her away from her furious cleaning.

"It's not just that," Jane said, growing vulnerability in her voice.

"What is it, sweetheart?" he asked, and her eyes flashed up to his face, shocked at the endearment.

She held herself still, willing herself to speak. But she held herself back. Whatever it was that she was hiding, she kept it in.

"I'm needed at home, is all," she said finally.

It was on the tip of his tongue to say, *Let me take you home. Let me call on you in your home. Don't keep me secret from your brother, from your father, from your friends.* But that would mean . . .

That would mean they were more to each other than a summer idyll.

And they could not have that.

When the time came, he would let her go. He would give her back. But not yet.

He held her close, let his hand snake up her back. "There are still five minutes till tea," he whispered, kissing the freckle at the corner of her mouth, feeling her whole body relax into a delightful little shudder.

"Five minutes?" she asked, her voice small, hopeful.

"Five minutes . . ." he agreed.

Twenty

JANE made it to tea that day, but just barely. The next day she was not so fortunate, coming in ten minutes late with a twig in her hair. Luckily, when her father pointed it out, she thought quickly and said it was from a tree that grazed her on her daily walk. It was an inept fib, but he seemed to believe it. Nurse Nancy, however, gave her a pointed look.

Jason was not in attendance to pass judgment, and Jane hoped that Mr. Hale and Mr. Thorndike had finally wrestled him into the library and to his books. But at dinner, while she was being besieged by Charles and Nevill's ideas for seating arrangements (they favored a few dozen smaller tables as opposed to one very large one) for the ball, Jason told them he had spent the day with Mr. Hale fishing on the Broadmill River.

"But we talked a great deal about the castle. Apparently there are a number of tenant cottages that could use some repair," Jason said as he shoveled food into his mouth. Jane looked over to Mr. Hale, who, after a confused moment, nodded vigorously. It occurred to Jane that Hale and Thorndike were enjoying this excursion more than they were meant to, taking rides and going fishing at length with her brother.

It also occurred to her that he was spending less and less time with his guests, Charles and Nevill—and they had been left to her to entertain.

But what to make of it, she wasn't quite sure.

She also didn't know what to make of planning a ball. There were so many more details than she expected! How many people the Cottage could accommodate, who to invite, who to exclude, how to decorate the hall versus the entryway, what crystal to use, should a band be called up from London if the York octet proved unworthy? Even what to serve evoked controversy among herself, Victoria, Charles, and Nevill.

"Roast beef? And French asparagus?" Jane cried, looking at the sample menu Charles and Cook had drawn up.

"Where on earth are we going to get French asparagus?" Victoria asked.

"France," Charles replied offhandedly, as he bit into a scone.

And so it went. Planning the ball. Spending time with her father, making sure she was there for him. Being heartbroken by Jason. And running, running, running to Byrne whenever she could.

Those moments. Those stolen moments were her salvation. She could forget herself then. Forget that her brother was willfully being useless, that her entire house was being turned upside down by Victoria, Charles, and Nevill in the search for the perfect spot to hang draperies, and just be herself.

In fact, she felt as if she were more than herself. She was flying high, a refined, pure version of Jane unseen before. Not the little girl with scraped knees who loved to dance, not the polished debutante with her nose in the air and a penchant for trouble, not the lost daughter—but some new Jane, who discovered the ability to be bold and vulnerable at once, and admit to herself that yes, indeed, she did have freckles . . . and someone who adored them.

Is it any wonder then, that some things began to be missed?

Victoria was remarkably helpful to Jane. Thinking they were on the verge of capturing the highwayman, the girl would wink and nod when Jane told the room she had to go speak with the head gardener about lighting paper lanterns in the trees during the festivities. (Which she did go and do—Jane was not a terribly great liar, but perhaps she exaggerated the time it would take.)

Charles and Nevill would marvel at how that was a wonderful idea, and then write out a note for a messenger to run to Manchester, and not come back until he had purchased several dozen paper lanterns in varying shades, that they could choose from.

Indeed, the committee was making such progress that the ball would likely turn out to be a great success . . . but as the day moved closer, it demanded more and more attention. Jane still managed to find moments to herself, fewer and farther between, but she seemed to make them stretch longer and longer.

She could be missing for another ten minutes, surely. Just enough time to enjoy a quick kiss, an embrace, a ramble in the woods. A hike past the creek, Byrne pointing out a particular species of swan . . . surely another half hour wouldn't hurt.

She missed luncheon once.

She and Byrne played chess. She lost every game.

She missed the tasting of the sample menu for the ball.

She missed Nurse Nancy bemoaning to Dr. Berridge, who had dropped by ostensibly to assist Victoria, that the Duke was not eating as well as he ought.

She missed her brother's attempt to get a fourth at whist after dinner (Hale and Thorndike being too worn out from that day's outdoor activities to join in, instead following the Duke up to bed after supper . . . as Jane was not there to play her evening game of chess).

Until one day, she was too missed to go unnoticed anymore.

They were in Byrne's sitting room when it happened. The small space with a few pieces of widow Lowe's embroidery still gracing the side tables was now covered in papers and drawings. Jane, whose limited artistic talent was marginally better than Byrne's, had drawn a crude map of the area—Merrymere, Reston, the Broadmill River, the fells and roads labeled quickly but legibly.

These past few days had been both the headiest and most frustrating of Byrne's memory. Headiest, because Jane was there, her cinnamon and honeysuckle smell filling the air as effortlessly as her bright energy . . . and most frustrating for exactly the same reason.

"But what I don't understand is how anyone who is in the town can then ride out and attack someone on the road without attracting notice," Jane was saying, looking down at the sketched-out map on the table. She tucked a fallen strand of hair behind her ear, her face a delightful mix of confusion and concentration. And Byrne could not stop looking at her. The way she bit her lip, the way her shoulder worked under the crisp linen of her day dress . . .

"Maybe they ride around Merrymere," Byrne suggested, popping out of his reverie as he came beside Jane and ran his finger along the charcoal coastline. "On the eastern side," he ventured, looking down at her, standing far too close to Jane for either of their comfort.

"But they'd have to cut across the Cottage's lands and come up over the fells," she argued, glancing up to meet his eyes and making him catch his breath.

"Doable when it's necessary," he replied, taking a pencil and tracing a path through the valley between the fells.

"Yes, but annoying to the family whose land he's using as a means of escape." She crossed her arms over her chest in the perfect imitation of a proper schoolteacher who has caught a child cheating.

Byrne smiled but kept his eyes on the map. "One man takes the goods to a secured location, likely south of Reston; the other comes back around the eastern side of the lake, then down the western, and coming into the village from the opposite side, no one's the wiser. Hell, if he's quick, and he's unsettled the victims of his latest attack properly, he might beat them into the town."

He stopped and put a small X on a spot between the fells on the eastern side of the lake. "Here. The valley between the fells. If he comes around this way, then he would have to come through this pass. There's no other option."

"Then that's where we can catch him!" Jane replied, the excitement evident in her voice.

"Where *I* can catch him," Byrne admonished, too pleased by the discovery to truly chastise her. "You promised you wouldn't endanger yourself, remember?"

"Oh all right, where *you* can catch him." Jane rolled her eyes. "But when?"

"Your ball," Byrne answered immediately. "People will be arriving dressed to the nines. It's too much temptation for any highwayman worth his salt to resist."

"You'd have to miss my ball?" Jane asked, her voice surprisingly small.

Byrne took in her disappointment, blushed with it. "It's too good an opportunity to pass up. And if I went to the ball, all I would be doing is thinking about how I missed catching the man and how much I wished I could dance with you."

Jane nodded, stifling a sniffle. "No, you're absolutely right. It's too perfect a chance." She squared her shoulders and smiled at him. "Byrne, this is wonderful! This will finally have the town believing you!"

She threw her arms around him then, enveloped him in honeysuckle and warmth, and really, what else could he do but twirl her and drink in her liveliness?

She laughed as he lifted her off her toes, and spun her around the room, stopping only when he bumped into a table.

"Would you look at that," she breathed, her face mere inches from his.

"What?"

"We're dancing." Jane smiled as she slid down his body, landing lightly on her toes.

He could feel every inch of her, and he knew she could feel every hardened inch of him. But she wasn't frightened this time. She invited him against her, pressed ever so slightly closer . . . and that was the permission he needed.

He swooped down, took her mouth.

It was unbearable, this want, and the need to give in to it. Fearful as he was of igniting her caution, he could not keep his hands off her. Nor could she him. He couldn't help but allow himself to sink into her body, to let his hands graze her breasts, to glory in her hand dropping to his flanks, pulling her into him, and . . .

"Well, I see you two are making progress," Dobbs's voice came from the doorway. Byrne broke away from Jane with a growl, unable to stop her as she skittered to the farthest corner of the room.

Dobbs, willfully oblivious, merely nodded to the maps and papers spread out over the small table, as he dropped his load of firewood by the stove.

"Yes," Byrne said, his voice clipped to the barest edge. "How do you feel about a little reconnaissance work?"

"Eh?" Dobbs brightened. He was always one for an adventure. "When and where?"

"Night after next," Byrne replied, his gaze never leaving Jane's, backed as she was to the other side of the room, her cheeks utterly flushed, her eyes dark and sparkling.

Dobbs came over and began to study the map, his nimble fingers running over the lines of the fells.

"The eastern side, eh?" he mumbled. "This spot here, between the fells?"

"Precisely," Byrne said, never once looking away from Jane.

"Huh." Dobbs shrugged as he grabbed a pail and ambled out the back and headed toward the barn.

". . . I take it he's agreeable to the plan?" Jane asked, her husky voice barely above a whisper.

Byrne nodded, barely. His eyes still locked with hers, each of them unable to move backward or forward. Locked in their current pattern.

"We can't do this anymore, Jane," Byrne said.

"What?" Her face fell in total shock.

"We cannot dance around it. What's between us," he took the barest step forward. She made no move, just stayed where she was, watching his approach with the thrill of a hunted animal. "Does what we share . . . suffice, any longer for you?"

Slowly, steadily, she shook her head. Just once.

"That is because there is more," he breathed. "I want more."

More. He could see the wheels turning in her head. More meant upstairs, in the loft. The softness of his bed. No clothes, no interruptions, no moments stolen from a day busy with planning and projects and a highwayman to catch. Just the two of them together.

"What do you want?" he asked, his voice the only sound in the air. No birds chirped outside the windows, no Dobbs singing to the horses beyond. They were the only two people in the world.

And he saw the moment, watched her eyes go dark with desire, heard her breath hitch, when she realized . . . she wanted more, too.

The smallest squeak from the front door broke their cocoon. Then a soft, hurried knock.

"Hello?" Victoria Wilton's voice came, small and scared as she pushed open the door. "Oh thank goodness!" she cried and ran to Jane.

The tears in the girl's eyes and the pure relief in her face upon finally finding Jane shook Byrne out of his reverie.

"Victoria, what is it?" Jane asked, worried.

"I'm so sorry to interrupt," the words came in a rush, "I know you are working very hard—but your father . . . Jason just got home and saw you weren't there, and your father . . . We didn't know what to do. The Nurse sent me out to find you."

"It's all right, Victoria," Jane soothed the girl briskly. "Byrne, I apologize, I must go."

Jane did not stop as she headed with Victoria to the door. Byrne had to scramble to catch her.

"Jane, what's wrong?"

"It's nothing," Jane covered.

"She said something happened with your father?" he asked. "Is he hurt? Injured?"

"No," Jane replied immediately. Then her forehead creased, and her chin wobbled dangerously. But whatever it was, it lasted only a moment, and soon enough she smiled at him. Polite, strained, but still a smile. "Thank you for your concern. I must be going."

And with that, she was out the door, leaving Byrne asking a single question: What had just happened?

"Victoria, would you be so kind as to go for the doctor?" Jane said, wiping the tears away from her eyes as they beat a hurried path through the woods back to the Cottage.

"They are there already," Victoria said, trotting to keep up with Jane's desperately long strides. "Dr. Berridge had been close by and thought I might like an escort home, when it happened. He sent immediately for Dr. Lawford."

"Charles and Nevill?" Jane asked, whipping through the trees and into the clearing of the Cottage's front lawn.

"They were surprised," Victoria conceded. "The Duke—" She hesitated, not sure how to begin. "Your father—I think they knew that he was growing absentminded in his old age. Everyone understood that. But . . . but he just came into the room and started throwing his food. Saying he had already eaten luncheon, and that the nurses were trying to fool him. He hit one," she whispered. "One of the nurses, with a broken plate. She cut her hand."

Oh God—it was worse than Jane had feared. She had ruefully been hoping that her father had only said something out of turn, had mentioned his wife as if she were living or asked who Charles and Nevill were, but this . . .

Jane should have been there.

How could she be so utterly selfish?

They walked through the front doors of the house, into the stillness that follows pandemonium. Jane glanced into the dining room without stopping, saw the broken plates and spilled food that three maids were now attempting to clean up. She then bounded up the stairs two at a time, with an uncertain Victoria falling behind. Victoria stopped in the foyer, apparently deciding to wait there.

Jane ran into Jason first.

"Where the hell have you been?" Jason asked under his breath.

Jane did not stop moving, did not stop until she got to her father's door and the doctors waiting outside.

"Never mind that," she breathed, arriving in front of Dr. Lawford. "How is he?"

The gray-haired man peered over his spectacles at her. "He's resting. Nurse Nancy managed to convince him to drink some tea, laced with a bit of laudanum. He'll sleep off most of his agitation."

"It's to be expected," Dr. Berridge added, with a nod from his colleague. "His memory loss is progressing. No matter how careful you've been with him of late, these episodes are going to happen."

But she hadn't been careful with him, she thought guiltily. She had been the exact opposite. She had been reckless. She hadn't been there for luncheon, and because of that, he thought luncheon had already occurred . . .

"The house being turned upside down for your ball," Dr. Berridge continued, "he can sense the upheaval. It's not your fault," he addressed Lady Jane but then nodded up to Jason. "Either of you."

Jane, for the first time, looked at her brother—his face wore the bereft, confused, and scared expression that it had when he first witnessed his father's episodes. But there was something else. There was blame.

He blamed her.

She blamed herself.

"Can I see him?" she asked, her voice as calm as she could make it.

The doctors shared a look and then nodded simultaneously. "Just for a few minutes. He's likely asleep; do not wake him."

Jane nodded and with a look to her brother, she ducked into her father's bedchamber.

He looked so small in the oversized, stately bed. Swallowed by gray silk sheets and a feather comforter. She approached the bed penitent, like a child caught at mischief. She had never been so scared to see her father as when she was about to be punished. But this . . . this was worse somehow.

He was sleeping, and she dare not wake him. But she didn't see her father there.

When had he stopped being a parent to her? Stopped being a person? Now, all she could see was her responsibility and how she had failed at it. When had her father morphed from the strong, bold man of her memory into this small, fragile creature? When had she decided to run away from it?

She couldn't do this. She couldn't be this person, who lost all sense and compassion in pursuit of her own pleasures.

"I'm sorry," she breathed, brushing the white hair back from his brow. He breathed lightly, peacefully. As she watched her father breathe in and breathe out, Jane wished, not for the first time, that there was someone who she could lean on. Who she could confide in, and who would know what to do for her father.

She wished her mother were here.

Twenty-one

AFTER Jane rushed out with Victoria, Byrne was left to pace the length of his sitting room for some time, its short distance no strain on his leg, as he worried out what had just occurred, its complexities and implications.

It was a truly rare thing when Byrne Worth did not know what to do. He was used to deciding his course quickly and taking it. But now he was without bearings.

Something was wrong. Lady Jane's reaction at Victoria's arrival was not based in embarrassment over being seen with Byrne but fear when her father was mentioned. It was the second time she had done so. The first time he had thought little of it, only that it had prevented her from entering his house. But now—now it was the first piece of a larger puzzle.

And this time, she had rushed off, shutting Byrne out as effectively as if he had never existed.

In his old life, as the Blue Raven, this lack of existence never irked him. Hell, it proved useful. Slipping into the shadows, standing on the edges of life—it let him watch, step back, and see the whole picture. But this—he was too close in. Too worried that his actions were causing her to be as skittish and frightened as a newborn colt. Too entrenched with Jane to be able to tell at a glance what was bothering her and what to do about it.

Byrne's head snapped up. Of course, it was too simple. What this situation required was some reconnaissance.

"Dobbs!" Byrne yelled. "We're going out."

It wasn't terribly difficult for Dobbs to amble up next to the Cottage's stables, ask a few easy questions while pretending to pick a rock out of his horse's shoe. The stable lads there were willing to lend a pick when necessary, as well as gossip, and by the time Dobbs led his horse away back onto the road toward Reston, they had completely forgotten he had been there.

Nor was it terribly difficult for Byrne, upon being relayed the information that the commotion in the house was located abovestairs, and that the Marquis had come home in a lather, and once Jane had arrived, left in one, to skulk around the side of the large manor house undetected, as everyone who might be outside was requisitioned within.

What was more difficult was climbing the side of the Cottage, its smooth stone face offering little to no foothold, as he moved from terrace balustrade to window frame, to second-floor balcony, which ran the length of the lake-facing side of the building. Once he nearly lost his balance and had to hook his cane around a banister for support, but he managed, and silently, too.

The family rooms would afford views of the water, he guessed. And wherever Jane was, so would answers be.

He found her in what must have been the Duke's rooms. He peered through the window, watched as she sat on his bed, her back straight and proud. She took a cup of broth handed to her from a nurse, brought a spoon of it to his lips. The old man shook his head weakly, forcing Jane to placate him into taking a sip. After a few spoonfuls, she put the cup of broth aside, tenderly fussed about the Duke's pillows, tucked him in, watched until he fell asleep.

Byrne knew instantly when he saw it.

The same tightly wound expression. The same buried pain, only now—when her father couldn't see—making its way to the surface. It was the same as when he first spied her, all those months ago, at the Hampshire Racing Party. The concealed strain, and grief. But there was something new now, something frightened.

She watched her father continuously. And Byrne watched her. Minutes on end, an hour. The sun began to dip lower into the afternoon sky, and yet they remained at their vigil: Jane watching the Duke rest, breathing evenly, Byrne watching Jane from outside the window.

And then a shaft of sunlight angled through the opposite window, warming Jane's back, setting her hair on fire as surely as tinder. She sat up, taken out of her reverie. She looked around.

And she saw him.

Her eyes locked onto his, never once betraying his position, kneeling at the base of the window, never uttering a sound. But her eyes—those dark lost pools, they told him everything.

They met at the creek. The sun setting red and orange, turning the lake beyond the trees into silken ribbons of pink and coral, lapping gently on the shore. They made no plans to meet there, but he must have known she would take this path to his door—the cowardly long way around, instead of the quick lakeside route, delaying the inevitable. He was waiting on the bench stone when she arrived.

She saw him outside her father's window long before she had met his eye. He had remained remarkably still, crouched there. His leg must have ached horribly. None of the other people in the room, not Nurse Nancy, and certainly not her father, noticed the interloper spying through the window. Just Jane. But then, she had always managed to see him. At the assembly. At the lake. Even as far back as the Hampshire Racing Party, she had managed to pick Byrne out of a crowd, her eye drawn to him like a moth toward light.

But now, sitting beside him on the stone, the creek babbling beneath their feet, Jane couldn't look him in the eye.

And so, after some moments, it was Byrne who spoke first.

"How long has he been ill?" he asked dispassionately.

"A while," Jane answered. "At first it was just as if he were . . . older. He would forget little things but then remember them. But then he began to forget bigger things."

Byrne held quiet, waiting, watching. Which was something he was very good at, Jane thought with bleak humor.

"He's still himself most of the time. But sometimes . . . today—" Jane didn't think she would be able to continue on that train of conversation, so she stopped. Taking a deep breath, she continued. "None of the doctors in London gave us any hope. So my brother and I brought him up here, to keep him away from the eyes of the world during the Season. To tend to him."

She let the silence fall between them, held there for some moments.

"I get the impression," Byrne replied at length, "that you do most of the tending."

"He has nurses," Jane replied defensively. But it was a weak defense, she knew. And so did Byrne.

"Why didn't you tell me?" he asked, finally turning his face to meet hers.

"I don't know," her voice was so small, it was barely a whisper.

"I mean it, Jane, why? I would have tried to help, or . . ."

"Because I didn't want you to know!" Jane cried, standing up, turning away, pacing. "Because I wanted to keep something of my own. Don't you understand? I needed to escape to a place where my father, my brother, they don't exist."

"And my house is that place," Byrne concluded. "But if it was making you unhappy—"

"It's the only place I *was* happy!" she replied despairingly.

"It doesn't work that way, Jane," Byrne stood, following her. "Take it from someone who knows about leading a double life and keeping hard secrets. There is no true escape. You don't get to break yourself in *half* running from one life to the other. They will bleed into each other, and something will fall through the cracks."

Something. That something being her father, she thought ruefully. And her peace of mind.

"You told me I could run to you," Jane replied after a time.

He looked at her then, nodding to acknowledge the truth of what she said. "I did. And that was selfish of me. I offered you a peaceful refuge because I wanted to see you. Steal as much time as I could."

Jane's heart leaped when he said that, his declaration of desire as potent as most men's poetry. Perhaps they could remain as they were, Jane could still hide at his house, they could still enjoy each other's company . . .

Then he said, "But I thought your problems were limited to too many houseguests."

Foolish hopes, Jane knew. And ones she couldn't entertain to begin with, thanks to her lies of omission. Everything was all her fault, it seemed. Suddenly Jane felt red sparks of anger behind her eyes. No, it wasn't.

"If I had told you about my father," she asked, rounding on him, her shoulders squaring, "what would you have done?"

Byrne's eyebrow went up.

"You would have told me to go home, and not see you again, correct?" Jane filled in for him.

". . . Probably," he acknowledged after a time.

"Because it's what would be best for me, of course. So you'd send me away and go back to living in your little house, in your little life, wrapped up in your own problems with no thought to the outside world." Jane began to rant, pacing as she spoke, knowing that Byrne only followed her with his eyes. "And if you gave yourself permission to crawl back into yourself, those tentative steps you'd been taking out into the world again forgotten, well, who is there to argue? Certainly not Jane."

She cocked her head to one side, regarded him. "I get angry with my brother for abdicating his duties, for not working, for going out and being a fool with his friends. But at least he lives in the world. At least he doesn't hide."

He didn't answer her. Instead his gaze bored into hers, those ice blue eyes blazing with suppressed fury.

"Maybe that's why I didn't tell you," she decided, closing the gap between them, her gaze narrowed, scrutinizing. "Because if I did, you would send me away—not for my own good, but because in Byrne's little house, in his little life, with his half a bottle of laudanum, no one is allowed to be broken but you."

She stood toe to toe with him, and from the fire in the gaze, barely contained fury, she thought (briefly and uncharitably) that he might hit her. She couldn't blame him if he did—she didn't know what possessed her to say what she did, to go as far as she did . . . but it didn't matter. Because at that moment, shaking with energy, he reached out and touched her.

Softly, tenderly. As if she would shatter . . . and she very well might. His hand caressed her cheek, his thumb dancing over her full lower lip, and oh, how she wanted him to kiss her. She wanted him to crush her to him, and to just take. To take all this shaking madness and anger and argument that coursed through her and through him and smother them into the ground. And for one, full, long, frightening and glorious moment, it looked like he would.

Instead, he leaned down, and with infinite restraint, placed the most chaste of all kisses on her forehead, and said, "Go home, Jane."

And whatever illusions she had about their friendship and their time together fell apart, revealing the hardest of truths.

"Of . . . of course," she whispered, pulling away from him, out of his reach. Because if he touched her again, she would die from it, she was sure. "Good-bye," she said, turning, and before she could stop herself, walked away.

As she made her way back to the Cottage, she held back any tears that might threaten to fall, by thinking of the absolute logic of this conclusion.

She needed to be with her family now. And if he refused her because of that, well, then damn him anyway. As she climbed the steps to the Cottage, met at the door by the butler, telling her supper was waiting, she knew she had returned to her rightful place.

After all, they had known it would end. It would simply be a few days earlier than expected.

They were never meant for more than the summer.

Byrne sat by the creek as night fell. For once, he didn't want to go back to his little house and his little life. He had a feeling that what had once felt cozy and safe would now seem empty.

Jane had made a rather cruel and astute point—that he was hiding from life.

But he had been making progress, hadn't he?

You really think so? That little voice came back, and Byrne rolled his eyes in the dusky light.

"Yes, I do," he countered, his voice echoing against the creek. He'd gone to the assembly. He'd been trying to be kind to everyone in the street. He'd . . .

When's the last time you wrote to your brother? Or bought a new shirt? Or paid a call? No, you just shut yourself up in your little house, just like she said.

But it's not the same! he thought vehemently. I'm . . .

You're what? That little voice shot back. *Broken?*

Byrne remained silent, unable to reply to that.

Are you broken anymore? The voice needled.

No. He realized it, and it made him so calm. No, he wasn't. For the first time in a very long time, Byrne felt whole. He felt able to venture out into the world.

So why was he holding back? What was keeping him in his little house? What was making him give Jane back to her world without a fight? Why had he ever agreed to let her go?

Why do you keep that half bottle of laudanum?

It was fully dark now, twilight giving way to stars. Byrne looked up, and through the trees, he managed to find the Big Dipper in the inky black sky.

And he made a decision.

He went back home, did not pause at the table of papers in the sitting room, did not answer Dobbs as he asked if they were ready to head out to the Oddsfellow Arms for supper that evening. He went up the stairs, pried open the floorboard, and pulled out the satchel hidden therein.

Then, marching down the stairs and out the front door, he came to stand at the edge of the water.

For too long, he had let Jane feed him. He'd taken her energy, her vibrancy, without thinking what it might have cost her.

As he poured out the remaining golden liquid into the lake, those precious drops falling away, becoming lost in the water, he decided it was time for him to become the man Jane needed.

The next day was terribly hectic at the Cottage. It was the day before the ball, and on top of all the preparations, and every different faction of the party (culinary, musical, decorations, accommodations, gardens) having some form of catastrophe occur (the gardener in particular nearly incited homicide when it was suggested that the stakes and pitch for the game of horseshoes be removed), the household had to tiptoe around the Duke's health and his daughter's careful watch over it.

For her part, Jane's emotions were equally divided between hovering with mad attention to detail and listless with despair. No, *despair* may be too harsh a word. Apathetic maybe, possibly bereft, but Jane refused to despair. She was too much like her own mother, in that whatever challenge faced her, she would sigh for five seconds, then square her shoulders and face it. However, it was more difficult to square her shoulders knowing that she had nothing to look forward to.

The plans for the ball did not hold her interest—in fact, they never really could. But before, she had tried, to please her brother, Victoria, the entirety of the town. But now, it just lost all its color to her. The breathless anticipation everyone else felt translated solely to nerves for her. Charles and Nevill's assistance was proving invaluable, but when the two got into a fight about which year port should be served (Charles insisting on the '93 and Nevill adamant for the

'91), they went to their rooms for an hour to sulk, leaving Jane to talk them out again.

She was softly knocking on Charles's door, begging him to come out, when Jason happened by, riding crop in hand.

"Where do you think you're going?" Jane asked, eyeing him apathetically.

"Out of this madhouse," Jason replied, as a footman and two maids carrying table linens made their way past him in the hall. Jason then knocked on Charles's door. "Charles!" he barked. "I'm going for a ride. Come along!"

There was no response from within, just the sound of feet shuffling on carpet.

Jason shrugged at Jane. Then Jane spied a footman carrying an armful of cut roses, and pounded on Charles's door. "Charles, the flowers have arrived!"

The door opened immediately.

"Good! Just in time. Did they bring only long cut roses, or did they happen to include wildflowers like we requested?" Charles said as he stepped out of the room, straightened his coat, and went off in pursuit of the blooms, without waiting for a reply.

Immediately thereafter, Nevill emerged from his rooms, obviously having heard Jane's latest news. "Flowers are here? If Charles tries to put in his accursed wildflowers . . ." he grumbled, and set off after his brother.

Whether or not he even noticed Jason standing there was a matter for debate.

"What have you done to my friends?" Jason asked once Nevill was gone, bewildered. Then, shaking his head, he said, "Well, at least you're keeping busy. Ta, Sis."

As Jason whistled his way down the hall, Jane called after him. "We haven't touched the library," she ventured, causing her brother to turn. "We've left that room closed to the party. That is, if you wanted to seek refuge there, I'm sure Hale and Thorndike would be happy to get to working." At his silence, she tried a new tack. "Or, if you seek company on your ride, you could go with Father."

"Father?" Jason's head shot up.

"He's feeling much better today. And he used to love to ride. I'm sure he would appreciate it."

Jason looked for a moment as if he considered the prospect, but then simply shook his head. "No, it might rain." It was cloudless. "Besides, I'd have to get a mount for his nurse, too . . ."

"You'd be with him; he'd be all right without his nurse for an hour." Jane didn't know if this was strictly true, but was willing to chance it. Jason had not spent so much as five minutes in their father's company alone that summer. Nor had he begun his study with the stewards. If he chose either option, Jane would have been elated. But Jason shuffled his feet and backed away.

"It wouldn't be a very good ride for Father," he muttered. "Besides, you're so much better with him than I am . . ." he trailed off dumbly, his body already halfway down the hall, fleeing. "I'll see you later."

And Jane was left alone again, amid the chaos.

Victoria needed her attentions in the kitchen—the cook kept shifting the menu to accommodate the latest count of people who would be attending. The stables were having difficulty preparing for all of the carriages they expected. Charles and Nevill were likely to kill each other in increments with rose thorns, but whereas Jane may have been running here and there, solving one crisis and blundering another, her mind was constantly on her father.

He had awoken this morning, after a rather tumultuous night, his mind again his own, and horrified that he had put his family through any ordeal. Dr. Lawford had come by shortly thereafter and determined that the Duke was fit enough to resume his daily schedule of exercise and activities.

Jane didn't want to leave her father's side, no matter how much Nurse Nancy assured her it was all right, that he would be fine taking his exercise today without Jane, knowing she had a million other things to do. But even so, knowing that her father was in good hands, Jane couldn't help but want to oversee every tiny detail of his comfort. Making certain the soup was to his liking, that he was comfortably occupied, that the stress of the preparations for the ball would not disturb him again.

This made her very short with everyone else.

"For the last time, Charles, I do not care about the year of the port!" she yelled, rubbing her hands over her eyes. Apparently the flower argument had been easily solved, and they were back to the Great Port Debate of 1816. Charles had gone so far as to put the two bottles side by side, and make everyone in the room taste each to decide which was best.

"The '93 is superior!" he argued.

"But the '91 will finish much better after a roast!" Nevill argued back.

Jane was about to knock together the heads of the two men who a mere week ago were her party-planning saviors, when a deep rumbling voice came from the door.

"Why not serve both?"

All eyes turned and saw Byrne Worth, standing in the foyer, dressed in what had to be his finest morning coat and breeches, cane in hand. It was so idiosyncratic to see him in anything other than shirtsleeves that Jane had to blink twice before she remembered herself enough to be shocked at his arrival in general.

"You can offer up the '91 or the '93 as a choice, and let the public decide," Byrne continued, as he entered the dining room, where the debate raged.

While Charles and Nevill considered this simplest of options that they had managed to not think of, Jane went to Byrne.

"What are you doing here?" she whispered.

He shrugged. "You said I was welcome anytime," he replied with a smile.

"I did?"

"Yes, you did." Byrne winked, then said low, "Or do I need to remind you of every word from your lips during our swimming lesson?"

Jane's pallor dropped instantly, turning a shade of white heretofore unseen outside of the Himalayas.

"I say, Jane, are you all right?" Charles ventured over, two glasses of port in hand, discriminatingly taking tastes out of each.

"I'm quite well," Jane replied.

"Maybe you should try the port," Nevill added, his eyebrow going up. "Get your color back up. Mr. Worth," he turned to Byrne, bowing.

"Mr. Worth is it?" Charles said, and then, quizzically, "Byrne Worth? Do I know you from somewhere?"

"Yes." Nevill rolled his eyes. "We accused him of having robbed us. A pleasure to see you again." He nodded to Byrne.

"No, that's not it," Charles replied, trailing off into his own memory, trying to decide where he knew Byrne from.

Byrne smirked and bowed to Nevill. "Tea, I think, would be better for Lady Jane than port," he replied. "Jasmine blend, correct?"

Twenty-two

O VER the course of the next two hours, Byrne managed to organize it so every single difficulty that arose regarding the ball was taken care of. No longer did they run to and from one crisis to another, everyone looking to Jane to provide the final say. Instead, they sat in the drawing room, tea and scones at the ready, all in a row. Victoria, Nevill, Charles, Jane, and Byrne, who with the assistance of tea and port, held court on all difficulties that were brought their way.

The cook said she needed at least three more servers and an assistant for the pastry chef to make the tarts for tomorrow's dessert. She claimed her niece was ready and able to take the position.

The tribunal deliberated, and the request was granted.

The stable lads needed room for all the extra horses they expected. Byrne suggested establishing a small section of the woods by the stables to tie up any extra horses.

A dozen heart-stopping, party-ending questions, a dozen simple answers. Jane's particular favorite was when one of the kitchen staff was worried about purchasing enough fish for the fish course, Victoria was the first to point out that there was a lake right outside the front door, full of fish for the catching.

"Honestly," Nevill laughed as he sipped his port-laced tea. "You'd think they'd never thrown a party before."

"They haven't," Jane replied. "The older staff, yes. When my mother threw parties, they were here, but it was only once a year. The newer staff are as inexperienced in executing a ball as we are planning it."

"Speak for yourself!" Charles cried, with Nevill nodding.

This camaraderie in the midst of chaos continued as the Duke joined them for the rest of tea—adding his voice to his appreciation for the octet (who had arrived unexpectedly a full day early and were unable to get rooms in Reston, as they were fully booked due to the ball) when they obliged him with a quick reel, which he danced with his daughter, to the delight of the entire room.

The newfound pleasantness continued on into supper, where Jason joined them.

Jason was shocked by Byrne's presence, to say the least.

They were seated in the dining room, everyone except Victoria, who had been summoned home for supper at her house. The meal was simple, to allow the cook to prepare tomorrow night's opulence, and the mood merry. That is, of course, until Jason decided to question Byrne.

"Mr. Worth," he said, as he violently sipped a spoonful of soup—if one could do so violently, "why have you decided to grace us with your presence today?"

"A long overdue call," Byrne replied smoothly, smiling charmingly at the assembled party—all of whom had paused mid-soup to hear his reply. "I should have paid my respects to your family when you first arrived, but was remiss."

"I promise you it was unnecessary," Jason replied through gritted teeth. "After all, we've already met."

The audience's eyes shifted back to Byrne.

"But I had not called upon your father. He has the right to know who is living on his grounds," Byrne said. "Besides, I was aware of the commotion here and thought I could lend a quiet hand."

"And he did, too!" Charles interjected. "In fact, we were at raw ends until he showed up!"

"Indeed," Nevill drawled. "Came in and commanded everything. Almost makes me feel sorry for mistakenly accusing you of thievery."

Byrne tipped his glass to Nevill, who raised his back.

"They thought you a thief?" the Duke asked, his eyebrows rising in surprise.

"Yes, it's how we were introduced," Nevill supplied.

"Why does no one tell me these things?" the Duke replied. "I haven't had a good bit of gossip in ages."

"I never believed him a thief, Father," Jane spoke up, and gave a pointed look to Jason. "Neither did Jason, which is why we didn't mention it."

"It's an easy mistake to make," Byrne interjected. "I'm not well known in the community. And, after all, it's not as if man is ever above such things."

"You consider yourself capable of disreputable acts?" Jason interjected, his eyes narrowing and then sliding to the side, to his sister.

"Jase, don't get us started on your disreputable acts!" Charles sniggered. "There was that one time, in . . . where was it, Barcelona, that—"

"Thank you, Charles," Jason said sharply, eliciting no small amount of giggles from the table.

"All humor aside," Byrne said, his gaze never leaving Jason's quickly reddening face, "yes, I consider myself capable of disreputable acts. When I was in the army, I did things for King and Country that I would rather not own. But I've moved past them."

"Besides," the Duke said, "you were under obligation to the Crown. Whatever sins you committed were for the protection of this country. There is a difference between sinning for something and sinning for idleness or greed. Which is what this highwayman must be doing." A surprised look from his daughter had the Duke saying, "Yes, I know all about the highwayman. Except that this young man was accused of it. For heaven's sake, child, I have ears."

But that aside did not avert the staring match between Jason and Byrne.

"But what about during peacetime?" Jason asked, not even deterred by the changing of the courses. "How would you assuage yourself of guilt over disreputable acts committed then?"

Byrne held his gaze level with Jason. "I don't know," he said slowly. "How do you?"

Before Jason's face could turn more florid, Mr. Thorndike thankfully changed the subject.

"Mr. Worth, you say you were in the army?" he asked, biting into his lamb with fervor. "Then surely you must be familiar with the game of horseshoes."

Byrne nodded appreciatively. "I am. A few boys in the Seventeenth Regiment learned the game from their American cousins. Everyone was wild for it . . . I know more than one soldier who lost his week's pay on that game."

"Well, then you must indulge us in a round!" Thorndike cried, and Charles and Nevill joined in. For his part, Hale rolled his eyes. "After dinner. There's a pitch out back."

"Thank you, but I thought I might challenge His Grace to a game of chess after dinner."

"I'll take you on, Thorndike," Nevill said. "Don't look so sad."

The Duke's ears perked up. "I would happily accept your challenge, Mr. Worth." Then he turned to his daughter. "You don't mind, do you? Jane is my usual partner," he explained, "but she's not terribly skilled at it."

"No, she's not," Byrne agreed, earning himself a shocked and annoyed look from Jane. The Duke began laughing, and Jane soon enough joined in. However, no one seemed to notice that Byrne had made an alarming admission of familiarity. No one, that is, except a livid Jason.

After dinner, Byrne and the Duke played a very intense game of chess, and Jason watched his sister as she wrote on a piece of paper, checking things off a list . . . presumably for the ball tomorrow.

She seemed glad to be getting to it, Jason thought, humming to herself with every check mark, but she kept sneaking glances toward where their father and their uninvited guest were locked in a battle of wits. As Byrne began rolling his cane between his hands, studying the board, Jason watched Jane smile wistfully.

His stomach turned.

Damn it all, planning the ball was supposed to keep her *away* from him. But somehow their connection had not been strained; instead, it had deepened. Obviously she had been with him when Father had his episode yesterday, but that hadn't deterred her from mooning over the man today.

Damn it, he should have just sent Jane away when he first overheard their . . . swimming. But he couldn't do that. He couldn't be left alone with his father. And now with the ball . . .

He would just have to remove Mr. Worth, he thought as he narrowed his eyes shrewdly.

Which should be simple enough.

The chess game finally ended. Byrne Worth placed his king down, conceding defeat.

"I thought I had you for a moment there," Byrne said, rising from his seat.

"You brought out your queen too early," the Duke replied as he wiped his forehead with a handkerchief. "But I will admit there was a moment of fear when you cornered me and I had to castle." He then turned to his daughter. "Jane, you could learn a few things from this young man here."

Jane shared a smile with Byrne. "I'm sure I could."

Jason nearly groaned aloud.

Luckily, Nurse Nancy chose that moment to discreetly nod to Jane, who went over and took her father's arm. Those two had a rhythm worked out, Jason realized, as Jane steered her father out of the room, after good nights were exchanged with Mr. Worth.

Leaving Jason alone with Byrne.

"You must be a very skilled player," Jason commented, smiling. No reason to be unpleasant about the matter. Yet. "To nearly best my father."

"*Nearly* being the operative word," Byrne replied, coming to sit in one of the high-backed wing chairs by the low embers of the fireplace. It was still too warm for a full blaze, but no one wanted to keep the Duke cold.

Jason wandered over to the sideboard. "I've never beaten my father at chess. Jane only wins when he lets her. If you had actually managed to triumph, I would have had to accuse you of cheating. Care for a brandy?"

"Certainly," Byrne replied without missing a beat. "But I wouldn't have cheated. It would be a disreputable act."

"Ah yes," Jason replied. "Disreputable acts. In peacetime, no less." He came and sat in the chair opposite Byrne, handed him a short glass of brandy. "I'm curious: What would you say qualifies as a disreputable act?"

Byrne shrugged. "Besides cheating and thieving? Lying."

"Fighting?" Jason supplied.

"Idleness?"

"Seduction."

Byrne regarded Jason for a moment, a slight smirk on his face. "Now we come to the point."

"I know you have an interest in my sister," Jason said, lounging in his chair. "But you should be aware, she's a flirt. Always has been up to mischief. You shouldn't take her seriously."

"No?" he answered. "Someone should."

"She's a Duke's daughter, used to getting her way, but she knows her place—that she will end up with someone of import. And I won't have a summer romance ruining that. She's passing time with you, nothing more."

"If that's the case, why would you feel the need to warn me away?"

"I simply think it's to her benefit if you are aware of the circumstances." Jason idly sipped his brandy. "And it could be to your benefit as well."

Byrne paused in lifting his drink to his lips. "To my benefit? How?"

"Perhaps you'd like to find a house in a less isolated corner of the world. And I've been thinking of reintegrating the widow Lowe's house back into our property. Fifty thousand pounds would go a long way toward both ends."

The little house wasn't worth five thousand pounds, and both men knew it.

Byrne's eyebrows shot up. "But, my lord, what on earth would I do with a hundred thousand pounds?"

"Don't get greedy," Jason snapped. "The offer is for fifty, an immense sum—one that could buy *this* house."

"I know it's an immense sum. I wasn't being greedy, I was simply adding. You see," he said with a smile that made Jason's own falter, "I already have fifty thousand pounds in the bank. If I haven't spent that, how on earth would you expect me to spend another fifty?"

"How . . . but you live in that little shack!" Jason exclaimed, but Byrne just shrugged.

"I was very good at what I did for the army. Now"—he leaned forward, his smile gone—"what is between me and your sister, remains between me and your sister. And in no way does it qualify as a disreputable act. Not in my eyes and not in hers." He looked daggers at Jason then, his gaze steady and unnerving. "I am appalled that you can dismiss her needs so easily. Yes, you have," Byrne said before Jason could argue. "You say she's used to getting her own way, but I don't think she's had her own way in quite some time. I came here today to try to be a friend to Jane, to help her—she bears the weight of the world on her shoulders, and you do nothing to assist. In fact, you hinder, you hide—you leave her to take care of everything, while you avoid doing the most basic of tasks that are asked of you. Idleness," he added. "That's your disreputable act."

"Don't you dare judge me so!" Jason jumped out of his chair. "I came up here at Jane's insistence, putting my own life on hold . . ."

"What life?" Byrne asked. "Riding? Getting sotted with your friends? From what I've seen, you've done that here."

"I'm just trying to have some fun," Jason said defensively. When had the conversation turned on him so? "You're only young once."

"I told you when we met to grow up, remember?" Byrne countered calmly. "Likely not; you were drunk. Well, grow up now. Take your place. You are done being young. Be a man now. For your father. For Jane's sake." And then under his breath, he added, "And so will I."

Byrne shot down the last sip of his brandy, stood, and walked to the door. "Thank you for dinner. I'm afraid I must be going."

And with that, Byrne left. Left Jason sitting alone, with his words echoing in the room, against his brain . . .

. . . and up the chimney.

Jane, having far more curiosity than any lady of quality should, once she ascertained her father was comfortable and Nancy had everything in hand, rushed to the chimney of the second-floor family rooms, where she hoped she would be able to catch a word or two of Byrne and her brother's conversation.

She was not disappointed.

Jane had spent the majority of the afternoon and evening in a state of awe. Byrne, showing up out of nowhere, after she had been so terribly mean to him the day before, forcing together the two worlds that she had worked so hard to keep separate, exposing her sham.

And he had fit. She had no idea how difficult tonight was for him, but he never showed any strain, and he *fit* perfectly. He was kind and understanding but not pitying to her father. He was entertaining and charming with her guests. He saw her at her absolute wit's end with the preparations for the party, and instead of running and hiding as anyone sane would do, he stepped in and helped. He took a look at the shape of her life, and contorted himself into the voids that she didn't even know were there—but remained himself. It wasn't some man intent to please her and win over her family, sending flowers and flirting artfully. It was Byrne. It was all Byrne.

She may have spent the majority of the day in awe, but it wasn't until she was kneeling by a cold and empty fireplace, listening to her brother parse words with Byrne below, that she was at turns appalled by her brother, her face burning with shame, and then an overwhelming sense of protection and hope at Byrne's words. And then, she knew.

She was in love with him.

She could hear the voices fade as they moved away from the fire. She strained, listening for the click of the door. Then she ran out of the room.

She reached the top of the staircase just as the front door closed behind Byrne.

She should run after him, shouldn't she? She should fly down the stairs and try to catch him before he rode home.

But she didn't. She held still, at the top of the staircase, with the realization of love falling like leaves around her, and she simply stared at the front door in complete shock.

As she stood there, she saw her brother emerge from the drawing room, cross and brooding. He didn't notice her watching as he called out to one of the footmen. "Send Mr. Hale and Mr. Thorndike to me. I'll be in the library," he said authoritatively.

"Certainly, sir," the footman replied. "May I tell them what you require of them?"

"I require them to show me the accounts!" Jason growled. "It's what they're here for."

With that, the door to the library closed, and Jason in it. The footman abandoned the hall.

And Jane abandoned the stairs.

She fled the house, flying across the grounds. She could hear the men at horseshoes in the back of the house, but it gave her no pause.

She found the path along the shore with a lifetime's worth of practice, knowing each footfall, every time to duck and avoid a branch. She moved so quickly, she came into the clearing of widow Lowe's house in no less than ten minutes, guided by the moonlight, and did not stop moving until she stood before Byrne's door. And knocked.

No one answered.

She knocked again. Again, no one answered.

Jane became very aware of the awkwardness of it all. What if he was avoiding her? What if he knew it was she and he didn't want to see her? What if he had fallen asleep immediately? She couldn't imag-

ine walking back to the Cottage without telling him . . . without seeing him . . .

"Jane?" She turned and saw Byrne standing behind her, still in his
coat, cane in hand.

She started laughing, relieved. "You took the creek path—the long
way around?" she asked, breathless.

"Yes," he acknowledged. "And you took the lake path."

She nodded, smiling, her breath still coming in heavy gulps from
the run over—which had caused her to beat him here.

"What are you doing here?" he asked, his expression wary as he
climbed the steps, came to stand right next to her, right above her.
Her mouth went dry. She hadn't been this near to him all day, and
suddenly, Jane wanted nothing more than to get closer.

"I . . ." she said, her voice a rasp on the wind, "I came to kiss you
good night."

He took another step closer, his eyes never leaving hers, as he
shook his head. "No."

"No?" she squeaked.

The corners of his mouth lifted, as he pulled her to him and
whispered.

"Not yet."

Twenty-three

THERE were words to be said. Simple words, holding words, words that turned lives on the point of a pin . . . but they would not be said tonight. Tonight, words felt cheap and gaudy. Words would not do for what was between them. Only action, and purpose, and the vast comfort of a blanket of stars.

They could only see each other. The night sky evaporated, the stairs under their feet. Byrne's hand at the small of her back pressed her against him, but he didn't kiss her. Not yet. He just looked. Looked into the face of the most beautiful woman he'd ever seen, luminescent, lit by stars. Watched her eyes change in the dark . . . go from wonder to confusion to desire in the space of a moment.

He couldn't help but smile.

She smiled back.

Because she knew.

Their eyes remained locked as he slowly reached past her and opened the front door behind her. Jane had nothing to lose. She had exposed herself entirely, coming here. She had known full well the ending they had in store and rushed to greet it, and him, anyway. She wanted this. This look in his eyes, this deep focus on what he held, this strange and yet utterly familiar sensation that shot down from her shoulders and pooled where his fingers lay, where their bodies pressed together.

She took the step back, into the darkness of the little house. He did not let her go, and instead followed, leading her as if dancing. It was pitch-black in the small sitting room, and Byrne was certain he was going to bump into a side table or a chair, but his equilibrium and memory found him, maneuvered him and Jane to the base of the stairs that led to his spare loft. Not once did he let go of her, break contact. It would have destroyed them . . . cool air shattering them back to reality.

Byrne stopped at the bottom of the stairs. Paused. He reached out and touched the side of her face, and she leaned into his palm. But it was too dark, and he needed to see her. Needed to see if certainty still reigned in her eyes. Slowly, he hung his cane over the end of the banister, pulled at the knot of his heavy cloak, let it pool on the floor at their feet. He chanced his whole soul then and let go of her, removing his hand from her waist. She could pull away now, if she wanted. She could seek the sanity of space.

She didn't.

He reached over and struck a match, the flare of light burning their eyes for the briefest moment. They both flinched away from it. He lit a candle that rested on the small shelf along the wall—useful for when you wanted to find your way up the stairs late at night, and useful now. The candle burned between them, and Byrne sought her eyes—and momentarily panicked.

Even in the candlelight, it was too dark. Her eyes too dark, the night too dark, the room too dark to read what she truly felt. All he knew was they were set wide, vulnerable. Intent.

Calm.

Then she took the candle from his hands. And in answer to a million unspoken questions and one in particular, her eyes never leaving his, she took the first step of the staircase. And the next. And the next.

It was a fractional second of unending relief, before the stark realization settled in that there was far too much room between them, and so he followed. Caught up. Breathed in that honeysuckle scent of her hair that proved more intoxicating that the sweetest liquor, the strongest medicine.

They reached the top of the staircase, the small loft, where the soft bed was made with patchwork quilts, a slight breeze from the open window the only reminder of the world beyond their own. Byrne and Jane were alone. None of the ordinary sounds—the creak of a servant's footsteps on the floor or the rattle of carriage wheels could reach their ears and rip them from their cocoon.

The rush of noiselessness enveloped them, and Byrne could think of no reason not to kiss her any longer.

This raw want, from a day spent in her company, unable to reach out and hold, made him ravenous. As for Jane, the whole of the afternoon and evening, counting the times his arm had accidentally brushed hers, the number of moments she had caught him looking at her mouth, was finally, *finally* being acted upon. It wasn't her imagination or her wandering daydreams. It was real, and what they both wanted.

It was more.

His mouth tore at hers, a configuration both normal and new to them. He lifted her off her feet, held her to him. She used her free hand to support herself on his shoulders, clinging with all the strength she had, holding nothing back. She squeaked once, jerked. Their heads broke apart, their nearness mourned for the space of time necessary to realize Jane had hurt herself—still holding the candle, their jostling had caused the wax to spill over onto her hand. Byrne set her on her feet, took the candle from her poor, injured hand. He kissed said hand gently, the white wax cooling rapidly on her skin, then placed the candle on the small table covered with books, by the stuffed chair. Then he returned his attentions to Jane.

Fumbling brought out their humor. Her nervous fingers danced lightly on his shoulders, pushing back his coat; his hands tried like hell to work open the ridiculously small buttons at the back of her dress. They stopped, caught their breath, sought each other's eyes.

And then they laughed. Giggled like schoolchildren caught at mischief. Little kisses on her eyes, the corners of her mouth—devouring her by inches brought them back to themselves, to the moment, the candlelight, and the patchwork bed in the corner of the room.

He danced her to the edge of that bed. Byrne felt his hands shake as he dropped them to his sides. He would not press her into the mattress, as every nerve in his body begged him to. No, he couldn't do that. He couldn't have her here by his will; she had to be here by hers. She had come to his door, she had climbed his stairs, all on her own. And now, looking into her eyes, he asked her to take this next and last step on her own. He held perfectly still as she went on tiptoe and kissed him deeply, reverently.

And then, her eyes never leaving his, she sat on the bed, inviting him to join her.

The next came quickly. His jacket was thrown to the side. His cravat torn away, finally allowing him to take the deep, gulping breaths he desperately needed to fuel his blood. His shoes clunked to the floor, discordant sounds that made her grin. But when he knelt before her, her attention became fixed. The pinpricks of awareness stilled any smiles, because up until this point, she knew basically what to expect. Now, with the simple motion of kneeling before her, Jane came to the startling realization that they were headed deep into unknown territory.

She sucked in her breath as he removed her slippers. First one, then the other, he tossed them over his shoulder with a wicked smile. His finger ran over her silk stocking lightly, up from her ankle, to her knee, making her shiver. He found the garter, tied just above her knee, and slowly pulled at the ends. As his fingers caressed the now-naked back of her knees, he watched as Jane's chest rose and fell rapidly . . . and when he slid the stocking down her leg, she stopped breathing entirely. Byrne couldn't help but feel mildly triumphant. He'd been racking his brain, since the moment he'd seen her standing on his porch, trying to remember the flair and ease he used to have with women.

Stockings had always been one of his better tricks.

By the time he was done with the second stocking, Jane was certain she was drunk. She'd had too much wine with dinner. Too many sips of Charles's port. Because her legs were inching open, allowing him access to her skin, as his lips replaced the brush of his fingers. On her ankle, her calf, her knee. He pushed her gown up, watered silk rasping against skin. And she felt every fraction. His lips reached her inner thigh, and she had to bite her lip from crying out at the intensity, the newness of it all.

As much as Byrne wanted to continue his journey up her leg, he knew she wasn't ready. He could tell in the jolt of her flesh, the flicker of apprehension that stiffened her spine. Instead, he came to lean up over her, a predator ready to feast. He started at her throat, more confident in his seduction now, more certain of his effect on her. The small gasp that escaped her lips pulled him in, and even as he laid her back against the bed, he finally managed to work those damn buttons open on her dress. He rolled her with him, working her dress over her head, freeing her of its weight and him of its obstruction. She only wore her chemise now, a plain scrap of linen with lace on the hem.

Well, this wasn't particularly fair, to Jane's mind.

Buttons opposite what she was used to, it took more than one try to get his shirt open and off, but it fell away easily enough, with some assistance from him. She had, of course, seen his upper half naked before and even been close enough to touch—but then, in the water it had felt illicit. Stolen. Now, with time stopped outside the door, she could admire at leisure. She could feel the planes of strength that had come back to him in the recent months from exercise and health. The muscled flanks that roped around his sides. The springy hair that dusted his chest, at once silly and wholly masculine. And her hands could dance lower, to places she hadn't seen, hadn't had opportunity or courage to admire before.

As she let her hands burrow beneath his waistband, sought and found the curiously hard length of flesh straining therein, his head came up, and he grabbed her wrist. Slowly, his breath exhaling in one long, shaky sigh, he pulled her hand out of his trousers. Then, before she could make a sound of protest, he flipped her with ruthless efficiency, came to lie on top of her, trapping her wrists above her head.

She held his gaze, too surprised by his angry reaction to look away, too curious to see what would happen next. Slowly he released her wrists, bent to kiss her again. But this time, his lips trailed down as his hands slid up, pushing the chemise up from her hips to her waist, finally bringing it over her head. He caught one dusky nipple in his teeth, the sensation beyond bearing. Her hand wound its way into his hair, held him there. But no, he would not be deterred. He trailed lower.

Oh good Lord. Her head lolled back as he placed a kiss on the place where her legs joined. She forced herself not to snap them together, did not resist the easy pressure of his hand on her knee. This pooling of feeling, where his mouth touched, where his tongue reached . . . this was new. This was something she had not thought existed. She found herself being pulled toward something, lulled by her blood and skin and the air and his mouth . . .

But then he stopped.

No, he couldn't *stop*.

Her head came up, any protest allayed when she saw he had backed away only long enough to remove his trousers and drawers. She came up on her elbows and could see in the dim candlelight as he sprang forth, but he was unconcerned by it. Instead, he was gloriously naked, as naked as she. But what would normally reduce Jane to blushing instead made her bold. They were both as vulnerable as could be in that moment, and yet it made them strong. She accepted him when he came back to her, his mouth dancing its way up her soft frame, one hand supporting her as the other dipped between them, tested her headiness.

She was slick with want, her skin pink with desire, as ready as they could hope her to be. He entered her swiftly, held his breath, and pushed forward. He felt the tightness of her, the small tear, her body giving way. She stiffened but did not cry out—no, instead, she bit his shoulder. He took it, took back the fraction of the pain he knew he had caused her. But the grating of her teeth on his shoulder had a lucky side effect. It kept him from losing himself entirely, from taking a running leap over that ledge that beckoned him. The pain was over. He had to hold himself together long enough to make sure she experienced the pleasure, too.

Lazily, with far more grace than he ever thought he'd manage, he slid his hand up her velvet thigh, cupped her rear, squeezed, pressed himself even deeper into her. Her whole body relaxed as she arched into him, a motion founded entirely on instinct but blindingly erotic. She hitched her legs higher around his waist. And they began to move.

They slid into the rhythm without any question or fear. He kissed her throat, her mouth, drugging her with sensation. She was being lured. Lured into rejecting everything beyond feeling. Slowly being dragged under by this incoming tide of heat and pressure. With every push and pull, she wanted what he had promised. She wanted more.

She wanted every inch of his skin to touch every inch of hers. Wanted his hands in places she hadn't even known existed. Wanted his eyes. Wanted his mouth. Wanted it from the moment she had seen him emerge from the water, months ago. Her mind lost to everything else, it crystallized on this one thought: that this night, this act, was the consummation of all that came before. That she had wanted him from the beginning. After all, they had known each other instinctively, before they ever had the opportunity to know one another, before they ever spoke. She could spot him at a thousand paces, and he her.

And suddenly it was all too much. The tide swallowed her whole, and she cried out, lost entirely to this shuddering sensation, this burst of life that racked her body and had her laughing out loud. He gripped her to him as she convulsed, tiny little shivers throughout her entire body that left her sated and breathless.

Byrne kissed her as he continued to move, faster now, urgent in his own need, his own breath ragged. He gripped her shoulder, his hand raked her back. She bit his lip, toyed with his ass, her hand finding that ugly mangled scar on his thigh. She pressed him into her as he finally shuddered and found his own release.

It was some moments before either could move, could bring their heads up and open their eyes. When Byrne did, the first thing he saw in the faint glow of the dwindling candlelight was her shoulder. She wore his marks. Her freckled, sensitive skin was indented and burned by his rough fingers. But instead of regretting them, he felt a surge of pride, as if with those ugly, delicate scratches he had claimed her as his.

She was his.

He brought his head up, and her eyes caught his in wonder, as both their breathing slowed, both floated back down to the reality they had left behind. But before they landed, she found his ear, mumbled those words she had come here to say and only now, in this state of total loss and freedom, had the audacity to speak.

When he repeated them back, pushing a lock of hair back behind her ear, he became acutely aware that for the first time in his life, everything he wanted was granted, and he could think of nothing else to ask for.

Except to keep her.

They lay there for minutes, for hours, as the candle by the chair flickered its way down, extinguished in the early hours of the morning. As sleep drifted in, she felt his lips on her cheek and a mumbled, humorous, "Good night, Jane," float across the room on a summer breeze.

No, not summer, she realized, as she lost herself to slumber. For it was past midnight.

It was the first day of fall.

Twenty-four

Morning came, and it was the day of the ball. Victoria was excited. It was impossible not to be, having put so much hard work and expectation on this one evening . . . Was it any wonder that the night before she had found sleep impossible? Luckily, her ankle was quite strong enough for dancing, but there were so many details to finalize, so many little things that Victoria was certain would go wrong that she had spent the gray hours before dawn composing a list of things to double-check.

Around noon, Victoria was near collapsing with exhaustion.

"Now, you are going to take a nice long nap," Lady Wilton said to her youngest daughter as she escorted her to her bedroom.

"But if the paper lanterns are not secured properly, the whole garden could catch fire!" Victoria whined, as she let her mother unbutton the back of her dress, unlace her corset.

"Now, now," Lady Wilton tutted. "The ball will be lovely. I'm so proud of you, you know," she said, the tears in her voice not unnoticed by even the very tired Victoria. "I cannot wait to see what you girls came up with."

"I'm shocked you managed to stay out of the planning entirely."

Victoria sighed. Later she would be vaguely embarrassed by her bold speech to her mother, but right now she was too exhausted to care.

Luckily, Lady Wilton just chuckled. "It was difficult. But I knew that this was important for you and Lady Jane to do on your own, cementing your friendship for life."

It was on the tip of Victoria's tongue to say that Jane had spent much less time planning the party than anyone thought. But instead, drained as she was, and completely without pretense, she asked her mother the question she had long been curious about but never dared broach.

"What about Jason?" Victoria said and felt her mother's fingers still on her laces. "Did you wish me to cement my friendship with him, too?"

"The Marquis is a very nice young man," Lady Wilton replied noncommittally, without feeling.

"Mama." Victoria turned then, faced her mother. "You must know that I find the Marquis . . . that I have a preference for him." She watched her mother carefully here, gauging her reaction. "The minute I learned he was coming to Reston, I had to go out and purchase a new gown. Why have you never encouraged me toward him? Or vice versa?"

Lady Wilton sighed and busied herself turning down the bed. "The fact that he broke your sister's heart is not enough?"

"That was long ago, and Penelope's heart survived. In fact, it thrived," Victoria countered. "Mama . . ."

Lady Wilton straightened and said very softly, "Get into bed, Victoria." She obliged her mother but would not let her leave without an answer, holding her gaze steady and strong.

"Why, Mama?"

"Oh my darling," Lady Wilton sighed. "Lord Jason Cummings is likely the most eligible bachelor any of us will ever meet. I have very likely failed in my motherly duties by not thrusting you into his path. But . . ." She paused here, took a deep breath. "But he has never seen you. He has never looked at you as a man should look at a woman."

Victoria felt the whole world go still. "He has never looked at me?"

"I want nothing more," Lady Wilton said wistfully, "than to have my daughters situated with men who truly see them. Because if a man doesn't see you, he can't love you—no matter how much you love him."

Victoria watched, stunned, as her mother wiped a stray tear away from her eye. "One day," her mother said, "you will be minding your own business, and you will look up, and find a man, a good man, looking at you as if you are the only person in the entire world. And that day, you'll know what I am talking about."

Victoria was about to ask her mother how she knew this, how she would be able to discern one look from another, when they heard the door slam and Sir Wilton cry out.

"Matilda!" he yelled, his footsteps impatient on the stairs. "It has happened! Finally!"

Another voice that she recognized as Mr. Cutler's said, "Red-letter day, my friend!"

"Matilda!" her father called out again to his wife impatiently.

Lady Wilton kissed her daughter's forehead and, with an order to "get some rest," left her daughter to attend to her husband, leaving Victoria to ponder her mother's words as she drifted off to a dreamless sleep.

જૐ

That night, Victoria prepared herself very carefully. Not only her beautiful new gown (a cream silk with a single perfect sky blue ribbon at her waist, brought all the way from London, Mrs. Hill professed), or her hair, or face, but for once, she was determined to discover, to see what she had not before.

Was what her mother had said true? She had been helping with the ball preparations for over a week, spending the majority of her day at the Cottage, not watching her brothers or spending time with her sister and her family. And in all that time, she couldn't think of an instance where Jason had paid her particular attention. She had been certain that having been thrown into his presence constantly, as she hadn't in the past, he would take notice. But had he?

He was rarely around during their planning sessions, but he was a busy man, surely. One of the great men of society, he must have been working toward that end. Else he would have spent more time with Charles and Nevill. But he had come in for mealtimes, and he spoke with her then.

Didn't he?

Or did he say no more than was polite? His conversation could be put down to Victoria being his sister's friend and an old family acquaintance.

But he'd come to ask her specifically to help with the ball. *He'd* come.

By the time Victoria pinned the last of the flowers into her hair (Dr. Berridge had been kind enough to send over bouquets for herself, her mother, and Penelope), she knew two things definitively: First, that she had never in her life looked more beautiful than she did right now.

And secondly, that she had to end her torturous wanting and discover Jason's feelings for her.

To find out if he saw her.

So, when Victoria arrived at the Cottage, she made certain to make an entrance.

She had promised Jane and Charles and Nevill that she would arrive early, simply to quadruple-check any last details. Besides, she had a certain sense of pride in the endeavor. This was her first ball. The first one she had a hand in, and in some ways it was as much her party as theirs. Her parents sent her ahead in the carriage, which would then return to pick up the rest of the family.

She was admitted by the Cottage's butler and entered a world unlike any she had ever seen. Overcome with a delicate sense of awe, she could not help but stare openmouthed, just for a moment.

The theme they had chosen was Summer Night. Yes, technically, it was fall, and true, the theme was not particularly original, but it did evoke a certain feeling of magic, bringing the outdoors in. Seasonal blooms (roses and wildflowers—apparently Charles had won that particular argument) festooned the foyer. Ribbons of fabric hung from the ceiling, dark blues and greens, set with beading at intervals to sparkle like stars.

As she removed her cloak, the first person that came to greet her was Jason, looking far too handsome in his evening kit for her state of mind.

"Miss Victoria," he said, walking across the hall, dodging any number of panicked servants as they moved things from one corner to the other or opened a window and then closed it again. "I do say you look lovely," he observed as he bowed over her hand.

Victoria tried very, very hard to keep from swooning. Old Victoria would have fallen to the floor in a puddle, but new Victoria—clear-eyed Victoria—had to keep her distance and her wits.

"Thank you, my lord," she replied, looking up demurely through her lashes.

"You'll find Jane and the others in the ballroom." He nodded toward the great room's entrance. "I should congratulate you all on a job well done."

"Then come in with me and do so," Victoria offered prettily, somewhat surprised at her own flirtatiousness.

Jason seemed to be surprised as well, for his eyebrow went up, but then he dismissed the thought. "No, I intend to keep to my library for the time being. I have some work to occupy me until the madness is in full swing. But," he continued with a wink, "let Jane know where I am, so I'll be fetched in time to greet the guests."

Then he made haste to his library, leaving Victoria to find her way to the ballroom.

And she had the sinking feeling that even given her perfect hair and beautiful new dress and her newly composed self, that Jason hadn't noticed a thing.

She kept her eye on him as the ball began. Had him dutifully fetched when the guests began to arrive. When the dancing began, she had hoped he would come to request a dance, but Jason was nowhere to be found.

"Your mind is elsewhere tonight," Dr. Berridge surmised, who had been kind enough to partner her on the first two dances. "You should allow yourself to enjoy the party—stop worrying over the details. Everything is perfect."

"Hmm?" Victoria asked, distracted. "Oh, it's not that," she blushed, "I'm simply trying to . . . to find someone."

"Well, I have the advantage of height," he offered, "perhaps I can help you. Who are you trying to find?"

Victoria kept silent, kept to her moves in the dance. But he must have been able to see through her. Because in those short seconds, Dr. Berridge lost his good humor and stopped in his own steps, in the middle of the dance floor, much to Victoria's surprise. Then, without any explanation, he guided her to the side of the floor, having them fall out of the dancing.

"What is it?" Victoria asked, confused. "What is wrong?"

But the good physician said nothing, instead just lifted a hand to touch one of the small soft flowers that dotted her hair. "Nothing," he said finally, his kindness in place if not his usual happiness. "I'm simply tired."

"We should go into the refreshment room then. I know we had champagne and lemonade set up—" Victoria offered, but he shook his head.

"The Marquis is at the door—I believe there are a few guests still arriving, and he and his sister are there," Dr. Berridge said abruptly. Then, his face darkening, he turned on his heel without bowing and walked away.

Victoria suddenly realized he was angry—as angry as Andrew got, at any rate. He had abandoned her in the middle of the dance, and she couldn't help but feel it was her fault for some reason. But she shouldn't think about that now. Not being under any obligation to anyone for the moment, and not having any real idea what to do, she decided to use the information she had been given and go seek out Jason, continuing her clear-eyed course of action.

She ducked and weaved her way through the crowd, the happy townsfolk, the gentry from farther out in the county, the world she knew assembled and glittering and greeting her as she passed, complimenting her on her looks, begging a few words of conversation. It stalled her from her goal, but it did not deter her. However, when she got to the main entrance, where Jason and Jane and the Duke had been greeting the guests, she was shocked to find herself stepping into what looked like a near fistfight.

Jason had his hand out, trying to pull Jane back into line, but she was speaking very rapidly to an increasingly red-faced Sir Wilton who, next to Victoria's mother and Mr. Cutler, was having a rash of words. The Duke sat in a nearby settee, his ever-present attendant Nancy holding his hand, as they watched the exchange.

Her father was saying something, something Victoria could not hear as she approached, but she did manage to catch Jane's reply, which managed to shock all assembled.

"Because I was with him."

ॐ

Jane had been floating through the whole day as if on a cloud. Nothing disturbed her. Not the last-minute fracas of the kitchen (they had a lack of blackberries necessary for the crème fraîche tarts), nor her brother's needling on her sleeping late or his inability to be found once the guests started arriving—Victoria later mentioned she saw him go into the library, thank heavens. No, nothing would bother her today, if for no other reason than after she snuck home at dawn and subsequently woke up past noon, there were wildflowers in her room. Beautiful long cut daylilies, blazing orange and bright. There was no note, and her lady's maid could not account for how they had gotten there, but she knew they were from him.

She knew she could not expect him at the ball—he would be out hunting highwaymen with Dobbs. But somehow, with the flowers, she felt as if he were there.

And so, an orange daylily tucked into the waist of her white silk gown, Jane stood with her brother and her father and greeted their guests as they arrived for the ball that had at once been so difficult to arrange but at that moment had been so worthwhile.

The Morgans came, dressed in their absolute best clothes—a few years out of date, but beyond impeccable in terms of make and cleanliness. Mrs. Hill and her family arrived, admired all the bolts of fabric that hung from the ceiling that she had supplied. Mr. Davies told them that he'd had the invitation framed and would hang it in his shop forever. Eventually, the Duke had to sit down, he'd grown so exhausted with the rounds of people. Guest after guest, friend after friend came in and smiled, admired, enjoyed.

"Why are you smiling?" Jason asked, seeing the permanent upturn of the corners of her mouth.

"I was simply thinking of the first day we came. Do you remember?" Jane said in between receptions. "You left me to fend for myself as I suffered the assault from the town."

"Not much difference today," Jason surmised.

"Not from their perspective—except we are all better dressed. But I find it very different." Jane smiled at her brother.

Jason regarded his sister and then said, "Yes, I suppose I see your point. Ah, Sir Wilton! Lady Wilton, lovely to see you!"

"And Mr. and Mrs. Brandon," Jane smiled at the newly arrived party.

"Lovely to see you again," Penelope said to Jane, and then turned to Jason. "My lord, my dear Brandon and I did not know if we would be able to come but were so happy to receive your note."

"Note?" Jane asked. Sir and Lady Wilton were turned to speak with Mr. and Mrs. Cutler behind them, allowing Jane to insert herself into the conversation.

"Yes," Mr. Brandon spoke up, "he said how pleasant it was to see that his old friend had grown up into such a wonderful wife and mother and specifically asked us to join you for the ball."

"Brandon had returned to fetch me and the girls back to Manchester a few days ago but decided to stay," Penelope finished, as she and Mr. Brandon executed formal bows and moved into the ballroom arm in arm. Jane shot her brother a look of utter surprise, but Jason simply kept his gaze firmly ahead and shook hands with Sir Wilton.

"Marvelous party, my lord, marvelous day!" Sir Wilton pumped Jason's hand vigorously.

"Wonderful to see you, too, sir," Jason responded.

"You seem to be in excellent spirits," Jane commented, smiling at Sir Wilton.

"And he has cause!" Mr. Cutler spoke up.

"Now, now, Cutler, we shouldn't spread any stories just yet," Sir Wilton said with a modesty no one believed.

"You cannot keep secrets," Jane admonished, drawing him out. "Not in Reston."

"Oh, go on, dear," Lady Wilton said, "after all, you knew all along."

"Well, my lord, Lady Jane"—Sir Wilton beamed—"you no longer have to be afraid of any assault on our roads; the highwayman has been captured!"

Jane's eyes widened. Could it be true?

"Hearty congratulations are in order then!" Jason replied. "How did you manage it?"

"No manage about it—the man finally slipped up," Mr. Cutler provided.

"Yes, attacked a carriage on the road into Windermere in the wee hours of last night. Just a messenger coach, but the lad recognized his cloak and cane and identified him this afternoon! We took him to the town jail then and there!" Sir Wilton finished with no small amount of puffed-up pride.

Jane's smile froze on her face. "I'm sorry, Sir Wilton, did you say *cane*?"

"Yes, of course." Sir Wilton's own smile faltered a bit. "For all his protestations of innocence, and the good turn he did my little Joshua, I'm afraid the slippery Mr. Worth's greed got to him in the end."

Oh God. Oh no, it was impossible.

"Sir Wilton, I'm afraid you must be mistaken," Jane protested, as Jason, no longer smiling as well, put a hand on her arm. But she would not be deterred and attempted to pull Sir Wilton to the side.

"No mistake about it," Mr. Cutler interjected. "We took the mes-

senger over to the widow Lowe's house this afternoon; he identified
Mr. Worth as the culprit, as was proper."

"But surely, Mr. Worth did not stand for it . . . after all, he had
dinner here with us last night!"

"Jane, come back," Jason whispered in her ear, "we'll talk about
this in the library."

But Jane was beyond thought at that point, and Sir Wilton was
ignorant of her frenzy.

"Attack occurred at one in the morning. Lad had no alibi, said he
was asleep in bed by midnight," Sir Wilton replied.

"He was!" Jane replied.

Lady Wilton had moved aside with Mrs. Cutler, but they, and the
Duke and Nurse Nancy, and everyone else within the vicinity was
listening intently.

"Forgive me, my lady, but you cannot possibly know that for
certain."

Jane didn't stop, didn't think, just said what she knew to be the
truth.

"Yes I can . . . because I was with him."

Twenty-five

NEEDLESS to say, the ball ended rather abruptly at that point. Rumors spread like wildfire that the Duke's daughter had consorted with and provided the alibi for the notorious highwayman, and while people danced and drank and ate the food provided, Jane was immediately taken into the library and shut in there, with strict orders to not emerge until Jason came for her. Her father joined her shortly thereafter, Nancy keen to keep him out of the fracas that was about to inevitably ensue.

Jason gave orders to the whole of the household staff to cease serving food and wine, and instead to usher the guests out to their vehicles. Charles and Nevill, once apprised of the situation by a grim-faced Jason, fell in line and made it their work to root out the more-curious-than-intelligent hangers-on and escort them out. The music was brought to a stop, the silver and summer night taken away. And in the space of a half hour, the work of ten days, four fervent minds, and innumerable staff was trampled under a ruthless heel.

Victoria rode home with Lady Wilton, Penelope, and Brandon in complete silence—Sir Wilton had to stay to question Lady Jane more thoroughly. Well, Victoria, Penelope, and Brandon were silent; her mother kept muttering to herself in the most dramatic and appalled fashion she could muster.

"Scandalous!" she would say, as the carriage rocked along. Victoria kept her eyes firmly out the window.

"Utterly wild, that girl!" She then sighed. "And with *him*!"

And then . . . "We should have known she would turn out bad—running around the square naked as a child!"

"Mama," Penelope once breathed, but a squeeze of the hand from her husband told her not to engage. He was right, Victoria knew. They would be home soon enough.

And they were. But Lady Wilton's conversation did not die with the opening of the carriage door. No, it simply found room to breathe.

"And it cannot be hidden," she said as she stepped into the darkened house, the boys and little girls long since put to bed. "Absolutely everyone knows. She'll never be able to show her face anywhere again."

"She could marry him, Mama," Victoria said, finally unable to keep her countenance.

"Marry him? The Duke's daughter? No, I think not," Lady Wilton cried. "And he'll be run out of town, highwayman or no, I promise you that."

"But why?" Victoria asked, aghast. She could feel the hot pink of anger flush across her cheeks and saw out of the corner of her eye Penelope and Brandon discreetly step upstairs.

"Victoria, how can you ask me that?" Lady Wilton replied. She shook her head and tutted. "This is all my fault for allowing you to ingratiate yourself with that . . . wanton child. You feel far too much sympathy for her situation. Even though it was one of her own making."

"Mother, not six hours ago, you told me you were proud of our friendship!" she argued.

"And that was before we knew the extent of her true character! These London people—the Duke's family always thought themselves higher than everyone else, but why should they be allowed to operate without scrutiny? And while I had thought that Jane in particular had outgrown her debauched wildness, but when fostered, it's fostered deep. Why else would she consort with such a man with impunity?"

Lady Wilton was yelling by the end of the speech, causing lights to be struck in the upper levels of the house, but she did not seem to care. In fact, if no one on the entire street slept tonight, it would be considered due course.

Victoria thought back over the course of the evening, how she had been so blindly trying to look for any sign of affection from Jason, living and dying with every spoken word, and without success. But then she happened upon the end of Jane's conversation. The most important conversation of Jane's life, most likely, and how she had hung her heart in the balance without fear.

Then, she remembered with a moment of unblinking clarity, the occasion two days ago when Victoria had run to the widow Lowe's house to fetch Jane. She had been frightened, and so blind to it then, but now she could recall the scene perfectly: Jane and Mr. Worth, at opposite ends of the room, but their eyes locked, everything in the whole world laid out between them.

"You consider Mr. Worth low?" Victoria replied slowly. "A man who saved your son from drowning?"

Lady Wilton sighed. "It doesn't make him the same as . . ."

"As what?" Victoria asked. "As Lady Jane? As us?"

Lady Wilton approached her daughter with fury, grabbed her by the chin, pinching hard.

"You stop your snippiness now, young lady. This is how the world works. Something you are now old enough to understand."

Victoria pulled away from her mother, out of her reach. Then, straightening her shoulders, she took determined steps to the stairs. But not before turning and saying, "You ask how she could consort with him. The answer is simple, Mama." She paused, her hand on the banister. "It's because of how he looks at her."

And with that, Victoria flounced up to her room, locked the door . . . and began to pack a bag.

It would be an hour before Lady Wilton felt well enough to send for the doctor, to get something to calm her nerves. Sir Wilton had arrived home by then, in need of some nervous reduction himself. When Lady Wilton tearfully imparted to Dr. Berridge the verbal fight she'd had with her youngest daughter, it was the chagrined physician (conscious of his own bad behavior toward Victoria that evening) who thought it might be best to check on her.

And it was he who discovered she was gone.

The muffled sounds of guests being escorted out of the house fell on deaf ears, as Jane was very much wrapped in her own mind. The shock of her announcement was followed by a surprising calm, as if all shame and fear and repercussion were softened by the fact that the truth was known, and now they could move on from it.

Of course, the longer she waited in here for Jason's return, the more the calm dissipated. She paced by the desk, saw the numerous account books there, the dust cleaned off them for once, the work being done. Then she settled into one of the velvet chairs by the library fire, next to her father. Nancy had bustled out to find tea, something soothing, she murmured, patting Jane's hand as she left.

Jane could not help but fear what her father thought of her. He must be disappointed. Somewhere, inside his lost mind, he was disappointed in her. She could see it in the set of his jaw, in the way his eyes refused to stray from the fire.

"Your brother is very angry with you," the Duke finally said.

"Yes," Jane replied softly.

"He has reason, I assume. He's never that angry without cause. A little angry yes, but . . ." He paused and came to look Jane dead in the eye. "You should listen to him. He only wants the best for you," her father added. Then his eyes returned slowly to the fire.

"I cannot . . ." he said, then cleared his throat and started again. "I'm sorry," he finally said.

"Whatever for?" Jane asked.

"I never thought this would happen to me," he said sadly.

Jane looked up and saw before her the father that she loved, but not the one that she had known her whole life. He hadn't the strength of mind anymore to be the authority. He was passing it on to the next, while he still could.

She never thought this would happen, either.

"Listen to your brother," he repeated, this time reaching out and patting her hand comfortingly. Then his mind shifted. "Do you know," he said, smiling, "I played an excellent game of chess yesterday. Against a very fine opponent."

But before Jane could respond, the door opened, admitting Jason, with Nancy at his heels. A nod from Jason had Nancy turning to her patient and kindly escorting him from the library. But not before the old man placed a peck on his daughter's cheek.

Then Jason and Jane were alone.

Jane remained in her seat, her hands folded in her lap, while Jason remained still at the door, in silence for some few moments.

"Do you know what Father said to me when I came to him at nineteen and told him I wanted to marry Penelope Wilton?" he began softly.

Jane looked up, shook her head.

"He said that I was bigger than this place. And he would not let me tie myself to it until I had seen the world." He paused, lost in the memory. "We left for London the next day."

They held silent again for some time.

"Take it back," Jason said finally.

"No."

"Sir Wilton is still here; you can tell him that you were simply too overwrought, wanting to provide an alibi for . . . a friend from London."

"No, Jason."

"How could you, Jane?" Jason finally yelled, coming away from the door. "How could you do something so foolish?"

"What was foolish—the act or the telling of it?" Jane asked pertly.

"Do not start with me on this," Jason said warningly. Then, hand to his head, he began to pace. "I should have sent you away. When I knew you were . . . too friendly with him. But I thought it would be too difficult for Father, too many people would question it. And I thought you could be controlled."

"Controlled?" Jane replied, offended.

"Kept occupied," Jason equivocated.

"Oh, thank you, that's so much more flattering." Jane cocked her head to one side. "You mean with the ball? You thought to keep me occupied and off-kilter planning the ball?"

"Yes, and I'll blame Charles and Nevill for their interference later. But Jane, you have to recant. You have to!"

"The damage is done, Jase." She shook her head. "Even if I did recant, no one in the village would believe me. And besides, Byrne is not the highwayman! He deserves to be set free!"

"He deserves to have his balls cut off."

"Jason!" she cried, admonishing.

"He'll be set free; I'll see to it," he promised. "But you're never going to see him again."

"That's not up to you," she said softly.

"Yes it is. Don't you realize that I understand?" he came and sat before her, "Jane, I've *been* you. It's this place. It's the summer heat. It's this strange insular little world that makes you forget that life exists elsewhere."

"It's not the same," she replied, shaking her head. "Byrne and I are not you and Penelope. I won't forget him like she forgot you."

Jason stood again, paced.

"It's more than a summer romance. He's more. He's been my strength ever since we arrived. Do you know what I thought the first time I saw Byrne?" she could not help but grow a bit wistful, a bit misty-eyed at the now-important memory. "I was at the Hampshire Racing Party, and I was sent to fetch Byrne by his brother, and when I found him—he was so sad, and trying so hard to hide it. It was like looking in a mirror for me. I don't think you ever understood how hard this past year has been."

"It's been hard for me, too," Jason defended. "You think I don't miss Mother?"

"You do?" Jane asked.

"Every day." Jason paused, cleared his throat conspicuously. "And what do you think she would say about your behavior?"

And now the tears did begin to fall. Because Jane knew what their mother would think. She would be scared and ashamed and angry. And Jane felt every one of those emotions course through her at once.

"Your trunks are being packed as we speak," Jason said, as she cried quietly into her handkerchief. "Your maid will await you in the carriage. It will take you to London, and then from there . . . Italy? I think you would like Italy."

"Jason, please don't send me away." She breathed gulps of air.

"You'll have to say good-bye to Father—try not to upset him too much," Jason continued, distracted. "You cannot stay, Jane. You yourself said, no one in Reston will believe you."

"But, don't you remember?" she asked, her voice barely audible above the tears. "It's you and me. We're in this together."

He looked as if he would say something then, something of importance, and maybe reach out and embrace her. But he held himself back and simply said, "I'm sorry," before he walked out the door.

❧

It was another hour before Jane was ready to leave. Her maid had packed her trunks, she had said good-bye to her father, which she feared he interpreted as little more than a good night, and in the morning would wake with renewed confusion. She refused to leave, however, until she knew that Jason had gone and had Byrne released from the little cellar behind Mr. Davies's shop that served as the village's jail. When Jason returned, she climbed into her carriage dry-eyed. She did not embrace her brother. The last hour had wiped her of sympathy. She was cold and bereft. The world outside of Reston seemed bleak, but it was where she was being sent, alone.

But not as alone as she might think.

After little more than a mile rumbling down the road, Jane turned to her maid, who had kept her hood up against the chill.

"I can never sleep in a carriage, Mary, but I might try for a while. It's been a harrowing day," Jane said, settling into the cushions.

"Mary has a sweetheart in Reston." The light, sweet voice of Victoria had Jane's eyes opening wide. "She was rather reluctant to leave him."

Jason did his duty by Jane and fetched Byrne back from behind Mr. Davies's shop, much to the grumblings of Sir Wilton. He dutifully bore him home and dutifully deposited him back at the widow Lowe's house.

But that was as far as duty bore him.

"Thank you," Byrne said as he rubbed his wrists, happy to have them free of the manacles, happy to be back home.

That was when Jason decked him. A quick right fist to the jaw, faster than Byrne thought the boy capable of. It connected with his left cheekbone, knocking him into the sofa, and would leave a healthy bruise soon enough, but it was the bones in Jason's hand that cracked audibly.

"Ow!" Jason exclaimed, holding his hand tightly.

"I have to agree," Byrne groaned, coming up off the sofa.

"That was for touching my sister," Jason growled.

"I need to speak with her," Byrne said, making sure to back up a few steps, out of Jason's reach. "She shouldn't have told them, just to set me free, I would have—"

"Damn right she shouldn't have said anything. Or done anything." Jason's eyes narrowed. "But you won't be speaking to her ever again."

"You sent her away?" Byrne surmised. "I'll find her," he said, grabbing a spare cane as he stalked to the front door. He wrenched it open, only to discover the two burliest footmen standing guard with blunderbusses in hand and pistols at their waist.

"Mr. Worth, I would like you to meet my, er, groundsmen," Jason replied with a smirk. "Since you own only the house, not the land that surrounds it, if you step foot outside, you are trespassing." He leaned in, and said with relish, "And they are under strict orders to shoot any trespassers on sight."

Byrne turned to the smiling face of Jason Cummings. "I know you never liked me, my lord, but just out of curiosity, is it because I told you to grow up all those weeks ago, or because I was right to?"

But as much as Byrne could tell Jason wanted to rise to the bait, and as much as Byrne would have loved a little engagement himself, he was glad to see the boy back down.

After all, there was no time to waste.

"You've been exonerated, at the expense of my sister. You'll forgive me if I don't wish you a good evening."

And with that, Jason turned on his heel and strolled out the door to his waiting Midas, who bore him home.

Byrne was alone again in the little house, the one that still smelled of cinnamon and honeysuckle. After a very long afternoon spent in that dirty little cellar, he needed a bath, a meal, a drink. But more than that, he needed Jane. And he needed to take care of some unfinished business.

Dobbs's hat and coat were not hanging on the hook by the door, like they normally did. Neither was his bag present. He had likely hit the road the moment Byrne had been arrested that afternoon.

But then he heard it. It was the smallest sound, a shuffle of feet on hay from the barn. And he knew what it meant.

Silence fell over the room as Byrne moved with quiet insistence. He grabbed a jar of jam, left from one of Jane's visits, and a stale loaf of bread. Then, leaning more than necessary on his cane, he ambled to the front door, opened it, and smiled to the two men who stood outside, guarding him.

"I'm just going to go upstairs, go to bed," Byrne said, his voice cool and calm. Hell, it could be described as nonchalant. "It's going to be a long night, I wager. Either of you two hungry? I have some blackberry preserves . . ." He held the jar out to the men. The darker, more wide-eyed of the two looked to his partner, then shrugged and advanced.

They never saw the cane coming.

After making quick and quiet work of his two unfortunate guards, Byrne moved silently, like a cat in the night to the small stables behind the little house.

He found Dobbs loading up his horse with all manner of supplies— enough so the man would not have to stop running as long as the horse could carry him.

"You shouldn't have come back here, Dobbs," Byrne said, jolting the man out of his movements.

"Oh, Captain!" Dobbs said with a start, his hand going to his chest. "You scared the piss out of me!"

"You should have just run." Byrne advanced slowly.

"Why, uh, whatever do you mean?" Dobbs smiled nervously. "Say, aren't you supposed to be in jail? You escaped again—mighty clever of you, sir."

"Cut the chatter," Byrne said, his face like granite, his voice deceptively calm. "I know you are the highwayman, Dobbs. I just want to know why."

Twenty-six

"Do I not pay you enough?" Byrne asked. "Is that it?"

"Actually, that's part of it," Dobbs said, his shoulders dropping. "There was a while there you were taking so much medicine that you forgot to pay me, and the butcher, and the blacksmith . . ."

Byrne swallowed, unwillingly acknowledging his complicit past. "But that's not how it started, is it?"

"No. It's not that easy to explain." Dobbs shook his head. "It began a while ago."

Byrne waited for Dobbs to settle into his story. While he waited, he casually fingered his cane, knowing Dobbs was watching. And Dobbs knew what he could do with that cane.

"It began in the winter. That night, I was late coming back from Manchester, and you had to go into town for firewood? When I got home, I found you on your bedroom floor, cradling that satchel of stolen medicine in your arms."

Byrne's face burned with the very blurry memory. With shame.

"I knew that the town would come for you, so I thought . . . maybe I could distract them," Dobbs continued. "So I went into Reston and threw a rock through the window of the printer's shop. Ransacked the place, made sure I put down a mess of hoofprints so it looked like the thief was on horseback. You couldn't ride very well then." Dobbs tugged his hat down off his head, played with its edges nervously. "And maybe another storefront or two."

Only the horses made a sound. A small nickering oblivious to the intensity in the air.

"Anyway . . ." Dobbs coughed nervously, then continued. "Big Jim the blacksmith? He caught me at it. But he dinna turn me in, like I thought he might."

"Big Jim is your accomplice?" Byrne's head came up. An image flashed into his head of Big Jim's imposing figure, muscled and callused through long years of backbreaking work. This might be more difficult than previously thought.

"He said he wanted a little fun," Dobbs replied. "Tired of waitin' for what he wanted. And that's when we decided to try robbin' coaches. Only in January there ain't no coaches, so we took the mail . . . and I have to say we did it really badly. Don't know how we managed to get back to town. We was unloading what we took in the smithy, and Mr. Cutler comes in, sees what we've got."

"Cutler?" Byrne's head snapped up. "The town solicitor?"

"Aye." Dobbs nodded furiously. "He's in a right state, too, says he followed our tracks from where we took the coach. Me and Big Jim are beggin' for our lives, but Cutler just looks at us and says we have to do it better if we don't want to get caught."

"Don't want to get caught?" Byrne repeated, incredulous. "I don't understand—did he want a portion of your bounty?"

"No! That's just it!" Dobbs started talking fast now, his hat flying up and down as he gesticulated wildly. "He dinna want money, he wanted to be magistrate. You see, he recently came into a bit of property and thought Sir Wilton was doing a shoddy job of his offices, and thought his background in the law would make him a better magistrate . . . but he knew Sir Wilton would never step down, so he needed to make him look really bad—and he decided a crime spree would do it."

It was an unsettling amount of information to receive at once, and

Byrne took a moment to adjust to it. But there were still pieces left out. And apparently Dobbs had questions, too.

"When did you know?" Dobbs asked.

Byrne worked his jaw. "Little over a week ago, I decided to analyze the dates of the attacks versus when the men of Reston were in or out of town. I did so by first recalling where I was . . . and then recalled *you* were out of town during every single robbery. Every last one. I thought that was a little suspicious, so I decided to test you."

"By asking me to stake out the eastern side of the lake with you?" Dobbs asked, and Byrne nodded in response.

"And it scared you enough that you fell out of pattern. Attacked a carriage and decided to frame me."

"But it wasn't me that wanted to frame you!" Dobbs replied vehemently. "Even when you were lost to your medicine, you were still a good man to work for . . . didn't hit, let me be myself, and I want you to know I appreciate it."

"Really, Dobbs, you're not going to escape punishment via flattery."

"It was Cutler and Big Jim who insisted we use your cloak and cane. They thought you were getting too close, and we needed a way out. You should know . . ." Dobbs coughed, and began again. "You should know that Big Jim—he began to enjoy the money a little much."

"And you didn't?" Byrne drawled sarcastically.

But Dobbs just ignored him. "He's become obsessed with getting a big score. He nearly lost his mind when he saw the inside of the Cottage. All that money, just hanging off the walls, he said. And he went on and on about the diamond earbobs Lady Jane wore to the assembly. Thought the lady must drip with jewels, even on weekdays."

Byrne paused, became very still. "Jane is being packed in a carriage right now," Byrne growled, "and about to ride out."

And since Jane created a scandal at the ball, everyone in a the village would know it.

Byrne looked at the horse, already saddled, ready to go. Ruthlessly, he tossed away all the excess supplies that weighed the horse down and swung himself into the saddle.

"Dobbs—you have been a very good friend to me for a very long time," Byrne said, as the horse danced, adjusting to him in the seat. "So I am going to do you a favor."

"You're not going to tell Sir Wilton about me, are you?" Dobbs breathed a sigh of relief. "Oh thank you, sir. You won't regret it, I promise—"

"No," Byrne interrupted him. "I'm afraid he will have to be told. But I'll give you a head start."

And with that, Byrne burst out of the stables, his horse attuned to his desperation.

He needed to get to Jane.

Jason paced the length of the carpet in the sitting room. Charles and Nevill were, for once, silent, simply watching him as he walked a hole in the rug. If Jason were feeling himself, he would take this opportunity to get good and stinking drunk. But he wasn't feeling himself. He wasn't feeling himself at all.

Jane's look as he had packed her into the carriage and instructed the second-burliest footmen he had to not let her out of their sight until she was on the ship to Italy . . . she didn't stare daggers at him or look ready to spit fire, which was her custom. Instead, she just looked disappointed. But not in her actions—in his.

"You've done the best thing you can, old boy," Nevill broached. "Jane acted recklessly. She knew better than to fall in love with a nobody like Byrne Worth."

Fall in love. Had she truly fallen entirely in love? He was willing to grant that it could be the folly of summer love that he had experienced in his youth, certainly, but what had she said? That it was deeper.

It was more.

"But he's not a nobody!" Charles cried. "I finally remembered where I know his name from!"

"And where is that?" Nevill asked.

"From the papers, of course. Right before we left London. It came out with the latest list of men honored with knighthoods. Byrne Worth and Marcus Worth are to be knighted by the Crown. For services performed during the war."

"That doesn't make him not a nobody," Nevill argued, rolling his eyes as he stood up and walked to the window that looked out over the back gardens, where Hale and Thorndike had recently abandoned a game of horseshoes. "It just makes him Sir Nobody."

"But he's a gentleman of honor, certainly," Charles argued. "No one gets knighted without being a man of honor."

"Yes, well, Jase—that man of honor is cutting across your back gardens on horseback right now."

Jason's head snapped up, as he ran to the window beside Nevill. He just caught a glimpse of the black steed and the man who rode it like he was being chased out of hell.

"Where do you think he's going?" Charles asked, coming behind them, jumping to see over their shoulders.

"I don't know." Jason narrowed his eyes. "But we are going to find out."

❧

"Victoria, what on earth do you think you're doing?" Jane cried, shocked to her core, as the carriage rumbled along at a clip. The smaller blond woman was swallowed by the large black cloak, looking more like a child than ever—but the set of her mouth, the defiance in her eye . . . those were very adult, as if she finally saw the world as it was for the first time.

"My parents are wrong," Victoria said, absolute conviction shaking in her voice. "You should have heard them, Jane—actually, I'm rather glad you didn't. My mother was horrible, condemning you as if you were . . . a . . . a *fallen* woman!"

Jane didn't feel the need to point out that technically, she was fallen. Fallen rather hard and publicly.

"But why would you stow away in my carriage?" she asked.

"Because you're my friend," Victoria replied, her eyes wide with astonishment. "And I could not let you be condemned and sent away alone! You don't deserve it. And . . ."

"And?" Jane's eyebrow went up.

Victoria bit her lip, hesitating. "And I realized something tonight . . . and suddenly I didn't want to be in Reston anymore."

Jane reached out and took her friend's hand. Victoria smiled bravely, then looked down, started playing with the long sleeve of her oversized cloak.

"You knew the whole time, didn't you? That Jason would never love me."

Jane nodded curtly but not unkindly. She understood. Victoria's realization would make anyone want to run away, to go to a new place and become someone different. Jane had tried it once, tried losing herself in the frivolity of London after her mother's death. It hadn't worked.

"Victoria," Jane began softly. "Disappointment, and difficulty . . . you cannot deal with them by running away."

"I know," Victoria replied. "I feel nothing but foolish over the whole thing now, but . . . more than that, it made me realize that to find someone that looks at you the way Mr. Worth does, and to look back in the same manner—it's not something to be ashamed of. And my parents and their friends in Reston, and the whole world wants to make you ashamed." Victoria looked up then, her cheeks streaked with silent tears. "I do not believe you should be ashamed."

Without thinking, Jane left her seat and went across the carriage to Victoria, wrapping her arms around her and holding tight. Victoria was no more surprised by this emotional display than Jane herself was.

"Thank you," Jane whispered, her voice wobblier than she had expected. Oddly, they had been the first words of support she had received since she told the world of her involvement with Byrne, and it was so good to have someone on her side. Someone who wanted to be her friend, no matter the consequences. She hadn't known she needed it, and she was so grateful. However . . .

"I can't kidnap you, Victoria," Jane said as she pulled back from the embrace, wiping away an errant tear.

"It's not kidnapping if I come willingly," Victoria protested weakly, making Jane smile.

"You know what I mean," Jane said ruefully. "Your parents will be mad with worry."

Victoria shrugged, then gave a small nod as she fell back against the seat, exhausted by her mad rush to get here and now resigned to returning home.

Victoria knocked on the roof of the carriage, then waited for the carriage to slow to a stop.

It didn't.

She knocked again. When it still yielded no return, Jane set her mouth, and put her head out the carriage window.

"Excuse me!" she yelled against the wind up to the driver and his partner. "We must turn around!"

The second man (whom Jane recognized as Freddy, a footman) turned his bulky frame, leaning down cautiously as they moved at a gallop down the main road into and out of the district. "Apologies, ma'am," he yelled. "We were instructed by the Marquis to not stop until we put you on a boat!"

Rolling her eyes at her brother's unrealistic expectations (they would have to stop to change horses sometime, after all), Jane replied, "Circumstances have changed! We have a stowaway!"

"A what?" Freddy said, trying to hear over the wind and the sound of hooves beating against the dirt.

"Another person!"

Freddy looked at her for a moment, uncomprehending. Then he turned and exchanged a few words with the driver of the carriage, gesturing wildly. Finally the driver slowed to a canter, then to a stop. Once the carriage had stopped moving, Freddy turned back around in his seat.

"Thank heavens," Jane breathed.

"I'm sorry, milady, I couldn't hear what you were saying," Freddy said. "What do we have?"

"We have a—"

But Freddy was never to hear the full answer, never to know that Victoria Wilton was hiding in the depths of the carriage. Because at that moment a shot rang out from the fells that lined the road.

Jane whipped her head around, but the echoes made it impossible to discern where the shot originated.

But it was easy to discover where the bullet ended up.

Jane looked back up at Freddy, confused surprise on his face. He reached his hand up to his chest, where Jane could see the patch of red growing, almost black against his white shirt in the spare starlight. He slumped over and fell off the carriage, just as the driver, scared beyond belief, whipped the horses into a lather, and they ran.

Jane ducked back inside, closed the window, and pulled closed the curtains, as the carriage rocked wildly on its springs.

"What happened?" Victoria asked, breathless.

"Victoria, get on the floor with me," Jane ordered, and was readily obeyed. "One of the drivers was shot—he fell off the carriage . . . I think we're under attack!"

Another shot rang out, followed by another, and another. Jane ducked her head, crouched on the floor of the carriage, her arm around Victoria, covering the younger girl's body with her own. They rocked and swayed for some moments, not knowing what was going on outside, their imaginations running wild.

Suddenly another shot sounded, this one closer. And just as suddenly, they screeched and jolted to a halt, one side of the carriage falling with a thud.

Victoria squealed in shock, shaking. "What was that?"

"Shhh!" Jane replied, furiously whispering. "Don't say a word. I think we broke a wheel, or an axle. We're stuck here."

Victoria stilled under her, as Jane listened intently. She heard the horses whinny and snort. She heard the driver's muffled voice, his words indecipherable but his tone scared and placating. Then they heard another shot. And the driver's voice was silenced.

And then there was nothing but the footsteps outside, and the sound of Jane's and Victoria's breathing.

"Lady Jane!" the rough male voice called out from the outside. His tone mocking, singsong. "Come out, come out, wherever you are!"

Jane was frozen in fear. He knew it was her. She had no men to guard her, no weapon. If she came out, would he kill her? What to do? What would Byrne do?

"Don't make me come in. Not enough room for us both in there," the man said, a voice that Jane recognized but could not place. Then she heard the clink of metal snapping into place, the gun reloaded now.

"Victoria," Jane whispered. "No matter what, do not leave this carriage. Whoever it is doesn't know you're here. Do not make a sound, all right?"

"You can't go!" Victoria mouthed.

"I must."

Victoria saw the determination on her friend's face and nodded once, curled into a ball on the floor, and practically disappeared within the cloak.

Jane reached for the latch of the carriage door, turned it slowly. Then, with as much dignity as she could, she exited the carriage.

And stared down the barrel of a gun into a manically smiling, half-masked face.

One she knew.

"Jim?" Jane asked, before she could stop herself.

"You know it's me, then?" Big Jim asked. "No matter. You would've learned soon enough. Hallo, my lady," he sneered. "You're lookin' fine this evening."

He took a long, leisurely perusal of her form.

"Very fine, indeed."

Twenty-seven

"WHAT do you want, Jim?" Jane asked, as calm as she could manage, her hands coming up. Suddenly, everything came into sharp focus. The rough metal of his pistol. The large, shaggy black horse that danced impatiently a few steps away from Big Jim. She knew that every move she made, every word she said, had to be just right. "Money, jewels?"

"That'll do for a start," he replied, his black eyes hard.

Big Jim the blacksmith—he'd been a resident of Reston since before Jane was born, apprenticing under the old blacksmith, then taking over the shop. She'd known him her whole life. Taken their horses to him, run past his smithy as a child.

But now, it was as if she was seeing his true self for the first time.

He wore a disguise, of course. Nondescript, dark clothes, the mask with holes for the eyes, but Jane knew his voice, his stance, his oversized, roughly muscled body. He was the highwayman; she knew it now like she knew her own face. And he didn't seem particularly at ease. In fact, he seemed a bit mad with power.

She had to be very, very careful.

"Well, my jewel box is in my trunk, up there," Jane replied, cautiously pointing to the back of the carriage, where all of her luggage was piled high and strapped down.

Jim glanced to where she indicated and then leveled the gun back at her head. "Unfortunately, m'friends aren't with me today, so you're gonna have to assist me, aren't you?"

She didn't blink. Didn't move. She just waited.

"Climb up there and untie the trunks," he commanded.

Jane walked slowly but steadily to the back of the carriage, and after one heart-stopping misstep, managed to gain a hold and climb up to where large leather straps belted and secured two trunks, two suitcases, and a heavy satchel onto the back of the carriage.

It suddenly occurred to Jane that he was being very reckless. He had gotten down off his horse. What kind of highwayman got down off his horse?

And he had killed two men.

The highwayman had never killed anyone before.

Jane slowly, steadily reached up and took hold of the first strap. It was attached tightly, and she grunted with the effort to unbelt it.

"Now, Lady Jane, don't dawdle," Big Jim admonished. "We can't linger here too long. People might come by."

For the first time, Jane looked about her, understood where they were. Big Jim had forced the carriage off the main road during his pursuit, into a field, down a bit of a hill. It was removed enough from the road that the average passing carriage might not see them, but the sound of gunfire carried, so someone might have been alerted to the situation. Someone might be looking for them.

Please let someone be looking for them.

Suddenly Jane couldn't catch her breath. She took big gulps of air, but none filled her lungs. Her hands started to shake. The driver sat slumped in his seat, his arms falling at unnatural angles. And where was Freddy? Where had he fallen? Was he still alive, up by the road?

She could feel Big Jim's eyes boring into her. She could do this, she told herself. She just had to breathe. She would give him the jewelry, and he'd ride away.

Then she felt the warm metal of the gun barrel slide up her ankle. And suddenly, Jane knew he didn't just want the jewelry.

"You grew up right pretty, Lady Jane. Would've never known it when you was a girl."

Even as her stomach turned, Jane's mind found its anger. And its focus.

She had gotten one strap unbelted. She moved to the next.

He followed her.

"You was always scraped up, completely wild," he said, and she could feel the gun barrel move up her leg, to her knees, her heavy gown lifting with it. "No more scrapes," he leered. "But you still got that wildness—don'tcha?"

She unbelted the second strap, let it fall loose. Her hands went to the heavy satchel on top.

"You went wild for that Mr. Worth, after all," he said, as his hand replaced the barrel on her limb.

One chance.

She heaved with all her might, and swung the satchel around, catching Big Jim across the face, knocking his half mask off. His head snapped back, and he stumbled, the gun flying to the ground, lost in the tall grass.

Jane jumped down off the carriage and *ran*.

If she got to his shaggy black mount, she could gain the advantage. He couldn't take the carriage, not with its broken axle. He'd be forced to lose time by unhitching one of the horses. Then, once he followed her, Jane prayed, Victoria would be free to make her escape.

Her plan had to work—she just had to reach the horse.

She didn't make it five steps before Big Jim tackled her to the ground.

Jane fought, scratched, kicked. But it was no use. He was so much stronger. So much larger—he held her still with as little effort as a lady would hold her fan.

"Do you know what I've learned, these past months?" Jim growled at her, his teeth near enough to her ear that she could feel his warm, spit-flecked breath as it spewed its venom. "I learned that if I want something, I can take it, *Lady* Jane."

Keep fighting, Jane. Just keep fighting and do not ever stop. If you stop, he will win, and he cannot win. Just keep fighting.

But she wasn't strong enough.

He slammed her back by the shoulders, rocking her head against the hard earth. The already dark world became darker. The edges of life fell away, as her head fell to the side.

The last thing she saw was horse hooves, galloping toward them.

When Byrne had seen the body of the footman, he knew he was too late. Scanning wildly, he found the tracks of the carriage as it ran off the road, making decisive, parallel lines in the tall grass, and he followed.

Blind rage took hold of his body when he saw them. He no longer felt worry or pain or fear. He kept the horse going at full speed and launched himself off the saddle, knocking all his weight against the solid mass of Big Jim, forcing him off of the unconscious form of Jane.

They rolled, landed, Big Jim using his size to advantage and pinning Byrne to the ground. He managed a solid hit to the side, but his meaty hands were too slow to knock Byrne across the face. He ducked and weaved as Jim thundered and plodded. Byrne was more precise, more lethal in his focused red haze. He managed a direct hit to the kidneys. Big Jim reared back in pain, allowing Byrne to squirm out from under him and gain his feet.

Unfortunately, it allowed Big Jim to gain his feet, too.

"Do you know what I'm going to do to you, Worth?" Big Jim slurred, as he spat a streak of blood onto the ground. "I'm gonna string you up by your entrails, and then finish with your lady over there—let you watch."

"If she dies, you die," Byrne growled, desperate to turn around and see if Jane was all right, alive, breathing. But he couldn't turn his back on Big Jim, not for a second.

"Then," Big Jim continued with a little laugh, as if Byrne had never spoken, "I'm gonna tell the town that I come upon you trying to thieve Lady Jane's carriage. You killed her men, and were trying to take what you wanted. Including her."

Byrne felt every muscle in his body tense in anticipation. Every cell, every hair was awake, aware, and controlled. And his voice—his voice became like ice.

"That's very elaborate," he said calmly, almost conversationally. "And here I was just going to fucking kill you."

The black gleam in Big Jim's eye faltered ever so slightly at Byrne's tone.

"It has been some time since I've killed anyone with my bare hands," he continued. "Generally I prefer blades, knives, pistols—that sort of thing. Even my cane works well as a blunt instrument. But"— he grinned, baring his teeth like a panther hunting his prey—"there is something to be said for variety."

Byrne lunged.

Fists met bone in blinding fury, and both crunched under the impact. Big Jim had power, but Byrne had skill. Jim met Byrne hit for hit, bloodying his eye, but Byrne managed to pin Big Jim against an outcropping of rock, managed to get his hands around the larger man's throat. Big Jim struggled and choked, his arms flailing out. Just when Byrne thought he had him down, Big Jim scored a lucky hit— his meaty fist connected directly with Byrne's wounded thigh.

A thousand needles stabbing at his leg had Byrne crumpling over in pain. His hands loosened on Big Jim's neck, but he didn't let go. Instead, he pounded. He let what pain he had focus him. Once across Jim's face. Once again. Pound after pound after pound. Big Jim's face became nothing but a jumble of flesh. A jumble of flesh that, upon hearing the beating of horseshoes on the ground, began to laugh.

Byrne paused in his frenzy enough to look up. Up by the road was a group of five riders, coming from Reston, and scanning the country-side like mad. The great blond Midas and his rider Jason were easily recognized at the lead—and they had spotted the lifeless form of Jane on the ground and were riding hell-bent for leather toward her.

"You're too late," Big Jim laughed, his words garbled by the blood in his mouth. "They'll never believe you."

"They'll believe me," came the small, shaky, feminine voice from behind them.

Byrne let go of Big Jim's face and turned fully.

Standing behind them, leveling an unsteady pistol at Big Jim, was Victoria Wilton.

Needless to say, the next few minutes were total chaos.

Jason, Charles, and Nevill arrived with Dr. Berridge and Sir Wilton, who had met up at the head of the main road—and upon discovering both parties were looking for someone, decided to join forces. They found their individual quarries—Victoria and Byrne Worth—together, one pointing a gun in the direction of the other, who had been beating the town blacksmith to a bloody pulp, while Jane lay unconscious several feet away, the driver of the carriage shot in his seat, and a footman dead up by the road.

It was Dr. Berridge who leaped into action.

"You two!" he snapped, pointing to Charles and Nevill, who jumped to attention, "go up and bring down the driver, see if he's breathing." Charles and Nevill moved with alarming speed for people used to lethargy. "My lord," he addressed Jason, "your sister."

Jason snapped out of his haze, came down off his horse, and followed Dr. Berridge to Jane, who was slowly coming round. Dr. Berridge gently but efficiently examined her head for any contusions, her body for any physical harm, and then nodded to Jason.

"Sit her up," Dr. Berridge commanded, "slowly. Find some water, see if she can drink."

With Jason yelling to Nevill to see if he could find some water in the carriage, Dr. Berridge ran over to where Byrne was frozen, hovering over the woozy form of Big Jim, where Victoria was explaining to her father just why she couldn't release the gun from her unsteady hands.

"Big Jim did it!" she cried. "He came for Jane—he shot the men!" Her gun shook as she spoke.

"I know, sweetheart, you told us," Sir Wilton was saying consolingly, "but that doesn't mean you can shoot him."

"It should!" Victoria cried. "He's the highwayman."

Sir Wilton's eyes shot back and forth to where Dr. Berridge was now pulling Byrne off of Big Jim. He wasn't proving too successful, Byrne being intent upon keeping Big Jim from running away, from hurting anyone. And Big Jim, who, at the sight of having his own discarded gun trained on him, went mad with rage, pain, and thwarted power and fought to get free of the now two men who restrained him.

"No! This is not how it happens! I get what I want!" he yelled, his voice carrying across the field. "I get what I want!"

"Not this time," Dr. Berridge said, as he pulled out a rope (from where, it is unknown) and with Byrne worked the oversized man to the ground and bound his hands tightly behind him.

"Can you handle him?" Byrne asked the doctor, who nodded.

"Now that he's on his face without hands. That's a bad cut above your eye," Dr. Berridge commented, but recognized too easily the man's impatience, and with a tilt of his head, sent Byrne moving—limping heavily but moving as fast he could—for Jane.

"You see, Victoria?" her father was saying. "Big Jim cannot hurt anyone anymore. You're just pointing a gun at Dr. Berridge." Sir Wilton reached out and placed his hand gently over the barrel of the gun. "You don't want to hurt the good doctor, do you?"

And in that moment, Victoria, for perhaps the first time in her life, truly looked at Dr. Berridge. He was kneeling over the man who had tried to harm her friend and kill Mr. Worth, this screaming wretch of a man, and Dr. Berridge was tending to his injuries, as he would any other injured person. Just not as gently, perhaps.

"Does this hurt here?" Dr. Berridge said, as he pressed hard on Jim's shoulder, which seemed out of alignment. A scream was his answer. "Is that a no? Are you sure?" Dr. Berridge asked as he pressed again.

A small laugh fell from Victoria's lips. Her hand fell down, the gun falling into her father's possession. And Dr. Berridge's gaze met hers.

Victoria realized then that her mother was correct. She would know when a man truly saw her. However, her mother had never mentioned what it would feel like when she saw him in return.

It took her breath away.

But this exchange went unnoticed by the rest of the party. Sir Wilton was simply glad to have the gun in his possession, not his frightened daughter's; Charles and Nevill had worked the driver to the ground, and while Charles discerned if the man had survived being shot (sadly, he had not), Nevill ransacked the carriage looking for water (or possibly spirits) for Jane.

Jane was still rather groggy, so it was a bit of a surprise to her to have Jason leaning over her, as kindly as he could, supporting her weight against his arm.

"Take it easy," Jason whispered, as she winced with every little movement. "Drink this." He put the flask of water that Nevill handed him to her lips. She sputtered but managed to get a few sips down. "Careful," he cautioned.

"Byrne . . ." she croaked, looking about. Oh, turning her head like that hurt.

"What did he do?" Jason asked quickly, his eyes narrowing.

"He saved me," she breathed.

Then he was there.

Limping madly, blood caking the side of his face, but he was there.

"Are you all right?" Byrne asked wildly. Then, turning to Jason, "Is she all right?"

"She was unconscious," Jason grumbled. But Jane waved him away, her eyes never leaving Byrne as he knelt before her.

"Are you all right?" she asked, seeing the state of his face for the first time. He nodded gruffly, reaching out to touch her, his roughened palm gently playing over the side of her face.

Suddenly, every emotion and worry that Jane had been keeping at bay broke forth, tears falling freely. Byrne swept her up in his arms, cradling her as she sobbed and sniffed and shook like a vibrating wire.

"I was so scared," she cried, the shoulder of his coat becoming her handkerchief. "I tried to get away, but he caught me."

"I know, love. You were so brave. I'm sorry he touched one hair on your head. I'm sorry I didn't get here in time," Byrne whispered in her ear.

"You came. You saved me."

"Actually, Victoria saved you. And me," Byrne replied, which made Jane's shoulders shake in a laugh. He rocked her back and forth, giving and taking calming comfort in each other's arms. Sanctuary found and held.

Privy to this intimacy was Jason Cummings, mostly due to the fact that the moment Jane and Byrne saw each other, they had forgotten he was there. And Jason Cummings had a realization of his own.

He had thought to protect his sister from a mistake, one that she would come to regret. But he'd failed to understand one fundamental truth.

He couldn't protect his sister. Not from herself and not from this. Not from a man who would fight dragons for her, storm the gates of the Cottage and brave her family.

And he didn't want to. Jane had chosen. She had chosen a man who was recalcitrant, brooding, and injured. She had chosen a man who showed caring and kindness in unexpected ways—playing chess with his father and saving the life of a small boy. She chose a man who loved her without boundaries.

She had chosen well.

As Jason stood, relinquishing the care of his sister to the man who loved her, he overheard one final exchange.

"I won't give you back this time," she breathed. "So don't let me go."

"Never, love," he replied with a smile. "I'll never let you go."

Over the course of the next few minutes, Big Jim spewed his venom at the assembled party but was quick to reassign blame, pointing his finger at his associates, Dobbs and Mr. Cutler.

Within the next hour, Mr. Cutler was found in his home, as he was throwing silver trays and candlesticks into a trunk, intent, it seems, upon fleeing from his sleeping wife and seven children.

Within the night, Jason managed to find the wherewithal to shake Byrne Worth's hand. After, of course, the two guards that had been left at Byrne's door and subsequently knocked unconscious, were found relatively unharmed.

Within the next few days, Jane, Byrne, and Big Jim recovered from most of their wounds. Big Jim, of course, did this from inside a Manchester prison, awaiting deportation.

Within the next few weeks, the whole of Reston returned, in most part, to its normal self, as did the weather. It was harvest time, after all. The Morgans had graciously allowed the cow path, and Reston had begun parading their livestock along it. Michael and Joshua Wilton, no longer able to swim daily, were caught by Mr. Davies red-handed, as they pilfered some of his overstock of red ink. The church bells rang on the hour, and Lady Wilton's knitting circle met for tea.

The days became shorter and shorter, and the tourists became fewer and fewer, both the sun and the travelers abandoning Merrymere for southern climes. But one thing, in all the time that passed, in all the days and weeks and years to come, never happened.

Byrne never let Jane go.

Epilogue

BITE stung the air of the Lake District by the end of October. There was no hope for a warm breeze or a lazy shaft of sunlight dancing across the lawn to momentarily remind them of that heady summer they had spent together—the days being too short, sunbeams too precious. But there was no shortage of smiles or jubilation or conversation.

Two conversations in particular stood out.

The first took place between Mr. Byrne Worth and Lord Jason Cummings, Marquis of Vessey, as they awaited the approach of the former's bride and the latter's sister, standing as they were, at the front of the church.

Byrne's brother Marcus, acting as best man, stood between them, so some maneuvering was done to allow for this conversation. It began thusly:

"I have a proposal to put forward to you, Worth," Jason stage-whispered, leaning around the tall form of Marcus to make himself heard.

"Oh?" Byrne replied. "I'm curious to hear it."

"I'm school friends with the son of the Chancellor of the Duchy,"

Jason began, alternating between leaning forward and backward around Marcus. "He appoints the magistrates in this county."

Byrne's gaze shot immediately to Sir Wilton, who sat in the front row of the church next to his wife and Victoria, whose arm was locked with Dr. Berridge's. Sir Wilton was watching the badly whispered conversation closely enough to hear it—but instead of seeming angry or embarrassed, he nodded ever so slightly, ever so encouragingly.

"I'm aware of the role of the Chancellor of the Duchy, Jason," Byrne drawled, leaning around Marcus to address him. "But I don't feel that—"

"Why not?" Jason asked immediately.

"Would you care to exchange places with me?" Marcus asked Jason, bemused. "I am more than happy to slide down a spot and facilitate this conversation."

"Not necessary, Marcus," Byrne answered.

"No, of course not," Jason agreed. "Just say yes to being Reston's new magistrate and be done with it."

Byrne smiled and shook his head. "I cannot say yes, Jason, but thank you."

"Why not?" Jason asked.

"Yes, why not?" Marcus echoed.

"First of all, the town has a magistrate," Byrne argued.

"Sir Wilton is considering retirement and would very much like to take you under his wing, show you the ropes," Jason answered offhandedly.

Byrne shot a glance to his brother, hoping for some commiseration but not receiving any. Instead, there was an upshot eyebrow and a wry smile. Byrne looked to Sir Wilton, who was still following the conversation intently but pretending to casually listen to Dr. Berridge . . . who wasn't actually speaking.

"Magistrates have to be men of property," Byrne replied. "And I doubt my little house qualifies."

"No, but the Cottage does," Jason countered with a preening smile. "We're giving it to you as Jane's dowry." He wiggled his fingers in the air. "Surprise."

"Surprise," Marcus added with the same finger wiggle.

"I don't want the Cottage given to me," Byrne said with a small frown.

"Why ever not?"

"Yes, why ever not?" Marcus repeated.

"Would you stop repeating everything he says?" Byrne snapped at his brother.

"Sorry, I'm simply curious."

Byrne's eyes narrowed. "I don't want you to give me the Cottage, because I'm not marrying your sister for your house. And she would agree with me."

Byrne actually didn't know if Jane would agree with him; he had a sneaking suspicion she fully expected to still live at the Cottage . . . but there was the small matter of his pride.

"Fine," Jason said, backing off immediately. All three men stared ahead, watching the doors at the end of the aisle, festooned in bowers of fall blooms, oranges and reds that guarded Jane from the audience that eagerly awaited her.

"But," Byrne conceded, "I might be willing to buy the Cottage from you."

"You wish to buy the Cottage?" Jason asked, taken aback.

"At the discounted family rate, of course." Byrne grinned. "Do you think that can be managed?"

Jason just looked from one brother to the other, the elder smiling and the younger shrugging.

"I still don't know what one does during a war to earn so much money." Jason sighed and luckily missed the look shared by the brothers at the altar.

"What's taking so long?" Jason grumbled, as he checked his pocket watch, echoing the sentiments of the assembled crowd. Everyone from Lady Wilton to Mrs. Morgan and all in between were desperate to know what Lady Jane would wear as her wedding gown. To see the odd and oddly heroic Byrne Worth marry the daughter of a Duke. "Maybe Jane's decided not to marry you," Jason added with a smile. "Maybe she's making a run for it."

Byrne shot his soon-to-be brother-in-law a glance. "You really don't know your sister at all, do you?"

The second conversation took place in the antechamber of the church. While everyone awaits the arrival of the bride (most of all the groom), it is customary for the father of the bride to take this opportunity for one last talk with his daughter. And this moment was no different.

The Duke of Rayne sat on a stone bench, in his very best coat, and stared out the window of the church, admiring the crisp autumn leaves on the oak trees of the village square. Jane sat beside him.

The past few days, with the preparations, had been difficult for him, she knew. But she, Nancy, and Byrne had done their best to keep things as normal as possible. But the good days . . . they were fewer and farther between now.

"Hullo, dear," the Duke said with a satisfied smile as he took Jane's hand and returned his gaze to the outdoors. "I cannot believe how quickly autumn came this year."

"I know," Jane replied with a smile.

"And we are still at the lake! Jason must be chaffing himself raw to get back home." The Duke laughed, encouraging Jane to join in as well. "Well, at least we know Jane must be having a fine time. She always loved it up here. Almost as much as you, darling."

Jane paused and let the disappointment in. She glanced over her shoulder. There was no Nurse Nancy here to offer support; it was just her and her father alone again. But instead of worrying, despairing, she squared her shoulders and squeezed her father's hand.

"I am your daughter, Jane," she said, as the Duke turned to look at her. "And I am getting married today."

"You are?" the Duke asked, his hazel eyes awed with possible recognition.

"Yes," Jane nodded.

The Duke looked down for a moment, his brow pinched in confusion. "Have I met the man?"

"Yes," she replied softly, "and you like him very much."

"What about you? Do you like him?"

The question caught Jane off guard. "Yes," she stuttered. "Father, I love him."

"And he loves you?" the Duke asked, his hand coming underneath Jane's chin, looking her in the eye like he did when she was a child and he wanted a serious answer.

"Yes. Very much."

They held there for a moment, Jane kneeling before her father, her hand over his, his other hand under her chin. And then a rare shaft of sunlight came through the church windows, warming them both.

"Am I to give you away, then?" the Duke asked, his voice filled with its old authority, its old gruff humor.

"You are." Jane blinked back a few threatening tears.

Then the Duke's face broke into a beatific grin, and Jane could not help but join in.

"Well," he said, as his gruffness gave way to emotion. "Aren't I lucky?"

And they were.